Runic Revolt

Books by Clayton Taylor Wood:

The Runic Series
Runic Awakening

Runic Revelation

Runic Vengeance

Runic Revolt

The Fate of Legends Series
Hunter of Legends

Seeker of Legends

Destroyer of Legends

Magic of Havenwood Series
The Magic Collector

The Lost Gemini

Runic Revolt

Book IV of the Runic Series

Clayton Taylor Wood

Special thanks to my brothers and to my loving wife for their invaluable advice.

And to my son, for whom this book was written.

Table of Contents

Runic Revolt

Prologue

The streets of Osa were packed with carriages leaving the city, commuters returning to the surrounding towns after a long day's work. Children walked in long lines down the sun-baked white stone sidewalks, dressed in colorful shirts and shorts, most of them wearing sandals or no shoes at all. Tessa walked among them, glancing behind herself on occasion, peering through the crowd.

Where is he?

Darren must've gotten out of school a little later than her, she supposed. Probably talking to his friends, or maybe that dumb girl he was obsessed with. Ever since he'd turned twelve, her brother had become preoccupied with girls. Overly-preoccupied, if you asked Tessa. It was weird; he'd never even noticed them before. She wished that he was more interested in spending time with *her*, like he used to be. Dad had warned her this would happen at some point, but she hadn't believed him.

Of course Dad had been right, as usual.

She sighed, turning to face forward again, her arms aching a bit from carrying all her books. While most of her friends hated books, she loved them. She read all the time, especially since her brother had started ignoring her. Either that, or she played at her friends' houses. It wasn't like she could play with her friends at *her* house, after all.

1

She stared at her feet as she walked, wishing her brother were by her side. He *knew* she didn't like to go home by herself.

She glanced up, spotting her house ahead. Someone bumped her from behind, and she startled, realizing she'd slowed down. Tessa moved to the side, onto the short grass of her neighbor's lawn, which prickled her bare feet. She stared at her house; it was the biggest one on Zucker street, which had the biggest houses in Osa. Dad was an important person, and as far as Tessa could tell, important people had bigger houses. Which meant that Dad was the most important person in Osa, besides the governor of course.

The other children walked past her as she stood on the lawn, and she watched them go, hoping to spot her brother among them. But he wasn't there. She glanced at her house again, picking at her lower lip.

Come on, Darren!

She waited until all of the other kids had passed, the sidewalks now deserted. A few carriages still came down the road, pulled by big, burly horses, their hooves *clopping* on the cobblestones. She watched them pass, her guts squirming. She glanced at her house again, knowing full well that she couldn't wait much longer. She didn't have a choice; she'd have to go in alone.

She took a deep breath in, then stepped back onto the sidewalk, trudging toward her house. Up the front steps to the porch she went, opening the front door.

A large foyer greeted her, high ceilings painted white, and a grand staircase leading up to the second floor. Walls with colorful murals painted on them, and a beautiful, dark wooden floor polished to a mirror-shine.

Tessa stepped into the foyer, then felt a sharp pain in her heel. She jerked it back, seeing blood welling up there, a small piece of glass sticking out of her heel. There was broken glass all over the floor, she realized, along with the unmistakable – and familiar – smell of alcohol.

Her books fell to the floor with a *thud*.

"Tessa?" she heard a voice call out. A woman stumbled into view, staring at Tessa. A woman with light brown skin, her eyes red and bleary, her wavy hair a mess atop her head. She glared at Tessa. "What're you standing there for?" she slurred. "Close the damn door!"

Tessa obeyed instantly, shutting the door behind her, then pressing her back against it. She stood there, a small puddle of blood forming around her right heel, glass still embedded in it.

"What's this?" her mother demanded, gesturing at the broken glass. "What did you do?"

"I didn't..." Tessa began, but her mother held up one hand, standing before the mess, swaying slightly.

"Don't even," she warned. "Wait until your father..."

The door opened suddenly, shoving Tessa forward. She stumbled, stepping onto another piece of glass. She cried out, hopping to the side on one foot, then falling onto her butt on the floor. Blood poured from her feet, and she stared at them in horror.

She burst into tears.

"Mom?" she heard a voice say. She jerked her gaze up, seeing Darren standing there. He was nearly as tall as Mom was, with short black hair and deep brown eyes. He stared at the bloodied glass on the floor, then at Mom.

"Close the damn door!" Mom shouted.

Darren ignored her, turning and spotting Tessa sitting there. She stared back at him mutely, her vision blurry with tears.

"Look at what your sister did!" Mom exclaimed, gesturing at the floor. Darren turned on Mom, his expression furious.

"You mean look at what *you* did," he shot back.

"Don't you talk to me like..."

"Shut up, Mom," Darren retorted. He stepped carefully between pieces of glass, reaching for Tessa. Tessa grabbed his hand, but shook her head when he tried to pull her onto her feet.

"My feet," she whimpered. Darren looked down, seeing the blood all over the floor. All over her feet. He turned to Mom, balling his hands into fists.

"Look at what you did!" he shouted, pointing at Tessa's feet.

"What *I* did?" Mom retorted, her voice rising. "You *dare*..."

3

"Go to hell, Mom," Darren interrupted. He turned to Tessa, reaching down and sliding one hand under her knees, the other under her back. He lifted her off the floor, using one hand to open the door.

"Don't you walk out on me!" Mom shouted.

Darren ignored her, stepping out onto the porch, then down the stairs. He walked across the short path to the sidewalk, carrying Tessa in his arms. She looked up at him, wiping her tears away with one hand.

"Sorry sis," he mumbled.

Tessa nodded mutely, glancing over his shoulder. The front door was still open, and she could hear her mother screaming through it. A bottle hurtled through one of the windows, shattering it, then landing on the grass beyond, rolling a few yards before coming to a stop.

"It's okay," Darren murmured, smiling down at her. It was forced, she knew, but she appreciated him trying. "Dad'll be home soon."

He took her rightward down the sidewalk, then turned right again, down a narrow path. It led to the backyard...to the white sand beach. And the ocean. She smelled the tang of saltwater in the air as they approached it, a slight breeze cooling her sun-baked skin. She gazed across the sand, blindingly bright with reflected sunlight, watching as wave after wave crashed upon the shore.

Darren walked all the way to the shore, then stepped into the water, waves lapping at his sandals. He lowered her gently, so that she sat on the dry sand, her feet dipping into the water. A wave rushed toward her, bathing her feet, then taking her blood back with it into the endless blue.

"Let's take a look," her brother said, crouching down and peering at her feet. There was a piece of glass stuck in the bottom of each foot. He glanced up at her. "I'm gonna pull them out, okay?"

She nodded, taking a breath in, then holding it.

Darren grabbed one of the pieces of glass, then pulled, and she bit back a yell, watching as blood gushed from her foot into the water.

4

"That's one," he said. "One more, okay?"

He pulled out the piece of glass from her other foot, and this time it hurt…a lot. She cried out, yanking her foot back. But the deed was done, and Darren tossed the piece of glass into the ocean before she could get a look at it. He rinsed the blood from his fingers, then smiled at her.

"All done."

"Thanks," she mumbled.

He crouched there, looking at her, his smile fading.

"I'm really sorry."

"It's okay," Tessa insisted, forcing herself to smile. "Really."

"No it's not," he retorted. "I shouldn't've been late."

"I could've waited for you," she countered.

"Tessa…"

She heard shouting in the distance, and looked over her shoulder to their house in the distance. The shouting grew louder, followed by a scream.

"Dad's home," Darren guessed.

Tessa said nothing, turning back to gaze at the ocean. The waves lapped at her feet gently, the water warm and gentle. Her feet stung where it touched her wounds, but she didn't mind. The water was cleansing. She closed her eyes, feeling the breeze on her skin, hearing the endless crashing of the waves and the hiss of foam on the sand.

"Do you really think he'll leave her?" she asked, keeping her eyes closed. Even asking the question made her guts squirm.

"After this?" Darren asked. There was a long pause. "Maybe."

Tessa opened her eyes, staring at him.

"What's going to happen to us?"

Darren smiled, sitting beside her. He wrapped an arm around her, pulling her to lean her head against his shoulder.

"Dad'll get us," he answered. "Everyone knows about Mom now."

"What if he doesn't?" Tessa pressed, picking at her lip.

"He will," Darren promised, giving her a squeeze. "I promise."

5

"Yeah, but what if he *doesn't?*" she insisted. "What if they split us up?"

"No way," he replied. "Not gonna happen."

"Yeah, but…"

"Look at me," Darren interjected. She lifted her head from his shoulder, staring at him.

"I won't let it happen," Darren interjected firmly, his expression dead serious. "Dad won't let it happen."

Tessa lowered her gaze, tears welling up in her eyes.

"You don't know that," she mumbled.

"Tessa," Darren insisted, grabbing the sides of her head gently, lifting her gaze to his. He leaned in, kissing her forehead, then pulling away. "I promise you, I will *never* let them separate us."

"You promise?"

"I promise," he repeated. "I'll always be here for you, sis. Always."

She dared to smile, ignoring the shouting in the distance. The waves drowned out the sound anyway, cleansing the air as they'd cleansed her foot. The ocean always made things better.

They sat there for a long while, neither of them speaking. Tessa watched wave after wave advance, kissing her toes before retreating back into the sea. The sun felt marvelous on her bronze skin, her long wavy hair blowing in the ocean breeze.

"Love you Darren," she murmured. She felt him stir, then give her a squeeze.

"Love you too sis."

Tessa heard someone calling her name, and fear gripped her. She twisted around, spotting a man trudging through the sand toward them. She immediately relaxed, standing up and limping toward him.

"Daddy!" she cried. She limped up to him, leaving bloody footprints on the white sand.

"Tessa!" Dad exclaimed, rushing up to her and bending over to look at her. He was a big man, tall and broad-shouldered, and impressively muscular. "What happened?" he asked. "Are you okay?"

"I cut my feet," she answered. He took one foot at a time, peering at her wounds. His expression darkened.

"On the glass," he stated. It wasn't a question, but she nodded. His jawline rippled, and he scooped her up in his arms, bringing her back to the waves lapping at the sandy beach. He lowered her gently into the water, rinsing the sand from her wounds, then turned back toward the house. "Come on," he urged Darren.

"No," Tessa blurted out, clutching him tightly. "I don't wanna go back inside."

Dad hesitated, then turned toward the street instead of the house. He walked back to the sidewalk, stopping there. To Tessa's surprise, the streets were packed with people – kids and adults – all of them looking upward.

Tessa followed their gaze, and saw a dozen large black objects floating high in the sky, just below the clouds. They descended slowly, spreading over the city.

"Dad, look!" Darren cried.

"I see them," Dad replied tersely. He grimaced, glancing down at Darren. "Come on," he added.

"But I don't want to."

"You don't have a choice," Dad retorted. "You have to come."

"But Dad…"

"Don't argue with me," Dad interjected. Darren stared up at his father, his face paling. But he stood his ground.

"We could go back inside," he insisted. "We can hide from…"

"No one can hide from them," Dad snapped. Darren's mouth snapped shut, his eyes turning moist. Dad's expression softened. "It'll be fine," he added. "Nothing bad is going to happen."

"But last year…" Darren protested.

"I know what happened to Elan," Dad interjected. "But it's not going to happen to us."

Darren hesitated, then nodded, and they joined the others on the street, watching as the black objects continued to descend toward the city. One of them, Tessa realized, was falling toward *them*. As it got closer, it was clear that it was a black, oval-shaped ship. Four men in black robes levitated around it, holding long staves with white crystals on top.

The crowd parted as the ship lowered itself toward the street a few dozen yards ahead. The ship slowed its descent as it reached street-level, stopping to levitate a few feet above it. The black-robed men surrounding it eyed the crowd, their expressions flat.

"Come on," Dad urged, walking forward through the crowd, squeezing past the people ahead of them. Tessa saw other parents doing the same, squeezing past the adults with their children, making their way closer to the ships and the robed men. A ring of parents and their children began to form a few yards away from the ship. More than a few of the children were crying...and some of the adults, too. Tessa pulled on her father's shirt.

"Daddy?" she asked. He looked down, smiling at her. But only with his lips.

"It'll be okay," he tried to reassure her. But she knew he was telling himself that as much as he was telling her.

The black-robed men formed a line in front of the big black ship. One of them came forward; he did not walk, however. His black boots hovered over the ground as he levitated forward a few feet ahead of the others, then stopped. He stared at the crowd for a moment longer, then slammed the butt of his staff onto the street.

A gust of air shot out from him, striking the crowd, whipping through Tessa's hair and clothes. She clung to her father tightly, her guts squirming.

"I am Finder Warren," the black-robed man declared. He had a book in his other hand, and held this out before him, letting go of it. The book levitated in mid-air, the pages turning of their own accord, then stopping suddenly.

"As your name is called," Warren declared, "...come forward. If I call a name and no one comes forward," he added, "...we will find you, and the punishment will be severe. If you come forward for someone else, we will know, and the punishment will be severe."

Tessa glanced at Darren, then at Dad. They were both staring at Finder Warren. Tessa clung to Dad, wondering what was going

8

to happen next. She'd never been to one of these before, although all the kids talked about it. Dad had always insisted that she and Darren stay in the house every year it happened.

But this year was different, of course.

"Balister of forty-six Abaxter Street," Finder Warren called out, his voice booming over the crowd. Moments later, a boy came forward, and Warren gestured at the robed man to his right. Balister walked up to this man, staring up at him silently. Balister's eyes were as wide as saucers, his face pale. The robed man pulled a clear crystal orb from his robes, holding it before the boy.

"Touch the orb," the man commanded.

Balister hesitated, then placed his hand on top of the orb.

The black-robed man paused, then inclined his head.

"You may go," he stated. Balister practically ran back to his family, vanishing into the crowd.

"Valerie of forty-nine Abaxter street, Grennan of fifty-four Abaxter street," Finder Warren called out. An older girl and boy walked up, and Warren gestured for each to stop before one of the other robed men. They touched the orbs hovering before the men; a moments later, the robed men gestured for them to go back into the crowd.

Finder Warren called out more names, and each time two children would come up, touch the orbs, and be asked to leave. Most stayed in the crowd however, watching each pair of children as they were called, all eyes on the two black-robed men...and their orbs. Tessa realized that Finder Warren was calling them by street, from A to Z. Which meant that their street was going to go last. That meant they'd have to be out here for a good while longer. She didn't mind, of course...not with Mom still home.

As the minutes passed, the crowd began to dwindle, people gradually losing interest in the endless parade of children being sent away by the cloaked men. Tessa's mind wandered, already planning what she'd be doing after this. Mom was probably already asleep, so she could get a snack, and spend the rest of the day...

"Darren of 34 Zucker Street."

9

Tessa snapped out of her daydream, glancing down at Darren, who'd stiffened. He turned to look up at Dad questioningly, and Tessa did as well. Dad nodded at Darren, smiling reassuringly.

"Go on," he prompted. "We'll have ice cream when we get home."

Darren smiled back, then glanced at Tessa, who was suddenly nervous.

"Don't go," she urged.

"Don't worry sis," he reassured her. "This'll only take a sec."

He walked up to Finder Warren then, who gestured for him to go to the cloaked man on his left. He obeyed, stopping in front of the man. The clear orb levitated between them, and Darren hesitated, glancing back at Tessa and Dad. Then he put his hand on top of the orb, holding it there.

Nothing happened.

Darren gave a relieved smile, and was about to take his hand off when the orb changed, turning a slight yellow. He stared at it, then looked up at the cloaked man, the blood draining from his face.

Finder Warren grabbed the book floating before him, shutting it was a loud *snap*. Darren flinched, taking a step backward. His hand slipped off the orb, and it shifted back to clear once again.

"Come," Finder Warren ordered, putting the book back into the recesses of his cloak, then gesturing at the ship. A door swung down from it, forming a ramp that led inside.

Darren shook his head mutely, taking another step back. Finder Warren gestured at the ship again.

"I won't ask you again," he warned.

Darren bolted.

"Darren!" Tessa cried, watching as her brother sprinted toward her. She felt her Dad's arms tighten around her, and he burst forward, pushing through the crowd toward Darren. He ran up to him, then stopped suddenly, as if hitting a wall. Darren did as well, ricocheting off an invisible barrier between them. Darren recovered, leaping at Dad. But the invisible wall stopped him.

"Dad!" he shouted, his eyes wide with fear. "Daddy!"

Finder Warren lifted a hand, and Darren lurched upward suddenly, levitating a foot off the ground. He began floating backward toward the ship.

"No!" Dad yelled. "Don't take him!"

Finder Warren stared at Dad for a moment, then turned his back to him, levitating back toward the ship. The other two cloaked men placed their orbs back within their cloaks. Darren continued to be pulled toward the open door of the ship. The air rippled slightly around him, under the strange power of the cloaked men.

"Dad!" Darren pleaded. "Make them stop! I don't wanna go!"

"Darren!" Dad cried. "You can't take my son. You can't take my son!"

But Finder Warren ignored them, and Darren disappeared within the ship, the ramp swinging shut. The cloaked men resumed their positions around it, and the ship began to rise into the air.

"Darren!" Tessa screamed, struggling out of her Dad's grip and jumping to the ground. She ignored the pain in her feet, bursting forward. The invisible wall was gone, and she ran toward the rising ship, her soles leaving bloody footprints on the street. "Darren!"

The black ship flew upward, rising faster and faster, higher than the tallest building in Osa now. Tessa stopped, watching as it shrank against the pure blue sky. Watching until it was so small she couldn't see it anymore.

And then her legs wobbled, and she fell to her hands and knees. She lowered her forehead to the sun-baked street, and wept.

Chapter 1

"Try again," Ariana urged.

Kyle sighed, pushing himself up from the ground, then standing up. He brushed dirt and grass from the front of his white shirt and pants, grimacing at the stains they'd just acquired. There was a reason Runic students wore white; it was because they stayed indoors, doing research and inventing things like civilized people, instead of going outside trying to blast each other to pieces.

"All right, all right," Kyle muttered. He faced Ariana, taking a few steps back, then nodding. Ariana smiled at him, running a hand through her long black hair. Her skin was terribly pale in the light of the noon sun, but that was hardly surprising. She wasn't technically alive, after all...she was undead, kept animated only by the strange power of the hidden magical green crystal buried in her brain. Only a handful of people knew Ariana's true nature; everyone else assumed she was just a normal young woman. Which she was, mostly. Sure, her skin was as pale and cold as a corpse's. And she was immortal, and possessed of enormous strength and incredibly keen senses, and never ate or slept. But other than that, she *was* perfectly normal...and the best, most loyal girlfriend he could ask for.

"Remember your shield," Ariana reminded him. Kyle nodded, focusing inward. He felt power there, vibrating in the bones of his skull, and *pulled* it inward to the center of his mind's eye. It formed a thin thread of magic, and he wove it into a tight knot, then sent it outward. A faint blue sphere appeared around him. It was a gravity shield, capable of repelling just about anything that was thrown at it.

"Ready," Kyle called out.

"Neutralize my shield first," Ariana instructed. A single gravity shield appeared around her, its outline a faint blue to Kyle's eyes. To anyone else the shield would be nearly invisible, marked only by a faint distortion of light, but Kyle was capable of *seeing* magic...a trait he'd inherited from his god-like grandfather.

"Okay," Kyle replied. He studied Ariana's shield; it was actually *two* gravity spheres, the outer one shoving outward, the inner one pushing inward. In order to neutralize her shields, he had to create a shield of exactly the same strength around her, but in opposite directions. So the outer layer had to suck inward, the inner layer push outward. That would completely nullify the shield, making her vulnerable to his attack.

In theory.

Kyle wove the appropriate patterns in his mind, *pulling* the magic from the edges of his mind's eye and shaping them. Then he sent them out at Ariana's shields, streaming magic to the pattern. He saw the blue sphere around her darken slightly.

"I think I got it," Kyle stated, not at all sure that he had.

"Now let's spar," Ariana replied.

"Are you *sure* this is safe?" he asked nervously. The green crystal in Ariana's skull – shoved through her forehead, hidden beneath her flawless skin – had magical defenses automatically programmed into it. Her Weaving teacher, Master Owens, had nearly died trying to spar her.

"I can suppress my shard's reactions now," Ariana answered. "I've been practicing it for the last week." Which meant, of course, that she'd been practicing every night, while everyone else slept. Not being able to sleep had its perks.

"All right," Kyle decided. He nodded at her, creating a gravity shield around himself. "Ready?" Ariana smirked.

"You're about to find out."

Kyle smiled despite himself, then took a deep breath in, letting it out slowly, and nodded at her. He felt his heart start to pound in his chest, butterflies flitting about in his stomach.

Here goes...

A fireball shot out from Ariana, flying through the air right at him!

Kyle dodged left, magic automatically weaving in his mind's eye, creating a gravity sphere to the left of the fireball. The fireball clipped the gravity sphere, sucking leftward...and directing it right into his shields. The fireball bounced off, landing on the grass below.

"Oops," Kyle blurted out.

"Silly," Ariana teased, grinning widely. A stream of water appeared over the burning grass, extinguishing the flames. "Try again."

"Okay," Kyle replied. He sighed, then nodded. Another fireball shot out toward him with unnerving speed, and this time he dodged left, creating a gravity sphere to the *right* of the projectile. The fireball swerved rightward toward the sphere...and away from him.

"Ha!" Kyle exclaimed triumphantly.

Then he saw his shields vanish, and a force sucked him rightward, pulling him right into the path of the fireball. The projectile stopped in mid-flight right before hitting him, and he stumbled to the ground.

Again.

"Damn," Kyle muttered. He picked himself up off of the ground, shaking his head at Ariana. She laughed, walking up to him and giving him a quick peck on the cheek. He tried to glare at her, but found it impossible to do so. Just looking at her made him melt.

"Don't rely too much on your shields," she counseled. "Remember that they can be taken away from you."

"Yeah yeah," Kyle mumbled. While he knew *how* she'd nullified his shields — by creating gravity fields of equal strength but opposite polarity to his own – he hadn't even come close to perfecting the technique.

"Don't worry," Ariana soothed. "Practice enough and it'll become second nature."

Easy for you to say, Kyle thought, wisely keeping it to himself. After all, Ariana had an extra eight hours a day while everyone else slept. Not to mention the time saved by not having to eat or drink, or rest. Ariana never got tired...unless she ran out of magic.

"Had enough?" Ariana asked.

"Yeah," Kyle admitted. "It's been a long day." And that it had; he'd been up since sunrise receiving lessons from Master Lee, his Runic instructor. He'd only finished later this afternoon...and then met up with Ariana to learn Weaving. As a Runic, Kyle was destined to learn how to create magical items called runics, while Weavers learned how to use magic to fly, throw fireballs, and do other flashy, heroic things. Kyle had accepted his role as a Runic, for the most part. He still felt jealous of Ariana's abilities from time to time. That's why she'd agreed to teach him Weaving, in secret.

"What did you learn from Master Lee today?" Ariana inquired.

"A lot," Kyle admitted. "Nothing exciting," he added ruefully. "Mostly just about different minerals and stuff."

"What do you mean?"

"Well, different minerals interact with magic in different ways," Kyle answered. "I'm supposed to memorize a whole bunch of them by tomorrow." He walked toward a small book he'd set on the grass, picking it up. It was, he knew, a book for young children, with more pictures than words. He was still practically illiterate here on Doma, the language being completely different than English back home. If it weren't for the magical earring in his right ear, he wouldn't be able to understand a word of what Ariana was telling him.

"Good luck," Ariana offered.

"Thanks," Kyle muttered. He glanced up at the sky then. "It's getting dark," he noted. The sun had already kissed the horizon, the few clouds above cast in a deep purple hue.

"Oh, right," Ariana replied, her face lighting up. "We're having dinner with Kalibar tonight!" She grabbed Kyle's hand, steering him back toward the Great Tower in the distance. Forty-two stories tall, with a huge crystalline pyramid at its peak, the Great Tower was the tallest building in the city of Stridon – and the home of the highest government officials in the land. That included Grand Weaver Kalibar, the co-emperor of the Empire...and Kyle and Ariana's adoptive father. Even though Kyle's real father and stepfather were back on Earth, Kalibar was Kyle's father in *this* world.

"I'm glad he's back," Kyle stated, smiling back at Ariana. Kalibar had taken a much-needed vacation after Sabin's defeat, bringing Petra to his mansion in Bellingham and showing her around. They'd returned yesterday for the celebratory parade, but Kalibar had been so busy with that, he hadn't been able to spend any time with Kyle and Ariana. Tonight was the first time they'd get to spend time together in nearly a week.

"Me too," Ariana agreed. She went faster, nearly sprinting from the grass onto the cobblestone path that led back to the Tower. Kyle struggled to keep up; not only did Ariana never get sleepy, her muscles never tired either. She could walk – or run – at a brisk pace indefinitely. A feat that she sometimes forgot others couldn't replicate.

"Hey, slow down," Kyle protested. Ariana did so, and they walked hand-in-hand, the Tower growing nearer with every step. Kyle glanced at Ariana, remarking on how happy she seemed. Seeing her smile had been rare before Ampir had killed Sabin; now she smiled all the time. It made her all the more lovely when she did so.

They walked the rest of the way in silence, reaching the huge open double-doors of the Tower and stepping inside the lobby beyond. Three stories tall, the lobby was magnificent beyond description, with polished granite floors and stone columns that rose to the ceiling far above. Powerful gravity fields allowed people to walk upside-down on the ceiling – as they could on almost every floor of the Tower. In the center of the lobby was a tall statue of a Battle-Weaver, standing atop a solid gold pedestal. They walked past this, continuing on to the long hallway beyond, their gravity boots *clopping* on the granite floor. Eventually, they reached the riser at the end, and stepped onto it. A magical elevator of sorts, the riser brought them upward with remarkable speed, coming to a stop rather abruptly at the 41st floor. They stepped off, continuing down another hallway until they reached the door of Kalibar's retirement suite. Ariana knocked on the door, and within moments the door became translucent. Kyle saw a stern man clad in black plate armor staring down at him from the other side. The man was an elite guard, one of Kalibar's personal bodyguards. Only the most skilled of the Battle-Weavers earned the right to wear that black armor. The guard's expression softened as soon as he recognized Kyle and Ariana.

The door became opaque again, and then it swung inward. The guard ushered Kyle and Ariana through into the massive suite beyond. There, sitting around a long table, were Kalibar, Erasmus, and Petra. Kyle broke into a huge grin.

"Kalibar!" he exclaimed, rushing up to the table. Kalibar turned to Kyle, then smiled broadly, rising from his chair and walking forward to embrace Kyle, then Ariana.

"Kyle, Ariana!" Kalibar greeted. He stood back from his adopted children then, his brown eyes twinkling. Despite his sixty-odd years, Kalibar appeared much younger, his tall frame toned and muscular. His white hair – completely shaved off a week ago – was starting to grow back in, as was his white goatee. He was quite handsome, the very picture of a regal emperor.

"How was your vacation?" Ariana asked. Kalibar gestured for the two to sit opposite himself and Petra, and they did so.

"Very relaxing," Kalibar answered. "I spent a day in Bellingham, and then took Petra on a flying tour of the Empire."

Kyle glanced at Petra, feeling his cheeks flush as he did so. A member of the Barren tribes, she was somewhat shorter than Kalibar, but equally toned, her skin nearly black. Tattoos covered almost every inch of her body, coming up the sides of her neck and ending at her temples. Thin, raised scars extended from the sides of her neck to her temples like the bones in a bat's wing. Her hair was black, and as usual was tied back into a ponytail. She wore a white shirt that would have been loose on just about anyone else, but given her impressively feminine proportions, found itself barely adequate to its task. Kyle found himself staring, and jerked his gaze away, feeling his cheeks grow even hotter.

"What did you think of it?" Ariana asked Petra, rather pointedly ignoring Kyle's consternation.

"It was...big," Petra replied.

"I assume you're referring to the mansion and the Empire," Erasmus said with a grin, nudging Kalibar with his elbow.

"You didn't invite your wife to dinner," Petra observed, ignoring Erasmus's comment. Erasmus cleared his throat.

"Yes, well," he replied. "She doesn't like to come when I'm with Kalibar, on account of how much I drink."

"You could drink less," Petra quipped.

"You haven't met my wife," Erasmus shot back.

Just then, the door opened, and a tall man clad neck to toe in shimmering golden armor strode into the room, stopping before the table.

"Darius," Kalibar greeted. "Come, join us for dinner."

Darius nodded, glancing at Kyle as he sat down next to Erasmus. The portly Grand Runic shot the bodyguard a sour look. He'd never taken a liking to Darius, almost certainly because the bodyguard was a bit of a jerk. Erasmus took great pleasure in trying to insult the man, although that pleasure was always short-lived. Darius never lost their battle of words...or any other battle, for that matter.

"Ah, damn," Erasmus muttered. "I just lost my appetite."

"Probably for the best," Darius retorted, eyeing Erasmus's protuberant belly.

"I'll fetch Jenkins," Kalibar stated, ignoring the exchange. He put a hand on a crystal sphere sitting on an end-table next to where he sat, and within moments, a man wearing a blue shirt and black pants entered the room. It was Jenkins, Kalibar's loyal butler.

18

Jenkins took everyone's orders with his customary quiet efficiency, then left the suite as quickly as he'd come.

"So," Erasmus stated, leaning forward and rubbing his hands together eagerly, his eyes on Kalibar. "Now that you're back, what's next?"

"I've been thinking about that all week," Kalibar admitted. "With Sabin gone, the Empire is relatively safe...but we still have all of the Death Weaver camps to deal with." Kyle nodded; even though Ampir had killed every last one of Sabin's Chosen, there were still countless underground lairs filled with thousands upon thousands of Death Weavers to consider.

"I'm not too worried about them threatening the Empire," Erasmus replied. "But they might stir up trouble in the surrounding towns."

"We also have to finish rebuilding Stridon," Kalibar reminded them. Nearly a quarter of the city had been destroyed by the Void Behemoth a couple of weeks ago. Erasmus's Runics had worked day and night to rebuild, their remarkable efforts having inspired many talented students in the Secula Magna to consider becoming Runics instead of Weavers.

"Well under way," Erasmus declared proudly. "The Southwest Quarter is going to be the most technologically advanced in the whole city when my Runics are done with it!"

"I don't doubt it," Kalibar agreed. While Kalibar's strength lay in strategy and warfare, Erasmus was remarkably gifted when it came to developing systems and infrastructure. As co-emperors of the most powerful country in the world, they made a formidable team.

Jenkins returned, followed by one of his assistants, and soon the table was filled to overflowing with silver platters and bottles of wine. Jenkins removed the lids from each platter, revealing Kyle's favorite dish – roasted duck. From then on, there was only the sound of smacking lips as everyone devoured their meal. The food, as always, was fit for a king...or in this case, two. When everyone had finished – which didn't take very long – Jenkins returned to whisk away the remains. Kyle noted that Petra's plate was still half-filled; she ate modestly, no doubt her secret to maintaining her remarkable figure. Ariana, being dead, ate nothing at all.

"How is the political climate in the Council?" Kalibar asked Erasmus, leaning back in his chair and sipping on his wine.

"They haven't turned on us yet," Erasmus answered. "We're about as popular as we're going to get." He leaned forward eagerly. "I say we take advantage of it and push as much legislation as we can."

"Within reason," Kalibar agreed. "We don't want to alienate anyone by appearing to take advantage of them."

"Like they wouldn't do the same," Erasmus scoffed. "Bastards'll turn on us first chance they get!" But he sighed, leaning back and sipping his own wine. True to form, he was already on his third glass. Kyle caught Petra eyeing the portly Grand Runic disapprovingly. She'd barely touched her own wine; apparently she wasn't much of a drinker.

"We'll enjoy their support as long as we can," Kalibar stated. Then he shook his head. "Ah, look at me, carrying on about work." He turned to Ariana. "How have you been, Ariana?"

"Good," Ariana replied. "I've been training every day with Master Owens. I'm learning a lot."

"I don't doubt it," Kalibar replied. He knew – as did just about everyone else – that Ariana had already far outmatched every Weaver student in her age range. Her daily sparring matches with Master Owens, the second-best Battle-Weaver in the Empire, had honed her skills considerably. "And how have you been, Kyle?" he asked, turning to Kyle.

"Not bad," Kyle admitted. He'd been training nearly as intensely with Master Lee, Erasmus's mother. Lee was an extremely effective teacher, albeit far less pleasant than Owens. "I'm learning a lot too."

"I bet you are," Erasmus agreed, grinning from ear-to-ear. "Can you imagine what I had to go through growing up?" He raised his wine glass. "Now you know why I drink!"

"I thought it was because of your wife," Petra retorted with an arch of her eyebrow. Erasmus smirked at her.

20

"They say a man marries someone just like his mother," he shot back. Then he took a robust gulp of his wine.

"Yes, well," Kalibar interjected. "I'm glad you're both doing well," he stated, smiling at Kyle and Ariana. Then he turned to Erasmus. "And how are you doing, old friend?"

"Busy," the Grand Runic replied with a rueful grin. "Between running the damn Empire, working on your idea about magical vacuity, and discovering new patterns with the K-Array, I've barely had time to sleep!"

"How many new patterns have you found?" Kalibar inquired. Based on an idea Kyle had a few weeks ago, the K-Array allowed Runics and Weavers – for the first time in millennia – to discover new magical patterns from plants and such. It had revolutionized the study of magic throughout the Empire...and made Kyle quite popular among the academic elite of the Secula Magna. Kyle knew he hardly deserved all of the credit; after all, it had been Kalibar who'd fleshed out his idea and made it actually work.

"Four," Erasmus replied. "I still think the invisibility pattern is the best of them. I'll have one of my Runics send you a debriefing."

"Much appreciated," Kalibar replied. "Anything else new?"

"Well, yes," Erasmus answered, glancing at Petra. Kalibar raised an eyebrow.

"What is it?"

"Remember all those bodies we found the day you came back from Orja?" Erasmus asked. Kyle saw Kalibar nod. When they'd returned from killing Sabin, reports of nearly forty people dropping dead – at the same time – had come to the Council's attention. Then came the reports of hundreds more having dropped dead throughout the other cities and towns of the Empire...also at the same time.

"Well," Erasmus continued, "...the coroner's office finished the autopsy of the first body they'd found...a butler in the Tower. They found a hole in the front of his skull...and that the front of his brain had been vaporized."

"What?" Kalibar exclaimed.

21

"That's what I said," Erasmus replied. "Then the coroner started the other autopsies at the head, and found the same thing in every other body they found."

"Interesting," Kalibar murmured.

"Damn right it's interesting," Erasmus agreed. "Autopsies on the other bodies found throughout the Empire showed the exact same findings. Nobody can make any sense out of it."

"I believe I can," Kalibar countered, leaning back in his chair and sighing. He glanced at Petra. "Remember the Chosen...the Immortals that nearly killed us when we were searching for Ariana in the Barrens?"

"I do," Petra replied.

"They dropped dead suddenly," Kalibar continued, "...with holes in their skulls where their shards had been."

"On the day Sabin was killed?" Erasmus asked.

"That's right."

"Well I'll be damned," Erasmus breathed, slumping back in his chair. Then his eyes widened, and he jerked forward. "Wait, that means..."

"Every one of the forty people found dead here in Stridon...and every one of the hundreds found elsewhere...were Sabin's hidden Chosen," Kalibar concluded.

"My god!" Erasmus blurted out. "You mean all this time we've had a few dozen Chosen living here, right under our noses?"

"Not anymore," Darius piped in with a smirk, taking a gulp of wine.

"Sabin's infiltration of the Empire was greater than anyone expected," Kalibar murmured. He shook his head. "We're lucky Ampir struck when he did."

"I agree," Erasmus replied. "And I for one plan on celebrating. A toast," he declared, raising his wine glass. "To peace throughout the Empire at last!"

With that, everyone raised their glasses – except for Ariana, of course – and took a generous gulp of their drinks. The conversation turned back to happier topics. Within another half-hour, everyone was ready for bed. Kyle retired to his room, washing up and flopping onto his bed. He rolled onto his side and closed his eyes, a smile on his lips. Kalibar and Petra were back, and the Empire was at peace. There was nothing more to fear, no Sabin threatening to kill them, no Chosen hiding among them waiting to strike.

Kyle gave a contented sigh. At long last, after months of terror, everything was finally going their way.

Chapter 2

Master Lee stared at Kyle from across the small wooden table they were both sitting at on the first floor of the Runic Archives, her thin, wrinkled arms folded in front of her. So old that she was almost painful to look at, his teacher's expression was sour, deepening the wrinkles on her face to the point that he could have hid pennies in them. Kyle stared back at her, wracking his brain for the answer to her question.

Which class of minerals is least resistant to magical flow?

He'd forgotten to study after the dinner last night...and now he was paying for it.

"I'd like an answer before I die," Master Lee stated dryly, drumming her wrinkled fingertips on the table. Kyle nodded, feeling sweat dripping down his armpits. No matter how many days he'd spent training with her, Lee still terrified him. He looked away from her, absently gazing at the shelves of books and various artifacts around him. His gaze stopped on a painting of a boat on the far wall, making him think of the *Defiance*...the ship he and Ariana had traveled to Orja on. It'd had metal beams in its hull to conduct magic away from the cargo hold and into the ocean.

"Metals," Kyle answered, turning back to Lee. She stopped drumming her fingers and nodded grudgingly.

"Took you long enough," she grumbled. "Which minerals are best at storing magic?"

"Um...quartz, diamond, mica..." Kyle answered.

"And?"

Kyle stared at her blankly, and she sighed.

"You failed to study," she observed. Kyle lowered his gaze, feeling his cheeks flush.

"Kalibar came back," he protested. "We..."

"Stop," Lee interjected. Kyle's mouth snapped shut. "Don't make excuses. Own your failure."

"I'm sorry," Kyle mumbled.

"Of course you are," Lee replied. "Failure feels terrible." She leaned in, a smirk on her lips. "That's why it's such a good teacher."

"Is that why *you* make me feel terrible all the time?" he asked. Lee chuckled.

"Now you're catching on."

"I don't get it," Kyle muttered, shaking his head. "Why do I have to learn about all these minerals?"

"Explain."

"Well, diamonds store magic the best, and metals conduct magic, so isn't that all I need to know to make runics?" Kyle asked.

"Take a cube," Lee ordered, gesturing at the dozen or so brown crystal cubes sitting on the table before him. Kyle did so. "Inscribe the fire pattern like this," she continued, drawing on a sheet of paper. Kyle studied the pattern she'd drawn; it was the fire pattern, but inscribed deep within the cube, with an unusually long crystalline "wire" extending to the top of the cube. The longer that wire, the higher up above the cube the flame would appear. He'd learned that lesson the hard way, scorching his cubes with the first few fire patterns he'd inscribed because he'd made the wire too short.

Kyle obeyed, picking up the cube and placing it near his forehead, then closing his eyes and weaving the inscribing pattern. He completed the task quickly, setting the cube down on the table.

"Activate it," Lee instructed.

Kyle streamed magic to the cube, and a small flame appeared an inch or so above the cube.

"Do it again," Lee ordered. "This time make the flame appear a foot above the cube."

Kyle stared at her blankly.

"I can't," he protested.

"Why not?"

"I can't put the pattern any deeper into the cube," Kyle answered.

"Exactly," Lee agreed. She reached up with one hand, grabbing at thin air, and a crystal cube appeared between her fingers. She set it down on the table before him; it was, Kyle realized, half-brown and half-clear.

"What's that?" he asked.

"The brown half is dravite, like your other cubes," she answered. "The top is quartz. Dravite conducts magic better than quartz."

"Okay."

"Inscribe the fire pattern in the dravite, and extend the wire through the quartz to the top," Lee commanded. Kyle nodded, inscribing the pattern as instructed. Then he set the cube so that the quartz half was facing up.

"Go on," Lee prompted impatiently.

Kyle streamed magic to the cube...and a small flame appeared over a foot above it.

"Whoa," Kyle breathed.

"Exactly," Lee agreed. "Now, quartz conducts magic more poorly than dravite...and more slowly. What would happen if you made a wire out of a mineral that barely conducted magic?"

"It would take a while to conduct it," Kyle reasoned.

"Precisely," Lee confirmed. She reached into her pocket, retrieving a diamond. "Inscribe the fire pattern into this," she ordered. He took the diamond from her, doing as she'd asked. "Now stream magic to it," she commanded. Again, he complied.

A moment later, a flame appeared above the diamond.

"Inscribe another fire rune deeper within the diamond," Lee continued, "...with a long wire going up to the top of the crystal." Kyle did so. "Now stream magic to the crystal."

He complied, and one flame appeared above the diamond. A second later, a second flame appeared several feet above the first.

"Ahhh," Kyle murmured. "Got it. The longer the wire, the longer it takes to conduct the pattern outside of the crystal."

"Correct," Lee agreed. "And the worse the conductor, the longer it takes."

"So I can time patterns," Kyle realized. Lee nodded, a smile deepening the wrinkles in her cheeks.

"Exactly."

Master Lee reached into her pants pocket then, retrieving what looked to be a silver amulet. It had a glittering diamond in the center, with gemstones of various colors at the edges like numbers on a clock. Between these were a ring of strange symbols etched into the metal. She handed it to him.

"Look at this," she ordered.

Kyle obeyed, grabbing the amulet and taking a closer look. The outer gemstones had tiny glowing runes embedded within them, and multicolored mineral "threads" that connected them to the central diamond. The diamond itself had more runes inscribed within, glowing faintly to Kyle's eye.

"What does it do?" Kyle asked, glancing up at Lee.

"No one knows," Lee answered. "Not yet, anyway. It was dug up a week ago."

"Dug up?"

"From an archaeological dig site in Meros," she explained. When Kyle stared at her blankly, she smirked. "An island seven hundred and fifty miles west of here. You've been close to there, I believe."

"Wait, what?"

"It's near the Shimmering Isle," Lee said. Kyle's eyes widened. He and Ariana had taken the *Defiance* – a shipping vessel – to the Shimmering Isle on their way to the Barrens over a week ago. That was where the Captain and his crew lived now.

27

Just then, Kyle heard footsteps from behind, and he turned to see Erasmus and Petra walking toward them. Petra was wearing her traditional Reaper uniform, made of rough black fabric that covered her from her neck to her toes, and even her hands. The uniform was skintight, and it was quite clear that Erasmus was having as hard of a time not staring as Kyle was.

"Good morning mother," Erasmus greeted, walking up to Master Lee and bending over to kiss her on one wrinkly cheek. "Good morning Kyle," he added. He gestured to Petra. "Mother, this is Petra, from..."

"The Barrens," Lee interjected. She stood from her chair, walking up to Petra and extending a hand. Petra shook it. "A pleasure to meet you."

"Likewise," Petra replied.

"I was just, ah, showing Petra around the Archives," Erasmus stated. "She wants to see our collection before she returns to the Barrens," he added.

"Wait, you're leaving?" Kyle blurted out. Petra glanced at him, and he immediately felt his cheeks flush. Damn his traitorous body!

"Soon," she confirmed.

"But isn't Kalibar supposed to...uh," Kyle stammered, stopping himself abruptly. Petra arched an eyebrow.

"Teach me magic?" she asked. Kyle blushed again, knowing how self-conscious Petra had been in the past about Kalibar besting her in combat. She was proud and competitive, and hadn't taken the loss well...at first. "He has been," she answered. "Every day for the last week."

"Oh."

"Don't let us stop you," Master Lee stated, sitting back down in her chair. Kyle glanced down, realizing he was still holding the amulet, and handed it back to Lee.

"What's that?" Erasmus asked, pointing at the amulet. Lee handed it to him.

"Latest find from Meros," she answered. "Came in yesterday."

"What a marvelous piece," Erasmus declared, turning it over in his hands. "Fully intact?"

28

"It appears so."

"Any idea what it does yet?"

"Not a clue," Lee admitted. "It's similar to the other runic artifacts we've found recently," she added.

"Mmm," Erasmus mumbled, running a hand through his white beard. "Was it found in the deepest levels of the ruins?"

"Yes."

"So strange," he stated. "Everything we've found there is completely different than any of the other pieces we found over the last few years." He frowned then, peering at the amulet. "Same style of symbols inscribed in the metal," he observed. "Still no luck in deciphering them?"

"They're not like any language our linguists have ever seen," Lee answered.

"Fascinating," Erasmus murmured.

"May I see?" Petra asked, holding out one hand. Erasmus snapped out of his reverie, glancing at Petra, then handing the amulet to her. Petra stared at it for a moment, then turned it over.

"How goes the training?" Erasmus asked Kyle, slapping him on the shoulder good-naturedly. Kyle smiled.

"I'm learning," he replied. Master Lee smirked.

"Your dinner made him forget to study," she countered. "He's as distractible as you were at his age."

"And look how I turned out," Erasmus replied, spreading his arms wide and grinning at Kyle. Lee crossed her arms over her chest.

"Indeed."

Petra stirred then, glancing up at Erasmus, the amulet still in her hands.

"Where did you find this?" she inquired.

"From an island off the coast of Orja," Erasmus replied. "Why do you ask?"

"These words," she answered, tracing a finger over the symbols etched into the metal, "...are an ancient tribal dialect."

Erasmus stared at her blankly.

"What?"

"These symbols," Petra clarified. "They're from the Old tongue, the language of our ancestors before the Immortals."

"Wait," Erasmus interjected. "You *recognize* those symbols?"

"Yes, of course," Petra confirmed.

"But that doesn't make any sense," Erasmus protested, turning to Lee. "Why would Ancient artifacts have symbols from the Barren tribes on them?"

"Indeed," Lee murmured, turning her eyes on Petra. "Do you recognize the runes in the crystals?"

"Yes," Petra replied. "Some of them. This is more advanced than the relics we have in the Barrens."

"So let me get this straight," Erasmus stated, running a hand over his bald pate. "We found a two-thousand-year-old runic device from the Barren forest...every bit as advanced as Ancient technology – in the ruins of a temple on some random island seven hundred miles away?"

"It appears so," Lee agreed, steepling her fingertips together.

"Describe this temple," Petra told Erasmus.

"Well we *think* it's a temple," Erasmus corrected. "It's in an ancient, secluded city near the center of the island. Our archaeologists have been digging out the lower levels for years ago. We've found more runic artifacts there than anywhere else in the world."

"But these are different?" Petra asked, pointing to the amulet. Erasmus nodded.

"We found the entrance to the lowest levels of one of the buildings," he replied. "We've only begun to explore it...all of the artifacts there have these symbols on them. So do the walls, the floors...everything. We sent our best linguists there, but no one could decipher them." Then he smiled at Petra. "Until now, I suppose."

Petra nodded absently, then stared off into the distance silently. Lee frowned, leaning back in her chair and crossing her arms over her chest.

"What are you thinking, Petra?" she asked. Petra snapped out of it, focusing on Lee.

"The symbols are in the Old tongue," she answered. "My ancestors must have built that temple. And this," she added, gesturing at the amulet. Erasmus shook his head.

"That doesn't make sense," he protested. "The upper floors of the ruins had Ancient artifacts in them, and the manuscripts we found there were written in Imperial standard."

"Unless," Lee countered, "...the Ancient ruins were built on *top* of the tribal floors."

"Granted," Erasmus conceded.

"But our ancestors would not leave the Barren forest," Petra countered.

"Regardless," Master Lee interjected, "...there are tribal symbols on that amulet, and on the ruins on Meros," she stated. "It warrants investigation."

"Damn right it does," Erasmus agreed. He turned to Petra. "And right now you're the only one who can read these symbols."

"What are you suggesting?" Petra inquired.

"Well," Erasmus ventured, "...you have to get back to the Barren forest, right?"

"Yes."

"And Meros is on the way," he continued, putting a hand on his generous pot-belly. "If you could make a stop there and help our researchers translate the ruins..."

"I have to get back to my people," Petra countered. "They depend on me for their protection. I've been gone long enough as it is."

"Think it over," Erasmus pleaded, reaching over and putting a hand on her shoulder. She stared at the hand, then at Erasmus, and he removed it rather quickly. "In any case," he continued, "...let me show you the rest of the Archives!"

"I'll show her," Lee interjected, standing up from her seat and pushing in her chair. Erasmus shot his mother a murderous look, which Lee ignored. Lee turned to Kyle then. "Many Ancient runics had dozens of different minerals in one device," she stated. "...like this amulet. If you ever want to be as good as them, I suggest you take your studies more seriously."

"Yes Master Lee," Kyle mumbled.

* * *

Kyle sighed, slinging his backpack filled with books over his shoulder and walking out of the Runic Archives. Two elite guards followed from behind, his constant companions. As the son of the most powerful man in the Empire, he was constantly under guard. He'd grown so used to their presence that he often forgot they were there.

He continued down the long hallway toward the riser at the end, reaching it and taking it up to the 41st floor. He made it to Kalibar's old retirement suite, opening the door and crossing the suite to reach his room. Closing the door, he activated its magical lock, then sat on his bed with a sigh.

You should've studied, he scolded himself. Not only had he disappointed Master Lee, he'd also been reprimanded in front of Erasmus...and more embarrassingly, Petra.

He sighed again, taking off his backpack and pulling out a few books. He opened one of them, glancing at pictures of various gemstones. They were organized from best magic storage – and therefore worst conduction – to best conduction and worst storage.

Kyle flipped through more pages, dismayed at how many minerals he had to memorize. There were a few dozen of them...and Master Lee expected him to learn them all over the weekend.

Well, better get to it.

He went back to the beginning of the book, seeing a picture of a diamond. Diamonds were incredibly good at storing magic...the best, as far as anyone knew. He flipped a page. Quartz was pretty good, but the various varieties of quartz, like amethyst, were less capable. But *why*? Kalibar had mentioned long ago that diamonds with the fewest impurities stored magic the best. From what he remembered from school back on Earth, amethyst was like quartz, but with impurities that changed the color. So he supposed it made sense that amethyst wouldn't store magic quite as well.

But why did diamonds store magic better than quartz? And why didn't metals store magic at all? There *had* to be a reason. Magic was just another science, after all.

Kyle sighed, resigning himself to memorizing the list of minerals. He flipped through the pages over and over, trying to guess at the next page's mineral each time. Then he heard a knock on his door.

"It's me," he heard Ariana call out.

"Coming," Kyle said, knowing full well she could hear him getting up from the bed and walking up to the door. He disabled the magic lock, and Ariana walked in. She was dressed, as usual, in the Reaper uniform Petra had given her. The skintight black fabric covered her from her toes to her neck, the hood pulled back behind her. The suit protected Ariana from her only real weakness...it prevented her from losing magic. Without magic, Ariana entered a state of suspended animation, a state she said felt exactly like death. And she would know.

"What are you up to?" Ariana asked, pecking him on the cheek and sitting down the bed next to him.

"Memorizing these minerals," he answered, gesturing at his book. "I was supposed to memorize them last night," he confessed.

"Which ones?" she asked, leaning in to look at his book. Kyle told her what had happened with Master Lee, feeling embarrassed about his failure. "I can quiz you," she offered immediately.

Kyle smiled; Ariana was always eager to help him. And she had a near photographic memory – another perk of the Dead Man's shard in her brain. One quick look through the book and she would be able to recall it verbatim.

"That'd be great," he replied. He paused for a moment, then shook his head. "I just wish I understood *why* one mineral stored magic better than another. Then I wouldn't have to memorize them."

"Yeah," Ariana agreed. "Well, at least I can test you to make sure you've got them."

Kyle sighed, knowing she was right. Still, the thought of studying more – especially after a few hours with Master Lee this morning – was suddenly overwhelming.

"What's this?" Ariana asked. Kyle glanced at her; she'd pulled his notebook from his backpack and was flipping through it.

"Just a few ideas I had," he answered, reaching over to grab the notebook from her. She pulled away, glancing at one of the pages. He'd drawn a picture of a grenade there, with various notations...in English, of course. Consequently, she couldn't read it.

"What is it?" she pressed.

"It's a gravity grenade," he answered.

"How does it work?"

"You just hold down this button," he replied, "...and it pushes a connecting metal rod between the magic storage crystal and the crystal with the runes in it, so that magic flows through the rod and activates the device."

"Right," Ariana breathed. "It's like your book said...magic flows best through metal." Then she frowned. "What does it do?"

"Well, when you press the button, it sets a timer. After a few seconds, it creates a gravity field that sucks everything around it into it, then create an opposite gravity field to shove everything away really fast, like an explosion."

"Oh," she replied. "Got it."

"But it won't work," he confessed. "If I stream magic to it, it'll activate instantly, and make both pushing and pulling gravity fields all at the same time. I don't know how to time everything."

"It's a good idea," Ariana said. "I'm sure you'll figure it out."

"Wait," Kyle blurted out. "Master Lee taught me how to use different minerals to time patterns!"

"So you *could* make this thing?" she asked.

"Yeah, I think I could," he agreed. "In fact, I could use each of these minerals," he continued, pointing at the book he'd been studying, "...and test them to figure out which ones give me the best timing for the grenade!"

"And that would help you remember each of the minerals," Ariana concluded. Kyle nodded, feeling a sudden burst of excitement. She was right, of course; it made perfect sense.

"But I'll never get it done by the end of the weekend," Kyle realized, his excitement waning. "Master Lee is going to test me."

"Well, I'll help you study now," Ariana consoled. "But I still think you should make this later on."

"Okay," Kyle agreed. Ariana put the notebook back in his backpack, then gave him a conspiratorial look.

"Want to learn a new pattern?" she asked.

"Of course," Kyle agreed. He wasn't technically supposed to learn Weaving, but they'd long ago agreed to teach each other what they were learning, in secret. He doubted Kalibar would mind; the Grand Weaver had dabbled in making runics himself. "What is it?"

"A magnetosphere," Ariana answered. "A magnetic field. It sucks metal into itself."

She searched around for something with metal in it, and found a small coin, placing it on the bed. Then she wove magic, and a small, faint blue sphere appeared above the coin. It shot upward instantly, hovering within the sphere.

"Cool," Kyle murmured. "How do you weave it?"

She showed him, weaving it slowly within her mind. He could follow the light at her forehead, the magic threads visible to him. Within moments, he'd learned the pattern, and recreated it, making a much brighter sphere above the coin. It shot up into his magnetosphere...as did his pen, hovering over the bed.

"It's like a regular gravity sphere, but it only works on certain metals," Ariana explained. Kyle nodded; he remembered from school that only iron, nickel, and cobalt were affected by magnetic fields. Why he would use a magnetic field over a gravity field, however, was beyond him.

"Thanks," he said, leaning in to give Ariana a smooch.

"No problem," she replied. Then she grabbed his book of minerals, handing it to him. "All right," she declared. "Time to memorize these. When you're done, I'll quiz you."

Chapter 3

Captain Apep stared out of the third-story window of the governor's home, one hand on the large glass window overlooking the street below. Throngs of dissidents filled the street, overflowing onto the lawns of the neighboring houses. Most of them barely more than kids. Students who'd congregated after school, all marching because of one damn girl. He searched for her, finding her quickly in the crowd, at the front of the line. A tall, slender woman with long brown hair that fell in loose curls to her hips. An unlikely leader.

Apep stared at her, grinding his teeth.

Ignorant fool.

"Ignore them, Captain."

Apep turned away from the window, facing the governor. A tall, well-built man, Governor Candric was physically intimidating...and knew it. He was in his forties, but looked younger on account of how well he'd taken care of himself over the years. Heavily muscled, with a bald head and intense brown eyes, he'd been the wealthiest businessman in Meros before taking office, and was well-accustomed to being obeyed. Apep grimaced.

"They're intruding on private property," he complained, gesturing at the crowd. "They're clearly violating the law."

"No one has complained," Candric reminded him. His tone was patient...too patient.

"Yet," Apep countered irritably. "If they do, we're well within rights to arrest them."

"Only those that violate the law."

Apep turned to face the window again, staring down at the people in the street. At the woman leading them. She was nineteen, technically an adult. What passed for one nowadays, anyway.

"She's a menace," he muttered, knowing that it was pointless to argue with the man. Governor Candric was hardly neutral when it came to these protesters...especially their leader. The damn girl was little more than an entitled brat...but her connections made her exceedingly dangerous. What she was doing took organization and money, and Apep was pretty damn sure he knew who was supplying the latter.

She *was* Candric's daughter, after all.

If he could prove that Candric was secretly involved in all of this, he'd have all the evidence he needed to take the governor – and the upstart bitch – down. And then the rest of these so-called revolutionaries would scatter like leaves in the wind.

"She's well within her rights," Candric countered. "Whether we agree with her or not."

Apep turned to Candric, eyeing him for a moment.

"Do *you* agree with her?" he asked.

"I understand her point of view."

"But do you agree with her?" Apep pressed.

"I believe in the rule of law," Candric answered. "As do you."

Apep said nothing, keeping his expression carefully neutral. It was a typical answer from a politician, in that it answered nothing. He turned to gaze out at the protesters again. They were chanting now, some drivel about their rights. Holding signs that accused the Empire of various atrocities, most of them demanding the end of the annual Testing of its children. He fidgeted, knowing that the Finders would be here soon. That they would see these protesters and think that Meros was disloyal to the Empire.

"They'll make a fool of us," he warned.

37

"If we're in the right, then they'll make fools of themselves," Candric countered. "If we're not, then we have every right to feel foolish."

"You're hardly neutral," Apep grumbled. He'd meant to say it under his breath, but it came out louder than he'd planned. A chill ran through him. He'd crossed a line.

"The law is the law," Candric replied calmly. But Apep heard how carefully Candric had said it. He only spoke that way when he was angry. Apep had rarely seen the governor lose his temper, but the few occasions he'd witnessed had been...memorable.

"I'm sorry," he apologized, hating that he was doing so. But to his relief, it came out sounding sincere. "It's just..."

"You believe in the Empire," Candric interjected. "I understand."

That's the problem, Candric thought. *You're* too *understanding.*

The protesters chanted in unison, thrusting their signs in the air as they marched down the street. Captain Apep clenched his fists, staring down at them silently. This was the wealthiest neighborhood in the city, and the protesters knew it. Just as they knew that the governor was home, and would see them marching down the street.

"Ninety-nine percent," the crowd chanted. "We will represent!"

A clever slogan, Apep had to admit. The latest census for the Empire showed that over ninety-nine percent of its citizens could not use magic. A fact these dissidents had used to their advantage.

Apep turned his gaze to his men lining the sidewalks, guards armed with spears and shields. With a word, his men would detain these upstarts. These *kids*. Fools with no respect for authority, no understanding of how the world worked. Two decades of peace and prosperity, and these idiots appreciated nothing that they had. That the generation before them had handed to them. They rebelled against the very government that had given them freedom, wealth, and security...all the things they were now taking for granted.

"Do it for the people," they chanted. "Do it for your kids!"

They were, Apep knew, just another anti-Empire, anti-magic group. Against something for the sake of being against something.

"If it weren't for the Empire," he groused, "...they'd all be slaves for Verhan."

"They want a better Empire," Candric retorted. "Just because they don't like one thing about the Empire doesn't mean they hate the whole thing."

"Don't they?" Apep countered, gesturing at the crowd. "They have signs saying 'down with the Evil Empire!'"

"There are radicals in every group," Candric reminded him.

"I don't see anyone disagreeing with them," Apep retorted. "No one's forcing them out of the crowd. That makes them *all* complicit."

"Perhaps."

"So what happens when the Finders come?" Apep demanded.

"We're about to find out," Candric replied, gesturing at the window.

Apep gazed out of the window, spotting small black dots in the sky high above the city. He felt a burst of trepidation...and a grim sense of satisfaction. These hooligans could march and chant all they wanted, but what could they do against the might of the Finders? They were invincible, untouchable. And they wouldn't tolerate these pathetic dissidents.

They don't know what power is, he thought. *But they're about to find out.*

The dots grew, black ships descending toward the city. Ten of them, each with three Finders. A handful of men with the power of ten armies.

A ship lowered itself toward the protesters, landing in the street a block away from them. The protesters immediately started marching toward the ship...and the three cloaked men levitating around it.

"This reflects poorly on you," Apep warned. "It reflects poorly on *us.*"

Candric said nothing, stepping up to Apep's side and staring out of the window. They watched as the crowd of protesters made their way down the street, now only half a block away from the ship. The three Finders levitated forward, facing the crowd. One of them raised their staff high in the air, then slammed the butt of it down on the ground.

The air between the Finder and the crowd *rippled*.

A powerful wind ripped through the crowd. Some of the protesters stumbled backward, while others fell. Signs were torn out of their hands, flying down the street. The wind intensified, howling loud enough for Apep to hear it through the reinforced glass.

Apep watched with no small satisfaction as the protesters tumbled down the road away from the Finders. As they scattered like insects from the wrath of the Empire. Still, he was irritated with the governor.

"They shouldn't have had to do that," Apep accused, glaring up at Candric. "It's our duty to keep the peace." Candric turned away from the window, eyeing Apep calmly.

"Those people are well within their rights," he reminded Apep. "We cannot legally intervene unless they break the law."

Captain Apep grit his teeth, turning away from the governor and staring down at the dispersing crowd. At the tall woman leading them away from the Finders, back down the street toward the center of town. Tessa, the daughter of the governor. Cocky, arrogant, and belligerent, the bitch knew that she was untouchable. That daddy would swoop in and rescue her if things got out of hand.

But there was only so much that daddy could do, Apep knew. Candric's time was running out. A new era was about to begin, and soon – very soon – these dissidents would be silenced.

It was all just a matter of time.

* * *

Kalibar sat in his office, a large corner room in his suite. His desk was covered with various stacks of paper, bills that he was supposed to sign or veto. He'd read most of them, but there was still one left...and it was over a hundred pages long. He sat back in his chair, rubbing his eyes wearily. Then he sighed, staring at the stacks of paper before him.

So this is it, he muttered to himself.

The first few weeks of his second term as Grand Weaver had been the most difficult of his life. With Xanos threatening to destroy the Empire, Kalibar had fought valiantly to save his country and his people. It had been a horrible experience...but through it all, he'd felt more alive than ever before. Now that it was all over, he couldn't help but feel that he was...done. That the Empire didn't need him anymore.

He sighed again, running a hand over his short white hair. Then he stood, walking to the glass wall facing his desk. It gave him an incredible view of Stridon, and of the campus of the Secula Magna. He'd given himself this view purposefully. A constant reminder of what he'd been fighting for.

And now what?

He stared at the cityscape in the distance, feeling a now-familiar glumness come over him. He knew full well why he was feeling this way. He'd spent a lifetime throwing himself into his work, spending every waking moment on accomplishing his goals. He'd given up a great deal to get to his current position, never taking another wife or having a family after his wife had committed suicide four decades ago.

But now...

He heard a knock on the door, and moments later it cracked open, revealing Petra on the other side. Kalibar smiled.

"Come in," he called out.

Petra strode in, clad in her Reaper uniform. No matter how many times he saw her, he still found himself captivated...and at a loss of where to look. It was safest to focus on her eyes...and that is exactly what he did.

"Good afternoon," she greeted.

"Afternoon," Kalibar replied. "Have a seat," he added, gesturing at the chair opposite his desk. She obliged, sitting down in one graceful movement. She moved quietly and deliberately, a result of a lifetime of living in the forest. "How are you doing?"

"Still recovering from yesterday," she answered. They'd sparred the day before – as they had every day since she'd come to Stridon. Kalibar had killed two of her tribesman back in the Barren Forest, but had spared her life, and as punishment he'd been ordered to train her in Battle-Weaving.

"A good effort," he stated, his smile hardly apologetic. She was an excellent Weaver, if prone to using brute power over finesse. He'd beaten her handily every time, of course.

"I'm still learning your patterns," Petra replied, her tone flat.

"And I yours," Kalibar countered. "But I still won."

"Barely," Petra retorted, crossing her arms under her chest. Kalibar smirked.

"A teacher's job is to bolster his student's confidence," he replied, spreading his arms out wide. Petra's eyes narrowed.

"Your teachers may have overdone it."

"My confidence didn't come from my teachers," Kalibar stated smoothly. "It came from winning."

"So will mine," Petra replied. "Today."

Kalibar grinned, leaning back in his chair.

"I look forward to you coming out on top," he quipped. "Tell me...when do you want to do it?" Petra arched one eyebrow.

"Are we still talking about a lesson?" she inquired. Kalibar shrugged.

"I think I could show you something."

"A short lesson then," Petra stated coolly. Kalibar smirked.

"I'm sure we could find a way to extend it."

Petra stared at him for a long moment, saying nothing. Then she stood up, pushing her chair in.

"What time should I come?" she asked. "For the sparring match," she added quickly. Kalibar sighed, leaning forward.

"I have an opening at six."

"Six then," Petra agreed, nodding slightly. She turned and left then, closing the door behind her ample behind. Kalibar found himself staring, and tore his gaze away, idling scanning the papers on his desk instead.

Damn.

He leaned back in his chair, putting his hands behind his head. He pictured Petra back in the Barrens, when he'd first met her. He'd been instantly attracted to her, and not just because of her figure. She was proud, talented, and confident, with a hard exterior hiding a warmth and softness he'd only experienced the day that Sabin had been destroyed. It had been tantalizing, that experience...the one time she'd kissed him. He found himself thinking about it...more often than he'd like to admit.

He sighed, lowering his hands. The last week – spending every day together, traveling the Empire with her – had been some of the happiest days he could remember having. It'd been a long, long time since he'd felt like this. Despite their difference in age, despite having been born on different continents, with entirely different cultures, they had a great deal in common. She, like him, had chosen a life of solitude, honing her body and mastering Weaving to protect the ones she loved.

Everything just...clicked.

And now I want more than this, he mused, turning to stare at his desk. He felt a sudden pang of fear, wondering if Petra was changing him, weakening him. Making him value his own desires over the good of the Empire.

Not that any of it mattered, of course. He knew all too well that she would be leaving soon...and almost certainly never returning. Her duty was, like his, to protect her people. She had to return to the Barrens, and his duty was to stay here. It was no wonder that Petra had remained relatively distant for the last week, despite their banter. At first he'd assumed it was due to her grappling with her feelings about the Immortals, her ancestors that had been made into Chosen by Sabin. Petra's tribe had worshipped them, hoping one day that their ancestors would speak to them, providing their ancient wisdom. But the Immortals Petra had encountered had only tried to kill her, and Ampir had killed them all…along with every Chosen on the planet. She'd been devastated, of course…not that she'd ever speak of it.

It'd been a week since she'd started pulling away from Kalibar, and that distance was enough to drive Kalibar mad.

There was a knock at the door, and Kalibar snapped out of his reverie.

"Yes?" he called out. The door opened, revealing one of his elite guards, who saluted crisply.

"At ease," Kalibar stated. "What is it?"

"You have a visitor Grand Weaver," the guard answered. "The Verhanian ambassador has arrived."

"Bring him in," Kalibar ordered. The guard nodded crisply, bowing, then leaving the office. Kalibar sighed, sitting back down in his chair. He'd known about the ambassador's visit for about a week now. Verhan hadn't sent a representative since Kalibar and Erasmus had been elected. It was a symbolic gesture to send the ambassador now, to congratulate him on his re-election.

A man walked into Kalibar's office. He was tall, and dreadfully thin, with short, carefully combed black hair and a perfectly manicured mustache. He wore a deep purple shirt and pants, with gold cuff-links and buttons. He was a different ambassador than the last time Kalibar had been Grand Weaver; Kalibar had never met this man.

"Grand Weaver," The ambassador greeted, giving a curt bow. Kalibar smiled, standing and shaking the man's hand. They both sat down, facing each other over Kalibar's desk. "I am Rodric," the ambassador stated.

"Good afternoon ambassador," Kalibar replied. "I trust your travel went smoothly?"

"Without incident," Rodric confirmed. His words, like his mustache, were spoken perfectly, without a hint of a Verhanian accent.

"I appreciate your visit," Kalibar stated. "I trust everything is well in Verhan?"

The corner of Rodric's mouth twitched, and he didn't immediately answer. Kalibar kept his expression carefully neutral, waiting for the man's response.

Something's wrong, he realized.

"Things are stable," Rodric replied. "And in the Empire?"

Kalibar smiled inwardly, knowing full well that Rodric's spies would have already notified the ambassador of what had been occurring in the last few months.

"We're recovering nicely from the war," Kalibar answered. "We're almost finished rebuilding the city."

"So this...Xanos," Rodric stated. "He's truly dead?"

"He is."

"One less thing to worry about, I suppose," Rodric murmured. "Although he never gave us trouble."

"It would only have been a matter of time," Kalibar countered. "Xanos was interested in total control...and he opposed anyone who fought for self-governance."

"Yes, well," Rodric replied, "...as I said, one less thing to worry about. We have more pressing matters to consider now."

"Such as?"

"Surely you've heard of our...difficulties," Rodric stated. Kalibar nodded slightly. It was no secret to Rodric that the Empire had legions of spies in Verhan...and vice versa. While he didn't have much in the way of specifics, Kalibar knew that something unexpected had recently happened in the upper echelon of Verhan's government.

"I have," he admitted.

"How much do you know?" Rodric asked. Kalibar shrugged.

"Nothing specific," he admitted. "Just that..."

"The king is dead," Rodric interrupted.

Kalibar stared at the ambassador mutely, then blinked.

"Excuse me?"

"Our king is dead," Rodric repeated. "As is his heir."

Kalibar leaned back in his chair, running a hand through his hair.

"How?"

45

"He was found by an aide," Rodric answered. "Lying on his bedroom floor, with a hole in his head."

Kalibar frowned, leaning forward.

"A hole? Where specifically?"

"In the center of his forehead," Rodric replied, pointing to his own forehead.

"Unbelievable," Kalibar breathed. A chill ran through him. "Absolutely unbelievable."

"So you *weren't* aware," Rodric stated, eyeing Kalibar. Kalibar glanced at the man.

"Hmm?"

"You weren't aware of our king's passing," Rodric clarified. Kalibar shook his head.

"I was not," he confirmed. "Pardon me," he added. "I'm just a little...taken aback."

"As were we."

"Were there any others found in this way?" Kalibar asked. "Dead, with a hole in their forehead?"

"As a matter of fact, yes," Rodric replied. "How did you know?"

"Let me guess," Kalibar ventured. "They all died a week ago, on the same day, at the same time?"

Rodric leaned back in his own chair, his brow furrowed.

"An excellent guess."

"One week ago, forty people in Stridon – and hundreds elsewhere in the Empire – suffered a similar fate," Kalibar informed. "They dropped suddenly, a blackened hole burned into the center of their foreheads. It turns out that they were Xanos's Chosen," Kalibar revealed. "Xanos had infiltrated our government, with spies and traitors throughout the Empire. When Xanos was killed, his Chosen were destroyed with him."

"So," Rodric replied, steepling his fingertips together. "You're saying our king...and a quarter of the lords...were Xanos's Chosen?"

"Unfortunately yes," Kalibar answered apologetically. "Xanos did the same to the Empire," he added. "One of our Councilmen was secretly a Chosen, and I nearly became one."

Rodric leaned back in his chair, staring off into space for a moment. Then he shook his head.

"Unbelievable," he muttered. "Just...unbelievable." He glanced up at Kalibar. "So Xanos was controlling us all along."

Rodric sighed, rubbing his face with both hands. Then he gave a rueful smile.

"And now I get to bring this wonderful news back to the lords," he muttered. "I'm beginning to regret having taken this position."

"So without the King, the lords are running the government?" Kalibar inquired. There were eight lords, appointed by the King himself, who carried power second only to their monarch. If a quarter of them had been Chosen, now there were only six lords.

"Yes," Rodric answered. "They've set to vote on crowning a new king in three days."

"They can only vote for one of their own, I assume," Kalibar guessed. Rodric nodded.

"Correct," the ambassador agreed. "One of the lords will be voted king by their peers. It will be an open election, by necessity."

"Indeed," Kalibar murmured. A risk for all involved, of course. The newly crowned king could use his absolute power to demote...or even put to death...the lords that voted against him. There was no love lost between most of the lords, after all. Their respective families had been waging shadow wars against each other for generations, jockeying for the king's favor – and the power and prestige it granted. But a secret ballot would run the risk of being corrupted. If the person tallying the lords' votes were bought off, no one would be the wiser.

"Needless to say," Rodric said, "...the results of this election will be critical."

"Agreed," Kalibar replied. "It will have a profound effect on the Empire as well," he added. Many of the lords were none-too-fond of the Empire, and disapproved of their late king's trade agreements with their former enemy. "I'm guessing that's the reason for your visit," Kalibar ventured. If the lords were in control of Verhan, and were fighting against one another for the throne, then it was likely that Rodric had been sent here by one of the

47

lords...whichever lord the ambassador had managed to ally himself with.

Rodric smiled, inclining his head.

"Correct."

"Which lord sent you?" Kalibar asked.

"Lord Devlin," Rodric answered.

"I see," Kalibar murmured. Of all of the lords, Devlin was most sympathetic to the Empire. "And Lord Devlin wants my help in securing the throne?"

"Also correct," Rodric confirmed. He gave a rueful smile. "Your reputation is well-earned," he added. Kalibar was known as a master strategist, both politically and on the battlefield.

"What would Lord Devlin have me do?"

"He asks for your support," Rodric answered. "You have influence with a few of the lords. If you could use your considerable resources to make it...preferable for them to vote for Lord Devlin instead of themselves, we would be most grateful."

Kalibar leaned back, tapping his goatee with one finger. It was a sound plan. Having Devlin as king would ensure a strong relationship between Verhan and the Empire...the best-case scenario for both governments. Neither government would benefit from a deterioration of their already tenuous trade agreement.

"I'll have to discuss it with Grand Runic Erasmus and the Council," Kalibar answered.

"Of course," Rodric replied. "I appreciate your consideration." He hesitated for a second, then grimaced. "I would hope for a favorable decision," he stated. "Sentiment toward the Empire is not exactly positive at this point."

"What do you mean?"

"Well," Rodric replied, "...I hear you've adopted children."

"I have," Kalibar confirmed. "A girl and a boy."

"What were their names again?"

"Kyle and Ariana," Kalibar answered. Rodric smiled.

"Ah yes," he murmured. "I hear they're quite extraordinary, your children."

"Oh yes," Kalibar agreed. "That they are."

"I hear your son was able to sink one of our warships single-handedly," Rodric stated.

Kalibar's breath caught in his throat.

"Ah yes," Kalibar muttered. "That." He cleared his throat. "A terrible misunderstanding. The warship attacked a pirate ship," Kalibar explained. "One they could not have known carried two stowaways...my children," he added. "My children acted in self-defense."

"I see," Rodric replied, steepling his fingertips. "And these stowaways were attempting to enter the country illegally?"

Kalibar grimaced.

"Please don't be offended," Rodric stated hastily. "You must understand that Lord Devlin doesn't take any of this personally. But our public isn't as understanding. You can imagine how it looks to them, your children conspiring with criminals to sink our warship, killing hundreds of men."

"I can," Kalibar agreed reluctantly. It had been two thousand years since the Ancient Empire had conquered Verhan, but modern Verhanians still considered the Empire their enemy. Luckily, their government had adopted a more neutral position, agreeing to limited trade with the Empire.

"Some are calling it an act of war," Rodric warned. "Two of the lords are seizing the opportunity to strengthen their positions by condemning the Empire. One of them even went as far as to blame the Empire for the devastation in the Barrens...and the assassination of the king and his heir."

"Nonsense," Kalibar retorted, feeling his frustration mount. "Who said that?"

"Lady Damia, of course."

"Of course," Kalibar grumbled. Of all the lords, Lady Damia was the least sympathetic to the Empire. She was a formidable woman despite her relatively young age, and extremely popular among the people. No doubt her famed beauty had something to do with that. "What utter nonsense."

"Any reasonable person would agree," Rodric stated. "But you know as well as I do that most people are not reasonable." He sighed. "Lady Damia will set our people against the Empire, and she may even be able to win the crown if she gains enough support among the Lords."

"I find that hard to believe," Kalibar replied. "Lady Damia is popular, but most of the other lords don't like her. They would never nominate her."

"You'd be surprised," Rodric countered. "Our spies tell us that one of the lords has already agreed to endorse her."

"Damn," Kalibar swore. "With Damia voting for herself, that leaves four lords left to vote." Rodric nodded.

"You can see how very important it is to act quickly in this matter," he replied. Kalibar sighed, running a hand through his hair and leaning back in his chair. Several members of the Council were away from Stridon, returning tonight.

"Very well," Kalibar decided. "I'll assemble a meeting with the Council tomorrow."

Chapter 4

By the time Kyle and Ariana made it to Kalibar's suite for dinner, Jenkins had already set the table with steaming plates of what looked to be fish. Kalibar, Petra, and Erasmus were already there, as was Darius...and Master Lee. Kalibar had made it clear before he'd gone on vacation that he wanted to have dinner with his family every night if possible. Kyle loved the fact that he got to see his adoptive father every night now, especially considering how rarely he'd been able to see Kalibar in the last few weeks. Kyle sat down at the table, with Ariana on his left and Master Lee on his right.

"Good evening," Kalibar greeted, nodding at his children. "How was your day, Ariana?"

"Good," she answered. "Master Owens taught me how to create magnetospheres."

"Ah yes," Kalibar stated. "A very useful pattern. And you Kyle?"

"Um," Kyle began, glancing sidelong at Master Lee. "I learned about the magical resistance of different minerals," he answered. "And how to make runes weave magic at long distances."

"A tricky art," Kalibar stated. "I remember you teaching me a few years ago, Erasmus," he added. Erasmus snorted.

"More like a decade ago," the Grand Runic corrected. Kyle noticed that Erasmus had a glass of water by his plate instead of his customary glass of wine...and that he was in a rather sour mood. No doubt the two were related. Master Lee turned to Kyle.

"I trust you're prepared for your test next week?" she asked. Kyle paused, then nodded. He'd practiced with Ariana until he'd memorized those minerals backwards and forwards.

"You better be," Erasmus pitched in, taking a sip of his water. "You don't want to be on her bad side...trust me."

"Where's your wine?" Petra asked Erasmus. Dressed in her Reaper uniform, she was a sight to behold...as long as one didn't get caught beholding.

"I'm abstaining," Erasmus grumbled, taking another sip of his water. Petra glanced at Master Lee, then back at Erasmus.

"I thought you said you drank because..."

"Don't you have a forest to get back to?" Erasmus interrupted. Petra smirked, but took mercy on him, saying nothing more.

"About that," Master Lee said, turning to Erasmus. "Have you told Kalibar about that artifact from Meros?"

"Ah, right," Erasmus stated, brightening up. The Grand Runic told Kalibar all about the artifact they'd examined that morning, including Petra's discovery that she could recognize the mysterious language inscribed on it. Kalibar's eyebrows rose.

"Fascinating," he murmured. "What do you make of it, Petra?"

"I don't know," she admitted. "As far as we know, the tribes would never have left the Barrens. But there is much we don't know about our ancestors."

"They *must* have reached Meros," Erasmus opined. "What I don't get is why the tribal ruins and artifacts are *beneath* the other ruins."

"Maybe the tribes colonized the island first," Master Lee suggested.

"Perhaps so," Kalibar agreed. "And you say you understand this tribal dialect?" he asked Petra. Petra nodded.

"I can read it."

"You should see the runic artifacts we found there," Erasmus gushed. "They're unlike anything we've ever found...they seem to be as sophisticated as Ancient technology," he added. "But the runes are completely different...and Petra says she recognizes some of them."

"I do," Petra confirmed.

"The Barrens tribes do use remarkably different runes than we do," Kalibar stated, tapping his goatee with one finger. "Petra has been showing me some of them. There is some overlap, of course, but we have a great deal to learn from them."

"Well, I was wondering," Erasmus ventured. "Petra told me she has to head back to Orja soon. What if she were to make a stop at Meros, to help our archaeologists translate the symbols on the ruins there, and to study the runic artifacts?"

Kalibar and Petra glanced at each other, and Kalibar grimaced.

"Yes, well, it certainly makes sense," he said.

"It could advance our understanding of those ruins by years," Master Lee agreed. She turned to Petra. "What do you think?"

"I have to get back to my tribe," she replied apologetically. "They need me to protect them."

"Ampir promised to protect them until you got back," Erasmus countered. "Right now they're as safe as they can be."

"Yes, well," Petra replied. "How long will this take?" Erasmus shrugged.

"How quickly can you work?"

"Reading the ancient tribal symbols is easy," Petra answered. "But tracing the runes will take much longer. I have to sense the vibrations from each rune, then decode them."

"There are dozens of new artifacts ready for processing there," Master Lee interjected. She'd taken over Erasmus's duties as Head Archivist for the Runic Archives ever since Erasmus had been elected Grand Runic. "Most of them are still on-site in Meros."

"It could take months," Petra stated. "I can't spend that much time away from my tribe."

"But..." Erasmus began.

"I won't," Petra interrupted.

Erasmus slumped back in his chair, staring down at the tabletop. He glanced at his glass of water, then drummed his fingertips on the table. Ariana stirred at Kyle's side.

"Bring Kyle along," she proposed, breaking the silence. Erasmus frowned.

"What?"

"Bring Kyle along," Ariana repeated. "He can help Petra decode the runes."

"I don't get it," Erasmus admitted. Then his face lit up. "Wait, you mean by using the K-Array?" The K-Array was a machine that could reverse-engineer runes it was placed near. Kyle had come up with the original idea, but Kalibar had been the one to really make it work. The K-Array still took a great deal of time to decode runes, however.

"No," Ariana replied. "Petra takes a long time to decode runes because she has to *feel* the magic in them. Kyle can *see* magic."

"Ah, right!" Erasmus exclaimed. "I forgot about that. That's brilliant!"

"Wait," Petra interjected. "Kyle can see magic? Like you?" she added, turning to Kalibar.

"Yes, he can," Kalibar confirmed. "My sight was a gift from Ampir," he added. "Kyle is Ampir's grandson; he inherited the gift."

"So if Kyle goes with Petra," Erasmus stated eagerly, "...he'll be able to sketch each of the runes within seconds...and Petra can decode them!" He turned to Ariana. "Did I mention you're goddamn brilliant?"

Ariana gave a small smile, clearly uneasy with the praise. Kyle was sure she would have blushed, if she'd been capable of it.

"Excellent idea Ariana," Kalibar agreed. "My children continue to amaze me."

"And me," Master Lee piped in, nodding at Ariana.

"Well?" Erasmus asked, turning back to Petra. "What do you think?" Petra crossed her arms over her chest, turning to face Kyle, who immediately lowered his gaze further, having already lowered it to rather intriguing territory. He felt his cheeks flush, and kicked himself mentally. No matter how often he got caught staring, he couldn't seem to help himself!

"I'll do it," Petra decided.

"Excellent!" Erasmus exclaimed.

"Hold on," Kalibar interjected. "We must consider Kyle's safety."

"What do you mean?" Erasmus asked. "He'll be perfectly safe!"

"Meros is...unique," Kalibar reminded him. "Half of the island is owned by Verhan, the other half by the Empire. Our relationship with Verhan is...tense," he added. Erasmus snorted.

"Thousands of tourists travel to Meros every year," he countered.

"Yes, but they aren't the son of the Grand Weaver."

"Then send a few elite guards with him," Erasmus offered. "He'll have Petra there to protect him too."

"True," Kalibar conceded.

"Why don't I go with them?" Ariana offered.

Kalibar and Erasmus looked at Ariana, then at each other. It made perfect sense, of course. Ariana was incredibly powerful, with superhuman strength and senses...and she never slept. She was the perfect bodyguard.

"She has a point," Erasmus stated with a grin, nudging Kalibar.

"She does," Kalibar conceded. Still, he looked reticent. "I'll think about it."

"Oh come on," Erasmus complained. "It's the perfect plan and you know it!"

"I'll think about it," Kalibar repeated.

"Fine," Erasmus grumbled. He grabbed his glass, taking a gulp of his water. Then he made a face, clearly having forgotten that it wasn't wine. He glared at Master Lee, and then at Petra, who was smirking at him.

Having finished their meals, everyone sat back in their chairs, allowing Jenkins to clear the table. The dutiful butler made quick work of it, leaving a few bottles of wine on the table. Kalibar, Darius, and Master Lee indulged, leaving Erasmus staring at them in envy. The Grand Runic turned to Darius, who was already on his second glass.

"What are *you* celebrating?" he asked the bodyguard. "Another day of accomplishing nothing?" He turned to Kalibar. "How much do you pay him, anyway?" Kalibar ignored the question, but Darius put down his glass.

"My last day on the job," Darius answered. Erasmus snorted.

"I could only hope," he shot back. When Darius didn't reply, Erasmus frowned. "You're not serious, are you?"

"Yep."

Erasmus stared blankly at Darius.

"Wait, what?"

"Darius, what do you mean?" Kalibar asked. Darius turned his blue eyes on the Grand Weaver. Kyle glanced at Ariana, feeling suddenly uneasy.

"You're kidding, right?" he piped in.

"No," Darius replied. "I'm resigning effective today."

Everyone stared at Darius, their mouths agape. Finally, Kalibar broke the silence.

"Why?" he asked.

"You don't need me anymore," Darius replied.

"You're my bodyguard," Kalibar protested. "I'll always need protection...and so will Kyle and Ariana."

"*They* don't need me anymore," Darius countered.

"Darius..." Kalibar stated, "...you've done so much for us. And for me. If it weren't for you, I wouldn't be alive...and neither would Kyle or Ariana."

"Or Erasmus," Darius added, taking another sip of his wine. Erasmus grimaced.

"And you'll never let me forget it, will you," the Grand Runic grumbled.

"You're sure about this?" Kalibar pressed.

"I am."

"Well," Kalibar muttered. "I can't say I'm happy about it, but if that's what you want..."

"What are you going to do instead?" Ariana asked.

56

"Travel," Darius answered.

"Wait, you're not staying here?" Kyle exclaimed. Darius shook his head. "But how long will you be gone?"

"A few months, maybe longer."

"Where are you going?" Ariana inquired.

"I have other work to do," Darius answered. But in typical fashion, he offered no other information.

"You're coming back though, right?" Ariana pressed.

"I'll stop in to visit."

"Well," Kalibar stated, clearly taken aback. "I'm sorry to lose you Darius." He poured more wine in his glass, then poured some into Erasmus's empty water glass. Erasmus took a long gulp of it, avoiding his mother's disapproving gaze. Then he shook his head at Darius.

"You know, I actually think I'm going to miss you" he mused. "Now I've got to find some other fool to insult."

"Pick an easier target," Darius counseled. "Try a mirror."

"Ha!" Erasmus retorted, taking another gulp of his wine. But he didn't take the bait. To Kyle's surprise, the Grand Runic looked genuinely dismayed.

"I don't think I've ever seen you speechless," Kalibar observed, patting Erasmus on the back. "I actually think you're going to miss Darius."

"Well," Erasmus muttered, "...he did save my life, you know."

"All of our lives," Kalibar agreed. He turned to Darius. "We had quite an adventure together, didn't we?" Darius smiled.

"That we did."

"Marcus was right to recommend you," Kalibar stated. "I can't say that I understood why initially," he added. "You didn't exactly sell yourself very well."

"He still doesn't," Petra observed. Kyle couldn't help but smile; Darius had hardly given Petra the time of day since he'd met her. He was likely the only man Petra had ever met who seemed immune to her charms.

"Yes, well," Kalibar stated. "You certainly surprised all of us." He smiled. "I still don't understand how you managed to escape

57

your cell in the Arena," he admitted. "And how you killed that Dire Lurker..."

"Yeah," Ariana agreed. "That was amazing."

"Not to mention killing the Dead Man," Kalibar continued.

"Well," Erasmus piped in, "...I'd give you credit for killing Ibicus, but considering I built the weapon that you used to kill him, I really just saved myself."

"Uh huh," Ariana replied.

"Right," Darius muttered.

"Where are you thinking of traveling to?" Kalibar asked Darius.

"Not sure yet," the bodyguard replied. "But I have a few ideas."

"I have a few war zones I could recommend," Erasmus chimed in, taking another gulp of his wine. Everyone ignored him.

"Hey, you could come with us," Ariana offered. "To Meros!"

"No thanks," Darius replied.

"Come on," Ariana pressed. "It would be fun! And you could be our bodyguard," she added. Darius shook his head, making Ariana frown. "Why not?"

"You don't need me anymore."

"Well," Kalibar interjected, "...whatever you decide to do, I want you to know that you'll always have a home here, Darius." He smiled at the bodyguard. "You're as much a part of this family as any of us." Darius smirked, but said nothing. Little did Kalibar realize how right he was!

"We should do a toast," Master Lee stated, standing up from her chair and raising her glass, facing Darius. Everyone followed her lead, except for Darius, of course. "To Darius!" she exclaimed.

"To Darius!" everyone cheered.

Chapter 5

Kyle sat across from Ariana on one of the many white couches in Kalibar's retirement suite, sipping on the tea that Jenkins had included in their breakfast. Or rather, Kyle's breakfast; as usual, Ariana didn't eat or drink. He'd slept in quite late, it being the weekend. Ariana had waited patiently for him to wake, spending most of the night and early morning practicing Weaving.

"How'd you sleep?" Ariana inquired.

"Not great," Kyle answered.

"Thinking about Darius?"

Kyle nodded, staring down at his steaming tea. His mind had been whirling all night, thinking about Darius's unexpected news.

"Me too," Ariana admitted.

Kyle sighed, putting his tea down and crossing his arms. He'd also been thinking about their upcoming trip...and hoping that Kalibar would allow Ariana to go with him and Petra.

"I hope Kalibar lets you come to Meros," Kyle stated. Ariana smiled.

"He will," she replied confidently. "Or I'll sneak out again." Kyle smiled back, recalling their escape to the *Defiance*, the ship that had taken them to Orja. Ariana had masterminded that mission, against Kalibar's wishes.

"I guess we're leaving tomorrow morning," Kyle said. Jenkins had told him earlier, and had already arranged for his things to be packed for the trip. Ariana smirked.

"I heard."

"Right," Kyle mumbled. He always seemed to forget how good her hearing was now.

"You're sure you want me to come?" Ariana asked, still smiling. "You could spend a whole week alone with Petra, you know."

Kyle blushed, immediately hating himself for doing so. The prospect of being around Petra for any length of time was intriguing, but also exhausting. After all, he'd spend most of the trip staring at his feet, so as not to get caught gawking at more intriguing scenery. Ariana's presence would be a welcome distraction from that constant battle!

"No way," Kyle replied. "I want you to come." Ariana grinned.

"Hey, I offered."

Kyle said nothing, sipping his tea. He'd picked up the habit each morning after Sabin's defeat; it had become his ritual. There was a sudden knock on the door, and Ariana perked up.

"It's Darius," she informed. She magically unlocked the door from across the room, and the bodyguard strode through, his golden armor shimmering in the sunlight. Darius stopped before them.

"Good morning," Ariana greeted. Darius nodded at her.

"Morning."

"You're heading out today?" Ariana asked. Darius nodded, then turned to Kyle.

"We need to talk."

"Oh," Kyle replied. "Okay."

"Let's take a walk," Darius suggested. He turned to Ariana. "We'll be back soon," he added. "I want to talk to you afterward."

"Sure," Ariana agreed. She glanced at Kyle. "Go ahead, I need to go to town in a bit anyway."

"What for?" Kyle asked.

"You'll see," Ariana answered, grinning at him and kissing him on the forehead. "Go on," she urged. "I know Darius doesn't want me to see him cry his goodbyes."

Darius smirked, but didn't take the bait. Kyle sighed, standing up from the couch. Darius turned away from Kyle and walked toward the door.

"Come on," he urged. Kyle followed dutifully, walking out of the suite and down the hallway to the riser. They made their way down to the lobby, walking through the double-doors to the campus beyond. After a few minutes following one of the cobblestone paths away from the Tower, Darius turned to Kyle.

"I'm leaving tonight," he declared.

"Why?" Kyle asked. "Why leave now? I don't get it."

"Sabin's dead."

"Yeah, but the Empire still needs you," Kyle protested. Darius shook his head.

"The Empire is on its own now."

"But *why*?" Kyle pressed. Darius smirked.

"It's time for it to take care of itself," he replied. "Besides, I have things to do."

"What things?"

"Things on Antara," Darius answered. "And on Earth." Kyle frowned.

"What..."

"Things," Darius interjected. Kyle sighed, knowing that he would get nowhere with the man. As usual.

"But what about..." Kyle began, stopping himself. He dropped his gaze, swallowing with difficulty. Then he took a deep breath, letting it out slowly. "What about *me*?"

"What about you?"

Kyle grimaced, clenching and unclenching his hands.

"*I* need you."

Darius smiled, putting a heavy, gauntleted around Kyle's shoulders.

"Not anymore."

"But you're my grandfather!" Kyle protested, looking up at Darius. "You can't just leave, and...and that's it," he added. Darius chuckled.

"I'll visit."

Kyle sighed, kicking a pebble lying nearby. It bounced over the uneven ground, rolling to a stop some ten feet away.

"You're impossible," he grumbled. "Why can't you just be like a normal person sometimes? And like *talk* to people?"

"Doing is better," Darius replied. Kyle raised an eyebrow.

"Doing people?" he asked. Darius smirked.

"That too."

Kyle followed alongside Darius for a silent minute, mulling over things in his head. Then he glanced up at his grandfather.

"What about Marcus?" he asked. The old man – Kalibar's mentor, now living as an immortal on Antara – had promised to spend some time with Kyle soon. "When can I see him again?"

"Soon."

Well, at least there was that. Marcus – unlike Darius – loved to talk, and usually helped Kyle understand just what it was that Darius was trying to do. He was certainly much easier to talk to than Darius. Still, the bodyguard had been with Kyle since his arrival on Doma, a near-constant companion. To think that he wouldn't be there anymore...trading barbs with Erasmus, or having dinner with them every night...was profoundly depressing.

"They're going to miss you, you know," Kyle said. Darius nodded.

"I know."

Kyle kicked another pebble off the path, watching it roll off into the grass.

"*I'm* going to miss you," he added. He felt Darius's arm tighten around his shoulders for a moment, and looked up to see the bodyguard smiling down at him.

"I know."

Kyle frowned, feeling a surge of annoyance at the man.

"Are you going to miss *us*?" he pressed. Darius chuckled.

"I think I'll miss Erasmus the most," he answered. Kyle rolled his eyes at him.

"I take that back," he grumbled. *"Maybe I won't miss you."*

Darius chuckled, and they walked in silence then, following the meandering cobblestone path through the huge campus of the Secula Magna. The air was warmer now, the sun a bit higher in the late-morning sky. He suddenly felt the weight of this moment, of the change to come. From now on, Darius wouldn't be at the dinner table at night, bantering with Erasmus. No more adventures with the surly bodyguard, deftly insulting Kyle with every chance he got. The implications weren't wasted on Kyle; he knew that his grandfather was effectively killing off his golden-armored alter ego.

After tonight, Darius would be gone forever...and only Ampir would remain.

* * *

It was nearly noon by the time Kyle got back to Kalibar's retirement suite, and by that time Ariana had already returned from her trip into town. Darius took her for a private walk afterward, leaving Kyle to his own devices in his room. With nothing to do but study, he did just that, pouring over the books that Master Lee had given him. When he'd bored of that – which didn't take long – he sighed, laying on his back in bed and staring up at the ceiling. There were no video games, no television, or any other modern distractions on Doma to pass the time...and the various simple games others found entertaining here didn't hold his interest.

He sighed again, twiddling his thumbs. The he turned his head to the side, spotting his notebook lying on his nightstand. He picked it up, flipping through the pages. He'd been jotting down notes about ideas for new inventions ever since he'd returned from Orja. The sheer number of things he could make – only knowing a few patterns – was incredible. But while he had no shortage of ideas, getting down to actually *making* the runic devices had proven more difficult. Partially because he hadn't had time, what with his classes, and mostly due to the fact that he still didn't know enough about crystals to actually make something that worked.

Kyle flipped to the page he'd shown Ariana earlier, the one with the gravity grenade. He desperately wanted to build it, but he still didn't have the right materials to do so. He flipped to another page, which showed a gun-like contraption. It was a *punk* rifle, a gun that shot small balls of flaming *punk*. In theory, it worked by first creating a gravity sphere within the barrel, then creating a small ball of *punk* within it. The punk would then be set on fire, after which another gravity field would shoot the punk out of the barrel. Again, the issue was with how to time all of these things…and that *punk* was sticky, and would almost certainly clog the barrel.

He pushed the notebook aside. So many things he wanted to do! To think that he'd once thought that being a Runic would be boring. Master Owens had been right all along…inventing Runic technology was far more to his liking than being a Weaver.

Just then, Kyle heard the door to Kalibar's suite open, and he hopped out of bed, stepping into the huge suite. Ariana had returned from her walk with Darius, and had a big smile on her face.

"Hey Kyle," she greeted, walking up to him and giving him a kiss. He kissed her back, then realized that Darius wasn't trailing behind her.

"Where's Darius?" he asked. Ariana shrugged.

"He went off to do something," she replied. She glanced down at his notebook, still lying open next to him. "What's this?" she asked, sitting down beside him and picking the notebook up.

"Just another idea," Kyle answered.

"What does it do?" she pressed.

"It's a gun," he replied. He described it to her, and she stared at it, a frown on her face.

"But why do you need a Runic device for this?" she asked. "Weavers can make *punk* fireballs really easily."

"Well, I want anyone to be able to use it," Kyle explained. "Even if they don't make magic." Ariana's frown deepened.

"That's not possible," she countered. "You need magic to trigger runic devices."

"True," Kyle agreed. "But remember how I made the invisibility field around the *Defiance*?" He'd used one large cubic crystal for the pattern, and other cubes filled with magic as "batteries" to supply the magic. When one "battery" had been drained, he'd slid another next to the runic device. On contact, magic had flowed from the battery to the device, powering the invisibility field...like turning on an electric switch.

"Yeah."

"Well I'm doing the same thing here," he explained, pointing to the trigger on the gun. "Pulling this slides a small crystal into place next to the crystal that has the runes for making the gravity fields and *punk*," he added. "That provides the magic for the device...the trigger acts like a switch, turning the gun on."

"So anyone can use it?"

"Right."

"Wow," she breathed, staring at the drawing for a long moment. "Kyle, this could change everything!"

"What do you mean?"

"If you could do this for other devices, that means *anyone* could use magic!"

"Well yeah," Kyle replied. He'd assumed that everybody *could* use runic devices, turning them on and off. "Can't they already?"

"No," Ariana countered. "I mean, people who can't make magic can only use runic devices that are always on," she added. "They have to have a Runic or magic storage crystal recharge their devices."

"Really?"

"Yes, really," Ariana confirmed.

"Well that's silly."

"But with this," she stated, holding up the notebook, "...anyone could use magic devices, and turn them on and off!"

"Right," Kyle agreed.

"Can you make this?" Ariana pressed. Kyle shook his head.

"It's too complicated," he admitted.

"Can you make anything else with a...what did you call it?"

"A magical switch," he replied. "Yeah, I guess so." He grabbed the notebook, flipping pages until he reached the sketch of the gravity grenade. He tapped his chin with one finger. "I could make this," he offered.

"The gravity grenade?"

"It's pretty straightforward," he said, rubbing his chin. "But I still don't have what I need to build it."

Ariana gave him a little smile, raising one eyebrow.

"You sure about that?"

"Huh?"

She gestured for him to follow her into her room – another bedroom off of the main suite – and they sat down on her bed. Her backpack was there, and she handed it to him.

"How was your..." he began, but she cut him off.

"Open it," she urged, gesturing at the backpack. Kyle looked down at it, then did as she requested. To his surprise, it was practically brimming with various gemstones.

"What's this?" he asked.

"Gems for your inventions," she answered, grinning from ear to ear. Kyle stared at her blankly, which only made her smile wider. "Go on, empty it out."

Kyle did so, gemstones spilling out onto the bed...along with spools of metal wire, a pair of wire cutters, and various other items. Everything he needed to make the gravity grenade.

"I went to a few stores," Ariana stated proudly. "I think I got everything you need to build it."

"Wow," Kyle breathed. "Thanks!"

"No problem," she replied. "I memorized the gems in the book you were studying and bought a few of each."

Kyle shook his head, unable to help himself from grinning. She'd given him exactly what he wanted.

"Thank you," he said for the second time. "This is great, Ariana."

"Anything for you," she said, pecking him on the cheek. "You should bring it with you on the trip," she added. "Just in case you get some downtime."

"I will," he promised. He stared at her for a moment, at her big brown eyes, her radiant pale skin. She was lovely inside and out, more than he could have ever asked for. He leaned in to kiss her, feeling her cool lips against his. Then he leaned back. "How was your walk?" he asked.

"It was nice," Ariana answered. "Darius was really sweet." Kyle made a face, and Ariana laughed. "No really," she insisted. "He's a good guy once you get to know him."

"I know," Kyle admitted, if grudgingly.

"So what do you want to do for the rest of the day?" she inquired. "Want me to help you start making your grenade? Or maybe we could go get the stuff you need to make the gun-thing!" Kyle smiled; he loved spending time with Ariana no matter what they were doing.

"Let's start with the grenade," he decided.

Chapter 6

Kalibar sat down at the large circular table in the conference room where he'd chosen to have his meeting with the Council, nodding at each Councilman as they entered the room. They took their seats at the table, and Erasmus came with them, sitting beside Kalibar. The last to enter was a tall man with black hair and an imposing black beard. It was Goran, now the Elder Councilman after Ibicus's and Jax's deaths...and, as usual, Kalibar and Erasmus's staunchest opponent on the Council. He nodded at Kalibar and Erasmus as he entered the room, walking to his chair opposite them and sitting down.

"I believe that's everyone," Kalibar stated. "Thank you for coming at such short notice."

"Of course," Goran replied. "What is this meeting about, Kalibar?"

"I called this meeting to discuss my meeting yesterday with the new Verhanian ambassador," Kalibar explained, leaning forward in his chair. "As we know, when Ampir killed Sabin, he also destroyed all of Sabin's Chosen...many of which we've discovered had been hiding in plain sight in Stridon and other parts of the Empire."

The members of the Council nodded; they'd all heard of the disturbing number of spies that had infiltrated the Empire.

"It appears that there were many Chosen in Verhan who met a similar fate," Kalibar continued, "...including two of the lords."

A few of the Councilmen gasped, and Goran leaned forward in his chair.

"You're saying that a quarter of the lords were Sabin's Chosen?" he exclaimed. Kalibar nodded.

"Correct," he confirmed. "And there was another high-profile victim," he added. "The king himself was found dead in his bedroom, a blackened hole burned into his brain."

Every Councilman – to a one – sat back in their chairs, their mouths in a perfect "O." Kalibar let the news sink in, remaining silent. Goran was the first to recover, shaking his head in disbelief.

"Incredible," he breathed. "Just...incredible."

"Damn right it is," Erasmus piped in. "Sabin had the two greatest superpowers in the world under his thumb, and we didn't even know it."

"So now that the king is dead," Councilman Hewes stated, "...who is running Verhan?" An Elitist like Goran, he was a bit younger, in his forties. Slight of build and with short graying hair, he lacked Goran's fiercely handsome demeanor, but typically followed the Elder Runic's lead.

"The king's heir was a Chosen as well, so the remaining six lords are governing in their absence," Kalibar answered. "According to the ambassador, the lords have agreed on an election to crown one of them King. They'll each have one vote, and in two days they will conduct the election."

"I see," Goran stated. "Who are the surviving lords?"

"Lords Devlin, Damia, Farwell, Lindon, Zellus, and Tristan," Kalibar answered.

"Lord Lindon is out," Erasmus stated. "He's pushing eighty. No one would vote for him."

"Agreed," another Councilman stated.

"And Lord Farwell is out too," Erasmus opined. "He's too comfortable enjoying his money to ever take on real responsibility."

"So their votes are up for grabs," another Councilman realized. "We can pay them off and secure their votes."

69

"We can," Goran agreed. "But we need to act strategically. After all, their votes could already be bought by other parties."

"Obviously," Erasmus concurred. "Which means we have to pay them more than anyone else will."

"Which we can," Kalibar stated. "The potential for future trade agreements will more than offset the cost."

"Of course," Goran stated. "Assuming that we're successful in crowning Lord Devlin. He would be our preferred candidate."

"How can we succeed if we don't try?" Erasmus asked. "Unless you want Lady Damia to win," he added sourly. Goran grimaced.

"Lady Damia is hardly a contender for the throne," he countered. More than a few of the Councilmen nodded in agreement. "Her anti-Empire rhetoric is so extreme that the other lords will never elect her."

"But she has a strong following among the people," another Councilman argued. "She blames the king's death on the Empire...and her people like having an enemy they can rally against, especially given our past."

Kalibar nodded in agreement. There was no love lost between the Empire and Verhan, not after the wars between them that had nearly destroyed both governments over two thousand years ago. He'd spent much of his first term courting the Verhanian government, establishing trade agreements and coming to a peaceful, if tense, relationship. They were nowhere near allies, but at least they weren't at each other's throats anymore.

"Lady Damia is an extremist," Goran stated. "She won't be crowned."

"Still," Erasmus countered, "...supporting Devlin would prevent her from winning the crown."

"That's not in question," Goran replied. "I'm more worried about the lords that actually have a chance of winning."

"Granted," Kalibar agreed. "So the remaining contenders are Devlin, Zellus, Tristan, and Damia."

"I agree that Devlin would be the best king for the Empire," Councilman Mudd piped in. "Lord Zellus and Tristan would be a big step back...and Lady Damia would be a nightmare."

"Agreed," Goran stated. "We need to ensure that Lord Devlin is elected." He turned to Kalibar. "What did the ambassador say about the election?"

"It's in two days, as I mentioned earlier," Kalibar answered. "The ambassador works for Lord Devlin. My operatives in Verhan confirmed that earlier today. He's supposed to represent all of the lords, but he secretly reports to Devlin...and he wants our support in ensuring that Devlin wins."

"He'll get it," Goran replied. "It would be stupid not to take advantage of this opportunity," he added. "We've fought tooth-and-nail to get to the tenuous agreement we have with Verhan now. With Devlin sitting on the throne, we could even become allies."

"Which would be better for both countries," Councilman Hewes agreed.

Councilwoman Hess frowned, leaning back in her chair and crossing her arms over her chest.

"I think we're getting ahead of ourselves," she interjected. "I understand the urge to positively influence the outcome of the election, but I'm not sure that it's a given that we should do so."

Goran – and several of the other Councilmen – frowned at her.

"What do you mean?" Goran asked.

"Well," she answered, "...Lord Devlin is already popular among the other lords. He's more likely to win than Lord Zellus or Lady Damia."

"Granted," Councilman Mudd conceded, "...but Lord Tristan is still a threat."

"But remember," Hess countered, "...Lord Zellus and Lord Devlin are friends. It's likely Zellus will vote for Devlin."

"Maybe," Kalibar replied. "But maybe not." He shook his head. "We can't leave the future of the Empire to chance."

"Agreed," Hewes stated. Most of the other Councilmen nodded as well...as did Erasmus.

"We're talking about the future of the Empire here," the Grand Runic piped in. "If we can get Devlin on the throne, it will be the greatest accomplishment of our generation." Then he smirked. "Not that we'll be able to tell anyone about it."

Councilwoman Hess looked none-too-convinced, but said nothing more. Kalibar stood then, sweeping his gaze across the Councilmen seated before him.

"We'll leave it to a vote. All in favor of funding Lord Devlin?" he asked, raising his own hand. Erasmus raised his hand, as did all but one of the Councilmen...Councilwoman Hess, of course.

"Then it's decided," Kalibar declared authoritatively. "We'll mobilize the funds immediately, and notify ambassador Rodric before he leaves for Verhan." He leaned back in his chair. "Now to discuss which lords we'll target...and the funds needed to win their vote."

* * *

Kalibar eased himself into one of the white couches in the main room of his suite, taking the glass of wine Jenkins had thoughtfully left him and sipping it. He sighed, rolling his shoulders backward, feeling the tension there. He'd been worried that the meeting with the Council would go badly...that the Council would have rejected the proposal to back Lord Devlin. It had been a baseless fear, of course. Ever since Sabin's defeat, the usually obstructionist Council had become quite favorable to Kalibar and Erasmus's proposals.

He stretched his legs, then glanced out of the windows in his suite. It was already sunset, the day having flown by. Which meant that Kyle and Petra would be leaving for Meros tomorrow...and Petra wouldn't be coming back.

Kalibar took another sip of wine, suddenly wishing he had a bottle.

Not only was Petra leaving, but Darius had already said his goodbyes before the meeting and had left Stridon. Kalibar had a strong suspicion that he would never see the bodyguard again. As silent and generally unpersonable as the man had been, Kalibar would still miss him.

Everything was changing.

He heard a knock on the door, and willed the front door of his suite to become translucent. It revealed Petra on the other side. He

72

paused for a moment, knowing that while he could see her, she could not see him. Clad in her Reaper uniform, she was quite lovely, and he found it enormously difficult not to stare. He pulled himself together quickly, feeling suddenly ashamed of his brief voyeurism.

"Come in," he called out, mentally unlocking the door. Petra strode in, closing the door behind her, and walked up to the couch. She put her hands on her hips, looking down at him.

"I've been waiting all day for our rematch," she informed him. Kalibar sighed, rubbing his eyes wearily.

"Ah yes," he replied. "Sorry about the wait...I had to call an emergency meeting with the Council."

"I heard," Petra stated. She frowned then. "What's wrong?"

"I'm tired, that's all."

"You'll have to wake up," she replied, "...if you plan on beating me again."

Kalibar gave a weak smile, then shook his head.

"I don't know if I'm up for it tonight, to be honest," he admitted. Petra stared at him for a long moment, then sat down on the couch next to him.

"What's bothering you?"

"Long day," he answered. When she didn't say anything, he felt the urge to fill the silence. "Things are....tense between Verhan and the Empire," he added. "Turns out their king was a Chosen."

"Oh," Petra replied. Then her eyes widened. "I see." She knew what that meant, of course.

"They didn't appreciate finding him dead," Kalibar stated wryly. "There's a power vacuum now...the lords are battling each other to become king."

Still, Petra said nothing, just staring at him. She had large, beautiful eyes, and he found himself getting lost in them. He tore his gaze away.

"One of the lords is sympathetic to the Empire," he continued. "The Council agreed to use the Empire's resources to help Lord..."

"What's really bothering you?" Petra interrupted, putting a hand on his arm. It was warm, and her touch sent a thrill through him. He paused for a long moment, staring at his lap. Then he sighed.

73

"Everything is changing," he admitted. "And I don't like it."

"What do you mean?"

"Darius is leaving us," he answered. Petra's look soured, and Kalibar couldn't help but grin. "He's an ass," he admitted, "...but he's a damn good man. And he's been with me ever since I met Kyle."

"Go on."

"Well, you know I retired after my first term," Kalibar continued. "The reason...the *real* reason I took a second term was to protect my family – Kyle and Ariana." He shook his head. "Now that the Empire is safe, I feel like I'm..." He trailed off, leaning back in the couch. "Like I'm not needed anymore."

"You're a good ruler," Petra countered.

"Yes, well so are a lot of other men," he pointed out. "The Empire needed me to protect the Empire against Xanos, and now Xanos is dead."

"So you don't want to be Grand Weaver anymore?" Petra asked. Kalibar stared at her, saying nothing more a long moment. Then he sighed.

"I don't know."

"What *do* you want?" she pressed.

"Something I can't have," Kalibar answered.

Petra arched one eyebrow, but said nothing. Kalibar rubbed his face with one hand, feeling enormously uncomfortable. They'd never spoken about...*them*. And other than when Petra had kissed him after Sabin's death, she hadn't shown any real interest in starting a relationship.

"It doesn't matter," Kalibar stated, breaking the silence. "My duty is to finish my term."

"I understand," Petra replied. "Mine is to protect my people."

Kalibar nodded, feeling suddenly depressed. She knew what he was thinking...and had just shut him down. But she was right, after all. She needed to protect her people, and he needed to finish his term. There was no way that they could be together without one of them sacrificing their duties.

74

They sat there for a long moment, saying nothing at all. Then Kalibar stirred.

"Thank you, by the way," he said. "For agreeing to go with Kyle and Ariana to Meros."

"So you've decided to have Ariana go too?" Petra asked. Kalibar sighed, then nodded.

"There's no one better suited to protect Kyle," he answered. "And those two are inseparable anyway. I doubt I could keep Ariana from him." He smiled at Petra then. "I feel better knowing that you're with them, though. Thanks again."

"You're welcome."

Kalibar hesitated, rubbing his hands together.

"They're very fond of you, you know," he added. Petra smiled, putting a hand on his knee.

"I'm fond of them too."

Petra removed her hand from his knee, and they sat there in silence. A long moment passed, and then Petra stood up.

"I should get ready," she stated. Kalibar sighed, standing as well.

"Good night," he said.

"Good night."

He watched as Petra left, then sat back down on his couch, staring at his knees. He glanced the glass of wine sitting on the end-table next to him, and picked it up, raising it to toast the empty room.

"To what could have been," he muttered. He lowered the glass, staring down at it for a long moment. Then he downed the wine in one gulp.

Chapter 7

Tessa strode quickly down the path leading to the front door of the governor's mansion, making her way toward the two guards flanking the entrance. One of the guards glanced at the other, giving them a look, then glaring at her. She ignored him, reaching the door and opening it, then stepping through. She continued onward through the obnoxiously opulent foyer, walking right up to one of the men standing there. It was Benton, the governor's head butler.

"Ah, miss Tessa," Benton greeted, bowing slightly. "The governor has been expecting you."

"I doubt that," she retorted. The man grimaced.

"Yes, well," he replied. "Should I tell him you've arrived?"

"I'll tell him myself," Tessa stated, stepping around him and making her way to the grand staircase leading to the third floor. A large, stately chandelier hung directly above her head, glittering in the magic lights hanging from the ceiling. She glanced up at it in disgust, taking the steps two at a time.

"Miss!" the butler called out after her. "You can't just…"

"Are you afraid the governor won't approve?" she retorted, not bothering to look over her shoulder. That shut the man up, of course. Still, he followed behind her as she ascended the stairs, reaching the third story of the large mansion. She turned right toward a long hallway, hearing the *clop, clop* of the butler's footsteps behind her. There was a door at the other end of the hall, and she strode up to it…just as it opened. She stopped, nearly colliding with a middle-aged woman stepping out into the hallway.

"Whoa there," the woman blurted out, taking a step back. It was Bae, her father's secretary. She was much shorter than Tessa, and stocky, with short salt-and-pepper hair. "You trying to kill me?"

"Sorry Bae," Tessa apologized. Bae smirked.

"On the warpath, eh Tess?" she guessed. Footsteps approached from behind, and Tessa glanced back to see Benton walking up to them.

"I tried to tell miss Tessa that…" the butler began, but Bae cut him off.

"Leave her be," she interjected. She smiled at Tessa. "Give him hell," she stated. "But don't kill him, okay sweets? I need this job."

Tessa smiled.

"Thanks Bae."

Bae smiled back, then grabbed Tessa's shoulder and pulled her closer, putting her lips up to Tessa's ear.

"Help him find his balls, will you?" she whispered. Then she let Tessa go, and glanced through the doorway. "Love you governor," she called out sweetly. Then she turned back to Tessa, giving her a wink…and promptly leaving down the hallway, grabbing Benton's arm and dragging the butler with her.

Tessa watched them go, then walked through the doorway into the room beyond. She didn't even bother to knock. Beyond, she saw a tall man in a white shirt and black pants seated at a large desk reading a book. He was quite handsome, with a bald head and a smooth-shaven face. He was well-built, muscular in a way that Tessa knew intimidated nearly everyone around him.

But not her, of course.

"You wanted to see me?" she asked coolly, standing in the doorway and crossing her arms over her chest. The man glanced up from his book, breaking out into a smile when he saw her. He stood up immediately.

"Tessa!" he exclaimed. He went around his desk, walking up to her and trying to hug her. She pushed him away.

"Don't even," she said, glaring at him.

"Tessa…"

"Those Finders had *no* right to use force against us," she interrupted. "I know you were watching."

"What was I supposed to do?"

"You were *supposed* to uphold the law!" she shot back. "We assembled peacefully, Dad. We had every right to be there!"

"But…"

"Those Finders broke the law," she continued. Candric grimaced.

"What was I going to do," he replied, "…arrest them?"

"Damn right," she stated, putting her hands on her hips.

"You know very well how that would've ended," Candric countered.

"I do," she agreed. "And that's the point, isn't it? They can do whatever they want because they have magic. We don't have any power, Dad. They've taken it away from us."

Candric said nothing, staring down at her. He was over six feet tall, and as tall as she was, he still towered over her. He'd always been the strongest man she'd ever known, in more ways than one. That is, until he'd become governor.

Now he was impotent. A mouthpiece for the Empire.

"It's good to see you," he stated at last. "You look good."

"So do you," she admitted.

He sighed, running a hand over his bald head, then giving her an apologetic look.

"I heard about your plans for the Festival," he confessed.

Tessa kept her expression carefully neutral, not wanting him to see her surprise. She crossed her arms over her chest again. If he knew about her plans, that meant that someone had ratted her out. Which meant that there was a double agent in her team.

"And?"

"I don't think it's a good idea, Tess," he warned.

"Well good," she replied. "I must be doing something right then."

"Tessa, staging a protest for the Finders was bad enough," he argued. "Doing it during the biggest celebration of the year is…"

78

"Is what?" Tessa inquired. He grimaced.

"Dangerous."

"Oh really," she shot back. "And why is that? You going to send your dogs after me? I know Apep is just *dying* to throw me in jail."

"*I'm* not going to do anything," he countered. "And Apep is a man of the law. But I can't speak for every member of the City Guard. Tensions are high, Tessa. People are still angry about what you pulled with the Finders."

"You mean with the people that just kidnapped three more of our children?" Tessa inquired.

"Tessa..."

"Are you honestly going to defend them?" she interrupted angrily. "After everything, you're going to tell me I need to hide under a rock while the Empire abducts our children?"

"I'm not saying..."

"You *are*," she retorted. "Three-quarters of our island lives in poverty, the Empire sends its businessmen here to exploit our workers for wages we can't even *live* on, they send Weavers to abduct our children and brainwash them into good little slaves, depriving us of even having the *chance* to benefit from magic...and you're *defending* them?"

"I'm not defending them," he retorted.

"So what then?" she pressed. "Are you afraid I'll embarrass you in front of the Empire's precious little children? I heard they were coming tomorrow. Are you that ashamed of me father?"

He grimaced, taking a deep breath in, then letting it out. Which she knew damn well meant she'd gotten to him.

"I'm not ashamed of you," he stated quietly.

"Bullshit Dad."

"I'm not," he insisted. "I'm worried about your safety."

"I'll be fine."

"You haven't sat in on my meetings with the City Guard," he retorted. "You don't understand how angry they are."

"I'm well within the law and they know it," Tessa retorted. "I have every right to march down here and protest!"

"You do."

"They just can't *stand* that we have rights," she complained. "Everything's all well and good until we start pushing back. What good is having rights if we don't use them?"

"Like I said, I agree," Dad insisted.

"Then why are you trying to get me to stop?"

"Because I'm selfish," he confessed. She glared at him.

"Finally you admit it," she shot back. "Taking money from lobbyists, spouting Populist rhetoric when you know it's all a bunch of crap. You're as corrupt as the rest of them."

"I'm selfish because I don't want something bad to happen to you," he pressed.

She stared up at him silently.

"You don't know how hard I've worked behind the scenes to keep the City Guard from cracking down on you," he insisted. "They're even considering changing the law to make what you're doing a disturbance of the peace." He sighed. "They could put you in jail, Tessa. You and your people…and it wouldn't look good if I paid your bail."

"Oh don't you worry about that, Daddy," she countered acidly. "I've got plenty of money for bail."

He frowned.

"How?" he asked.

"Anonymous benefactor," she answered. "They've been *very* generous."

He considered this for a moment.

"I see," he replied at last. "But that might not help if they change the law," he added. "You could still do jail time if they succeed in doing so…and they'll try to make an example out of you. If I intervene, they'll scream nepotism and try to impeach me."

"Corrupt bastards," she spat. "Taking away our rights so we won't scare away the tourists, eh?" She glared at him. "God forbid our freedom gets in the way of the Empire's profits!"

"I'm just telling you what I'm dealing with," he insisted.

"Let me tell you what *I'm* dealing with," she shot back. "Kidnapping, poverty, profiteering, systemic corruption…"

"I *know*," he interjected. "I'm working on it."

"Really?" she shot back. "How many years have you been governor?"

He grimaced.

"Three years, Dad," she stated. "And what exactly have you accomplished?"

"These things take time," he insisted. "You can't make changes by pissing people off."

"What, are you afraid of conflict?" she retorted. "Is that why you decided to become the Empire's 'yes' man?"

"I *am* making a difference," he countered calmly, not taking her bait. "I'm doing it through the proper channels, by changing the law. It takes time," he added. "You have to be patient."

"So how many more kids are going to be torn from their families while I'm being *patient*?" she demanded. "While we were being *patient*, the Empire took my brother from me!"

He took a step back, looking as if he'd been slapped. The color drained from his face, and he swallowed visibly. Tessa looked down, seeing that his hands were balled into fists…and his knuckles were white. But she didn't care.

"How much longer will we go without representation in the government?" she continued. "Us *regular* people aren't even allowed *near* the Secula Magna unless we're servants!"

"We have some power," Dad countered, his voice carefully neutral. "We have to use it to make change from the inside."

"Bullshit Dad," she argued. "The only power we'll get is the power we take. We outnumber the Runics and Weavers ten-thousand-to-one. We have to rise up and demand change! We have to refuse to serve them any longer. *We're* the ones slaving away for nothing while the Empire flourishes! And until we stop them from stealing anyone who makes magic from us, we'll never have the real power to beat them at their own game!"

Dad sighed, his shoulders slumping. He stared at the floor for a long moment, looking suddenly older.

"Okay," he said in a near-whisper. "Do what you can…do it your way. I'll keep fighting my way."

She hesitated, then nodded.

"Okay."

"Together we can make a change for the better, in different ways," he stated. He hesitated then. "If you need money…"

"I've got money," she interjected. "What if your way doesn't work?" she pressed. "What if you fail?"

Dad stepped forward, putting his hands on her shoulders. He gave her a weak smile, with his lips but not his eyes.

"If I do," he replied, "I'll do it your way." He hesitated. "And what will you do if I succeed?"

She pulled away from his grasp, taking a step backward.

"You won't," she answered. "Bye Dad," she added, turning and walking back down the hallway the way she'd come.

"Tessa!" she heard him call out after her. She didn't turn around. "What?"

"Put off the demonstration," he urged. "Just for one day."

"We've been putting off our equality for two hundred years," she shot back, nearing the end of the hallway. "I think that's long enough."

* * *

Kyle woke up to knocking on his door. He groaned, sitting up and rubbing his eyes. It was still dark, starlight shining through his bedroom window. He yawned, stretching his arms over his head…and heard another knock.

"Are you decent, sir?" he heard a voice on the other end of the door ask. It was Jenkins, of course.

"Uh, yeah," Kyle replied loudly. He yawned again, unlocking the door with a thought. It opened, revealing Jenkins.

"Grand Weaver Kalibar requests your presence. Your carriage is ready," the butler stated.

Kyle frowned, at first not understanding what Jenkins was talking about. Then he remembered; he was leaving for Meros today with Petra. Kalibar had mentioned that they'd be leaving very early, but Kyle hadn't expected it to be before sunrise.

"Uh, what should I wear?" Kyle asked.

"Your clothes are on the dresser," Jenkins answered. Of course they were...Jenkins set them there every night for Kyle, for the next day.

"Shouldn't I pack some stuff?"

"Your luggage is already in the carriage," Jenkins informed. Then he turned about, leaving the room. "I'll give you privacy," he added, closing the door behind him. Kyle stripped off his bedclothes, pulling on the fresh set of clothes Jenkins had left for him. Far from the plain white uniform of a Runic student, these were quite ornate. The shirt and pants were black, with golden patterns and gems sewn into them. They were incredibly comfortable, lined with what felt like silk on the inside. He pulled on his gravity boots, then hesitated, remembering the gravity grenades he'd made yesterday. He'd also made a few magnetobombs, small cubes that acted on a timer, creating a powerful magnetic field that would pull any metals around it into it. A small gravity shield protected the cubes themselves from being crushed by things flying into them.

Kyle grabbed these, along with a few blank cubes of various mineral types, stuffing them in his pockets. Then he opened the door. Jenkins was nowhere to be seen. Instead he found Kalibar standing in the middle of the suite.

"Ah," Kalibar said, spotting Kyle. "Good morning, son."

"Morning."

"Today's the day," Kalibar stated. "Are you ready for your trip?"

"I think so."

Just then, Ariana's bedroom door opened, and Ariana walked through. She was dressed in her Reaper uniform, a gift from Petra...and the same uniform Petra had worn as a girl.

"Morning dad," Ariana greeted. "Hey Kyle!" She practically skipped up to Kalibar, giving him a hug and a kiss, and gave equal treatment to Kyle. When she pulled away from Kyle, he found her grinning from ear to ear.

"What are you doing up?" Kyle asked. It was a silly question, of course...she was always up.

"Kalibar said I could go," she answered excitedly. Kyle's eyes widened, and he turned to Kalibar.

"Really?"

"Really," Kalibar confirmed with a smile. "I can think of no one I trust more to protect you." He gestured for them to follow him, and began walking toward the front door of the suite. "There are a few things I want to go over before you leave," he added, opening the door and leading them into the hallway beyond. "You'll be traveling to Meros with a few elite guards...and a guide."

"A guide?" Kyle asked.

"A man named Jagwell," Kalibar explained. "He's not a Runic, but he's spent a lifetime with the natives on Meros. He'll be an important asset to you...I'd listen to what he has to say."

"Okay."

"Also, keep in mind that, as my children, you'll be representing me while you're on Meros," Kalibar continued.

"We'll be well-behaved," Ariana promised. Kalibar smirked.

"I'm not worried about that," he replied. "Just keep in mind that half of Meros is owned by Verhan...and the Empire isn't too popular with Verhanian citizens right now. Keep a low profile while you're there."

"Got it," Ariana stated.

"You'll be staying at the governor's mansion in Meros, on the Empire's side," Kalibar continued. "Jagwell will stay with you, and he'll take you to the ruins each day."

They reached the riser at the end of the hallway and took it down to the lobby. Kalibar led them to the double doors exiting the Tower, stepping through them.

The air outside was cool and fragrant, the stars still glimmering in the moonless sky. A large carriage levitated above the ground before the entrance to the Tower, two more elite guards flanking it. The carriage was unlike any that Kyle had ever seen. Far from the typical horse-drawn carriage he'd become accustomed to, this was much larger, with no horses in sight...and no real front or back. Rather, it was shaped more like a large bowl turned upside-down, perhaps twelve feet in diameter, its golden-red wood polished to a mirror-shine. Elaborate patterns had been engraved on its surface, with countless jewels embedded into the wood, glittering dully. The jewels glowed a faint blue, evidence that they were more than just decoration.

"Where are the horses?" Kyle asked, gesturing at the carriage.

"There aren't any," Kalibar answered. "This is a flying carriage." Kyle frowned at him, not understanding. Flying carriages hadn't been invented yet, at least not by the Empire. Only the Dead Man had possessed them.

"How...?" he began.

"It doesn't fly by itself," Kalibar explained. "It levitates, and the elite guards steer it from the outside, flying next to it."

"Oh," Kyle mumbled. Immediately his mind went to work, imagining how he could make it so that they could steer the carriage from the inside. It wouldn't be difficult...just a control panel with gems for steering. The gems would create various gravity fields around the carriage, much like his gravity boots.

Kyle heard footsteps behind him, and turned to see Erasmus and Master Lee walking arm-in-arm out of the Tower.

"Hey kids!" Erasmus greeted. "Ready for your trip?"

"I think so," Kyle answered. Master Lee smirked.

"Well you'd better learn something," she warned. "We'll have a week of classes to make up when you get back." Kyle grimaced, hardly looking forward to the prospect.

"Ha!" Erasmus interjected, putting a hand on Kyle's shoulder. "Don't worry about her. Just keep coming up with those glorious inventions of yours."

"I'll try," Kyle replied noncommittally.

"Just have fun," Kalibar interjected. He turned to Ariana. "And keep him safe," he added.

"I won't sleep on the job," Ariana quipped, making Kalibar smile. Kyle frowned.

"Hey, where's Petra?" he asked.

"I'm coming," a voice behind Erasmus and Master Lee said. Kyle saw Petra walking out of the Tower toward them. She was dressed, as usual, in her Reaper uniform. Kalibar turned to her.

"Good luck," he told her.

Petra smiled, stepping in and giving Kalibar a hug. She pulled away then, and they both stood there awkwardly. Kyle glanced at Ariana, who shrugged.

"Well, as long as we're being awkward," Erasmus piped up, facing Petra with a grin and extending his arms to the side, "...how about one last hug for the road?"

Petra took a step back, giving the Grand Runic a suspicious glare.

"You're a dirty old man," she shot back. But still, she leaned in and gave Erasmus a hug...much to the Grand Runic's surprise. His face turned bright red, and he, for once, was speechless. She let go, then turned to Kalibar. "I see where you get it from now."

"Yes, well," Kalibar mumbled. "Say hello to your parents for me." Petra nodded.

"I will."

They all stood for a long, silent moment, until a man stepped out from behind the carriage, coming up to face Kalibar. He was short and wiry, with long black hair and a clean-shaven face. He was maybe forty, with skin that was tanned and leathery from a lifetime in the sun. He bowed before Kalibar and Erasmus.

"Ah, Jagwell," Kalibar greeted. "Thank you for coming on such short notice."

"Grand Weaver," Jagwell greeted. He spoke in a rather thick accent that reminded Kyle of the people from the Shimmering Isle. "Grand Runic." He glanced at Kyle, Ariana, and Petra. "This my crew?"

"Yes," Kalibar confirmed.

"Go in," Jagwell stated, gesturing at the three. "Through the back."

Kyle glanced at Kalibar, who gave him one last hug, then pulled away.

"Come on," Jagwell pressed. "Don't got all day." He walked toward the back of the carriage, clearly expecting everyone to follow him.

"Good luck," Kalibar said.

Ariana waved, then followed Jagwell to the rear of the carriage. Petra followed suit, and Kyle followed behind her. The rear of the carriage had a door that swung downward to rest on the ground, serving as a ramp up into the vehicle. Jagwell walked up the ramp into the carriage, and the others did so as well. The door swung up, closing behind them.

The inside of the carriage was as ornate as the exterior, consisting of a single circular room with polished wooden floors and a white ceiling. It resembled a small living room, with a U-shaped white couch in the middle, and bookshelves lining a portion of the otherwise transparent curved crystal walls. The center of the floor was also made of transparent crystal, revealing the cobblestones below the carriage. The outer perimeter of the floor was made of a cherry wood polished to a mirror shine.

Jagwell led them to the couch, sitting down and gesturing for them to do the same. Kyle felt a sudden pang of fear as he did so; if this was the only room, where was the bathroom? He'd forgotten to pee before he'd left.

"Bathroom's there," Jagwell informed, gesturing to a narrow door. "Make yourselves comfortable," he added, glancing around the cabin. "Shouldn't be hard."

"I'm Ariana," Ariana greeted. "This is Kyle," she added, "...and Petra. And you're Jagwell?"

"People who know me call me Jag."

"Nice to meet you Jag," Ariana stated. Jag's expression remained flat.

"Just doing my job."

Kyle felt the carriage start to rise, and braced himself on the couch. He looked down through the transparent floor; the ground was falling away beneath them with alarming speed. He fought off a sudden wave of nausea. Flying this quickly was one thing with gravity boots, when he was in complete control. It was entirely different when he wasn't.

"How long's the flight?" Petra inquired. Jag eyed her for a moment longer than was necessary.

"Four hours, give or take."

The carriage lifted higher into the air, the dormitories and Tower below looking like models in the distance. Kyle frowned, looking up at Jag.

"Wait," he stated. "What about the Gate shield?"

"What about it?" Jag grumbled.

"Won't we fly through it?" Kyle asked. The Gate shield surrounded the campus of the Secula Magna, and would obliterate anything that passed through it.

"Gate operators'll open a hole in it for us," Jag answered. Almost as if on cue, Kyle saw the shimmering dome of the Gate shield appear below them, a large hole in the dome immediately underneath. The hole closed as he watched. The carriage slowed its ascent, then began to accelerate forward. The campus of the Secula Magna passed by beneath them, until Kyle could see downtown Stridon below. The streets were empty, it still being obscenely early.

"You're not from around here," Jag noted, looking Petra up and down. And up again. Petra regarded him coolly, saying nothing. Jag leaned back in the plush couch. "Where you from?"

"The Barren forest," Petra answered. Jag raised an eyebrow.

"That so," he replied. "You're one of them savages then?" Petra arched an eyebrow of her own.

"Excuse me?"

"That's what people call your kind," Jag explained.

"And why," Petra stated icily, "...are my people savages?"

"You live in trees, don't you?"

"And you live in houses made of trees," Petra retorted, glaring at him. Jag chuckled.

"Fair point," he conceded. When she continued to glare at him, Jag smirked.

"If you ask me," he stated, "...we're *all* savages." He leaned forward, his eyes locked on Petra's. "And the more we have, the more savage we get."

Petra said nothing, staring back at him, and Jag leaned back in the couch, eyeing her curiously. Or perhaps he was appreciating her...uniform. It was hard for Kyle to tell.

The carriage stopped accelerating, now cruising at a constant speed, such that Kyle wouldn't have even known they were moving if it weren't for the window on the floor. The ocean was below them now, dark waters churning endlessly.

"Do you live on Meros?" Ariana asked Jag.

"I do."

"How long have you lived there?" she pressed.

"I was born there."

"What do you do?"

"Lots of things," Jag answered. Ariana frowned.

"Like what?"

"I help your researchers find artifacts," Jag replied. "And keep them from pissing off my people." He smirked. "Guess I get to add 'Royal Babysitter' to my resume."

"We're not babies," Kyle retorted rather indignantly.

"My apologies, your highness," Jag stated, bowing his head. But the man hardly seemed sorry.

"We're going to Meros for a reason," Ariana stated, crossing her arms over her chest. "...and we're perfectly capable of taking care of ourselves," she added. "Trust me."

"Ah, right," Jag murmured, eyeing her, then Kyle. "I forgot. You're the kids that sank that warship, aren't you?"

"We did," Kyle confirmed.

"Fine bit of work, murdering patriotic navy officers to save a bunch of criminals," Jag quipped. "Do me a favor and try not to cause any more international incidents on this trip."

"We didn't..." Kyle began, but he felt Ariana's hand on his knee. She shook his head at him. Jag leaned forward, gesturing at the three of them.

"So what're two kids and a Barren tribeswoman planning to do on Meros?" he inquired.

"We're helping researchers translate some artifacts," Ariana answered. "Petra knows the language on the artifacts, and Kyle can...he's really good at sensing magic."

"That so," Jag murmured. "Those artifacts are advanced Runic technology," he added. "How's she," he continued, nodding at Petra, "...going to read them?"

Ariana glanced at Petra, who shook her head slightly. Jag sighed.

"Look," he stated, "...I was brought here by *your* father to help you in Meros. He didn't exactly brief me...and I can't help you if I don't know what's going on."

"The artifacts deeper in the ruins are from the Barren tribes," Kyle revealed. Jag frowned.

"You're talking the big cavern they just found," he stated. Kyle glanced at Petra, then shrugged.

"I guess."

"That doesn't make any goddamn sense," Jag retorted.

"We know," Ariana agreed. "That's why Kalibar sent us," she added. "Kyle and Petra can translate the symbols and artifacts, and figure out what's going on."

"I see," Jag murmured. Then he glanced at Ariana. "So what's your role?" Ariana smiled sweetly.

"I'm the bodyguard."

Jag's eyebrows went up, and he leaned back in the couch.

"Of course you are," he muttered.

Ariana didn't reply, and it was just as well. Few knew of Ariana's true nature, and Ariana wanted to keep it that way.

"You're our guide," Petra stated. "Tell us about Meros."

"Meros," Jag explained, "...is an island seven-hundred and forty-three miles off the coast of Stridon, and twenty miles from Orja. It's got an area of ninety square miles, about half of which is owned by the Empire, the other half by Verhan."

"Why is that?" Ariana asked.

"Long story," Jag answered. "The island's been battled over for thousands of years," he added. "It's switched ownership dozens of times, but twenty years ago Meros declared independence from Verhan. Or at least half of it did; the other stayed with Verhan. A year later, the independent half joined the Empire for protection, so Verhan couldn't try to reclaim it. The Citadel, of course, remained neutral."

"The what?" Kyle asked.

"The Citadel of the Old Tree," Jag answered. "An ancient city built on a mountain in the center of Meros." He eyed Kyle. "That's where the *real* natives live."

"And where are the ruins?" Ariana asked.

"The Citadel," Jag replied. "The whole bottom is in ruins...except the Wall, of course."

"The what?" Ariana pressed. Jag frowned.

"They didn't teach you anything, did they?" he muttered. Kyle glanced at Ariana, who shrugged. Petra crossed her arms under her chest.

"Isn't that what Kalibar asked *you* to do?" she inquired.

"When a Grand Weaver asks," Jag replied, "...you don't say no."

"Then do your job," Petra shot back. Jag stared at her silently, his face unreadable. Then he smirked.

"This," he stated, "...is going to be interesting."

"Tell us about the wall," Ariana urged. "Please."

"You'll see it soon enough," he promised.

They sat in silence for a while, the carriage flying smoothly through the air. The only hint that they were even moving was the occasional cloud that passed by below, visible through the circular window in the floor of the carriage. After a few minutes, Ariana raised her hand.

"Why is it called the Citadel of the Old Tree?" she asked.

"Because of the Old Tree," Jag answered. "A massive tree with roots that go down all the way down to the base of the ruins," he added. "You can see its branches winding throughout the Citadel."

"Oh," she replied. She was about to ask something else when Jag put up one hand.

"I'll tell you more later, don't you worry," he interrupted. "But now I'm getting some sleep." He laid down on the large couch, resting his head on a pillow. "Dreamweaver pillows are over there," he added, gesturing to a cabinet on the wall. Within moments, he was snoring softly.

Kyle glanced at Ariana, who shrugged.

"Well that was interesting," he mumbled. Petra sighed, crossing her arms under her chest.

"This," she muttered, "...is going to be a long trip."

Chapter 8

Kyle felt someone shaking his shoulder, and opened his eyes groggily. He sat up from the couch, realizing that Ariana was sitting next to him...and had woken him up. Jag and Petra were sitting on the other end of the couch, and were eating something that looked like beef jerky.

"Here," Ariana said, handing him a piece. He sniffed it, then bit off a piece. It was distressingly spicy, making Kyle's eyes water. Jag chuckled.

"Food takes a bit getting used to," he said, chewing his own piece vigorously. Kyle looked around for some water, and was relieved when Ariana handed him a glass. He gulped it greedily, then glanced out of the window at the ocean beyond.

"How long till we get there?" he asked.

"Soon," Jag answered.

"So you live on Meros?" Petra asked. Jag nodded.

"Born and raised there," he confirmed. "Make trips to the Empire now and then, but mostly I stay near the Citadel."

"And what do you do, exactly?" Petra pressed.

"I'm a liaison between your researchers and the Temple," he answered. "Think of me as a guide and an ambassador rolled up into one."

"*You're* a diplomat?" Petra stated incredulously.

"Wait," Kyle interjected. "What's the Temple?"

"Ah, right," Jag replied. "Of course you wouldn't know." He grimaced, shifting on the couch. "The Temple of the Old Tree. It's the government and religious authority of the Citadel, all wrapped into one."

"Oh."

"The priests control the Citadel...they decide who goes in, and who gets out. Without the priests' blessing, none of your researchers would be allowed in the Citadel," Jag continued. "And until recently, the Empire didn't have their blessing."

"Why not?" Ariana inquired. Jag smirked.

"Turns out a lot of folks want to get into the Citadel," he answered. "Lots of important artifacts there...stuff from your Ancient Empire, and maybe even before." Jag took another bite of jerky. "Place is a gold mine."

"Like the ones in the Archives," Kyle deduced. Jag frowned.

"Those are replicas," he countered sternly. "The Temple would never allow original artifacts to leave the ruins." He leaned back. "That's where I come in."

"What do you mean?"

"I was the one who convinced the Temple to allow the Empire into the Citadel a few years ago," Jag explained. "And I make sure that your people behave while they're there."

"Behave?"

"The Temple forbids anyone from taking artifacts from the Citadel," Jag stated. "Your researchers have to take notes and leave the originals. I make sure they do that."

Kyle mulled that over, chewing on his jerky. It was far too spicy to eat quickly, or to have much, and his stomach grumbled in protest. He glanced out of the window, seeing an endless expanse of ocean far below, scattered clouds in the sky. He wondered how long he'd been asleep for...and how far across the ocean they were.

"Wait," Ariana piped up. "If half of Meros is owned by the Empire, and half by Verhan, which one owns the Citadel?"

"Neither," Jag answered. "The Temple controls the Citadel." He smirked then. "Although both countries would kill to get their hands on the place. Believe me, they've tried."

"Really?" Ariana pressed. "What happened?"

"Nice thing about having all those ancient artifacts," Jag explained, "...is that you don't have to know exactly how they work to use 'em." He shook his head. "No one has ever been able to take on the Citadel...not even your precious Ancient Empire."

Jag fell silent then, finishing his meal, then grabbing a bottle of green liquid from one of the cabinets on the wall. He took a healthy swig of it, then laid down on the couch, stretching his legs. Petra stared at him for a long moment, then crossed her arms.

"So we land in Meros," she stated. "Then what?"

"You'll be staying on the Imperial side of the island," Jag answered. "In a palace on the coast. We'll travel to the Citadel each morning to work."

"So what are we going to be doing there, exactly?" Kyle inquired.

"You'll figure that out soon enough," Jag promised. He gestured at one of the windows. "Take a look."

Kyle looked out of the window, seeing the ocean far below. In the distance, he saw a large island, a curved strip of sandy beach leading to a city beyond. Buildings dotted the shore, looking like miniature toy houses.

"Is that...?" Kyle asked.

"Welcome to Meros," Jag announced.

Ariana got off the couch, walking up to the window, and Kyle and Petra did the same. The island was circular, but with a large lagoon that extended from the edge of the island a third of the way to the island's center, like a slice missing from a piece of pizza. Toward the center of the island, Kyle could see a large mountain rising upward, its peak almost completely obscured by dark gray clouds.

"What's that?" Kyle asked, pointing to the mountain.

"That," Jag replied, "...is God's Peak."

"God's Peak?" Ariana repeated. Jag nodded.

"The home of the Citadel."

The carriage continued to descend, and through the crystalline floor below, Kyle eventually saw the ocean give way to land. They were flying over the island now. Jag pointed to a group of buildings past the shore, arranged around a circular building with a hole in its roof.

"We'll be landing there," he informed them.

The carriage moved toward the buildings, losing altitude at a steady pace, until it was directly over the circular building. The carriage went straight down then, landing *inside* the building. Kyle yawned, feeling his ears pop. Jag stretched, taking another swig of green liquid, then gestured for them to line up by the carriage door. They did so, and the door swung downward, fresh, salty air spilling into the cabin. Kyle took a deep breath in, smelling the unmistakable scent of the ocean.

"We'll need to pass through customs," Jag said. "Shouldn't take long, considering who you are," he added. "Follow me."

Jag stepped down the ramp, everyone else following behind him. Jag led them to a large doorway leading out of the building, which was guarded on either side by men in tan uniforms. The guards gave off a slight blue hue, a telltale sign that they were Weavers...or Runics.

"Welcome," one of the guards greeted, nodding at Jag. "How was your trip, Jag?"

"Can't complain," Jag replied. "I believe you know who these people are?" he added, gesturing at his charges. The guard nodded.

"Welcome to Meros," the guard greeted, bowing to Kyle and Ariana. "A pleasure to meet our Grand Weaver's family."

"Nice to meet you," Kyle replied. Ariana smiled, giving a curtesy. Petra just nodded.

"Everything is in order?" the guard asked. Jag nodded.

"Of course."

"Then enjoy your stay," the guard said. "Your carriage is waiting for you just outside," he added, gesturing past the large doorway. Kyle saw a medium-sized, ornate-looking carriage there, two large black horses tethered to it.

"Thanks," Jag replied. The carriage door was already open, and everyone got inside. Within moments, they were driving down a narrow street, passing squat buildings on either side. Unlike the buildings in Stridon, these were stark white, reflecting the brilliant sun. Brightly colored flags lined the street, which was paved with light gray stone.

"Is this where we're staying?" Kyle asked. Jag snorted.

"Hardly," he replied. "The governor's mansion is a few miles from here."

"Wait," Ariana piped in. "Why didn't we just land in the Citadel?"

"You can't just fly in," Jag answered. "And besides, we had to go through customs."

"Where are all the people?" Kyle inquired. The only people he could see were uniformed guards walking on the sidewalks. There were no civilians to speak of.

"This is a military base," Jag explained. Your daddy wouldn't approve of you using a civilian landing zone."

"Why not?" Ariana asked.

"You really need to ask that question?" Jag shot back, raising an eyebrow. Ariana frowned, but said nothing further. She glanced at Kyle, who shrugged.

The carriage stopped before a small gate guarded by more men in tan uniforms. The guards peered inside the carriage, then nodded briskly. The gate opened, and the carriage went through to the road beyond. In contrast to the paved stone road on-base, this was a dirt road. To the right was the sandy shore, with the ocean beyond. To the left, tall bordergrass with the occasional tree. The carriage picked up speed, its wheels bouncing over the rough road. Kyle could feel every bump in the road; he had a sudden appreciation for Stridon's levitating carriages.

"How long until we get there?" he inquired.

"About an hour."

Everyone fell silent then, the only sounds the horse's hooves and the carriage wheels on the dirt road. Kyle stared out of his window, watching as the bordergrass gave way to acre after acre of farmland and sprawling fields. The occasional run-down shack dotted the fields, buildings made of old, warped wood with thatched roofs. Jag noticed Kyle's gaze.

"Where there's tourists, there's money," he explained. "And the waves here are too strong for tourists. So people here gotta squeeze out a living farming." He gestured forward. "A few miles down is the lagoon," he added. "The water there is placid...all of the best resorts are there."

Minutes passed, and the fields gave way to more densely packed houses. They were as run-down as the farmhouses. People sat on their front steps and makeshift porches, staring at the carriage as it went by. A few food stands lined the street, with vendors hawking their wares. The people here were much like the ones Kyle had met at the Shimmering Isle, with bronzed skin and wavy black hair – a stark contrast to the rather pale citizens of Stridon.

"Who are those people?" Ariana asked.

"Imperials," Jag answered.

"Wait, like us?" Ariana pressed. Jag shrugged.

"When the Empire...acquired this half of Meros, natives had a choice. Join the Empire or go to the Verhanian side of the island."

"Couldn't they just go into the Citadel?" Ariana asked. Jag shook his head.

"The Citadel is for the priesthood," he explained. "Only the devout are allowed to live there."

"But aren't the priests natives too?" Ariana pressed. Jag gave a tight smile, but said nothing. Ariana frowned, turning to look out of her window. Kyle did the same, staring at the people as they stared back at him. None of the plants had a blue glow to them, and neither did the people.

"Why don't any of them make magic?" he asked. Jag looked at him as if he had two heads.

"You're joking, right?" he retorted. When Kyle just stared blankly back at him, Jag snorted. "First of all, *most* people don't make magic," he informed. "And the ones that do, your Secula Magna whisks away – by law – to their campus. So no, none of the natives here use magic."

"Oh."

Kyle glanced at Ariana, who was busy looking out of the window at the makeshift town that the road ran through. No doubt she could see a heck of a lot more than he could, given her superhuman senses. At length, the town came to an end, and once again large open fields dominated the landscape. No one said anything as the carriage continued onward, and at length Kyle felt his eyelids getting heavy. He let them close, and was just about to fall asleep when Jag spoke up.

"There's the lagoon," he stated, pointing out of the right window.

Kyle looked; there, in the ocean, he saw a thin crescent of rocky terrain extending from the shore as far as the eye could see. The water to the left of the crescent was a lighter shade of blue and relatively still, in contrast to the choppy waves he'd seen earlier.

"The resorts are coming up," Jag informed them.

The road turned leftward, pulling away from the shore, and after a few minutes the road transitioned from dirt to paved. Lush vegetation bordered the road on either side, interrupted every few minutes by huge gates with guards posted on either side of them. Tall stone walls extended from either side of the gates, elaborate designs carved into them.

"These are the resorts?" Ariana guessed.

"Yep," Jag confirmed.

The carriage continued down the road, which widened as it went. Other carriages passed by in the other direction, and soon they came to a town...this one more in keeping with what Kyle expected from the Empire. Finely crafted stone buildings two to three stories tall lined the streets, with tall, wrought-iron magic lamp-posts at regular intervals. There were outdoor markets, much like Stridon, with tastefully painted signs hanging above each store. Crowds of people milled about on broad sidewalks, and music played from bands every few blocks, their performers wearing brightly-colored costumes. It was all very festive.

"This is Osa," Jag explained. "The city by the lagoon. It's the capitol of Imperial Meros. You'll be staying at the governor's mansion in the middle of the city."

The carriage turned down a wide road flanked by more large stone buildings. Throngs of people packed the streets, coming in and out of shops, their arms filled with bags of goods.

"We're only a few minutes from the mansion now," Jag notified. "The governor will want a formal meeting with you before you get settled in your rooms."

"Why would he want to meet us?" Kyle asked.

"It's good politics," Jag answered with a smirk. "Pays to play nice with the children of the Grand Weaver."

"Oh."

"Don't be surprised if he asks you to go to the Festival tomorrow," Jag added. "He'll want everyone to see him with the great Kalibar's children, of course."

"The Festival?" Kyle pressed.

"A celebration of Meros' independence," he explained. Then he smirked. "Short-lived as it was. I for one don't plan on being anywhere near Osa when it happens."

"Why not?" Kyle asked.

"You'll see."

He fell silent after that, the carriage continuing forward through Osa. The road led them to a large building through which an archway had been constructed, allowing vehicles and pedestrians to pass through. The carriage passed through the archway and into a large central square. It was as big as a football field, with buildings on all sides. Before them was the tallest building of them all, a stately white mansion four stories high, guarded by a gated, wrought-iron fence.

And the square was filled to the brim with people…so much so that the carriage had no way forward. It stopped, and people marched toward the carriage, led by a young woman. She was tall, with long, wavy hair and olive-skin, and held her head high as she made her way toward the carriage.

"Bring them back!" they chanted. "Bring them back!"

Kyle glanced at Jag, who said nothing. Dozens of golden-armored guards carrying vicious-looking spears pushed their way through the crowd, shoving everyone away from the carriage. But some people in the crowd resisted.

"Bring back my baby!" one middle-aged woman cried, breaking through the guards and rushing up to the carriage. Tears streamed down her cheeks. "Bring her back!"

A guard rushed at her from behind, thrusting the butt of his spear at her temple and striking it with a loud *crack*. Kyle flinched, jerking away from the window. The woman fell to the ground, blood pouring from her head. The guard began dragging her away…and the crowd rushed in on him, tearing him free of the woman and throwing him to the ground. They swarmed over him, and the other guards rushed to save their colleague, forcing the crowd back with their spears.

"Get back *now!*" one guard ordered.

"Ninety-nine percent!" the crowd began to chant. "We will represent!"

"What's going on?" Kyle demanded. "Why'd they hit her?"

"Ask the governor," Jag muttered.

The guards managed to save their colleague, pulling him away from the crowd. The man's face was bloodied, his eyes dazed.

"Not all the world's like Stridon," Jag said. "People aren't happy with the Empire."

"Why not?" Ariana asked.

"Lots of reasons," Jag answered. "Take kidnapping for example."

"Kidnapping?"

"Finders came yesterday," their guide explained. "Took three kids. Including that woman's."

"Finders?" Kyle asked.

"Weavers that test kids for magic," Jag explained. "They come every year. Whoever makes magic gets taken to Stridon."

"I thought people were happy to have their kids chosen," Kyle stated. Jag gave him a look.

"Your daddy tell you that?"

101

Kyle grimaced. Kalibar *had* been the one to tell him that. He stared out at the protesters, trying to find the woman who'd been struck. He felt queasy knowing that she'd been hit because of him. There'd been no reason to strike her so viciously; the guard could've just dragged her away.

I could have stopped him, he realized. *I should have stopped him.*

The guards shoved the protesters back from the carriage, beating the ones who resisted. Eventually they forced a path through the crowd to the gate guarding the front door of the mansion ahead. The carriage moved forward, stopping before the gate. Guards on the other side of it swung the gate open, letting the carriage through. Kyle looked back as the carriage moved forward again, seeing the crowd spilling in toward the closing gate. Guards beat the protesters back, forming a line blocking the protesters from getting through the gate.

Then one guard threw a small green orb into the crowd.

The orb shattered, green smoke exploding from it. The smoke spread throughout the crowd, obscuring them in a light green haze. The protesters began coughing, then stumbled, falling to the ground. The crowd dispersed, fleeing the spreading green cloud. The guards chased after them, grabbing protesters and throwing them to the ground.

The gate closed behind the carriage, and a moment later the carriage rolled to a stop in front of the mansion, before a large set of golden double-doors.

"*That's* why I won't be at the Festival," Jag quipped. "Let's go," he added, opening the door on his side and stepping out. Everyone followed suit, stepping down to the cobblestones below. Four guards stood by the double-doors to the mansion, and they immediately saluted, opening the doors.

"Welcome to the governor's mansion," one guard greeted, gesturing for them to enter. Jag led them inside. The interior of the mansion was quite grand, with white marble floors and white walls with elegant wooden trim. Almost immediately upon entering, a tall, bald man in a white suit strode across the foyer toward them.

"Good afternoon," the gentleman greeted, walking up to Jag and shaking his hand. He turned to Kyle, Ariana, and Petra. "I'm Governor Candric," he introduced. "Welcome to Meros. I...apologize for the demonstration outside." He shook each of their hands, including Kyle's, his grip firm, but not painfully so. He had no hair whatsoever on his head, with thick arched eyebrows and a smooth-shaven face. His white suit was immaculate, with gold cufflinks and numerous expensive-looking rings on his fingers. He was extremely well-built, like the bodybuilders Kyle had seen back on Earth.

"Thanks for having us," Jag replied. Candric smiled.

"It isn't every day we get to host the family of our Grand Weaver," he stated, turning to Kyle and Ariana. "Few get the opportunity to choose their children," he added. "I hear that Grand Weaver Kalibar has chosen well."

Kyle glanced at Ariana, who smiled, grabbing his arm and squeezing it.

"Once again, I apologize for the ruckus outside," Candric stated. "Passions have been high of late, and our people don't often get a chance to...communicate directly with people so close to the Empire's rulers."

"They attacked an unarmed woman out there," Kyle accused. "Struck her in the head hard enough to make her bleed."

"I saw," Candric admitted. "The guards were protecting you."

"Protecting a magically shielded carriage from an unarmed woman?" Petra countered coolly. Candric grimaced.

"I admit they were...overzealous," he conceded. "There's no love lost between the City Guard and the protesters."

"What are they protesting?" Kyle asked. "The Finders?"

"That and more," the governor answered. "I would be happy to discuss it at length, but unfortunately I won't have time today." He gestured at a grand staircase leading to the second floor. "Let me show you to your rooms," he offered, gesturing for them to follow him. He led them across the foyer to the staircase, climbing it to the third floor. They went down a long hallway, eventually stopping at a set of double-doors at the end. Candric opened these, revealing a grand, spacious suite beyond. He gestured for them to step inside.

"This is your suite," he stated.

While not nearly as large or elegant as Kalibar's retirement suite in the Great Tower, the room was impressive nonetheless. A spacious living room filled with expensive-looking furniture led into a series of large bedrooms, all tastefully decorated. Large windows looked out over the city, with the beach and lagoon visible in the distance.

"Will you be staying here?" Governor Candric asked Jag. Jag shook his head, and Candric nodded. "Very well. I apologize for having to leave you, but I have business to attend to. We'll get a chance to speak at breakfast tomorrow. If you need anything in the meantime, use the communication orbs to summon a member of my staff. Good-bye."

With that, he left.

Kyle glanced at Ariana, who shrugged. Jag cleared his throat.

"Well, I'm off," he declared. "You'll be spending the rest of the day here. I'll come for you tomorrow morning, bright and early. Get your sleep...we got a busy day tomorrow."

Chapter 9

Kalibar strode down the hallway of the 40th floor of the Great Tower, Erasmus walking at his side. He felt exhausted, having slept poorly last night, plagued with baseless anxiety for his children after they'd left for Meros. A long morning filled with meetings hadn't helped him feel any more energized. He felt Erasmus looking at him, and glanced at the portly Runic.

"Why the long face, old friend?" Erasmus inquired. "The meetings weren't *that* awful."

"I didn't sleep well," Kalibar admitted.

"Ah," Erasmus replied. "Is it your children you're worried about, or your girlfriend?"

"She's not my girlfriend," Kalibar countered wearily. Erasmus snorted.

"Like hell she's not," he retorted.

"She made it very clear..."

"I don't give a damn *what* she said," Erasmus interrupted. "I've seen how you lovebirds look at each other. You're completely smitten, Kalibar. And if I know women, she is too." Kalibar raised an eyebrow at this.

"Your wife would disagree about you knowing women."

"Oh I know them *now*," Erasmus retorted. "If only I'd known them when I met my wife!"

105

"Is it really that bad?" Kalibar asked. Erasmus gave him a sour look.

"Priscilla is a fine lady," he declared. "Capable of making a me a very happy man, I'd add."

"If she left you?"

Erasmus grinned, punching Kalibar in the shoulder.

"That," he declared, "...is why you're my best friend Kalibar. No one knows me like you do!"

"I could say the same about you, old friend," Kalibar agreed, giving Erasmus a grudging smile. The Grand Runic always knew how to cheer him up. It was one of Erasmus's best qualities, that he remained ever-cheerful despite having every reason not to be. He and Priscilla were a terrible match; Kalibar had never met two people less suited for each other. But Erasmus had stayed true to her, and despite his constant bellyaching, would likely do so until the bitter end.

"Our personal lives may have gone to crap," Erasmus stated, "...but at least the Empire is doing well. Our bribes to the lords of Verhan went off without a hitch it seems."

Kalibar nodded. The bulk of his and Erasmus's meetings that morning had been about the Verhanian election tomorrow. Their strategic support of lords likely to swing Lord Devlin's way had indeed gone as planned. Discretion had been maintained, and each lord had reportedly been eager to work in Devlin's favor. Of course, each payment had been made through a string of intermediaries, so that the Empire would not be implicated in the swinging of an election. Kalibar was to fly to Verhan today to witness the coronation. Not that he had to. Most countries would be sending ambassadors or other dignitaries. The fact that Kalibar was attending would send a message to Verhan and its new king: that the Empire was committed to forging a stronger relationship with Verhan.

All *was* going well for the Empire, for the first time since he'd met Kyle back at his mansion in Bellingham. Kalibar knew he should feel happy, but he didn't.

The two men reached the riser at the end of the hallway, taking it up to the 42nd floor. They continued down another hallway, and Kalibar stopped at the door to his suite.

"Care for a drink?" Erasmus inquired, wagging his bushy white eyebrows. Kalibar shook his head.

"I think I'm going to take a nap."

"Ah well," Erasmus grumbled. "Suit yourself. See you around, old friend."

Erasmus left then, and Kalibar opened the door to his suite, stepping inside and making his way to his office. He sat in the plush chair behind his desk, putting his heels up atop it and leaning back, a heavy sigh escaping him. He glanced to the right, through the thick crystal window there. It gave him a marvelous view of Stridon far below, a bustling city at the center of the greatest empire in the modern world. A view that usually gave him a sense of pride…and reminded him of the importance of his station.

But now it only made him feel depressed.

He'd felt the same way after Kyle and Ariana had escaped to Verhan to confront Sabin. The same emptiness inside. But now it was worse, and he knew damn well why.

Petra was gone, and he was quite sure he'd never see he again.

Kalibar glanced down at one of his desk drawers. He hesitated, then opened it, rummaging around until his fingers met a very familiar object. Lifting it out, he set it on his desk. It was a small, framed sketch, done in charcoal so many years ago. Of his long-dead wife. A sketch he'd rarely allowed himself to gaze at.

He stared at it, marveling at how young she looked. She'd been beautiful, with pale skin and amber, wavy hair. Very slight, almost tomboyish in figure. The polar opposite of Petra.

Kalibar grimaced, setting the sketch face-down on his desk. He fidgeted, staring out of the window once again. He'd planned on spending the rest of his life as a bachelor. Indeed, he'd given up on romance for decades, partly out of loyalty to his wife and mostly out of fear. His memories had been enough.

And then he'd met Petra.

How he'd forgotten what it was like to fall in love! The powerful current of emotion, the ecstatic highs and torturous lows. The complete erosion of his peace of mind, replaced by a kind of sweet, desperate madness. It was the spark of life he hadn't realized he'd been missing for the last thirty years.

And now it was gone.

Kalibar gave a deep sigh, staring down at his lap.

I've wasted my life.

He'd filled it with goals and responsibilities, desperately trying to fill that terrible void in his heart with distractions. A poor substitute for what his heart truly desired: a family, and a woman to love.

Kalibar turned to gaze at his office, at the bookshelves and his desk, and the papers neatly stacked to one side atop it. He suddenly dreaded the thought of having to do this for another six years. Running the Empire through endless meetings, reams of paperwork. Feeling the weight of the world on his shoulders. He'd agreed to a second term as Grand Weaver to save the Empire and his children from Xanos. Now that they were safe...

I don't want this, he realized.

He didn't want to spend the rest of his life doing things he *had* to do. He wanted to take a wife and raise his children, and maybe even make one or two of his own.

He sighed again, turning his chair around to grab a bottle of wine from the shelf behind him. He popped the cork, grabbing a glass from the same shelf and pouring himself a drink. Then he leaned back in his chair, taking a sip. The crimson liquid burned as it coursed down his throat.

It was too late to find new love now, of course. The mere thought of going out and searching for another woman was exhausting. He shouldn't *have* to find anyone else. Erasmus had been right...he *was* in love with Petra. And he had to believe that, deep down inside, she felt the same way about him.

And that if he weren't Grand Weaver, he'd be with her – and his children – right now.

Where he belonged.

* * *

Captain Apep strode up to the door leading to Governor Candric's office, knocking loudly.

"Come in," came the muffled reply.

Apep opened the door, stepping through and closing it behind him. Candric was sitting behind his desk, a mountain of paperwork stacked before him...and his secretary standing beside him. They both looked up when Apep entered.

"What is it?" Candric inquired.

Apep grimaced. He hated the fact that the governor was always so polite, sometimes insultingly so. He'd rarely seen the man flustered. That, however, was about to change.

"I'll leave you two alone," Bae stated, standing up straight. She walked right up to Apep, stopping before him. "You can move out of the way," she suggested, "...or I can move you."

"I wouldn't advise that," Apep shot back, feeling irritated with the woman. She was far too mouthy for a lowly secretary. She had the gall to smirk.

"Well aren't you a tough guy," she said...and promptly shoved him aside, stepping right past him. He stumbled, catching himself.

"You miserable little..." he began.

"Enough," he heard Candric order. Apep grimaced, turning to face the governor. "What do you want?" Candric asked.

"I hear you had a meeting with your daughter," Apep revealed, stopping in front of Candric's desk and glaring down at the man. Candric nodded.

"I did."

"Commiserating with the enemy?" Apep inquired, his voice deceptively calm. That Candric tolerated his wayward daughter's insolence was bad enough. To be caught having clandestine meetings with her..._that_ suggested conspiracy.

"Hardly," Candric retorted calmly. "My daughter may have differing opinions on the best way to help our people, but that doesn't make her my enemy."

"But it makes her *my* enemy," Apep snapped. "What did she say?"

"Nothing we don't already know," Candric answered. "She reiterated her intent to protest during the Festival," he stated. "I asked her not to do so, and she declined."

"Do you really think she was going to listen to you?" Apep inquired.

"Of course not."

"Then why bother?" Apep demanded. "She's signaled her intent to disrupt the peace during our most sacred holiday. She's breaking the law!"

"Peaceful protest is not against the law," Candric countered.

"Disrupting the peace is," Apep argued.

"A fine line between the two."

"If she marches," Apep warned, "...I'll have her and every single damn agitator that dares follow her arrested!"

"Only if they give you reason to do so," Candric replied. "And I expect you to do so nonviolently."

"That depends on your daughter," Apep retorted.

"She won't resort to violence," Candric stated. "And neither will you."

"Like I said," Apep grumbled, "...that depends on your daughter."

Candric eyed Apep for a long moment, leaning back in his chair. Then he stood. He was a much larger man than Apep, and he clearly knew it. He stared down at the man, his expression stony.

"You are Captain of the Guard because I allow it," the governor stated, his tone icy cold. "Don't give me a reason to choose someone else."

Apep swallowed in a suddenly dry throat, a chill running through him. But he stood his ground, refusing to let Candric dominate him.

"That," Apep retorted, "...would be extremely unwise."

Candric stared at him silently for a long, uncomfortable moment, his eyes unblinking. He stepped around his desk, stopping inches from Apep.

110

"Threaten me again," Candric growled, towering over him, "...and you'll regret it for the rest of your life."

Apep stared back at the governor, resisting the urge to take a step back. To lower his gaze. He'd been Captain of the Guard for two decades, after all. He'd seen his fair share of governors come and go.

"I'm a man of the law," he stated quietly. "As are my *extremely* loyal men."

Candric stared down at Apep for a moment longer, then sat back down.

"Execute your duties within the confines of the law," he stated, "...and you'll have nothing to fear from me."

"I always do," Apep replied coolly.

Candric leaned back in his chair, staring at Apep for a long moment. Apep held his gaze, refusing to blink.

"Captain," Candric stated. "Despite our differences, I have always supported you in your role as enforcer of our laws. I don't require that my employees agree with me, only that they execute their duties with integrity. I hope that you understand that I value our laws as much as you do."

"We'll see," Apep retorted.

"I look forward to proving it to you."

Apep held the governor's gaze for a moment longer, then crossed his arms over his chest.

"Is that all?"

"That's all," Candric confirmed.

"I'll see you tomorrow then," Apep stated. He turned about, striding through the doorway leading out of the governor's office. He shut the door behind him, loud enough to make a statement. He strode down the hallway toward the stairwell leading downstairs, his mouth set in a grim line.

If Candric wanted to play hardball, then so be it. The governor was almost certainly going to fire him...there was no doubting that now. But as long as he was Captain of the Guard, he would see to it that the laws of Meros were enforced.

Even if he had to break them to do so.

Chapter 10

The next morning, Kyle, Ariana, and Petra were awoken by members of Governor Candric's plentiful staff, and – after a brief shower and a fresh set of clothes, save for Petra and Ariana, who wore their Reaper uniforms – they were led down to the dining room for breakfast. Governor Candric was already there, as sharply dressed as he'd been the night before. They all sat down at a small circular table instead of the larger dining room table nearby, at Candric's insistence. A smaller table forced a more intimate meeting, he'd said.

Kyle sat in his chair next to Ariana, who of course didn't touch her food. Petra sat on his other side, and the governor sat across from him. Breakfast was toast and tea, and a few pieces of fruit.

"I admit I've heard a lot about you," Candric said, nodding at Ariana and Kyle. He turned to Petra. "But not, I'm afraid, about you," he added. "Petra, I'm told you're from Orja?"

"I am," Petra confirmed.

"Where specifically?"

"The Barren Forest," she answered. "North of Verhan, by Mount Grimore."

"Ah yes," Candric replied. "I heard Grimore erupted recently. I wasn't aware it was volcanic."

Petra said nothing, and Kyle glanced at Ariana, who shook her head ever-so-slightly.

"Tell us about Osa," Ariana urged, turning to Candric.

"We're the capitol of Imperial Meros," he replied. "Ten thousand citizens live here, with another twenty thousand living on the rest of this half of the island. Our economy depends on tourists from the mainland, and exports of tropical produce and luxury goods. We're the main tourist destination for the Empire's coastal cities, including Stridon."

"Are you from here originally?" Petra asked.

"Yes," Candric confirmed. "I was born here, outside of the city. My family was very poor. I had a knack for business, and eventually came to own several of the resorts here."

"And then you become governor?" Petra pressed, crossing her arms under her chest. "To makes laws in your favor, I assume?" Candric gave a tight smile.

"Not at all," he replied. "My family was poor, and I've never forgotten what that was like. There is still a great deal of poverty on Meros, and my goal is to change that. As for myself," he added, "...I have quite enough already."

Petra looked skeptical, and Candric sighed.

"I have more money that I will ever spend," he continued. "As do many of the businessmen who own property here. Unlike them, I'm a native, and I live here. I understand my peoples' struggles. Much of my energy is spent convincing...selfish interests to agree to improve the standard of living of Meros' poorest communities. Since I've been governor, I've fought for a minimum wage, improved health care, and better infrastructure for our people."

Petra considered this, then nodded in approval.

"Unfortunately," he continued, "...it hasn't been easy. I'm a Populist, and most of the merchant class is Elitist. And as we all know, extreme wealth is what often separates a predator from its prey."

Candric turned to Kyle and Ariana then.

113

"But enough about politics," he stated. "I hear you're going to be visiting the Citadel. A high honor, to be allowed there. Few earn the privilege to do so."

"We're doing some research," Kyle offered.

"You'd have to be," Candric agreed. "The Temple of the Old Tree does not allow tourists." He paused. "Can I ask what kind of research?"

"No," Petra replied coolly. Candric nodded, hardly seeming offended.

"Understood," he stated.

"We don't mean to be rude," Kyle explained, glancing at Petra. "We would tell if we could."

"As I said, I understand," Candric reassured.

"What about those protesters yesterday?" Ariana interjected. Candric turned to her. "You mentioned that you'd talk to us about it today."

"Ah yes," he replied with a grimace. "It's...complicated." He paused, as if choosing his words carefully. "Meros is a place of extremes," he explained. "Very wealthy businessmen and tourists come here from the Empire. Many own homes here. Yet most of the natives are very poor, and either employed by the resorts or the local shops. The businessmen keep the wages low, because they can. After all, with a large percentage of the island being unemployed, there's a great deal of competition for each job."

"So the rich are enslaving the poor," Petra translated. Candric grimaced.

"Not enslaving," he countered. Petra's eyebrow rose.

"You're saying they have a choice?"

"Between working and not working," Candric replied. "I agree, it isn't much of a choice. It's why I became governor," he added. "I was the wealthiest native businessman on Meros...*am* the wealthiest...and I pay my people well. I want to change the culture – and the law – to give my people a better life."

"Then give them your money," Petra shot back.

"Money is useless without education," Candric countered. "Most poor people will quickly lose their fortunes unless they learn how to manage their money. And money should be earned," he added. "My goal is to give people a fair shot at being able to earn a good wage. But that's not the only reason my people are upset."

"The Finders," Kyle ventured. Candric nodded.

"Imperial law dictates that the Finders come every year," he explained. "They test children entering puberty for the ability to make magic. Those that do are taken away from their parents to the Secula Magna."

Kyle frowned, remembering the woman who'd come up to their carriage earlier. An image of the guard striking her in the head with the butt of his spear came to him.

"Kalibar said that parents were honored to have their children taken," he stated.

"Not on Meros," Candric countered. "And probably not in most cities in the Empire. You see, the vast majority of children taken to the Secula Magna rarely or never return to their families. And on Meros, the only magic-users that come here are the Finders, or the occasional tourist."

"So your children never get to see their families again," Ariana realized. "That's terrible!"

"At least until they graduate," Candric confirmed. "And in my…personal experience, few return even then." He sighed. "You can imagine the consequences."

"The people go without magic," Petra realized. Candric nodded.

"Magic is power," he explained. "And the Empire keeps that power for itself."

"And the rest are powerless to stop them," Petra finished. She leaned back in her chair, crossing her arms under her chest.

"Thus the protests," Candric concluded. "They're hardly confined to Meros, of course," he added. "The Resistance – that's what they call themselves – have chapters in nearly every major city in the Empire."

"How come Kalibar didn't tell us about this?" Kyle demanded. The thought that Kalibar would allow such a thing was hard to believe.

"You'll have to ask him yourself," the governor answered.

"Who was the woman leading them?" Kyle pressed, remembering the tall woman with long, wavy hair. Candric hesitated, then sighed.

"That would be Tessa," he answered. "My daughter."

Kyle blinked.

"Your daughter...?"

"Is the leader of the Resistance in Meros, yes," Candric confirmed.

"Wow."

"Our methods are different," Candric explained, "...but our goals are similar. We both want what is best for our people."

"I'd like to meet her," Kyle stated. He glanced at Ariana, who nodded in agreement. Candric grimaced.

"I don't know..."

"If people are unhappy with the way things are," Kyle insisted, "...then Kalibar will want to know about it. He's a good man...he can help you."

"I have no doubt of his character," Candric replied carefully, "...but the political realities are...complicated."

"We have to try," Kyle countered. Candric sighed again, then nodded.

"Very well," he decided. "I'll send word to Tessa that you want to meet her. I can't guarantee that she'll answer me," he cautioned.

"We appreciate you trying," Ariana replied.

Just then, a butler approached. Candric turned to him. "Yes Benton?"

"You have a letter, governor," Benton informed. Candric frowned.

"It can wait."

"It's from the Empire, governor," the butler pressed. "By a Weaver by the name of Darren."

The blood drained from Candric's face, and he gripped the edge of the table, his fingertips turning white. A long moment passed, and then he relaxed his grip on the table.

"I'll be there at once," he told Benton. He slid his chair back, standing up and stepping toward the butler. Then he glanced at his company, as if surprised that they were still there. He cleared his throat. "As much as I'd like to stay and get to know you better, I have to go," he stated apologetically.

"What about the Festival?" Ariana asked. "Jag mentioned there was a celebration tomorrow."

"There is," Candric admitted.

"I'd like to see it," Ariana stated. Candric paused, then nodded.

"Of course," he replied. "You're welcome to join me in celebrating it."

"We'd be honored," Ariana stated with a smile. Candric smiled back, with his mouth but not his eyes.

"Good," he replied. He hesitated then. "I have to warn you, there may be another...demonstration."

"Like today?"

"At best," Candric replied. "I pray there's no violence like there was today, but I cannot guarantee it. Just to manage your expectations."

"Consider them managed," Petra stated.

"Yes, well," he muttered. "I have to go now. Please, take your time with the rest of your breakfast," he added. "And consider this mansion yours while I'm gone. Feel free to make use of the pools and my butlers until Jagwell comes for you."

"Thanks," Kyle replied.

"See you tomorrow," Candric stated. He left then, following his still-waiting butler out of the room. Kyle glanced at Ariana, who raised an eyebrow, and then at Petra, who was staring at the tabletop, her expression unreadable. Then he glanced down at his half-finished piece of toast. Suddenly he wasn't hungry anymore.

"Wanna check out the pools?" Ariana asked. Kyle smiled at her.

"Thought you'd never ask," he replied.

* * *

The sun's rays shone upon Kyle's shoulders as he stepped out of the governor's mansion to the grounds in the rear of the property. He was greeted by a huge outdoor area with stone

117

flooring and multiple large in-ground pools with water so blue it rivaled the clear sky above. Each pool was larger than a tennis court. Stone fountains shot water high in the air, and Kyle noted the telltale blue glow of magic around them. It was one of the few times he'd seen magic on Meros.

He eyed the nearest pool, eager to jump in. Back on Earth, he'd loved to swim, and he realized he hadn't really gotten the chance to since his swim in Crescent lake so long ago. Luckily he'd changed into swimming trunks; he peeled off his shirt eagerly, tossing it aside and running to the pool. Ariana joined him, dressed in a one-piece bathing suit. She of course passed him easy, leaping high into the air and landing in the center of the large pool with a big splash. He joined her, leaping a much shorter distance, then jackknifing into the water. It was pleasantly warm, like tepid bath water, and enveloped him immediately. The pool was deep, far deeper than would be allowed back on Earth. He swam downward, trying to reach the bottom, but a sudden pressure in his ears stopped him. He made his way to the surface instead, his head bursting through.

Ariana was right in front of him, grinning from ear to ear.

"Nice, huh?" she said. Kyle smiled back. It *was* nice. With all the adventures he'd been on recently – and his intense lessons with Master Lee – he hadn't had much time for leisure. He'd almost forgotten what having fun was like.

"This is great," he admitted, looking around. There were tables set back from the pools, and a walk-up bar as well. A few staff members stood by watching them, no doubt ready to see to their every whim.

"Beat you to the bottom!" Ariana cried, plunging below the surface. Kyle joined her, swimming downward. This time he held his nose, blowing through it to equalize the pressure in his ears. It worked; he followed Ariana to the bottom of the pool, touching it, then immediately pushing off the floor and swimming back up. He reached the surface, then looked around; Ariana was nowhere to be seen.

"Ariana?" he asked. Then he looked down, spotting a shadow at the bottom of the pool. He shook his head; Ariana had no need for air, able to stay submerged indefinitely. He suspected she enjoyed being underwater, and not just for the novelty of it. With her incredible hearing, the constant din of the surface world was an ever-present stressor for her. Under the water, however, she wouldn't be able to hear anyone on the surface.

Eventually Ariana bolted upward, bursting through the surface and grinning at Kyle. Her dark hair was plastered to her head, a few strands falling in front of her eyes.

"I win," she declared.

"That's fair," Kyle grumbled. Ariana laughed, shoving him in the shoulder. He flew backward in the water, spinning around as he did so. He heard more laughter.

"Beaten by a girl!" she teased.

"Says the immortal with god-like strength," Kyle shot back. But he grinned. "This is pretty awesome, huh?"

"Yeah," Ariana agreed. "I could get used to this."

"Me too," he confessed. "Sure beats spending my mornings with Master Lee," he added.

"Enjoy it while it lasts," he heard a voice behind them say. He turned, spotting Petra standing at the edge of the pool. She was still in her Reaper uniform...a clear indication that she was not going to join them. Kyle couldn't help but feel a little disappointed.

"Hey Petra," Ariana greeted. "Want to join us?"

"I would," Petra replied, "...but Jag is already here. We have to get going."

"Oh, *man*," Kyle grumbled. He sighed, swimming toward the edge of the pool and getting out. Ariana joined him a moment later.

"We'll swim after," Petra promised.

They made their way back to the mansion, heading to their rooms and changing out of their swimwear and into their usual clothes. Then they met Jag downstairs in the lobby. Their surly guide was standing by the door, leaning against the wall.

"Took you long enough," he grumbled. "Come on, let's go."

The three friends followed Jag out of the mansion, to a familiar-looking horse-drawn carriage parked on the street beyond. They all got inside, and the carriage began to move, taking them away from the mansion and back through Osa's town center. The streets and sidewalks were just as crowded as they'd been yesterday, throngs of people – tourists, likely – visiting the countless shops lining the city streets. With all the traffic, it took some time for them to leave Osa behind. The going was much smoother from there on out, a deserted road taking them toward the huge mountain in the center of the island.

"How long will it take to get there?" Kyle asked. Jag gave him a look.

"You got somewhere else to be?" he inquired.

"Just curious."

"An hour to get to the base of the mountain," Jag answered. "After that, maybe another hour to reach the top of the wall."

"That long?" Ariana asked. "Can't we just fly up?" Jag smirked.

"If you want to get fried, sure," he replied. "Citadel's full of magic defenses," he explained. "You go up the way the priests tell you to, or not at all."

"Tell us more about these priests," Petra stated. Jag glanced at her.

"What you want to know?"

"Where did they come from?" she asked. "How did they get to live in the Citadel?"

"Depends on who you ask," Jag answered. "If you believe the priests, they're descendants of the gods that created this world. Each of 'em thinks they have a bit of the divine in them. Claim they can communicate with the Old Tree, the last surviving god."

"They think a tree is a god?" Kyle asked.

"They think a lot of things," Jag grumbled. "Bunch of nonsense if you ask me. My bet is they got lucky and got in the Citadel before anyone else did, then used the Citadel's defenses to stop anyone else from taking over."

"Who built the Citadel?" Petra asked.

"Like I said, the priests say it was the gods," Jag answered. "The real answer? Who knows? It's advanced, that's all I know," he continued. "Makes your Ancient Empire's technology look like sticks and rocks."

"I thought the Ancients were the most advanced civilization ever," Kyle interjected. Jag smirked.

"The Empire'd like to think so," he replied. "Nice propaganda there. Every nation fancies they're the best."

Jag fell into a brooding silence then, giving one-word answers to any questions they had. Eventually everyone gave up asking, falling into an uncomfortable silence. The carriage continued its long journey toward the mountain ahead, eventually reaching the base of it. The road transitioned from paved to a wide dirt path through a dense forest, a path that climbed up a gradually steepening slope; eventually the path ended, and so too did their journey via the carriage.

"Get out," Jag ordered, being the first to do so. Everyone followed suit, and Jag tipped the driver, then turned to the others. "Rest of the journey's on foot," he explained. "Come on."

They followed Jag as he hiked up the steep slope. They weaved around trees as they went, Jag leading the way, Petra close behind, and Ariana and Kyle taking up the rear. It was a strenuous hike, at least for Kyle. Petra didn't seem to be having any issues, on account of her being in extraordinary shape, and Ariana was tireless as usual. He sighed, focusing on keeping one foot in front of the other. He had half a mind to use his gravity boots, but thought better of it.

Eventually the trees grew sparser and shorter, their growth stunted by the thinning of the air. Kyle looked up, spotting the high wall of the Citadel less than a mile away…and at least a thousand feet above their current elevation. The wall was absolutely humungous, a monstrous cylinder of black stone rising from the mountaintop. It was nearly as wide around as the mountain itself – over a mile in diameter, Kyle guessed – and taller than any structure he'd ever seen. It had to be over a thousand feet tall, if not two…or more. It was so tall that the top of it was obscured by thick gray clouds. It was made of sheer, plain black stone interrupted at regular intervals by long half-columns along its length, huge runes inscribed on their surfaces. The columns were taller than the wall itself, ending in spires that curved inward.

"Wow," Kyle exclaimed. Jag glanced back, smirking at him.

"That's what they all say the first time."

"You could fit a whole city in there," Ariana remarked.

"They do," Jag revealed.

They trekked onward and upward, half-walking, half-climbing up the steep slope of the mountain. After a few breaks – and swigs of water from Jag's backpack – they neared the base of the massive wall. From here, Kyle could see that the wall wasn't made of bricks or stones. Its surface was utterly, perfectly smooth, as if it'd been carved from a single piece of stone. Nothing grew on it; no vines, no moss. No lichen. And it showed no signs of wear and tear whatsoever.

Jag stopped a few dozen feet from the wall, then turned right, following parallel to it.

"Where are we going?" Kyle asked.

"You planning on climbing up?" Jag inquired. Kyle glanced up at the smooth surface of the wall, then shook his head. "Priests built scaffolding that goes up the wall," he explained. "They'll lower a platform down if they let us in."

"What do you mean?" Ariana asked. "I thought we already had permission."

"The priests have been known to change their minds," Jag replied.

Eventually Kyle saw what Jag was talking about: scaffolding constructed of thick wooden beams that went all the way up to the top of the wall. The scaffolding was some thirty feet across, and heavily reinforced, forming a wide, hollow rectangle. Standing before the scaffolding was a cloaked figure wearing a bright green and white cloak. It covered them from head to toe, their face hidden in the shadows of its hood.

Jag stopped before the figure, nodding curtly.

"Morning," he greeted.

The cloaked figure raised their hands to the sides of their hood, drawing it back…and revealing a young woman. Her face was narrow, and she had olive-colored skin and eyes that were almost orange. Her hair was tied up into a bun atop her head.

"That it is," she replied. She eyed Jag with a look Kyle couldn't read. "Two visits in one day," she added. "What a treat."

"Just let these folks up," he grumbled. She glanced at Kyle and Ariana, then stared at Petra for a long moment. Her eyes returned to Jag.

"And you?" she inquired.

"I'll go with them," Jag answered. "And I'll leave with them too."

"A shame," she replied. "We still have hope for you, you know."

"Hope for what?" he inquired. "My indoctrination?"

"Your family misses you, Jagwell."

"Do they?" Jag retorted. The woman took a deep breath in, then let it out.

"More than you know," she stated quietly. Then she turned to Petra. "You must be Petra," she guessed. "It's been a long time since we've had a visitor from the Barren Forest." Petra's eyebrows rose in surprise.

"You know of us?" she asked.

"We do," the woman confirmed. She turned to Kyle and Ariana. "And you are Grand Runic Kalibar's adopted children," she continued. "Greetings."

"Hello," Kyle greeted. "What's your name?"

"Priestess Marja," she answered. "For what reason do you seek entrance into the Citadel?"

"To help our researchers," Kyle answered.

"And how will you do that?"

"I can read the runes of my ancestors," Petra explained. "From what I've seen, some of your artifacts use these runes."

"None of our native artifacts do," Marja countered. "But many that came later do." She turned to Kyle. "And what is your role?"

"I'm...good at deciphering runes," Kyle answered. Marja's eyebrows rose.

"So are many others."

"I'm better," Kyle countered. It felt self-aggrandizing to say so, but it was the truth. Marja glanced at Jag, who shrugged, then returned her gaze to Kyle.

"Prove it," she shot back. She pulled an amulet out from under her cloak, leaning over and showing it to Kyle. It had a large red jewel – probably a ruby – with silver metal around it. It looked quite simple at first, but a closer look revealed the truth: numerous tiny runes embedded within the ruby, glowing a faint blue.

"Wow," Kyle murmured.

"What do you sense?" she asked. He paused, studying the runes.

"Twenty-eight runes," he answered. "Ten of them look like sensory runes, the others are effector runes. All embedded in the ruby, but none on the surface."

Marja stood up straight, placing the amulet within her cloak once again. She was clearly taken aback.

"That took you seconds," she accused. "I've never seen someone sense runes so quickly!"

"Like I said," Kyle replied with a shrug, "...I'm good at it."

"That's not all," she murmured, eyeing him critically. "You're a wellspring of power. I've never sensed anyone who made so much magic."

"He's one-of-a-kind," Ariana agreed, flashing Marja a smile and patting Kyle on the back. Marja turned to her.

"And you're Ariana?" she inquired. Ariana nodded. "What's your role here?"

"I'm the bodyguard," Ariana answered.

"Really."

"Would you like a demonstration?" Ariana inquired, arching one eyebrow. Marja paused, then leaned forward, until her forehead was nearly touching Ariana's. Ariana stayed right where she was, hardly intimidated by the priestess. Being nigh invincible had a way of instilling confidence.

"That won't be necessary," Marja replied at last, standing straight once more "I've met one of your kind before," she added. "I have no doubt as to your abilities."

"Excuse me?" Ariana asked.

"Your entry is denied," Marja declared, crossing her arms over her chest. "Kyle and Petra may enter, but you may not."

"But why?" Ariana blurted out.

124

"You're compromised," Marja explained. "You think this is the first time your kind has tried to gain entrance to the Citadel?"

Kyle glanced at Ariana, who looked back at him. Her face seemed even paler than usual, which was of course impossible.

"How did you…?" Kyle began.

"We know many things."

"But she's not like the others," Kyle protested. "Her shard isn't linked with Sabin…and besides, Sabin's dead!"

"Who?"

"The man who controls people like Ariana," Kyle explained. "The Chosen."

Marja glanced from Kyle to Ariana, then back again, saying nothing for a long moment.

"Very well," she decided at last. "But your entry is conditional," she added, nodding at Ariana. "You will require vetting once we get inside. If you fail this, at best you will be removed from the Citadel."

"And at worst?" Ariana asked.

"If you are telling the truth," Marja replied coolly, "…then you have nothing to worry about." She turned to Jag then. "You've all passed initial inspection," she declared. "You may rise to the top of the Wall for further processing. Follow me."

Marja turned toward the scaffolding ahead, walking up to it and stopping a few feet from it. She closed her eyes for a moment, and then turned to the others.

"They're sending the platform now," she informed.

Kyle looked up, spotting something being lowered through the scaffolding near the top of the wall. It was, he realized, a wide wooden platform suspended by eight long ropes. The platform descended slowly, taking several minutes to each the bottom. Finally it did, landing on the ground with a *thump*.

"Come," Marja urged, stepping up onto the platform and gesturing for them to do the same. Jag did so immediately, Ariana and Petra following behind him…and Kyle taking up the rear. He hesitated for only a second, not wanting to seem nervous. He'd come a long way in curing his fear of heights – the ability to fly certainly helped with that – but still, the thought of going a couple thousand feet up the side of a wall in some rickety-looking wooden elevator was a bit much to consider.

Not that he had much of a choice.

Kyle joined the others, stepping onto the platform. It seemed well-built, as did the scaffolding itself, constructed of thick beams dovetailed together. Kyle supposed that its primary function was to prevent the platform from swinging left and right in the wind.

The platform shuddered, and then began to rise.

"Here we go," Jag stated. "Anyone afraid of heights?"

"Does it matter?" Petra inquired. Jag grinned.

"Just wanna know whose face to watch."

Petra rolled her eyes, and Kyle ignored the two, gazing out at the landscape as they went slowly upward. He could see down the slope of the mountain, all the way down to the valley below…and the city of Osa far in the distance. Beyond that, he spotted the great reef, the water going from a light blue within the reef to a deep blue beyond it. He kept looking until they got a bit farther up…and that's when his fear of heights started to kick in. Ariana leaned in, putting her lips to his ear.

"You alright?" she whispered. "Your heart's beating faster."

"I'll live," he muttered, so quietly no one could have heard him…no one except Ariana, of course. She nodded, grabbing his hand and holding it tightly. But not too tightly, thank goodness.

Upward they went, until they were so high that Kyle didn't dare look down anymore. He focused on Jag and Marja, who were standing on the opposite end of the platform. A strong wind blew through the scaffolding, making the wooden beams creak loudly…and causing the platform to sway a bit, slamming into the scaffolding on the left.

"You sure this thing is safe?" Kyle asked, gripping Ariana's hand so tight his knuckles were white. Jag smirked at him.

"Guess we'll find out, won't we?"

"How reassuring," Kyle grumbled.

After what seemed like an eternity, the platform jerked to a stop, swaying slightly within the confines of the scaffolding. It had stopped before a large tunnel with an arched ceiling some fifty feet from the top of the wall, made of the same flawless stone as the rest of the wall. Marja stepped off the platform into that tunnel, gesturing for everyone else to follow. Jag went first, followed by Petra, Ariana, and Kyle himself.

The tunnel was twenty feet tall, its walls covered from floor to ceiling in intricate carvings. These depicted crowds of people on either wall looking up to a series of much larger men and women on the ceiling, each of whom was depicted in a rather heroic pose. At the other end of the tunnel, Kyle saw a set of black stone double-doors guarded by tall statues standing at either wall, facing inward. They were of stern, muscular men in intricate platemail armor, holding staves whose ends pointed down toward the center of the tunnel before the doors. Marja stopped a few yards before the statues, turning to face her guests.

"I present Jagwell for passage," she stated, gesturing at Jag. "Advance through the doors."

Jag did so, striding up to the doors, ignoring the statues on either side. He walked between them, the ends of their staves pointing right at his head as he passed. He continued on to the double-doors, opening one of them and striding through. The door shut behind him, seemingly of its own accord.

"I present Petra for passage," Marja stated, gesturing at Petra. "Advance through the doors."

"Is this a test?" Petra inquired, eyeing the statues. Marja nodded.

"Those deemed unfit will be denied access," she explained. "Those deemed a threat will be destroyed."

Petra glanced at Marja, then at the statues. Then she squared her shoulders, stepping past Marja and continuing on toward the statues. She passed between them, their black, stony eyes staring down at her. To Kyle's relief, nothing happened. Petra continued to the doors, opening one, then stepping through as Jag had.

"I present Ariana for passage," Marja declared, gesturing at Ariana. "Advance through the doors."

Ariana glanced at Kyle, grabbing his hand and giving it a gentle squeeze. She smiled, and he smiled back.

"See you soon," she promised.

She let go of his hand, walking past Marja, then continuing down the tunnel toward the doors, glancing up at the statues as she went. Their cold black eyes stared down at her as she drew closer, judging all who passed with their eternal scowls.

And then their eyes began to glow.

Ariana froze, turning to glance back at Marja, but the priestess said nothing. The statues' eyes glowed a bright white; the light coursed down their cheeks like tears, then spread over their arms in vein-like cords. When the light reached their staves, it shot down them, making each staff glow extraordinarily bright.

And then the light shot *out* of the staves, striking Ariana where she stood. An explosion of white light assaulted Kyle's eyes.

"Ariana!" he cried, shielding his eyes from that horrible glare. He blinked rapidly, his eyes re-adjusting slowly, and stared at the spot where Ariana had been standing.

To his relief, she was still there…but something was wrong.

She was standing perfectly still, her hands out in front of her, shielding her eyes from the rightmost statue's former beam of light. Her hair was wild, blown backward, each strand frozen in time. *She* was frozen in time. Unmoving. Unseeing.

The statues' eyes faded, going black once again.

"What's wrong with her?" Kyle demanded, facing Marja. "What did you do to her?"

"I did nothing, Marja replied evenly.

"Let her go," Kyle ordered, clenching his hands into fists. Anger grew within him, and he pulled magic into his mind's eye, large cords of it. More magic than anyone else in the world could summon…even Kalibar himself.

If they hurt her, he thought grimly, *it'll be the last thing they do.*

"Kyle, don't be upset," Marja pleaded, her tone gentle. "Your friend is only being held until she can be properly vetted."

Kyle hesitated, then let the cords of magic go, feeling them suck back into the bones of his skull.

"Then vet her," he stated. "And let her go."

Suddenly the double doors ahead burst open, and...*something* came through. Something monstrous. Kyle gasped, stumbling backward, his eyes widening.

It was humanoid...sort of. It had the head and torso of a human, but fashioned entirely out of sleek silver metal, and a lone black eye in the center of its face with no mouth or nose. It's metallic chest and belly were also humanoid, as were its two metallic arms. But its torso fused with the body of what appeared to be a humungous metallic ant, six segmented legs carrying it forward quickly. The thing had to be at least eight feet tall.

It crawled up to Ariana with remarkable speed, stopping before her, its black, mechanical eye gazing down at her.

Kyle stared at the monstrosity, then at Marja.

"What *is* that thing?" he asked.

"An emissary," she answered.

"Emissary?"

"All in good time," she counseled. The emissary leaned forward, putting one metallic palm on Ariana's forehead. Kyle saw a faint blue light lining its hand for a split-second. Then the emissary lowered its hand, turning about and crawling back through the double-doors. They closed behind it.

Moments later, Ariana cried out, backpedaling quickly. She blinked, glancing up at the statues, then at Kyle and Marja.

"What happened?" she asked. "What was that bright light?"

"You were telling the truth," Marja answered. "You are not one of Sabin's Chosen. You may proceed," she added, gesturing at the double doors. Ariana glanced at Kyle.

"I'm not going without him," she countered.

"You must," Marja retorted. "Nothing will befall Kyle if he is being honest with us. You have my word."

Ariana turned to Kyle, who gave her a reassuring smile.

"I'll be fine," he stated. "See you soon."

Ariana's shoulders slumped, and she nodded, turning around and going through the double-doors. They closed behind her.

"I present Kyle for passage," Marja stated, gesturing at Kyle. "Advance through the doors."

129

Kyle took a deep breath in, letting it out, then striding forward. He couldn't help but glance up at the statues as he got closer to them. Would they freeze him like they'd frozen Ariana? If so, would he sense the passage of time, or would it be like he'd fallen asleep? What if...

The statues' eyes began to glow.

Crap!

Kyle froze, then took a step back, looking over his shoulder at Marja.

"Why are they..." he began.

And then there was a flash of blinding white light.

Kyle cried out, stumbling backward, dark spots burned into his vision. He caught himself, looking up at the statues. They were no longer glowing, their eyes having gone dark once again. He looked down, and was relieved to find himself intact.

"What happened?" he asked Marja.

"I don't know," Marja confessed. "You triggered the sentinels, but the emissary could not find anything amiss with you."

"Wait, you mean I was frozen like Ariana?"

"Correct," Marja confirmed. Kyle felt goosebumps rise on his arms. It'd been as if no time had passed at all; could it be spacetime-altering magic? Only Ampir was supposed to know of such things.

"How did they do that?" Kyle asked, looking up at the statues. The sentinels.

"The sentinels were made by the gods," she answered. "No one knows how they work. They just do."

Kyle frowned, studying the sentinel to his left. There was no telltale blue glow around it; indeed, there hadn't been, even when they'd started glowing. There was no blue glow *anywhere*, except...

He looked down, seeing faint rays of blue light pulling outward from him, radiating to the walls of the tunnel.

"This place is draining me of magic," he realized. Marja blinked, clearly taken aback.

"How did you...?" she asked. Then she caught herself. "The Citadel does not drain magic," she corrected. "It does not pull it out of us. Radiated magic is only wicked away by it."

Interesting, Kyle thought. He saw no void crystals, nor anything resembling them. But *something* had to be doing it. Perhaps it was the walls of the tunnel. It couldn't be the sentinels; his magic wasn't drawn to them any more so than the tunnel walls.

"Continue through the doors," Marja instructed.

Kyle complied, walking past the sentinels to reach the double-doors. He opened one, stepping through into the room beyond.

And frowned.

The tunnel continued forward a good twenty feet, stopping abruptly at a pitch-black wall ahead. A wall bordered by a half-ring of black stone identical to the material making up the walls, but with small runes inscribed into its surface along its entire length. It matched the curve of the ceiling perfectly...and beyond it, there was only blackness.

The room was otherwise empty.

Kyle stared at the blackness beyond the arch, then walked forward, stopping a few feet from it. He studied the blackness, trying to peer beyond it, but could see nothing. Weaving magic in his mind's eye, he conjured a small floating light ahead of him. Still, there was only blackness; not light reflected off its surface.

Strange.

He paused, then sent the light into the blackness...and saw it vanish. As did the stream of magic he'd sent to it. Which meant that this must be some kind of portal...one that Jag, Petra, and Ariana had gone through.

One that *he* had to go through.

Kyle took a deep breath in, then stepped right up to the black wall. He raised one hand, pressing his palm against it...and taking a sharp breath in when it passed right through, vanishing into the darkness.

He pulled back instinctively, but the wall resisted, holding his hand captive. He yanked back harder, but it was no use. His hand was stuck inside the wall. And, he realized, it was being pulled *into* it, slowly but surely.

Uh oh.

He streamed magic to his gravity boots, activating them and flying backward until his arm was pulled taught. But his hand didn't budge; in fact, it was sucked into the wall up to his mid-forearm now. And everything past the wall was completely numb.

Crap!

He streamed more magic to his boots, but it was no use. The wall of utter blackness continued to pull at him. He watched as his elbow passed through, and then his upper arm. His head was only a few inches from the darkness now. Kyle grit his teeth, turning his head away from the inky blackness, feeling his shoulder go numb as it vanished into the wall.

Then he felt the back of his head pass into the wall, and the world went black.

Chapter 11

Kalibar jerked awake, opening his eyes. He found himself sitting in his flying carriage, on a comfortable white U-shaped couch. Several of his elite guard – some of the best Battle-Weavers in the Empire – sat on either side of him. He looked out of the windows comprising the outer walls of the carriage, noting that the carriage was sitting inside of a large circular room. It took him a moment to realize why he'd awoken. The carriage had landed…he'd made it to Verhan.

He yawned, feeling exhausted despite his nap. He'd slept poorly again the night before, thinking of his children and Petra. This carriage was similar to the flying carriage he'd sent them to Meros in, although this one had more advanced defenses, most of them created by Erasmus and Jax, the late Elder Runic. Not that Kalibar thought he'd need them during this trip. He was merely here to witness the coronation of the next king of Verhan. It would be a short courtesy visit; witness the coronation today, then meet with the king tomorrow to discuss the future of the two countries.

The carriage door swung down, forming a ramp leading out of the ship. Kalibar sighed, gesturing for his Battle-Weavers to stand.

"After you," he offered.

The Weavers bowed, exiting the carriage. Kalibar followed them, finding himself in a vaguely familiar place. The Royal Hangar, a yellow-stone building with an open, domed ceiling, allowing flying carriages to take off and land. Magic was not allowed in Verhan, but in this case the country made an exception. The Royal Hangar was one of the few magic zones in the kingdom, but outside of its walls, magic was expressly forbidden.

The fact that he'd brought his Battle-Weavers as his guards sent a message: he would abide by Verhan's laws, but not because he had to. A quiet display of strength was vital to international relations. Of course, few would doubt Kalibar's strength. All of Verhan – indeed, most of the world – knew of Kalibar's reputation as a Battle-Weaver.

His guards formed a ring around him, and escorted him to the door leading out of the hangar. Kalibar allowed himself to be led, realizing that it'd been almost twelve years since he'd last made this trip, during his first term as Grand Weaver. He'd been the first Grand Weaver in over a century to do so, in hopes of securing an alliance with the Empire's old enemy. He hadn't succeeded, of course, but the uneasy truce that'd resulted had been victory enough.

They stepped outside of the hangar into the glaring sunlight, a warm breeze blowing past Kalibar, ruffling his simple black uniform. He squinted, removing a pair of glasses from his shirt and putting them on. They were Weaving glasses; not only did they protect his eyes from the sun, they also detected any nearby magic patterns, a glowing symbol appearing at the periphery of his vision whenever someone wove magic.

A large strip of well-manicured lawn lay ahead, a wide street cutting through it, extending a quarter mile to a large, circular building three stories tall with a domed ceiling. It was the Royal Amphitheater, where the coronation was to take place. A tall metal fence bordered the lawn on either side; beyond this was the city center. A truly massive crowd of people had congregated here, packing the streets as far as the eye could see, pressed right up to the fence on either side. Kalibar felt the eyes of the multitude upon him, and stood tall, knowing that everything he did – the way he held himself, the way he walked – would be endlessly dissected for weeks, if not months, to come.

He stood there for a moment, then strode forward, his pace neither languid nor hurrying. Too relaxed and he would give the appearance of being dismissive, of believing this coronation was beneath him. Too brisk, and he'd give the impression of being nervous, or just wanting to get it over with.

The endless theater of politics, he mused. An unfortunate truth, that people were far more interested in appearances than reality. Far easier to sway the masses with an appeal to emotion than with dry facts and reason. As an academic, that was a bitter pill to swallow. But the game had to be played.

He'd made it about halfway to the amphitheater when he heard shouting. A man pushed his way through the crowd to the fence, glaring at Kalibar.

"Murderer!" the man shouted. "You killed our king!"

He threw something at Kalibar – a rock – and Kalibar wove magic instantly. The rock stopped in mid-air before him…and then dropped to the ground.

"Magic!" the man yelled, pointing at Kalibar. "He used magic!"

Verhanian guards pulled the man away from the fence quickly, but more people starting shouting. Kalibar ignored them; it was as the ambassador to Verhan – Rodric – had said. These had to be followers of Lady Damia, who'd been quite busy inventing all sorts of conspiracy theories about the Empire. The agitators were quickly silenced by the guards, however, pulled violently away from the fence.

Kalibar sighed, knowing that his use of magic would be a minor scandal, although it had been justified. No doubt Lady Damia had planned the whole thing, and would twist the story to her benefit. Another unfortunate consequence of the endless theater of politics, that people could be so easily manipulated into believing lies. Once Lord Devlin took the throne, however, these fringe groups would lose what little power they had…and Lady Damia would be brought to heel.

He reached the amphitheater, striding toward the door marking its side-entrance. Six guards stood before it, and a man in a deep purple uniform. It was ambassador Rodric; the man smiled as Kalibar approached.

"Grand Weaver Kalibar," he greeted. "Good of you to make it. I apologize for the unruly crowd."

"Everyone is entitled to their opinion," Kalibar replied. "Whether I agree with it or not."

"Perhaps in the Empire," Rodric stated, "...but in Verhan, dissent is less...appreciated. Have no doubt that the man who threw that rock will have many more thrown at him. And that he will not survive the process."

Kalibar grimaced.

"That's not necessary," he insisted.

"It is our law," Rodric countered. "If you would kill someone with a stone, you will be killed with a stone."

"I see."

"Come," Rodric urged, opening the door to the amphitheater. "The ceremony will begin in fifteen minutes. I'll show you to your table."

"Who will I be sitting with?" Kalibar inquired.

"The ambassador to Tor-Tanga and the Prince of Ortepa," Rodric answered. Kalibar nodded. Tor-Tanga was a country south of the Empire, a close ally. And Ortepa was to the north, also friendly. A logical choice of table-mates, to minimize tension. But Kalibar would rather have met with people he could have forged new relationships with.

He allowed himself to be led into the building, his Battle-Weavers staying behind. Rodric led him through a short hallway with a door at the end of it. This too was guarded; Rodric nodded at the guards, who stepped aside, allowing them through...and into the huge room beyond.

It was a large, rectangular amphitheater with a raised stage at the far end. Small tables had been placed nearest the stage, with stadium-style seating behind them. Most of the seats were already filled; Rodric took Kalibar down to his table, where the Tor-Tangan ambassador and the Prince of Ortepa were already seated. Kalibar greeted them both, then sat down.

"Good afternoon, Grand Weaver," the prince greeted. A tall, thin man with pale skin and long black hair, he looked nearly identical to his ailing father, the king. "Congratulations again on your second term. I enjoyed the ceremony, and meeting your children."

"I appreciated your presence," Kalibar replied. The prince had of course been there for the ceremony.

"And I believe congratulations are due for your defeat of Xanos," the Tor-Tangan ambassador added. Kalibar smiled, wracking his brain for the man's name.

"Thank you, ambassador Hulsey," he replied. Not that the Tor-Tangan government had done much to help.

"Here's hoping that Lord Devlin wins the crown," the prince ventured. Hulsey nodded.

"Only palatable option," he agreed. "At best he'll be as innocuous as the old king."

"I have higher hopes," Kalibar countered.

"I'm cautiously optimistic," the prince agreed.

The ambassador harrumphed, then looked around, checking out the other tables.

"Not too many other countries sent representatives," he noted. "Most of these people are Verhanian aristocrats." He frowned. "They even invited the High Judicator and the sheriff, for god's sake."

"It was extremely short notice," Kalibar reasoned. "Not everyone has the resources to fly here."

A bell tolled, and the amphitheater went silent. A moment later, the sound of trumpets reverberated through the theater. A tall, slender man appeared from backstage, wearing a crisp white uniform. He began his prepared speech, welcoming the crowd in a booming voice that carried easily across the amphitheater.

"Cue the theatrics," Hulsey muttered as the man's speech continued. "God I hate all this pomp. Everybody's got to put on a show. As if anyone in this room gives a damn!"

137

"The Verhanians do," the prince countered. "For us, other peoples' traditions are to be endured, not enjoyed."

Kalibar said nothing, waiting for the man onstage to finish.

"And now," the man stated, spreading his arms out wide. "It is my pleasure to introduce the six lords of Verhan!"

The audience stood, and Kalibar stood with them, applauding as more people came onto the stage. Five men, most middle-aged, with one much older. That was Lord Farwell, who was too old to be chosen. Lord Devlin was among them, a tall, well-built man. Quite handsome, with a square jaw, short black hair, and olive-colored skin. Stagehands brought six large, ornate chairs out onto the stage, and each lord sat down on one...leaving one chair empty.

"Where's Damia?" the ambassador wondered.

A courier rushed down the aisle and up onto the stage, whispering in the announcer's ear. The announcer grimaced.

"I regret to inform you that Lady Damia will be voting in absentia," he declared. The lords glanced at each other in surprise, and the crowd broke out into quite a stir at the pronouncement.

"You've got to be kidding me," Hulsey blurted out. "This is ridiculous...everyone knows she's in the city!"

"I agree," the prince stated. "Her duty is to be here. This is most unwise on Lady Damia's part," he added. "The future king will see her absence as a snub. This won't end well for her."

"Perhaps she's sick," Kalibar offered.

"That's for sure," Hulsey muttered.

At length the crowd hushed.

"Do I have the lords' permission to continue?" he inquired, turning to face the seated lords. They all nodded, and the announcer faced the audience. "Then we shall proceed with the voting. Whoever earns the most votes will be crowned king. If there is a tie, a second round of voting will occur, and so on, until a majority vote is reached. Lord Farwell?"

The eldest lord stood.

"My vote is for Lord Devlin," he declared. Then he sat down.

"Lord Lindon?"

"My vote is," he stated, gazing across the crowd, "…for Lord Devlin."

"Well well," Hulsey said under his breath. "Maybe there is a god."

"Lord Zellus?" the announcer asked. The lord stood.

"My vote is for Lady Damia," he declared, sitting back down. Kalibar grimaced. That meant she had two votes, as she most certainly would vote for herself. One more vote for her and it would be, at best, a tie.

"Lord Devlin?" the announcer inquired. Lord Devlin stood.

"While I find it distasteful for one to vote for themselves," he declared, "…clearly my colleagues have confidence in me. Therefore I must vote for myself."

"As she is voting in absentia," the announcer declared, "…I have been notified that Lady Damia has also voted for herself. That makes two votes for Lady Damia, and three for Lord Devlin."

Which meant, Kalibar knew, that Lord Tristan's vote – the final one – would be the tie-breaker…or the tie-maker. A tie would be potentially disastrous, but it was unlikely. The Empire had paid an enormous sum for Tristan's support…and Tristan knew that Kalibar was here. Yet another reason why Kalibar had chosen to come; it was far more difficult to double-cross someone in person than to do it behind their back.

"And now for the final vote," the announcer declared. "Lord Tristan?"

The last lord stood, his eyes sweeping over the crowd. His gaze met Kalibar's for a split-second, and Kalibar kept his expression carefully neutral.

"My vote," he stated, his voice booming over the crowd, "…is for…"

Bam!

Kalibar jerked his head toward the rear of the theater, where the sudden sound had come from. He saw a woman standing by the rear door, which she'd just slammed shut. She was tall, slender, and breathtakingly beautiful, with skin as black as night, contrasting sharply with the gold and purple dress she wore. She had long dark hair that was pulled tightly backward into a ponytail that sprung wildly backward in tight curls. She was a marvel to behold, this woman…and reminded Kalibar instantly of Petra.

"Did I miss anything?" the woman inquired breezily, stepping gracefully down the aisle toward the stage. She walked with utmost confidence, a slight smile playing on her lips. The announcer – and Lord Tristan – grimaced.

"Lady Damia," the announcer greeted. "We were just receiving the final vote."

"My my," Damia murmured. "What *awful* timing. The suspense must be killing you."

She stopped before the stage…and only a few feet away from Kalibar's table. He found himself staring at her. She was, unlike the other lords – and the vast majority of the citizens of Verhan – not possessed of olive skin or wavy hair. Sure, there were citizens as dark as she was, but they were few and far between. An oddity that her family had attained lordship so many centuries ago.

"Your vote, Lord Tristan?" the announcer inquired. Lord Tristan cleared his throat.

"My vote," he replied, "…is for…"

"Oh come on," Lady Damia interrupted. Lord Tristan's mouth snapped shut, his jawline rippling.

"Lady Damia," he began, "…I'm warning you…"

"And I'm warning all of *you*," Damia interrupted, turning around and gesturing at the assembled crowd. "I'm afraid this is all a charade, my dear, dear guests. An expensive one at that." She smiled, turning to face Kalibar. "More for some than for others."

"What are you talking about?" Lord Tristan demanded. She held Kalibar's gaze for a moment, then turned to face Tristan.

"What a marvelous example of a rhetorical question," she stated, gesturing at Lord Tristan with one slender arm. "A question you clearly already know the answer to."

Lord Tristan's mouth set in a grim line, and he crossed his arms over his chest.

"My vote is for Lord Devlin," he declared. "The lords have decided…Devlin is king!"

"Oh *really*," Damia retorted, putting her hands on her hips. "Sheriff, if you would."

The sheriff stood then, a burly man with a thick black mustache and hard black eyes.

"A week ago," he stated, "...my office was warned of a plot by the Empire to influence this election."

Kalibar's blood went cold, and he gripped his armrests tightly.

"Ambassador Rodric?" the sheriff stated. Rodric stood from his own table, a few tables down from Kalibar.

"That is correct," Rodric confirmed. "Our intelligence indicated that the Empire planned to sway the election of Verhan's king to ensure that an Imperialist sympathizer gained the throne. I traveled to Stridon to meet with Grand Weaver Kalibar myself, and he told me personally of his intent to bribe our lords to secure their votes."

Kalibar's eyes widened, his breath catching in his throat. More than a few heads turned, and he felt hundreds of eyes upon him. He quickly recovered, his expression stony. But not quickly enough.

Damn it.

"I have kept in constant contact with the Sheriff's office and the High Judicator for the last few days," Rodric continued. "We traced the Empire's bribes through multiple intermediaries, and have the storage locations of each cash payment."

"This is preposterous!" Lord Tristan declared. The High Judicator stood then.

"The evidence is incontrovertible," he declared. "Lord Tristan, Lord Farwell, and Lord Lindon have all accepted bribes to vote for Lord Devlin as next king of Verhan." He eyed the three men coldly. "Their votes are, in this respect, unsurprising."

"This is a setup," Lord Devlin accused. "Manufactured evidence from *her*," he added acidly, pointing right at Lady Damia. Her eyebrows rose.

"Is it now?" she retorted. She turned to the sheriff. "What say you, sheriff?"

"As the High Judicator said," the sheriff replied coolly, "...the evidence is incontrovertible."

141

"The sheriff is correct," the High Judicator agreed. "I hereby deem this election unlawful and invalid. Seeing as the lords are compromised, they are no longer trusted to elect a king that will act in the best interests of Verhan."

"*What?*" Lord Farwell blurted out, standing up from his chair with some difficulty. "This is unprecedented! You don't have the authority!"

"And you gave up yours," the High Judicator shot back icily, "...when you colluded with the Empire. The law clearly states that I have the power to intervene in cases where the lords are impaired and the king is dead. And you, Lord Farwell, are most definitely impaired."

"You insolent swine!" Farwell shouted. "I'll have you hanged!"

"My my," Lady Damia interjected. "Temper, temper. Calm yourself, Farwell...you'll have a stroke."

"You'll fall before I do," Farwell growled, turning to her. "You scheming little *tramp*. Your soul is as black as your skin!"

The crowd gasped, but Lady Damia only smiled.

"I love my skin," she stated evenly, "...and my country. Which is more than any of us can say about *you*."

"It is already decided," the High Judicator interjected, turning to the crowd. "The lords are compromised. As per the law, the king shall now be elected by majority vote of the citizens of Verhan. Lords Farwell, Tristan, and Lindon are no longer eligible for the crown, by virtue of treason. Lord Devlin, by virtue of his compromised position and questionable loyalties, is also ineligible."

The rest of the lords – other than Zellus – stood then.

"And *we* hereby remove the High Judicator from his office immediately!" Lord Farwell declared.

"Very well," the High Judicator stated. He turned to the sheriff then. "As per our laws, you are now acting High Judicator, sheriff."

"Then as my first order as High Judicator," the sheriff stated, "...I hereby declare Lords Farwell, Tristan, and Lindon guilty of treason. Arrest them," he ordered.

Guards swarmed up to the stage then, overpowering the three lords and pulling them backstage. Their shouts echoed through the theater, then went abruptly silent.

"Lord Devlin," the sheriff continued, "...you are hereby sentenced to house arrest, awaiting sentencing by the next king of Verhan."

"You can't do this!" Devlin protested as guards grabbed him and pulled him toward the back of the stage. "I hereby..."

His voice was muffled as one of the guards put a hand over his mouth, and he was carried offstage. Only Lord Zellus remained onstage.

"Lord Zellus," the sheriff stated. "Have you anything to say?"

"I of course defer to the rule of law," Zellus replied. "And happily reinstate the High Judicator to his original position."

The High Judicator nodded in thanks.

"Then it is decided," the High Judicator declared. "In one week, the citizens will vote for the next king of Verhan." He turned to the crowd. "You are all dismissed."

"A moment," if you will," Lady Damia spoke up. The High Judicator nodded. She turned to Kalibar, gazing down at him with her black eyes. "On account of his very *personal* involvement with interfering in our sacred election," she stated, "...I propose we name Grand Weaver Kalibar an enemy of the state."

"That, as you know," the High Judicator replied, "...is a decision for the king."

Damia took a step toward Kalibar, a smirk twisting her lips.

"Or the Queen," she murmured, holding his gaze for a long moment. Then she turned away. "Very well," she declared. She began walking back toward the theater exit, giving Kalibar one last glance as she did so. The audience stood then, guards ushering them toward the exit.

"You'd better get the hell out of here," Ambassador Hulsey warned, giving Kalibar an apologetic look. The prince nodded, his jawline rippling.

"Agreed."

Kalibar grimaced, rising to his feet, then joining the crowd as they went for the exit. He spotted two guards striding toward him, and stopped, turning to face them.

"Keep your distance, gentlemen," he warned. "You won't find me so easy to drag away."

The guards hesitated, stopping short of him. Kalibar held their gazes for a moment longer, his expression neutral. But they saw the very real threat in his eyes, a smoldering anger that he seldom displayed. A vision of them assaulting him came to him, and of the terrible things he would do to them if they dared to. Attacking a Grand Weaver on foreign soil was tantamount to an act of war...and Kalibar would have to make a catastrophic example of why one shouldn't make the attempt.

And then what?

That reasonable side of him ticked through the possibilities, knowing full well that to attack these men – after having been so publicly outed as a conspirator to rig an election – would be political suicide. And worse, it could lead to war...and the needless deaths of countless men.

To his relief, the guards backed down.

Kalibar turned away from the guards, forcing himself to walk slowly toward the exit instead of pushing through the crowd. He passed through the side door he'd come in through, seeing his Battle-Weavers waiting for him.

"It did not go well," he warned them. "You may use magic. Be prepared."

The crowd of people pressed against the tall fences on either side of the path leading back to the hangar spotted him, a shout piercing the air. He ignored them, focusing on the hangar a quarter mile ahead.

And then the crowd hushed.

Kalibar glanced back, seeing Lady Damia stepping out of the main entrance to the amphitheater beyond the fence. He stopped to watch as she walked right up to the crowd, spreading her arms out wide.

"The election has been corrupted," she declared. "Lord Devlin has conspired against you. He is a puppet of the Empire – of Grand Weaver Kalibar himself – who spent billions to crown Lord Devlin king of Verhan!"

The crowd gasped.

"They tried to take your freedom!" she declared, gazing across the sea of people. "They tried to steal your country from you!"

The crowd burst into angry shouting, and Lady Damia waited, allowing it. Then she raised one hand for silence.

"I have seen to it that Lord Devlin will be put to justice," she shouted. "And I will see to it that *you*, the people of Verhan, the heart and soul of this great country, will have justice in the end!"

The crowd cheered, taking a while to die down.

"Should the lords have power to choose *your* king?" she asked.

"No!" the crowd answered.

"Who has the power to choose your king?" she demanded.

"*We* do!" the crowd cried.

"And so you shall," Lady Damia agreed. "I have demanded it. I give my power to you, my people. I give you the power that *you* should have had all along. The Empire wants to take our country away from us, as it did two thousand years ago. It wants to enslave us. But we are not slaves, you and I. Together, we have power."

The crowd hushed, hanging on her every word.

"The Empire didn't try to bribe me," Damia declared. "They knew – and you know – that there is no fortune large enough to make me betray my people." She paused for a moment. "Do you trust me?"

"Yes!"

"I am the *only* one you can trust," she continued. "I am the only one you can trust to fight for *you*. I and I alone can fight back against the Empire, against Grand Weaver Kalibar," she added, turning to point directly at Kalibar. The crowd turned with her, and Kalibar felt thousands of eyes upon him. "Rest your eyes upon your enemy, my people. *This* is the face of your oppressor! This is the man who would make us all slaves!"

The crowd went mad, the people closest to the fence hurling things at Kalibar and his Battle-Weavers. Stones, pieces of fruit, and even a few shoes flew at them. Kalibar stood where he was, faint blue shields appearing around his Battle-Weavers, who surrounded him. Kalibar resisted the urge to activate his own shields, knowing that in not using them, he was displaying fearlessness. Let the citizens of Verhan know that he was not afraid.

The endless theater of politics, he thought bitterly.

He strode toward the hangar in the distance, more projectiles bouncing off his Battle-Weavers' shields. He heard Damia's voice from behind.

"Are we slaves?" she shouted.

"No!" the crowd cried.

"Are we *slaves?*" she repeated.

"*No!*" the crowd roared.

"Then fight for your country!" she cried. "You have the power to choose your king. Use that power before they tear it from you!"

The crowd cheered, and Kalibar continued forward, only a hundred feet from the hangar now.

"Who do *you* want for your king?" Damia cried.

"Damia!" the crowd replied.

"Who will save you from becoming slaves of the Empire?"

"Damia!" the crowd roared.

Kalibar passed through the archway leading into the hangar, striding quickly up to his carriage. The door swung downward, forming a ramp for him and his Battle-Weavers. He stepped up into the ship, sitting on the U-shaped couch and watching as the ramp swung upward slowly. He heard chanting in the distance, the sound echoing through the hangar.

"Damia! Damia! Damia!"

Chapter 12

Kyle blinked.

He was standing in the center of a hexagonal room twenty feet in diameter. The floor was made of black stone, as were the walls and the domed ceiling high above his head. Sunlight streamed through tall, arched windows all around him, lighting upon four thick stone columns rising from the floor to support the ceiling. And directly ahead, he spotted Ariana, Petra, and Jag staring at him.

"Hey guys," he greeted, glancing behind him. He expected to see the other side of the portal he'd gone through, but it wasn't there. He'd apparently been teleported to the middle of whatever building he was in now.

"Glad you could make it," Jag stated, hardly seeming to mean it. "Come on."

Their guide turned about, walking toward a tall arched set of double-doors ahead. Everyone followed behind him, and Jag reached the doors, throwing them open.

Kyle gasped; beyond the doors was the most incredible sight he'd ever seen.

It was clear that they were near the top of the Citadel, but on the inside of it this time, in a building near the wall. The great wall completely encircled a vast city that spread out before Kyle, one unlike anything on Earth...or Doma, or even Ampir's home in

Antara. For while it extended for miles ahead of him, it also descended far below, countless levels of buildings built upon black stone platforms that were suspended by columns that plunged into the depths.

On the uppermost level of the city – where Kyle was now – there were six huge buildings. In the center of the Citadel rose the largest building of all. Constructed of the same black stone as everything else, it was like a giant church. It looked rather like St. Peter's Basilica, which he'd seen while on vacation to Rome with his mother a couple of years ago. It stood upon a huge stone platform suspended nearly a hundred feet above the buildings underneath, supported by shockingly few columns that connected to the platforms far below, or pass between them.

Five massive buildings as big as castles spread out along the periphery of the Citadel, each with a wide skybridge connecting them to the center building like spokes on a wheel. And this building – the building marking the entrance to the great city – was the sixth, with a much narrower bridge connecting it to the center of the city. A gracefully arching skybridge supported by a disturbingly few slender black stone columns.

And this bridge, Kyle realized, was where Jagwell was taking them to.

"You can shut your mouths anytime you want," their guide offered. Kyle blinked, then realized his mouth was hanging open, and shut it with a *click*. Ariana and Petra did the same. "Welcome to the Citadel," Jag declared, stepping onto the skybridge leading to the center building over a mile away.

"Holy crap," Kyle breathed, following behind Jag. Ariana and Petra followed close behind. The bridge was barely wide enough to accommodate two people side-by-side, and had railings three feet tall on either side. Not quite tall enough for Kyle, who made the mistake of looking over the edge. It was a precipitous drop to the tall towers of the buildings directly below…and the seemingly infinite distance below that, with crisscrossing skybridges connecting the innumerable buildings on each level extending thousands of feet down.

The view made him dizzy, and he clutched at the walls on either side of him, deciding it was wiser to keep his eyes straight ahead. He focused on the huge building far in the distance, the one in the center. Then his eye caught something beyond...something growing up the inner surface of the Citadels massive walls. They were vines, it looked like. Kyle followed one of them downward, realizing that they were incredibly long...extending as far down as he could see.

The vines were everywhere, he discovered. Crawling up the walls all around the Citadel and winding up many of the support columns of the skybridges. They had green, spear-shaped leaves, and he spotted a round white fruit growing from some of them.

"Almost there," Jag stated. And the man was right; they'd nearly crossed over the skybridge, the central building only a quarter mile away now.

"Where are we going?" Ariana asked.

"There," Jag answered, gesturing at the building.

"What is it?" she pressed.

"The Temple of the Old Tree," he replied.

"Ah."

"I'm taking you to meet the High Priest Kilson," Jag explained. "Don't speak to him unless directly spoken to. And bow when I do, as I do." He glanced back at them as he walked. "If he doesn't like you, your trip is over."

"Got it," Ariana stated. She paused. "Is he the leader of this place?"

"He is."

They reached the end of the bridge, and Jag took them onto the black stone platform beyond. Upon this grew a verdant lawn, where bushes and small trees stood in artful clusters. More of the vines were here as well, crawling up the sides of the platform and running along it, some even reaching the church a hundred feet ahead, crawling up its walls. They were surprisingly large, Kyle observed, thicker than his torso, with brown, peeling bark.

"What's with the vines?" he asked Jag, who glanced back at him.

"Those aren't vines," he countered. "They're branches. Of the Old Tree."

Kyle frowned.

"But I saw them all over the place," he protested. "They're all over the Citadel. How many trees are there?" Jag smirked, raising one finger.

"Just one."

"Are you serious?" Kyle blurted out. "Those branches go down over a thousand feet," he added. "This place has got to be a few miles wide. No tree is that big!"

"Now you know why they worship the damn thing," Jag replied. "They think it's eternal. The creator of life itself, they say." He shook his head. "They built a damn cult around it."

"What are those white fruits?" Petra inquired, pointing at one of the fruits on the branches Kyle had noted earlier.

"Pamaté," Jag answered. "Priests think it has mystical properties, allowing them to talk to their god. It's just a glorified hallucinogen."

A path cut through the middle of the courtyard, and Jag took them across it, reaching a short, wide set of black stone steps that led up to a huge arched doorway leading into the church. Two black-armored guards holding black spears stood at the entrance, blocking the way.

"Afternoon," Jag greeted, stopping before the two. The guards nodded at Jag.

"Good morning Jagwell," one replied. "Proceed to the Chamber of Communion. The High Priest Kilson will see you."

"Great," Jag muttered. "Come on," he prompted, stepping between the two men and gesturing for the others to follow him through the open doorway. They did so, stepping into a truly massive hall. It had a cathedral-style ceiling forty feet up, but no columns or other structural supports one might expect would be needed to support its massive weight. Despite there being no windows – and no obvious sources of light – the hall was well-lit, as bright inside as it had been outside. Again, Kyle could see no telltale blue glow of magic to suggest a source for this lighting.

Strange, he thought.

"What is the Chamber of Communion?" Petra asked Jag as he led them down the giant hallway.

"The priests think it's the holiest room in the Temple," he answered. "They perform the Communion there."

"And that is?"

"A ceremony," Jag explained. "They drug each other and have visions…think they're talking to the tree."

"Using the pamaté," Petra guessed.

"Right."

They reached the end of the hallway, passing through another arched doorway into a narrower hall. Continuing forward, they reached an intersection, and Jag took them rightward down yet another hall. This hallway extended an enormous distance, and it took several minutes until they reached the end of it, marked by a large set of double-doors guarded by a woman in white robes. She had long black hair that fell in straight tresses down the front of her white robe, and a narrow face with hazel eyes.

"Welcome Jagwell," she greeted. Jag stopped before her, looking suddenly uncomfortable. She arched one eyebrow. "Come to disappoint us yet again?"

"I'd hate not to," Jag replied.

"Well then," she stated, opening one of the doors, then stepping aside. She gestured for them to go through. "Don't let me stop you."

"A pleasure as always, Sasha," Jag muttered.

"I wish I could say the same," she retorted coolly.

Jag ignored her, walking past the open door into the room beyond. Everyone followed, except of course for Sasha. Kyle found himself in a small circular room…or at least small compared to every other room he'd seen in this place. It was perhaps a dozen feet in diameter, with three circular steps leading down to the center of the room. Situated there was a man seated cross-legged on a plush circular cushion of sorts, facing away from them. The man wore a simple white robe like all the others, and had long hair that was just as white flowing down his back. His spine was bent with age, his shoulders narrow and frail-looking. Kyle could see the faint outline of the man's bones through the thin fabric of his robe.

"I see the sun has returned," the man stated. His voice was deep and powerful, in contrast to his body. He gestured upward, still facing away from them. A beam of sunlight descended upon him, making his white robes seem to glow. Kyle looked up, realizing that the ceiling was at least several hundred feet above their heads, the room's wall extending all the way to the top of the Temple. Sunlight streamed through a hole at the very top. It must be high noon, he deduced. "Every time it comes 'round, it brings me great joy to see it. But if I behold it for too long, it causes me great pain."

"And blinds you," Jag responded.

The old man chuckled, then stood up slowly, smoothing out his robes, then grabbing a long black staff from the floor. He turned around.

"Only one eye," he replied. And indeed, the man *was* blind in one eye; his left pupil was milky white. The man was old, maybe seventy or eighty, and terribly thin. His paper-thin skin hung loosely from his bones, and was deeply tanned and liver-spotted. His white beard was long, like his hair, reaching his belly. "I find I see far more without it," he added. "It was a crutch...like your cynicism." He smiled. "I only hope your crutch is taken away as mine was."

"I brought guests," Jag grumbled, ignoring the man's comments. "These..."

"...are Ariana, adopted daughter of Kalibar; Kyle, adopted son of Kalibar; and Petra, of the tribes of the Barren Forest," the old man interjected. He nodded. "Welcome to the Citadel," he greeted. "And our less-than-humble Temple."

"Thank you," Ariana replied. "We're honored to be here. High Priest Kilson, I presume?"

"Such confidence in one so young!" Kilson marveled. "You're either an old soul or very powerful. Or perhaps both."

Ariana glanced at Kyle, who shrugged. It was as good a description of Ariana as any.

"I am Kilson," the man confirmed. "You're a Chosen, yet Sabin does not own you. How is this?"

"I was turned by someone more powerful than Sabin," Ariana answered. The old man's eyebrows rose.

"And who might that be?"

"I can't say," Ariana answered apologetically. "I'm sworn not to."

"Hmm," Kilson murmured. "A mystery then. Very well." He turned in the vague direction of Kyle. "I'm told you have a gift for runes, Kyle."

"I do," Kyle confirmed.

"And you, Petra, bring knowledge of your ancestral language," Kilson continued. "We have no need of it, but your researchers may find it handy."

"You seem to know a lot more about us than we know about you," Petra grumbled, shooting Jag a quick glare. "Our guide hasn't told us much of anything."

"Hardly surprising," Kilson replied with a rueful smile. "I suspect he finds us painful to think about. And yet he keeps coming back," he added, turning his head toward Jag.

"Just doing my job," Jag retorted.

"A job you chose," Kilson countered. "Your heart betrays you, Jagwell. A part of you yearns to return to your people."

Kyle frowned, glancing at Jag.

"Wait, you…?"

"He was born here, yes," Kilson confirmed. "Didn't he tell you?" He raised one eyebrow at Jag. "Are you ashamed of where you come from, Jagwell?"

"You really wanna get into this right now?" Jag shot back.

"Not in front of our guests," Kilson replied calmly. "But keep in mind that a tree that rejects its roots dooms itself."

"I'll keep that in mind," Jag grumbled.

"You're all here to help the Empire's researchers," Kilson stated, turning toward the other three. "Jagwell will take you to them without further delay." He gave a curt smile. "Interesting to meet you all," he added. "Jagwell, I expect you to dine with me tonight. Goodbye."

With that, he turned away from them, sitting back down on the mattress in the center of the room. Jag nodded at Kyle, Ariana, and

153

Petra, leading them out of the room quickly. The woman guarding the Chamber of Communion – Sasha – closed the door behind them.

"That was quick," she commented, smirking at Jag as he passed by. He didn't bother to turn around, continuing down the very long hallway, Kyle, Petra, and Ariana following behind. Kyle noted that Jag set a far quicker pace than he had before, forcing everyone to struggle to keep up.

"What was that all about?" Ariana asked.

"Nothing you need concern yourself with," Jag grumbled. But he slowed down a bit, glancing back at them. "Come on, I'll bring you to the Depths."

"The Depths?" Kyle asked.

"The lowest levels of the Citadel," Jag clarified. "Where you'll be working."

"What are those buildings around the Temple?" Ariana asked, gesturing at the five other huge buildings at the topmost level of the Citadel.

"The shrines of the Five," he answered. "The priests think that the original five gods created the Citadel, and that they lived here a long time ago. There's statues of the Five all over the place," he added.

"There were more than five gods?" Kyle asked.

"Sort of," Jag answered. "They were demigods, granted immortality by the Five. None were as powerful as the true gods, of course. The demigods have small shrines throughout the city. The more powerful ones have shrines on the higher levels, and the least powerful are just above the Depths."

"And what's in the Depths?" Ariana inquired.

"Mostly ruins," Jag replied. "Notice how everything here is made of that black stone?"

"Yeah."

"The stuff is called 'godstone,'" he explained. "It's invincible. Unbreakable. It never degrades. And magic can't touch it...it just absorbs anything thrown at it. You can't damage it. That's why the upper Citadel – and the Wall – are still standing. They'll be here long after we're dead."

"But the Depths aren't made of this stuff?" Kyle guessed.

"The columns supporting the upper levels are," Jag replied. "But the buildings there aren't. So they're falling apart, of course. No one goes down there much…they don't see the point. There's a ton of artifacts down there, probably from the people who colonized the Citadel before the priests gained control of it. But they're inferior to the runic technology of the upper levels. Everything is," he added. "Like I said, not even your Ancient Empire rivaled the technology of the Citadel."

"You don't believe in the Temple," Petra observed.

"Would you?" Jag shot back. "Bunch of people drugging themselves into a stupor and claiming to talk with a big tree?"

"When you put it that way," Petra replied, "…no."

"So what's the point of all this?" Ariana inquired. "The Citadel, and the Temple. What do they do, besides worship the tree?"

"Nothing," Jag answered.

"Nothing?"

"You heard me," Jag stated. "They don't do anything. They don't get involved with anything beyond these walls. Don't care about the world. All they care about is protecting the Citadel…as if it needs protection."

"What do you mean?"

"The Citadel's invincible," Jag explained. "It's not like anyone could destroy it. And its runes are all hidden within the walls. There's no way to reverse-engineer their technology. No one knows how it works, it just does."

They reached the end of the long hallway, and Jag brought them back to the huge main hall of the Temple, striding down it toward the entrance.

"Wait," Kyle protested. "If there's no way to see the runes, why are *we* here?"

"Like I said, the artifacts you'll be studying aren't native to the Citadel," Jag explained. "They're from later civilizations that populated it. It's inferior technology."

"Oh."

Suddenly Jag stopped in the middle of the great hall, turning to face the group. He gestured at the floor, and Kyle looked down. They were standing within a huge circle carved into the floor, one that surrounded a ring of smaller circles, each three feet in diameter. Jag walked to one of them, stepping inside of it.

"Stream magic to it," Jag instructed.

And promptly vanished.

Kyle stared at the spot where Jag'd been, then glanced at Ariana, who shrugged. She walked right up to the circle, and he saw a stream of faint blue light shoot down from her forehead into the floor. She vanished instantly.

"Well then," Kyle muttered. He glanced at Petra, gesturing for her to go to the circle. "Ladies first." She smirked.

"Nice try."

"Worth a shot," he stated. Stepping into the circle, he gathered a thread of magic in his mind's eye, sending it straight down into the center of the circle…

…and found himself standing in a familiar room. A hexagonal room with a cathedral ceiling…the same room they'd entered the Citadel through. Jag and Ariana were facing him, and Petra blinked into existence by his side a second later.

"We're back here?" Kyle asked. Jag smirked.

"Not quite," he replied. "Follow me."

He led them through the doorway out of the room, and Kyle stepped outside…and blinked. A city street was before him, with tall buildings all around. While the street was made of the usual godstone, the buildings were not. They were white and brown in color, well-maintained, and rather Victorian in style. A few people in white robes were walking down the street together, talking amongst themselves.

"Where are we?" Kyle asked.

"Look up," Jag replied.

Kyle did so, his eyes widening. Some fifty feet above the tallest building, he spotted a complex network of skybridges that connected a multitude huge black platforms to each other. Each platform was supported by several slender black columns. And beyond those platforms, Kyle saw *another* layer of skybridges and platforms…and another. And another, extending upward as far as the eye could see.

"Welcome to the Lesser Burg," Jag declared. "We're only a few levels above the Depths now."

"We teleported all the way to the bottom?" Kyle asked.

"Not quite," Jag corrected. "More like a third of the way down. We're about fifteen hundred feet below the Temple now."

"How is that possible?" Ariana asked. "The Citadel walls weren't even two thousand feet tall. You're saying this place goes down over four thousand feet?"

"It does," Jag confirmed. "Maybe deeper. No one's made it to the Floor of the World yet."

"The what?"

"The priests believe the Citadel has a floor deep within the mountain," Jag explained. "That it actually goes *deeper* than the mountain. A floor made out of godstone, so people couldn't try to dig their way underground and make it under the Wall."

He walked down the street, and everyone else followed. They passed a few buildings, and then Jag turned right down a narrow side-street, which ended abruptly in a short, three-foot railing. Jag walked up to it, as did Kyle, who peered down. He realized that the street they were standing on was just another godstone platform, with numerous levels far below. It was truly a vertical city, unlike any Kyle had ever seen.

"We'll take the stairs down," Jag stated, gesturing at a spiraling staircase to the right, at the very edge of the platform.

"Can't we just fly?" Kyle asked. Jag shrugged.

"Suite yourself."

Kyle streamed magic to his boots, feeling himself rise off the street a few feet. He glanced at Ariana.

"Wanna come?" he asked.

"I'll jump," she replied. And she did just that, leaping over the edge. Jag shouted in surprise, and they all watched as Ariana plummeted a hundred feet to the platform below. She slowed her ascent at the last minute, touching down safely.

"Show-off," Jag grumbled.

Kyle smirked, flying off the edge of the platform and descending to meet Ariana below. Petra followed him, landing next to them. Then they all watched as Jag made his way down the spiral staircase, reaching them after a few minutes, huffing and puffing.

"Thanks for flying me down," he grumbled, glaring at them. Petra smiled sweetly.

"You didn't ask," she replied.

"Fly me down next time," he stated. "Please."

Jag led them to the edge of this platform, and there was another hundred-foot drop to the next one. Ariana grabbed Jag, flying him down, and Kyle and Petra followed. They walked to the edge of this platform then; Kyle saw only ruins below, a rocky wasteland with crumbling brick buildings.

"Is that the Depths?" Kyle asked.

"That's just the beginning," Jag answered. "All that debris is from parts of the city that collapsed over the millennia. Anything not made of godstone."

"So the lower sections of the Citadel weren't made of godstone?" Ariana asked. "Why not?"

"You'll have to ask the gods," Jag replied sarcastically.

They flew down to the ruins below, Ariana once again taking Jag. They landed on the rubble, and Jag gestured at a large hole in the ground fifty feet away. It was a tunnel sloping sharply downward into the earth, big enough to drive a car through.

"That'll take us to your researchers' dig site. Come on," he added, walking toward it. "We've wasted enough time already. You have a lot of work to do."

Chapter 13

The twelve members of the Council were seated around the large circular table of the War Room, Kalibar and Erasmus seated side-by-side nearest the door. Kalibar felt all of the eyes in the room on him, and for the first time in his career, he felt like shrinking under their stares. An increasingly familiar shame crept over him, worming its way into his gut.

"This is…" Councilman Goran blurted out, shaking his head in disbelief. "This is unbelievable!"

"You're saying that ambassador double-crossed us?" Councilman Mudd stated incredulously.

"He did," Kalibar confirmed.

"So he was working for Damia all along," Goran concluded. Councilwoman Hess shook her head.

"Why didn't you double-check his claims?" she demanded, glaring at Kalibar.

"I did," Kalibar insisted. "My sources confirmed he was working for Devlin."

"Well your sources were wrong," she retorted. "Where are these 'sources' now?" she asked. Kalibar grimaced, lowering his gaze.

"It appears they've fled Stridon," he answered.

"Unbelievable," she muttered, crossing her arms over her chest. "So your compromised sources vetted the compromised ambassador. And now most of the lords are in prison, and Lady Damia is a rising star. Not to mention that we've embarrassed ourselves on an international stage. Now the world thinks *we're* corrupt." She shook her head. "How could you have been so gullible, Kalibar?"

"I did the best I could with the information I had," Kalibar countered, feeling a flash of anger at the insult. He forced himself to remain calm, knowing that losing his temper – particularly now – would not help him.

"That clearly wasn't good enough," Councilman Hewes retorted. "Damia made a fool of you," he added. "And you led us all right into her trap!"

"Now wait a goddamn minute!" Erasmus interjected angrily, glaring at Hewes. "*All* of you signed off on this. Kalibar gave you all the information he had, and *all* of you agreed to go forward with this!"

"Not all of us," Councilwoman Hess retorted. Kalibar grimaced. It was true, after all; she'd been the sole dissenter during their vote.

"Fine," Erasmus shot back. "But the rest of you were on board with this. And now you're all pointing your fingers at Kalibar like a bunch of sniveling cowards, refusing to take any responsibility for what *you* did!"

"How *dare* you..." Councilman Goran began.

"Enough!" Kalibar shouted. Everyone stopped, turning to face him, their eyes wide. Not once had Kalibar raised his voice during a Council meeting...not in six years. He glared at them. "We can sit here all day and assign blame," he stated. "If that's your goal for this meeting, then save your breath. I am Grand Weaver of this Empire," he added, "...and I take responsibility for what has happened."

"That's all well and good," Councilman Mudd retorted, "...but it doesn't change the fact that the wealthiest nation in the world was caught conspiring with foreign leaders to sway their elections. Our soft power is significantly diminished now."

"Granted," Kalibar conceded. "But only if we let Damia control the narrative."

"What are you thinking?" Erasmus inquired.

"Damia set us up," he explained. "But that doesn't mean we have to let her control the narrative. We can claim the evidence against us was manufactured by Damia…that she manufactured evidence of collusion so she could kill off her political rivals."

"He's got a point," Goran admitted. "Everyone knew she didn't have the votes to become queen, but that she's incredibly popular with the people. Of course she'd try something like this."

"That *is* a good idea," Erasmus admitted.

"I regret the necessity," Kalibar stated, "…but Lady Damia will not allow herself to be constrained by rules or decorum. If we're going to beat her at her own game, we have to pull out all the stops."

The Councilmen nodded, and Kalibar leaned back in his chair, glancing at Erasmus. His old friend gave him a weak smile, and Kalibar returned it, knowing exactly what the Grand Runic was thinking.

They'd managed to pull themselves out of total disaster for now, but their troubles had only just begun. The consequences of Rodric's betrayal – and Kalibar's decision to sway the Verhanian election – would not be resolved so quickly.

And the worst part was that, as much as he loathed to admit it, Kalibar knew that Lady Damia was right. The Empire *had* attempted to illegally influence an election…and in the end, there was only one person responsible for that. Kalibar could've ignored Rodric's request for help, could have taken the high road and allowed the election to happen without interference. Devlin would almost certainly have won, after all…and Lady Damia had known it. Which is why she'd concocted this scheme in the first place.

She'd set him up, it was true. But she'd really only provided an opportunity for Kalibar to do the wrong thing.

He'd been the one to take it.

* * *

161

Kyle knelt before the small row of artifacts set on the ground before him, holding back a sneeze. They'd followed Jag down a maze of tunnels below the rubble of the Depths, eventually reaching the dig site where the Empire's researchers – all Runics, of course – were working. Kyle had expected the dig site to be just another tunnel, but that was hardly the case. The tunnels Jag had led them down eventually opened up to a truly massive underground cavern. It was L-shaped, with a huge, partially-excavated stone wall on the far side. Countless strange symbols had been carved into the wall, which rose as high as the cavern itself, easily over a hundred feet above their heads. It was difficult to tell exactly how high; magical lanterns bolted to the rock walls lit the lower part of the cavern, but there were none higher up. Consequently, the ceiling of the chamber was shrouded in darkness.

And, to Kyle's surprise, gigantic branches could be seen extending upward, piercing through the massive stone wall. They were easily twenty feet in diameter, these branches, with thick plates of peeling gray-brown bark covering them.

They'd met the leader of the research team, a bookish man in his fifties with messy salt-and-pepper hair named Bopkin. He'd introduced Kyle, Ariana, and Petra to his team of Runics, and then had spent the next few minutes gushing over Kyle. Kyle had, after all, helped invent the K-Array, one of the most revolutionary runic devices in modern times. Not only that, he'd helped take down the Void Behemoth, a seemingly invincible war machine that'd nearly destroyed the Empire.

It'd been rather embarrassing to have so many grown men putting him on a pedestal, treating him like he was famous. Luckily, Petra had reeled Bopkin and the other researchers in, asking to be put to work. And they'd been at work ever since, minutes turning into hours as they'd studied artifact after artifact.

Kyle picked up one of the artifacts set on the ground before him, a metal pendant with a single ruby in the center. He streamed a small amount of magic to it – not enough to trigger an effect, but sufficient to make its runes glow a faint blue – and studied them carefully. Then he turned to a small notebook he'd been given, drawing the runes one-by-one. He felt a presence behind him, and glanced back to see the head researcher shaking his head slowly.

"I still can't believe how quickly you're rune-tracing," Bopkin declared, clearly awestruck. I've never seen anything like it!"

Kyle smiled, then set down the pendant, picking up the next artifact and repeating the process. Over his last few hours here, he'd managed to transcribe the runes within dozens of artifacts. A feat that Bopkin had said would've taken his men weeks, if not longer.

"He's something else, isn't he?" Ariana stated.

"He certainly is," Bopkin agreed. "We'll have our hands full processing all these runes." He glanced at Petra, who was standing nearby. "Do you recognize any of them?"

"Yes," Petra answered. "Most of them. They're ancient Barren Tribal artifacts. Even the materials are similar to the few artifacts we've saved from our ancestors' time."

"How strange," Bopkin replied, scratching his head. "You're sure the Barren tribes don't venture from their forest?"

"It is forbidden," Petra confirmed. "Our sacred mission is to protect our ancestral lands."

"So why would their artifacts be here?" Bopkin wondered. "Unless someone else stole them or replicated them, and populated the Citadel."

"It'd have to be a long damn time ago," Jag grumbled. The ornery guide had stayed with them at the dig site, much to Kyle's surprise. "The priests have been here for at least a thousand years."

"These artifacts are older than that," Petra stated. "They must be at least two thousand years old. They match the runics from the time of the Outsider."

Kyle frowned, stopping what he was doing and glancing up at her. The Outsider is what the Barren tribes had called Sabin.

"Fascinating," Bopkin murmured.

Kyle returned to his work, quickly sketching the runes in each of the artifacts before him. Within a few minutes, he finished.

"There," he declared. "Ready for the next batch."

"You'll have to wait for tomorrow, I'm afraid," Bopkin apologized. "We've still got to process our newest finds."

"Oh."

Kyle felt a hand on his shoulder, and realized it was Ariana. She looked disturbed.

"What's wrong?" he asked.

"Something's coming," she warned. "I can hear it from somewhere above. But whatever it is..."

"What?"

"It doesn't have a heartbeat," she finished.

Kyle felt the hairs on the back of his neck stand on end, and he glanced at Jag. The man seemed entirely unconcerned, as usual. But Kyle knew what Ariana was afraid of. The only thing that wasn't alive, but could still move.

A Chosen.

"Do you...sense anything?" he asked. Ariana paused, then shook her head. She had the ability to sense the thoughts of any nearby Chosen, but only if Xanos was controlling them. And Xanos – *Sabin* – was supposed to be dead.

Then Kyle heard it...a *clang, clang* sound echoing through the cavern, getting steadily louder. It was coming from high above, at the great wall of the partially-excavated building. A moment later, they saw it: a metallic monstrosity with a humanoid upper body and the lower body of a giant ant, crawling down the side of the building. Its body gleamed in the light of the magic lanterns as it made its way down the wall, until at last it reached the floor of the cavern. It crawled by them, ignoring them entirely...and made its way to one of the tunnels exiting the cavern.

Kyle watched it go, then turned to Bopkin.

"What exactly are those things?" he asked.

"The priests call them emissaries," Bopkin explained. "As to what they are or why they're here, no one knows."

"It looked the same as the one that studied Ariana," Kyle noted. Ariana frowned at him.

"What?"

"It came when you were, uh, frozen in time," he explained. "Back at the sentinels."

"Do you know what they are, Jag?" Petra asked. Jag shrugged.

164

"Priests call them emissaries," he answered. "Beyond that, I haven't a damn clue."

"They come from this wall," Bopkin piped in, gesturing at the stone wall. Petra arched an eyebrow at him questioningly. "We suspect it's a very large building," he explained. "One that is at least as old as the artifacts here. Maybe older."

"Why's that?" Kyle asked.

"Because we can't get in," Bopkin answered. "It has runic defenses so complex that no one has been able to get past them. And believe me," he added, "...it's not for lack of trying."

"But these emissaries can go in?" Ariana pressed. Bopkin nodded.

"They can," he agreed. "They usually emerge from high up on the wall. There's an entrance there...a sliding stone doorway that they somehow activate. We tried following one of them in once, but it was...unsuccessful."

"What happened?"

"Well, the problem is that the wall seems to drain our magic," Bopkin explained. "The entrance is very high up, you see. We have to fly up to it, but it doesn't take long for the wall to drain us, and, well..."

"You don't want to fall to your deaths," Petra guessed.

"Precisely."

"Huh," Kyle murmured. He studied the wall; it was a good hundred and fifty feet across, at least the part of it that'd been excavated. If it was a building, then that building had to be pretty darn big. There could be all sorts of interesting things inside...including powerful runic artifacts.

"Can we check it out?" he asked Bopkin. The Runic frowned.

"I don't think that's a good idea," he cautioned. "I don't want to be responsible if you get hurt when that thing drains your magic."

"I wouldn't worry about that," Kyle reassured. "I make a lot of magic."

"I noticed," Bopkin admitted. "But..."

"I'll go with him," Petra interjected. Bopkin turned to frown at her. "I cannot be drained of magic," she explained. "Not with my Reaper uniform, and my...other abilities."

She was of course talking about her Reaper vines, whose still-living roots were slowing burrowing into her skull. They produced magic for her on demand, but with a terrible price. For each time she summoned magic from them, they burrowed a little deeper into her flesh. And one day they would burrow into her brain, killing her.

"We really should get going," Bopkin countered. "We have to pack up the dig site and leave by sundown. No outsiders are allowed to stay overnight."

"That's alright," Jag piped in. "Let them go. Gonna take at least an hour to pack up."

Bopkin turned to Jag, who held his gaze for a long moment. Then he nodded.

"Ah yes, I forgot," he muttered. "Good idea." He cleared his throat then. "Yes, well. The entrance is about a hundred feet up. Good luck finding it though."

"Got it," Kyle replied, turning to Petra and Ariana. "Let's go."

They walked to the base of the wall, and Kyle and Ariana activated their gravity boots, flying upward. Petra didn't need gravity boots, flying perfectly well by Weaving. As they ascended, Kyle noted faint rays of blue shooting out from him. The wall was indeed draining magic from him, albeit at a slow pace. Or, as the best magic producer in the world, he was just too powerful to drain anymore.

"Let me know when you need magic," he offered Ariana, who nodded. He turned his attention to the wall then. It was getting darker due to the lack of magical lanterns; he created a few magic lights around himself, illuminating the area. There were countless intricate carvings in the wall, some of various flora and fauna, but mostly consisting of strange symbols. They looked similar to the ones he'd seen on the artifact Master Lee had shown him, and on the artifacts he'd studied today. That meant this structure had likely been created by the Barren Tribes. But how? And why?

166

And more importantly, how to get in?

"Do you see anything?" Ariana asked. Kyle shook his head.

"Not yet," he replied. "If there's a sliding door, it has to be either mechanically gated or magically gated. My guess is it's magically gated," he ventured. "Which means there's probably a sensory rune lock somewhere on this wall."

"Which you should be able to see," Ariana guessed. Kyle frowned.

"Maybe," he replied. "Only if it has some magic flowing through it though." And if this wall was absorbing magic, then it'd probably leech magic from the sensory rune lock, making it effectively invisible. A good way to prevent anyone from finding it, much less unlocking it. But if he were to stream magic to the wall, the sensory rune might light up, if only for a short while…

He tried it, streaming some magic to the wall as he flew upward slowly…more than was already being drained from him. Nothing…so far.

"I'm gonna have to scan this whole wall," he notified them, slowing his ascent. They were only a few dozen feet from the top of the cavern now. "I'll have to go in rows downward from the top."

"Ok," Ariana agreed.

Kyle reached the top, where the stone wall met the rocky ceiling, then flew leftward, streaming magic to the wall as he went. When he reached the far-left side of the cavern, he lowered himself a bit, then flew rightward, continuing to stream magic as he went. He continued this for a few more rows, until at last he spotted something glowing on the surface of the wall.

Runes!

"Guys!" he called out. Petra and Ariana flew to him. "I found the sensory runes. Now I just have to trace them."

He did just that, pulling magic into his mind's eye, then weaving it in a pattern identical to the sensory rune. The rune was incredibly complex, and it took Kyle almost a minute to trace it. When he was done, he threw the pattern outward at the rune.

Nothing happened.

"Huh," he mumbled.

"What's wrong?" Ariana asked.

"It didn't work," he replied. He tried again, but nothing happened. He frowned then, studying the wall. If activating the sensory rune wasn't working, that meant that either the rune didn't control the door, or…

He backed away from the wall a few feet, then streamed magic to the stone around the rune. Sure enough, two more runes appeared.

"There are two more of them," Kyle notified the others. He'd probably have to activate each of them at the same time…a considerable feat. He focused, weaving the first pattern, then holding it in his mind's eye. He grabbed another strand of magic, weaving it into the second rune, and then a *third* strand, weaving the third rune. By the time he was finished, sweat was dripping down his forehead. He threw the patterns outward.

A rectangular section of the wall caved inward before him, then swung inward as if on hinges, revealing a large rectangular tunnel through the wall.

"Nice!" Ariana exclaimed.

Kyle smiled, flying into the passage, Ariana and Petra following behind him. He deactivated his gravity boots, landing on the floor of the tunnel, then continuing forward. The tunnel opened up into an eight-by-eight-foot room with sheer stone walls. He looked up; the ceiling was a good fifty feet above. There were no doors or passages that he could see.

"Interesting," Kyle murmured.

"Looks like a dead-end," Ariana observed.

"We should look for more runes," Petra ventured. Kyle nodded.

"This place drains magic," Kyle reasoned. "My guess is the door's up there," he added, pointing upward. "Most people's magic would've been drained by now, making it so they wouldn't be able to fly up."

"Clever," Ariana murmured. "Speaking of magic, I think I'm running low."

Kyle nodded, streaming a large amount of magic to the shard in her forehead. It would drain magic from him automatically if it got low enough, but it was better to be proactive.

"Wait here," he ordered. Then he flew upward, reaching the top of the room. He streamed magic to the stone there, and saw another set of sensory runes. He unlocked them as before, another passage opening up. "Come on," he prompted, flying through. Ariana and Petra joined him. They were in another short tunnel; this led to yet another room, similar to the first, but with a ceiling only eight feet high. A quick scan showed yet another series of sensory runes on the far wall. "There's another door," he informed.

"Can you open it?" Ariana asked.

"Yep," Kyle answered. The runes were similar to the ones he'd unlocked before. He started to weave magic, then paused, letting the strands of magic go.

"What's up?" Ariana asked.

"Something's bothering me," Kyle explained. He looked about the room then. It was eight feet cubed, and entirely nondescript. Petra frowned.

"What's wrong?" she asked.

"Well, the first two doors had a purpose," Kyle answered. "The first one tested my ability to deal with my magic being drained while finding the door and unlocking it. The second one tested this again, making me have to fly up to unlock it."

"And?" Petra asked.

"But this door has similar locks with no other test," Kyle stated. "Or at least not one we know of."

"What are you thinking?" Ariana inquired. Kyle frowned, tapping his chin.

"There must be a third test," he theorized. He streamed a little magic to the sensory runes on the wall before him; they lit up a faint blue, just like before. Then he streamed magic to the ceiling; nothing happened. Then he tried the floor.

More runes lit up there, all across the floor, each connected to the sensory runes on the wall.

169

"Opening this door triggers runes on the floor," Kyle realized. "But I can't tell what they do. They look complicated."

"It's a trap," Petra reasoned. "We have to unlock the door and neutralize the trap at the same time."

"Right," Kyle agreed. "But the trap might hurt us...or worse."

"Then we should go back," Petra stated. "We can't risk getting hurt."

"And we have to get going anyway," Kyle agreed. "They'll be finished packing up soon."

"Maybe tomorrow then," Ariana offered. They made their way back outside, flying down toward the dig site to rejoin Bopkin, Jag, and the other Runics, who were nearly finished packing up the dig site. Kyle caught one of the Runics slipping an artifact into one of the backpacks they carried their lunches in, and nudged Ariana as they reached the ground, staring at the bag. She frowned at him.

"What?" she asked. Bopkin and Jag walked up to them, and Kyle grimaced.

"Nothing," he mumbled. "Tell you later."

"How'd it go?" Bopkin inquired.

"We found the door," Kyle answered. "No luck opening it, unfortunately," he lied. To Petra and Ariana's credit, they did not contradict him.

"No surprise there," Jag quipped. Bopkin was clearly disappointed.

"Ah well," he replied. "We're going to the exit," he added. "Come on."

They made their way back up through the tunnels to the surface, then flew upward, passing countless levels of godstone platforms. Eventually they reached the uppermost level, landing on the platform upon which the Temple stood. They entered the huge building, stopping in the center of the great hall. Kyle looked down, seeing a familiar ring of circles carved into the floor...the same ones Jag had used to teleport them to the lower levels.

"We're not going back the way we came in?" Ariana asked.

"Nope," Jag confirmed. "That's a one-way gate. Only exit we know of is through the Temple."

"Why don't we just fly out?" Ariana pressed. Jag smirked.

"Try it," he offered. "If you feel like dying young."

"Stand in the center circle and activate it," Bopkin instructed. He did just that, and promptly vanished. The other Runics followed suit, vanishing one after the other. Then Petra, and Ariana. Jag gestured for Kyle to go next, and he did, stepping into the center, then streaming magic to the floor...

...and found himself standing on a rocky ledge atop God's Peak, the island of Meros extending out toward the horizon thousands of feet below.

"Whoa!" he blurted out, stumbling backward. He felt cold hands grip his shoulders, and turned around to see Ariana smiling at him...and Jag, Petra, Bopkin, and the other Runics. They were standing at the base of the Citadel's massive wall, near the scaffolding for the elevator they'd taken earlier. Marja was walking toward them.

"Don't worry," Ariana reassured. "Petra and I had the same reaction."

"Everyone does the first time," Bopkin agreed.

"Good evening," Marja greeted, stopping before them. "I will check your belongings now."

Bopkin nodded, and the Runics lowered their backpacks to the ground, opening them up for the priestess to search. She did so quickly; Kyle watched as she searched the backpack carrying the artifact that he'd watch the one Runic steal, but to his surprise, he didn't see the artifact inside of it. After Marja was done, she patted down each of the Runics – and Kyle, Ariana, and Jag – skipping Petra. It was impossible to hide anything in her Reaper uniform, of course.

"See you tomorrow," Marja stated, going back to the elevator. Bopkin turned to Kyle, extending a hand.

"Well done, Kyle," he congratulated. "With your help, we got more done today than we would have in weeks. We'll have to double our efforts tomorrow just to keep up with you!"

"My pleasure," Kyle replied. Jag frowned.

"Tomorrow's no good," he countered. "Governor wants them at the Festival."

"The next day then," Bopkin conceded. Jag turned to Petra.

"Take the kids to the carriage," he ordered, I got to go back," he added with a grimace. "Dinner date with the High Priest."

And with that, they separated, starting their long journey back to their carriage at the base of the mountain...and to their home away from home.

Chapter 14

Jag shifted his weight in his chair, staring across the long wooden table at the High Priest Kilson seated opposite him. He couldn't help noticing how much more frail the man looked, even compared to a few months ago. Time was marching relentlessly forward, stealing the life from everything around it. Jag had never really considered a life without the High Priest in it, as much as he loathed the man. But now it was clear that it wouldn't be long before it became a reality.

He lowered his gaze to his plate, unable to look at the man's face any longer. Looking more and more like the skull it would soon become.

"You've barely touched your food," Kilson observed.

"I'm not hungry," Jag muttered. He felt the old man's eyes on him, and lifted his gaze to meet them.

"You're so far away," Kilson scolded. "Come, sit closer," he added, gesturing to the chair to his right. Jag hesitated, then obeyed, standing up and walking to the chair, then sitting down again. Kilson smiled. "That's better."

"What do you want?" Jag grumbled.

"A man can't just want to see his son?"

"You never just *do* anything," Jag retorted, crossing his arms over his chest. Kilson sighed.

"True," he admitted. "It's my work I think," he mused. "Being High Priest means putting meaning into everything I do. But this time I mean it," he insisted. "I miss you, Jag."

"Don't," Jag shot back, feeling a flash of anger. Kilson frowned. "What…"

"You always do this," he interrupted. "Drawing me in, pretending you care. But you don't."

"That's not true, Jag."

"It is," Jag insisted.

"How can you say that?" Kilson retorted. "I'm your father!"

"You care more about that goddamn tree than you ever did about me," Jag accused.

"I care about both," Kilson corrected. Jag snorted.

"This from the guy who spends ten hours a day drugged up and pretending to talk to a goddamn tree." He shook his head. "How much time did you spend with me growing up, *Dad?*"

Kilson sighed, looking down at his own plate, then pushing it away. He too hadn't eaten much.

"I made mistakes," he confessed. "I wasn't the father I could have been."

"And you never will be."

"Not if you don't give me a chance," Kilson agreed. He leaned forward. "That's all I'm asking for, Jag."

"Must be hard wanting a relationship with your family and having them push you away over and over again," Jag grumbled. "How's it feel, father?"

Kilson took a deep breath in, letting it out slowly.

"It feels terrible," he admitted. "To think I did this to you for so many years…" He stopped, his eyes brimming with moisture. "I'm sorry, Jag."

Jag didn't answer, swallowing past a lump in his throat. He kept his arms crossed, refusing to give in. To open himself up to this man. He'd been disappointed far too many times before to make that mistake again.

"It's too late," he muttered. Kilson hesitated, then nodded, leaning back in his chair.

"That may be," he conceded. "But I have to try." He gave a weak smile. "I still haven't given up on you, Jag."

Here it comes, Jag thought.

"I want to show you why," Kilson stated, leaning forward again. "Why I was so…distant when you were growing up."

"Not gonna happen."

"Please," Kilson insisted. "Just once, that's all I ask."

"I said *no,*" Jag retorted, glaring at the man.

"Jag…"

"I'm not taking your goddamn drugs to talk to your damn *tree,*" Jag interjected, pushing himself back from the table and standing up.

"Jag, sit down."

"No," Jag said. "I *knew* you were going to do this. You *always* do this. Every damn time!"

"I just want you to understand me," Kilson insisted.

"Bullshit," Jag retorted. "You just want me to join your stupid cult." He clenched his teeth. "It's the only way you'll ever love me."

"It's the only way you'll ever know *me,*" Kilson countered. "How can you love someone you don't know?"

"Exactly my point," Jag agreed. "You never took the time to get to know me."

Kilson sighed.

"You're right, I didn't," he admitted. "I was blind. Obsessed. I know that now."

"Great," Jag muttered. "Better late than never."

"I'm not blind anymore," Kilson continued. "My eyes are open, son. I want to know you before I die."

"Then stop trying to get me to join your club," Jag shot back.

Kilson stared at Jag for a long, uncomfortable moment. Then his frail shoulders slumped, and he nodded.

"Alright," he agreed.

Jag sat there, staring at the old man. He felt himself wanting to believe his father. Wanting to open up. This moment – his father actually *wanting* to have a relationship with him, without an agenda, and actually listening to him instead of just waiting for a chance to speak – was everything he'd ever wanted growing up. What he'd yearned for. But he knew all-too-well that his father was incapable of it. That Kilson was a broken man, unable to have a real connection with people. The only thing he'd ever loved was the Old Tree. There was no room for anything else.

"Thanks for dinner, Dad," Jag muttered. "See you around."

He turned away from his father, walking to the door leading out of the dining room. And to the High Priest's credit, for the first time in the man's life, he didn't try to reel Jag back in.

* * *

Governor Candric paced around his spacious office, the floorboards creaking under his feet with each step. He looked down at the piece of paper clutched in his right hand, hesitating, then unfolding it for the umpteenth time. He read it slowly, devouring each letter on the page.

Father,
I've completed my training. I will be arriving the night before the Festival. Tell Tessa.

- Darren

He re-folded the letter, stopping his pacing and staring at the door to his office. It was nearly midnight, and Darren still hadn't arrived. He'd sent a messenger to Tessa as instructed, and yet he hadn't heard from her either. She should've jumped at the chance to see her brother again. And as much as he missed his son, he also dreaded seeing the boy – the *man* – again. Hundreds of unanswered letters had tempered his enthusiasm. It was no surprise that his son's first letter to him in ten years was so…formal. Cold.

Candric sighed, walking up to his desk and setting the letter atop it. Then there was a knock on the door. He flinched, turning to face it.

"Come in," he stated.

The door opened, and Bae stepped in.

"You have a visitor Governor," she informed, and then winked at him. Candric smiled.

"Thank you Bae," he replied. "Please, bring him in."

A moment later, a man in a plain black uniform walked through the doorway, stepping around the butler. He was nearly as tall as Candric, but much more slender. He had hair so dark it was almost black, short and wavy, and a smooth-shaven face. A stranger except for his eyes...those familiar, deep brown eyes staring into his own. Eyes he'd waited a decade to see again.

"Hello son," he greeted. Though every fiber of his being wanted to rush forward and hug Darren, he did not. Darren nodded slightly.

"Father."

"I got your letter," Candric stated, gesturing at his desk.

"I see."

"I did as you asked," Candric continued. "I haven't heard from your sister yet."

"Are you two speaking?" Darren inquired. Candric grimaced.

"Sometimes," he confessed. "Tessa...she and I don't always see eye-to-eye."

"And why is that, father?"

Candric stopped himself from replying, sensing something in his son's tone. It'd been a rhetorical question. He took a deep breath in, squaring his shoulders. There was no point in circling the issue. It was time to get it all out.

"You never returned my letters," he stated bluntly. The corner of Darren's lip twitched.

"On the contrary," he replied. "I returned every single one of them."

"Why?" Candric asked.

"Ten years and you still don't know the answer to that question?" Darren retorted. "Have you given what happened to me any thought at all?"

"Every day of my life since you were enlisted," Candric replied immediately. Darren's eyebrows rose.

177

"Enlisted?" he shot back. "Is that how you see it?"

"Since you were taken from me," Candric corrected. "Since you were stolen from me."

"If that's how you really feel, why didn't you say so the first time?" Darren wondered. "Still protecting the Empire I see."

"I'm the governor now," Candric apologized. "I'm…used to speaking diplomatically."

"I'm not," Darren retorted. "And I trust Tessa isn't either."

"Has she answered any of *your* letters?" Candric inquired…and immediately regretted it. Darren had sent Tessa many letters since he'd been taken, and Tessa had refused to open a single one of them. It'd been a low blow to mention it.

"So you *can* get angry," Darren replied evenly. "Tell me, did you finally divorce Mom?"

Candric stared at Darren for a moment, then nodded.

"The day you were taken."

"So that's what it took," Darren observed. "Not the drinking. Not the countless times she hurt us and endangered us. Not the screaming and calling us worthless. Not the beatings."

"Darren…"

"You know, I always saw you as the strongest man I knew," his son interjected. "And you still are, physically." He tapped his own temple with one finger. "But here…"

"I tried to help her," Candric retorted. "She needed help, Darren. I did everything I could…"

"To help *her*," Darren shot back. "Not me, not Tessa. You always put *her* first."

"She was the mother of my children," Candric countered. Darren blinked, his eyebrows furrowing.

"Was?"

Candric froze, staring at Darren for a long moment. Then he sighed, lowering his gaze.

"She's gone," he revealed.

"How?"

"She…killed herself," Candric confessed.

"Drinking?"

"No," he admitted. "She…it was after you were taken, after I told her I was going to leave her. That same night." He hesitated. "I sent you letters about it."

Darren swallowed visibly, processing this. Then he nodded.

"I see."

"I lost you that day," Candric stated. "And your mother. And…Tessa."

"Why Tessa?"

"She never forgave me for letting them take you," Candric admitted. "She blamed me for letting it happen, for not using my money and influence to protect you."

"That makes two of us," Darren replied. Candric grimaced.

"And she never forgave you for leaving her," he retorted. "And not answering her letters."

"I didn't at first," Darren admitted. "I was in shock. My world ended…and I was guilty."

"Why?"

"I promised her I'd always be there for her," Darren answered. "And I broke that promise. I couldn't face that at first, and by the time I could, it was too late. She wouldn't answer my letters. Hell, she probably didn't even read them."

"She didn't."

"If she had, she would've known why I hadn't responded at first," Darren continued. Candric gave a rueful smile.

"So here we are," he stated. "Three people who won't talk to each other."

"We're talking now," Darren pointed out.

"We are," Candric agreed. "And…thank you for that," he added. Darren nodded.

"I owe you that much," he conceded. "You did what you thought was right."

"It wasn't good enough," Candric countered. He felt a sudden wave of shame, and blinked moisture from his eyes. "I wish I could go back in time," he added. "And be a better father for you two. I wish…I wish I'd left your mother sooner. I should've protected you and I didn't."

Darren stood there, saying nothing.

"I screwed up," Candric admitted. "And I'm sorry."

"Are the Finders still taking children?" Darren asked.

"Yes."

"Then you're not sorry enough," Darren stated coldly.

Candric dropped his gaze to the floor, swallowing past a lump in his throat. When he lifted his gaze again, his vision was blurry with tears.

"I'm trying," he said in a near-whisper. "I don't know what else to do."

Darren stared at his father for a long moment. Then he strode forward until he was only a few feet away. He hesitated, then reached out with one hand, putting it on Candric's shoulder.

"I'm sorry," he apologized. "I…I know it's not your fault, Dad. You can't stop the Finders. And I wouldn't have you stop them if you could. I understand the need for Weavers and Runics. Without us, the Empire wouldn't be able to protect itself. But that doesn't make it right."

"It doesn't," Candric agreed.

"What have you been doing?" Darren inquired, lowering his hand.

"I've petitioned the Empire to consider a mentorship program," Candric answered. "To keep children with their families by sending teachers to students. Or by allowing kids to return to their parents during weekends, or at least during vacations."

"A reasonable solution," Darren conceded. "But they already allow children to go home once a year. Any more than that is a logistical nightmare. We don't have enough Weavers to send every child back to their parents in a reasonable timeframe, not with how huge the Empire is. And we don't have enough Weavers to have a one-to-one mentorship."

"Then set up schools in every major city," Candric proposed.

"The Empire won't do it," Darren countered. "They want to be just like the Ancients, father. The Ancients had their students come to the Secula Magna, so we have to go there."

"That can change."

"Maybe," Darren stated. "And maybe you can change it. But I doubt it."

"I still have to try."

"For me?" Darren asked.

"For me," Candric corrected. "I lost everything when I lost you. I don't want any father to have to go through that like I did."

Darren nodded.

"I hear Tessa is leading protests throughout Meros," he said. "Anti-Imperial protests."

"She isn't anti-Imperial," Candric countered. "She just wants people who make magic to stay in their communities…and for people who don't to be equally represented in government."

"What do *you* think?"

"I agree with her goals," Candric answered.

"It'll never happen," Darren stated bluntly. "The Empire doesn't just take kids who make magic for logistical purposes. They do it because it gives them power…and takes it away from the people. We magic-users will always dominate normal people, Dad. It's just how it is."

"Governments can reign in that power," Candric countered. "The law is more powerful than the most powerful Weaver."

"The most powerful Weaver *makes* the laws," Darren countered. "No one is more powerful than Grand Weaver Kalibar. Trust me, I've seen him in action."

"The Council…"

"Is made of up of Runics and Weavers," Darren interjected. "Normal people can't serve on it."

"Not today," Candric admitted. "I hope to change that." Darren's eyebrows rose.

"You want to get on the Council?"

"Yes," Candric replied. "Being governor is only the beginning. I'm going to run for mayor of Stridon next year."

"Really?" Darren murmured. He considered this, then nodded. "I can see it…and I think you'd make a fine mayor."

"Thank you son."

"You really *are* going to try to change things," Darren observed.

Candric nodded, and Darren stood there for a long moment. Then he sighed.

"I'm sorry I didn't read your letters," he stated. "If you still have them, I'll read them."

Candric felt his lower lip quivering, and he nodded silently, not daring to speak.

"I'm a man now," Darren stated.

"Yes you are," Candric agreed, moisture blurry his vision. He felt tears dripping down his cheeks. "I'm proud of you, son. Of the man you've become."

"You don't know me," Darren retorted.

"I hope to."

Darren paused, then nodded at him.

"You will," he promised. "And maybe Tessa will too."

"All I want is my family back," Candric confessed, his voice breaking. He closed his eyes, and felt Darren embrace him. He embraced his son back, squeezing him tightly.

"Me too, Dad," Darren murmured. "You know I still love you, right?"

Candric smiled, patting his son on the back, his cheeks moist with tears.

"I do now."

Chapter 15

The sun had no sooner peeked above the endless blue sea when Kyle, Ariana, and Petra were awoken by Governor Candric's plentiful staff, insisting that they come downstairs for an early breakfast with the man. It'd taken Kyle a few minutes to wake up; they'd all gone to sleep late the night before, after their adventure in the Citadel. With bleary eyes, he'd made his way downstairs, sitting at the same dining room table as yesterday. Breakfast was some fruit and what appeared to be oatmeal, and everyone ate silently for a few minutes before speaking…and before a tall, slender man in a Battle-Weaver uniform joined them, sitting beside Candric.

"This is Darren," Candric introduced. "My son. Darren, this is…"

"I hardly need an introduction," Darren interjected, smiling at Kyle and Ariana. "I fought with both of them against the Void Behemoth when it attacked Stridon."

"You were one of the Battle-Weavers that used the killerpillar guns to shoot it down after we drained it," Ariana recalled. Darren's eyebrows rose.

"You have a good memory," he stated. Kyle smiled.

"You have no idea," he agreed.

"I've rarely seen such bravery in adults, much less children," Darren continued. "Without your help, the Empire would have

183

fallen." He turned to his father. "You should have seen it, father...it was – and probably will be – the greatest battle of my life."

"I wish I had," Candric murmured, looking at Kyle and Ariana with newfound respect.

"And what's your name?" Darren inquired, turning to Petra.

"I am Petra," she introduced. "I too have fought with them, and Kalibar."

"Ah," he replied. "You're Grand Weaver Kalibar's...visitor," he realized. "I heard of you, but never got to meet you."

"Yes, well," Candric stated, clearing this throat. "About your request from yesterday, about meeting with the Resistance."

"Yes?" Kyle asked.

"Their leader has agreed to meet with you this morning, before the Festival," Candric informed. "They're sending a carriage to pick you up in a half-hour."

"Oh, good," Kyle replied. With everything that'd happened at the Citadel, he'd almost forgotten about the whole thing. "You said her name was Tessa?"

Darren's eyebrows rose, and he glanced at Candric, who grimaced.

"They're going to meet Tessa?" Darren asked.

"Yes," Candric admitted.

"I'll go with you," Darren stated, turning to Kyle and Ariana. "I'm sure she'll want to see me."

"Are you?" Candric countered. "I don't think it's a good idea. She's not expecting you."

"I only have a few days of vacation," Darren countered. "If I don't see her now, it may be years before I get another chance."

"It's fine if he comes," Ariana offered. Candric sighed.

"I won't stop you."

One of Candric's butlers stepped in the dining room then, clearing his throat.

"Yes Benton?" the governor inquired.

"It appears the carriage for our young masters has arrived," Benton informed them.

184

"Thank you," Candric replied. He stood then. "Tessa can be...abrasive," he warned. "Good luck."

* * *

Tessa stretched her arms over her head, then sighed, staring across the large divination room of the ancient, renovated church that served as the headquarters for the Meros chapter of the Resistance. Centuries old, its ornate black stone was cracked and crumbling, its floor covered in a thin layer of dust despite daily sweeping. Built by worshippers of the ancient gods of the Citadel, it'd been long-since abandoned, still standing despite the death of the religion that had brought it into being. It was still beautiful, with huge rooms and domed ceilings, and stately black stone columns rising all the way to the ceiling twenty feet above her head...and above the heads of the dozens of volunteers who constituted the leadership of the Resistance on Meros.

A seemingly abandoned church at the foot of God's Peak, it was far away from the prying eyes of the City Guard. A great gift from Tessa's sponsor, a wealthy businesswoman whose name she still didn't know, and whom she had never met. An unfortunate necessity in a time where dissent – even lawful dissent – was fancied to be tantamount to treason.

"Okay guys," she stated, her voice carrying easily through the large room. The volunteers stopped what they were doing, turning to face her. "Gonna go over this one more time, alright?" Everyone nodded. "We meet up at Zucker street in six hours, then march to the governor's mansion by two o'clock. Each of you is in charge of your group. Make sure no one breaks the law," she warned. "The last thing we need is to give Apep a reason to shut us down."

Everyone nodded.

"If we stay within the law, and Apep tries to stop us, it'll look real bad for him...and he knows it. So we need everyone to be on point." She paused. "Any questions?"

"What if they attack us like last time?" one of the volunteers – a woman named Sandy – asked.

185

"Don't fight back," Tessa answered. "If you do, they'll insist you started it, and you'll go straight to jail…and they'll accuse us of instigating a riot. The stakes are high here, people. The highest they've ever been. The government doesn't want us ruining the Festival – especially with the Empire watching. We're embarrassing them, and they'll pull out all the stops to shut us down. We have to be perfect, and they don't." She paused. "Any questions?"

There were none, of course. They'd been through this many times. She swept her gaze over her people, unable to help herself from smiling. Many of them had been with her from the beginning, before this movement had even gotten started on Meros. Back when organizing a full-on protest during the Festival would've seemed impossible.

"Remember this day," she urged. "The City Guard will be watching us, but so will the people. All of Meros will be watching us. The Empire will be watching." Her smile broadened. "Let's show them something they'll never forget!"

The crowd cheered, pumping their fists in the air. Tessa grinned, then waited for the applause to die down.

"All right people," she stated. "Let's get to work!"

The crowd dispersed, everyone returning to their duties. Some were finishing up the signs they'd been working on for the last week, while others were putting food and water into backpacks. Everyone moved quickly and efficiently, driven by a singular, powerful purpose. The sight sent a chill down Tessa's spine.

We are powerful, she thought. The guards had weapons, and the Empire had magic. But everyday, ordinary people had each other.

She felt a tap on her shoulder then, and turned around. It was Gia, her second-in-command. A short, slender woman with curly black hair.

"Our guests have arrived," Gia warned. Tessa nodded, quickly sobering.

"I'll meet them outside," she replied. Gia nodded, leaving to supervise the others. Tessa took a deep breath in, letting it out slowly. She felt her heart starting to race, and forced herself to calm down.

This is it, she knew. Kalibar's children were here…had requested to meet with *her.* It was beyond her wildest dreams, this meeting. Her one chance to talk straight to power…the closest she would ever get to the Grand Runic and Grand Weaver.

You can do this.

She squared her shoulders, then strode across the large room, making her way to the church entrance. She stepped into the bright sunlight, spotting a lone carriage in the small courtyard in front of the headquarters. The doors to the carriage opened, and two children got out. One of them was a pale, slender girl in a black uniform. She had long dark hair, and was maybe thirteen or fourteen. The other was a slightly shorter boy with short brown hair wearing a stark white uniform. They both walked up to her, and she studied them as they did so. Both of them carried themselves well, walking with confidence beyond their years.

If I had magic, she thought, *I would too.*

Another person got out of the carriage – a tall, slender woman with jet-black skin. She was strikingly beautiful, with a formidable physique made obvious by the tight black uniform she wore. Tattoos crawled up the sides of her temples, with raised scars that seemed to grasp the sides of her head like long bony fingers.

"Good morning," the young girl greeted, stopping before Tessa and extending a hand. Tessa shook it; the girl's grip was shockingly strong, even a little painful. "You must be Tessa."

"I am," Tessa confirmed. "And you must be Ariana." Ariana smiled.

"I am."

"I'm Kyle," the boy offered, also shaking Tessa's hand. "Thanks for meeting with us," he added.

"I could hardly say no to the children of the Grand Weaver," Tessa replied with a smile. She immediately regretted the statement; it felt too much like pandering. "And who's this?" she asked, gesturing at the black woman.

"I am Petra," the woman greeted, standing back a little. "From the Barren tribes." Tessa's eyebrows rose.

"How do you three know each other?" she inquired.

"That is…complicated," Petra answered.

Just then, a fourth person exited the carriage. Tessa frowned; it was a tall, slender man in a black uniform. A Battle-Weaver uniform, she realized. As he strode toward her, she found her gaze locked on his eyes. Eyes from her past. Eyes she could never forget.

Darren!

Her blood went cold, and she froze, staring at him. He stopped behind the others, giving her a rueful smile.

"Hello Tessa," he greeted.

She nodded silently, swallowing past a sudden lump in her throat. Her heart thumped in her chest, a combination of surprise and fury. She hadn't wanted to see Darren. He hadn't been invited.

Dad set me up.

She glanced at Kyle and Ariana, clearing her throat. She couldn't afford to make a scene in front of them. She would have to accept Darren's presence. The cause was more important than her.

"What a surprise," she said, returning her gaze to Darren. "I wasn't expecting you."

"I know," Darren admitted. "I…don't have a lot of time," he added. "I needed to see you."

"And now you have," Tessa replied, a little too coolly. She turned her attention to Kyle and Ariana. "I'm curious," she admitted. "Why did you want to meet me?"

"I saw what happened at the governor's mansion," Kyle answered. His expression darkened. "The woman who was hit in the head…"

"Catalina," Tessa stated.

"Her child was taken by the Finders?" Kyle asked.

"That's right."

"They shouldn't have hit her," Kyle stated. "It wasn't right. She wasn't trying to hurt us."

"I agree."

"Kalibar told me about the Finders," Kyle continued. "But…he said that families were honored to have their kids chosen." Tessa raised an eyebrow.

"What do you think now?"

"I think he's wrong," Kyle answered. "And I think he needs to know how people really feel. That's why I wanted to meet you," he added. "I want to know what you're going through...why you're doing what you're doing."

Tessa felt a burst of hope, and quickly suppressed it. This was more than she could've asked for, but she couldn't get her hopes up.

"I'll tell you anything you want to know," Tessa promised. "Would you like to come inside?"

"Sure."

Tessa led her guests back into the church, bringing them to the divination room, where her volunteers were still busily preparing for the Festival.

"I'm heading the Meros chapter of the Resistance," she explained. "These are my organizers. They're all volunteers, and each is responsible for organizing protesters in different neighborhoods on the island. We're getting ready for the Festival."

"You're marching to Osa?" Kyle asked. Tessa hesitated, then nodded.

"That's right."

"Why?"

"The Festival is supposed to celebrate the day Meros gained independence from Verhan," Tessa explained. "That lasted about a year. Verhan was threatening to reclaim us by force, and take over our democratically elected leadership. So our government agreed to become a part of the Empire in exchange for protection."

"But isn't half the island owned by Verhan?" Ariana asked.

"Yes," Tessa confirmed. "Half of Meros didn't want to become part of the Empire, so Verhan took over again."

"So why march during the Festival?" Kyle pressed.

"The Festival marks our independence," Tessa answered, "...but we are clearly not independent. Even though we have democratically elected officials, they still ultimately answer to the Empire. The Empire takes away anyone who makes magic, forcing us to rely on magic and runics they provide...at ridiculous expense, mind you. Businessmen from the Empire have snatched up many of our most lucrative businesses, siphoning the profits back to the Empire instead of using them to help the island. We've become a tourist economy, but there aren't enough jobs to support our people. And the jobs we do get barely constitute a living wage. Thirty percent of our people live below the poverty line."

"That's terrible," Kyle stated. "But isn't your father trying to change things?"

"Yes," Tessa admitted. "He's trying. But everything is against him. We operate under the Empire's laws, and most of the businessmen who profit from Meros have a lot to lose if the status quo changes. They have a vested interest in keeping things the way they are, and lobby the government to ensure my father's hands are tied. Despite everything he's tried, he's gotten very little done."

"I see," Kyle murmured.

"The Resistance isn't just confined to Meros," Tessa continued. "We have chapters in every major city in the Empire. The biggest issue..."

She hesitated, stopping herself from continuing. Kyle frowned.

"Go on," he urged.

"I don't want to offend you," Tessa stated. Kyle smiled.

"I won't get offended," he promised. "I really want to hear what you have to say."

"The biggest issue is that the people...people who don't make magic," she added, "...constitute well over ninety-nine percent of the population, yet we have no representation in the Council. Members of the Council have to make magic, and so does the Grand Runic and Grand Weaver."

Kyle frowned, glancing at Ariana.

"I never thought of it that way," he admitted.

"Exactly," Tessa stated. "Neither have they. That's just the way it is...and it means that, whether they realize it or not, their policies will always favor the minority that makes magic, and not the majority of people. We don't have a voice in the Secula Magna."

Kyle considered this, lowering his gaze for a long moment. He looked troubled.

"You're right," he agreed.

"People like to say the Resistance hates the Empire," Tessa continued. "They say we're just anti-magic. But it's not true. We just want to level the playing field. People who make magic have most of the wealth in the Empire. They own the majority of the land. They dictate our wages, our laws. We just want a fair shot at having the opportunities that they do."

Kyle turned to Ariana and Petra.

"We need to tell Kalibar this," he stated. "This isn't right." Ariana nodded, and Kyle turned back to Tessa. "I promise that I'll speak with my father," he added. "And if possible, I'll try to get him to meet with you so you can tell him yourself."

Tessa's heart leapt into her throat, and she swallowed, nodding silently. She cleared her throat, smiling at him.

"I would be honored to have the opportunity to do so," she replied.

"Kalibar's an honorable man," Kyle stated. "The best man I've ever met. I'm sure he can help."

"I hope so."

"In my tribe," Petra stated, "...those who make magic serve those who don't. We sacrifice our lives to protect them." She shook her head. "To use magic to serve oneself is...it's unthinkable."

"But that is the reality," Tessa countered. "I'm sure the Council and the Grand Weaver and Runic *think* they're serving us," she added quickly, glancing at Kyle and Ariana. "But as you can see, it's not always the case."

"What else can we do to help?" Kyle inquired.

"If you can arrange for me to meet with Grand Weaver Kalibar," she replied, "...then you'll have done more than I could ever have dreamed."

Kyle squared his shoulders, nodding at her.

"Then that's what I'm going to do," he vowed. "And I promise you I won't stop until I've done it." He smiled then. "I look forward to seeing you at the Great Tower," he added. "Ariana and I will show you around personally."

191

Tessa smiled, extending a hand and shaking Kyle's. She held his hand in both of hers then, blinking away sudden moisture in her eyes.

"I've heard stories about you," she admitted. "And I thought they were tall tales. You've changed my mind."

"And you," Kyle replied with a smile, "...have opened mine." He withdrew his hand. "I look forward to seeing you at the Festival," he added.

"And I you," Tessa replied.

Chapter 16

Governor Candric sighed, easing himself into the plush chair on the third-story balcony of the governor's mansion. One of his butlers had already set a glass of water and one of wine on a small side-table to his left, and he chose the wine, sipping at it and gazing down at the large courtyard below. Throngs of people had already arrived for the Festival, held back from the center of the square by temporary barriers that had been placed by the City Guard the night before. Guards lined the barriers and stood among the crowd, their golden armor and long spears gleaming in the sunlight.

It was a perfect day for the Festival, not a cloud in the sky. A cool breeze blew over Candric's scalp, a pleasant reprieve from the sun's hot rays. He should be happy, he knew.

Candric shifted in his chair, taking another sip of his wine.

He heard footsteps approaching from behind, and twisted around to see Kyle, Ariana, and Petra stepping onto the balcony. He smiled, gesturing at the chairs to either side of him.

"Good afternoon," he greeted. "Come, have a seat."

They did so, choosing the chairs to his left. The two children were dressed in formal Imperial regalia; it was the first time Candric had seen Ariana not wearing her usual uniform, the one that looked like Petra's. Of course, Petra was clad in her usual outfit, forcing him to be mindful of his gaze. A moment later, Darren arrived, smiling down at his father. He sat down to Candric's right.

"How did your meeting with Tessa go?" Candric inquired, glancing at Kyle.

"Very well," Kyle replied. "She was very nice. We had a lot to talk about."

"I'm glad it went well," Candric said, somewhat taken aback...and a little jealous. It'd been far too long since he'd had a positive interaction with his daughter. He turned to Darren. "Did you get a chance to speak with her?"

"I did," Darren replied. Candric raised his eyebrows, and Darren gave a rueful grin. "I spoke with her after the others left," he explained. "She...wasn't happy at first," he admitted. "But I got to say what I needed to say."

"Good."

"She knows how I feel now," Darren continued. "We're...better. Not perfect, but better. She promised to read all of the letters I sent over the years." He paused. "It was hard," he confessed. "But good."

Candric smiled, patting his son on the knee.

"I'm happy for you," he replied. And he was. After all these years, the family was finally coming together again. The open wounds that each of them had suffered for so long were starting to heal. Candric could only hope that Tessa would be able to forgive *him* one day.

Then they could finally be whole again.

"Looks like the parade is almost here," Darren observed. Candric gazed past the courtyard below, to the main street running through Osa. Darren was right; long columns of people were making their way slowly toward them, carrying huge orange and white flags, the colors of Imperial Meros. A few floats, magically levitating a foot above the street, were being pulled by large black horses. Actors stood upon the floats, re-enacting the signing of the Letter of Independence, when Meros officially declared itself a sovereign nation.

But Candric found himself looking *past* the parade, to the empty street beyond.

Where is she?

He took another sip of wine, then realized he'd drank almost all of it. He grimaced, setting it down. He hadn't had much to drink since his wife died. A glass of wine a year at most. He wasn't about break that habit...or risk starting a new one.

The faint sound of music reached his ears as the parade made its way toward the courtyard, the beating of drums echoing off the mansion walls.

"Anything to eat?" he heard a voice inquire from behind. He glanced back, seeing one of his butlers standing there. He shook his head, as did everyone else. "Drinks then," the butler offered, handing out tall glasses of what looked like tropical smoothies to each of them.

"I'm done with this," Candric stated, handing the man his glass of wine. The butler took it, stepping back into the mansion, and Candric sipped on his drink. After the sweetness of the wine, it tasted slightly bitter.

"I remember watching the parade when I was a kid," Darren reminisced, leaning back in his chair and shaking his head. "It's the same as I remember," he added. "Almost like I never left."

"I remember watching it with you," Candric replied, taking another sip of his drink. "You and your sister took turns sitting on my shoulders so you could see." Darren smiled at him.

"That's right," he remembered. "And you were taller than anyone else, so I got to see everything." He shook his head. "Never thought I'd be watching this from the governor's mansion."

"And I never imagined you'd be a war hero," Candric countered.

"Just a veteran," Darren corrected. "The real heroes are sitting to your left."

Candric glanced at Kyle and Ariana, who were busy watching the parade and enjoying their smoothies. Or at least Kyle was; Candric had never seen Ariana drink, or eat for that matter. He heard footsteps from behind, and saw Captain Apep step up to the edge

195

of the balcony to his right, looking over the railing at the approaching parade. The man pointedly ignored Candric, which was just as well, as Candric had no desire to speak with the man. He already had a replacement in mind for the Captain of the Guard; Apep's escalating insolence and veiled threats had made him unfit for the job.

He turned back to the parade; the flag-bearers at the front had reached the intersection right before the square, and would end up turning right down another street, continuing onward. They would march all the way through the shopping district, Candric knew, a quarter-mile down the road.

But when they reached the intersection, the flag-bearers didn't turn. They continued right toward the square.

Apep gripped the railing.

"What are they doing?" he demanded, turning to Candric. "They're supposed to turn down Main Street!"

"I know," Candric replied. He realized he'd stood up, and walked to the railing, watching as the flag-bearers led the front of the parade into the square – easily a few hundred people. The rest of the parade turned down Main Street as planned.

"What's going on, Candric?" Apep demanded, glaring at him. Candric turned steely eyes back on the man.

"That's *Governor* Candric," he retorted. "And I know as much as you do."

The flag-bearers stopped a dozen feet before the governor's mansion, as did the people behind them. They stood in the town square, holding their flags high.

And then they parted in the middle, a lone figure striding forward between each half. A tall woman with long, wavy hair, wearing what looked like a sleeveless white kimono with a wide orange belt around her waist. She stopped in front of them, a flag of Meros in her left hand. Candric stared at her, his breath catching in his throat.

Tessa!

His guts squirmed, and he too gripped the railing, staring down at his daughter.

"Look," Ariana said, pointing at Tessa. Kyle stood up from his chair, as did Ariana and Darren. They watched as Tessa lifted her gaze to stare right at them. She turned to the crowd behind her then, raising her flag as high as she could.

"Citizens of Meros!" she cried.

The people in the square cheered.

"Twenty years ago, we fought for our independence from an occupying country," she declared. "We fought for the right to choose our own path, to end the tyranny and oppression of Verhan. To end the exploitation of our island, our people. To give every man, woman, and child of Meros a chance at a better future."

The crowd cheered again, and Tessa waited for their voices to die down.

"But our oppressors did not approve," she continued, her tone grim. "With Verhan threatening to use violence to enslave us, we turned to the Empire to protect us."

Apep turned to Candric, his mouth set in a grim line. He pointed a finger at Candric.

"*You* planned this," he accused. "You and your damn daughter!"

"I did no such thing," Candric retorted. "My daughter did this on her own."

"Well I'm going to end it," Apep promised, turning from the railing and striding toward the mansion. Candric grabbed the man's arm, stopping him. Apep whirled on him, shooting him an icy glare.

"Until my daughter breaks the law, you aren't doing a damn thing," Candric retorted. "If you do, not only am I going to fire you, I'm going to have you thrown in jail."

"Oh really?" Apep shot back, trying to yank his arm free from Candric's grasp. But Candric held fast, gripping Apep's arm with his formidable strength. Hard enough to hurt. Candric pulled Apep closer, leaning down until his face was inches from the Captain's.

"Try me," he growled.

Apep stared at Candric for a long, silent moment, then pulled his arm away, less violently this time. Candric allowed it, letting go of the man. Apep stood as tall as he could, squaring his shoulders.

"Stay," Candric ordered.

Captain Apep said nothing, but stood where he was, his fists clenching and unclenching. Candric glared at him a moment longer, then turned back to the crowd below.

"...now we see that the Empire has broken its promise to us," Tessa was saying. "They promised us the independence we had fought for...that we had sacrificed so much to earn. And yet now they take our children, stealing our magic from us. Ninety percent of our island is owned by the elites of Stridon. Our island is no longer ours. Our freedom is no longer ours. We beg and scrape for jobs, letting our owners pay us next to nothing for our hard work, while they hoard all the profits!"

The crowd booed, the sound echoing through the square.

"On this day," Tessa shouted. "We should not be celebrating our independence. We should be fighting for it!"

The crowd erupted into applause, and Tessa thrust her flag high into the air.

"She's inciting a riot!" Apep complained.

"Cheering is not rioting," Candric retorted.

"Not yet," Apep countered. "She's asking them to fight against us!"

"She's asking them to fight *for* us," Candric shot back.

"You're a fool," Apep growled. "What happens when they coming storming the mansion? When they turn into a damn mob? You're really going to let it go that far?"

"It won't," Candric promised.

Apep said nothing, turning to stare down at Tessa, gripping the railing so tightly that his knuckles turned white.

"We will be slaves no longer," Tessa declared. "We will not hand the fruit of our labors to our captors. If they want us to work, they will have to pay us what we're worth!"

The crowd roared.

"Shut it down," Apep ordered, turning to face Candric.

"No."

"I'm giving you one last chance," Apep warned. Candric ignored the man. It didn't matter what the fool said anymore. Apep didn't know it yet, but he was already fired.

198

Apep turned back to stare at Tessa, his jawline rippling. He shifted his gaze, and Candric followed it, spotting a man in the crowd, standing by the rightmost edge of the square next to a line of guards. A tall, thin man with short black hair and a goatee. There was something *off* about him, and it took a moment for Candric to realize what it was: he wasn't looking at Tessa like the rest of the crowd.

He was staring right back at Apep.

Apep nodded.

The man nodded back, then spun around, punching one of the guards in the face.

The other guards shouted, grabbing the man and pulling him past the barrier surrounding the square. He disappeared into the crowd of people beyond, just as guards began swarming into the crowd of protesters, shoving people to the side as they made their way toward the front.

Toward Tessa.

"Stop this!" Candric ordered, turning to Apep. But the Captain ignored him. Candric stepped up to the man, grabbing him by the shoulders. "Stop it now!"

"Stop what?" Apep retorted, pulling away. "One of those fools just attacked one of my men!"

"I saw what happened," Candric accused, jabbing a finger at Apep's chest. "You planted a mole in the crowd!" The corner of Apep's lip curled into a smirk.

"Prove it," he shot back, slapping Candric's hand away. Darren stepped to Candric's side, glaring at Apep.

"Touch my father again," he warned, "...and you'll regret it."

There was shouting from below, and everyone turned, seeing more guards swarming into the crowd from all sides, beating people back and making their way toward the front. One of them reached Tessa, grabbing her flag and tearing it from her hands. He threw it aside, then shoved her to the ground.

"Hey!" Darren shouted, stepping to the edge of the balcony and gripping the railing. "Stop!"

Two guards grabbed Tessa by the arms, hauling her to her feet. They pulled her away from the mansion, and she resisted, digging her heels into the cobblestones and swearing at the men.

"Stop it!" Darren shouted, turning to Apep. "Do something or I will!"

Apep smiled grimly at him.

"Go right ahead."

"Fine," Darren growled. He levitated upward and forward through the air, flying over the railing above the square, the telltale rippling of the air around him revealing his gravity shields.

Then Candric saw something in his peripheral vision, and turned to see Apep taking something out of the recesses of his uniform. A small white sphere.

Candric's eyes widened. It was a Neutralizer...a device that drained magic. A device made only in Verhan.

He turned, seeing Darren starting to fall, his son's gravity boots drained of their magic. Candric lunged for his son, leaning over the railing and reaching out to grab him. But he was too far away, and Darren plummeted helplessly toward the cobblestones forty feet below.

"Darren!" Candric cried, terror gripping him.

There was a blood-curdling scream from below, and Candric eyes went to Tessa, her arms held out to her sides by two guards, facing the mansion. She screamed again, trying in vain to break free of the guards' grasps.

A third guard rushed at her from behind, a spear clutched in his hands.

"No!" Candric shouted.

And then the guard thrust his spear into Tessa's back, its cruel point bursting through the left side of her chest.

Chapter 17

Kalibar leaned back in his chair, rubbing his eyes. He sighed, gazing across his large wooden desk at Erasmus and Goran. He'd invited them both into his spacious office in his Grand Weaver suite to brainstorm solutions to the mess they'd made – that *he'd* made – with Verhan.

So far, it wasn't going very well.

He'd seen people like Damia before. Seemingly minor players who'd risen to power by giving their people a common enemy. No matter how civilized a man was, in the end they all craved the same thing. A reason to exist...something to fight for. A mission. And no mission was more compelling – and more uniting – than the threat of a foreign aggressor. Men were born to protect their families, and their tribes. It was their very nature.

And Damia knew it.

"You're saying Lady Damia was seen leaving Verhan?" Goran asked. Kalibar snapped out of his reverie, nodding at Goran.

"My spies say she boarded a ship that left Verhan last evening," he confirmed.

"Any idea where it's going?" Erasmus inquired. Kalibar shook his head.

"Not yet."

"But why would she leave all of a sudden?" Goran pressed, clearly confused...and annoyed. "The election is in a couple of days!"

"You'd think she'd want to stay to make sure her followers were all riled up for the election," Erasmus agreed. "Leaving now doesn't make any damn sense."

"On the surface, no," Kalibar agreed. "But we can't assume anything with Damia."

"Not anymore," Erasmus grumbled. "She's been three steps ahead of us this whole time."

"Which means we have to assume she's up to something," Kalibar concluded.

"Something dastardly, the witch," Erasmus muttered, shifting uneasily in his chair. Goran shook his head, looking far from pleased.

"We're behind," he stated grimly. "We need to catch up to her, Kalibar."

"I agree," Kalibar replied. "Staying on the defensive will only benefit Damia." Much of politics was momentum, after all...and right now, Damia's momentum was considerable. She'd almost certainly already planned for whatever counterattack the Empire might come up with. Kalibar had to assume that every move he made offered Damia a devastating counterattack. He'd underestimated her once; he wouldn't dare do it again.

He needed to think things through before he acted.

"Whatever we do," Goran piped in, "...we have to make Lady Damia pay for having made fools of us. If we don't – and soon – it'll make the Empire seem weak."

"And then she'll walk all over us," Erasmus agreed.

"Yet if we attack too directly," Kalibar countered, "...it'll just confirm Damia's narrative that the Empire is out to get her. That we're out to depose her to install a sympathetic king."

"Aren't we?" Erasmus retorted with a wry grin. Kalibar sighed.

"Yes, well," he muttered. "If we're going to fight her, we need to know more about her."

"You mean we need to dig up some dirt on her," Erasmus interpreted. "She has to have some skeletons in her closet."

"And if she doesn't," Goran replied, "...we can create some, then spread the word."

"It won't work," Kalibar countered. "At this point, she can just blame the Empire for trying to smear her." He shook his head grimly. "She's in a position of strength now."

"So just because we got caught doing one thing, now we can't do anything?" Erasmus stated incredulously.

"Not publicly," Kalibar confirmed. Erasmus threw up his hands, leaning back in his chair and glaring at him.

"So what're we supposed to do, Kalibar? Send her a private letter telling her she's been a naughty girl?"

"Not quite," Kalibar replied with a smirk. Erasmus frowned at him, crossing his arms above his protuberant belly.

"You've got something up your sleeve, don't you?" he accused. Kalibar's smile broadened, and he nodded at him.

"I just might."

"Well don't just sit there," Erasmus grumbled. "Tell us what it is!"

Chapter 18

Kyle looked over the railing of the balcony three stories above the town square in front of the governor's mansion, watching as two guards grabbed Tessa by the arms, dragging her away. His heart leapt into his throat, and he glanced at Candric and Darren, who were looming over Apep in the rightmost corner of the balcony.

"Do something or I will!" Darren ordered. Apep gave the Battle-Weaver a grim smile, saying something that Kyle couldn't hear. Darren turned away from the man, multi-layered gravity shields appearing around him, and he flew upward and forward, clearing the balcony.

And then Kyle heard someone curse, and turned to see Candric staring in horror at Apep…and Ariana bolting toward the Captain with blinding speed. Apep was pulling something from his uniform.

A small white sphere.

No!

Rays of blue light shot outward from Kyle – and Ariana, and Darren – converging on that white sphere. Kyle felt the magic draining from him, saw Ariana collapse, tumbling to the ground at Apep's feet. And saw Darren's shields vanish instantly.

Right before the Battle-Weaver began plummeting toward the ground forty feet below.

Kyle *yanked* what little magic he had left into his mind's eye, weaving it into a tight knot and shoving it at Darren. A gravity sphere appeared around the Weaver, holding him in mid-air. He turned to Ariana then, streaming magic to her.

There was a blood-curdling scream from below.

Kyle followed the sound, looking down over the railing, spotting Tessa standing between two guards, her arms held out to her sides, facing the mansion. Right as a third guard rushed at her from behind, plunging a spear into her back.

"No!" he heard Candric scream.

The spear impaled Tessa, its wicked point bursting from the left side of her chest. The silver metal was smeared with blood, a crimson stain spreading rapidly over the front of her uniform.

Tessa's eyes widened in shock, her mouth opening in a silent scream.

"*Tessa!*" Candric cried.

The governor turned on Apep, who tried to back away. But he was cornered. Candric grabbed the man by the front of his uniform, lifting him clear off the balcony floor. The governor's biceps bulged out of his shirt.

"*You* planned this!" he shouted. Apep said nothing, but his lips curled into a smirk.

"I told you…" he began.

And then Candric threw the Captain of the Guard over the balcony railing, sending him plummeting toward the ground far below.

Kyle wove magic instantly, creating a second gravity sphere, this one around Apep. The Captain jerked to a stop in mid-air a dozen feet from the ground, right next to Darren.

"Ariana!" Kyle called out, spotting her rising to her feet. She looked utterly confused. "Get Tessa!"

Ariana blinked, then nodded, turning to look over the railing. Her eyes widened, and she leapt over the railing, falling all the way to the ground below. She burst forward then, reaching the guards holding Tessa within seconds. Ariana tossed them aside like ragdolls, then lowered Tessa to the ground. She turned to look up at Kyle, her pale face seeming to glow in the sunlight.

205

She shook her head.

Kyle swallowed in a dry throat, feeling numb.

She's dead.

He pushed the thought aside, trying to focus. Lowering the gravity spheres carrying Apep and Darren to the ground, he dropped his magic stream to Darren's, watching as the gravity sphere vanished. He activated his gravity boots then, flying over the railing and dropping down beside Darren. Petra followed close behind, landing and sprinting toward Tessa and Ariana.

It was then that Kyle realized that there were armed guards all around them...with weapons pointed right at them.

"Kyle, magic!" Darren cried. Kyle streamed magic to the Battle-Weaver, then created a gravity shield around himself. Darren did as well, then turned to face Apep.

"What..." Kyle began.

Apep *exploded.*

Kyle flinched as blood and body parts slammed into his shields, ricocheting off violently. Darren turned from where the Captain had been, striding toward the guards surrounding them. His dark eyes bore into the men, his lips set in a grim line.

"Darren," Petra stated, standing up from Tessa's body. "Don't..."

She flew backward, an invisible force sending her careening through the air.

A ring of fire burst outward from Darren, engulfing everything – and everyone – around him. A burst of intense heat struck Kyle, flames parting around his shields, and around a large gravity shield protecting Ariana and Tessa. But the guards surrounding them weren't so lucky. They screamed as the ring of fire struck them, their clothes and flesh igniting instantly as they were thrown back into the crowd of protesters surround them. The crowd panicked, fleeing as the guards fell to the ground, their screams echoing across the town square.

"Darren, stop!" Petra ordered, hovering above the flames. A beam of light shot out from Darren toward Petra, who flew to the side, dodging the attack. Darren ignored her, turning toward the fleeing crowd…and a few remaining guards escaping with them. Bolts of electricity shot outward at the guards, and they fell to the ground, their limbs twitching uncontrollably. Darren flew toward them, his mouth set in a grim line.

A gravity field sucked him backward, and he neutralized it a split-second later, turning to see Petra flying after him.

"Stand down," she warned, "…or else."

"Don't stand in my way," Darren growled. "My sister was right…they're all corrupt. They deserve to die!"

"Maybe so," Petra conceded. "But you will not be their executioner."

"Who's going to stop me?" he inquired, giving her a withering look. "You?"

Kyle hesitated, glancing at Petra. If she used too much magic, she'd have to get more from her Reaper vines…and he knew the consequences that entailed. He stepped forward, facing Darren.

"No," he stated. "*I* will."

Darren's eyes went to Kyle, and he hesitated.

"My quarrel isn't with you," he stated. "You know I hold you in the highest esteem, Kyle."

"Then listen to us," Kyle pleaded. He gestured at the burnt corpses of the guards strewn across the square. "Most of these men didn't do anything wrong."

"They were complicit," Darren argued.

"You don't know that."

"This is war now," Darren insisted. "Between the people and the Empire. *They* chose the wrong side."

"This isn't war," Petra countered. Darren glared at her.

"Tessa tried peace," he shot back. "My father tried peace. They both failed." His jawline rippled. "I won't."

"Don't do this," Kyle pleaded. "You're a good person Darren."

Darren swallowed visibly, then shook his head.

"That's what they count on," he replied. "That's why they win. Because we have to be good and they don't."

And then he turned to the soldiers twitching on the ground, and set them on fire.

Kyle wove magic, sending a veritable waterfall cascading over the soldiers, snuffing out the flames instantly. Darren whirled to face him.

"Don't," he growled. "I'm warning you."

Kyle grit his teeth, feeling anger rising within him. He used it, pulling huge cords of magic into his mind's eye. Darren was far more experienced, and a highly-trained Battle-Weaver. But when it came to sheer power...

"You don't want to make me mad," Kyle replied. "Trust me."

He saw the telltale flash of blue at Darren's forehead as the Battle-Weaver began to weave, and wove rapidly himself, thrusting the throbbing knot of power outward at the man. A large gravity shield appeared around Darren, so powerful that it glowed bright blue. Darren's eyes widened, and he wove magic rapidly...but to no avail. The Battle-Weaver only had the small bit of magic Kyle had given him...there was no way he could break past that powerful barrier.

Darren's lips moved, but no sound came out. The gravity shield surrounding him was airtight. Which meant that it was only a matter of time before the oxygen ran out.

"Ariana," Kyle called out. Ariana stood up from Tessa's body, walking up to him. "Drain him of magic, then detain him." She nodded.

"Got it."

A dozen gravity shields appeared around her, turning bright blue as Ariana poured magic into them, burning through her limited supply until there was little left.

Then her shard activated.

Blue cords of light shot outward from Darren, converging on Ariana. The gravity shield trapping Darren vanished, and Darren flew upward and backward, but Ariana was quicker, leaping after him. His shields vanished, his gravity boots deactivating as she drained the last of his magic. She caught him in mid-air as he fell, landing feet-first onto the ground, then shoving him onto his back, pinning him with one hand on his chest. He struggled, gripping her arm and trying to pry it from him, but it was no use; he might as well have been wrestling a statue.

"Get off me!" he shouted.

Kyle heard shouting behind him, and glanced back to see the near-abandoned town square...and a virtual army of guards running down the street toward them. One of the guards who Kyle had rescued sat up, waving at the oncoming guards.

"They killed the Captain!" he cried, turning to point right at Kyle. "Watch out...they're Weavers!"

Then Kyle saw blue light shooting backward from his arms, and turned around to see a guard standing at the open front double-doors of the mansion, holding a white sphere.

"Void sphere!" Kyle warned.

Ariana slumped on top of Darren, and Kyle cursed, flinging a stream of magic her way. Then he wove magic – or at least he tried to. After being drained twice, even he had barely any magic left. He cursed, turning to Petra.

"I'm almost out!" he warned. Petra nodded, flying up to him and pulling him to her side. A gravity shield appeared around them...just as the first of the guards reached Darren.

"Kill the Battle-Weaver!" one of the guards cried, rushing at Darren as he got to his feet. The guard thrust his spear at Darren's chest, the cruel tip gleaming in the sunlight.

A small, pale hand grabbed the shaft of the spear, stopping it dead in its tracks.

"Leave," Ariana ordered. She squeezed, the shaft bending, then snapping under her ungodly grip. She threw the broken piece to the side, flinging it so hard that it flew over a hundred feet in the air, sailing over city block after city block until it vanished from sight. She shoved the guard backward with one hand, sending him flying into his compatriots, knocking them over like so many bowling pins.

The guards around them stared at Ariana, their jaws dropping.

And then blue light shot outward from her, and she dropped like a stone...again.

209

"The Void sphere!" Kyle cried, turning to see the guard still standing by the mansion's double-doors. "Stop him!"

He tried to weave magic, but there was none left this time...and the other guards were getting to their feet, rushing after him. Petra's gravity shield had vanished temporarily, but she recreated it, grabbing Kyle's hand and pulling him toward the guard with the Void sphere. An invisible force knocked the guard back, and he dropped the sphere.

"I'll get the sphere," Petra stated. "You get Ariana!"

Kyle felt magic filling his mind's eye, quickly redistributing to the bones of his skull. Petra was giving him magic. With her Reaper uniform preventing magic loss, even the Void sphere couldn't drain her very much. He nodded, breaking away from her as her shields vanished. He wove magic of his own, creating a shield around himself...and facing the line of guards rushing at him. Ariana was nowhere to be seen...and neither was Darren.

"Stop!" he cried. But the guards ignored him, and one of them ran up to him, thrusting their spear at his chest. The weapon ricocheted off his gravity shield, and the guard stumbled to the side. Another guard reached him, trying to ram him with their shoulder...to similar effect. More guards ran at him, forming a circle around him, their spears pointed at him.

"Stand down!" one of them ordered.

Kyle stared at their spears, then at their armor, their metal breastplates and greaves glittering in the sunlight. He reached into his pocket, feeling the cubes he'd placed there. The magnetobombs and gravity grenades he'd created.

He threw one over the guards' heads, then shot a stream of magic to it.

"Runic!" one of them cried.

And then the guards' spears flew out of their hands, shooting toward the cube. The soldiers were next, tumbling to the ground, then sliding backward toward the cube, which bounced off the ground a few times, rolling to a stop at one corner of the square. The guards – and their weapons – slid over the cobblestones after them.

Kyle searched for Ariana, but all he saw were the burnt bodies of the guards that Darren had killed. No Ariana…and no Darren. One or more of the guards must've taken her and ran.

"She's not here!" Kyle called out, walking back to Petra, who'd taken out the guard with the Void sphere. She held it in one hand, glancing at the guards Kyle had neutralized – still stuck in the magnetobomb's field.

"She was taken," Petra replied grimly.

"There isn't much magic on Meros," Kyle warned. "Ariana won't be able to recharge." Which meant that if he didn't get to her, she'd be as good as dead. "We need to find her soon. Let's fly," he suggested. "We can get a bird's-eye view of the city."

Petra nodded, and they both flew upward, rising high above the rooftops. Kyle looked down, scanning the streets. Protesters were fleeing across the main street leading away from the city, but he didn't see any guards among them.

"Do you see her?" Kyle asked.

"No," Petra answered. "She could be anywhere," she warned.

"The guards couldn't have gone far," Kyle reasoned. "We could split up and sweep the area."

"Too dangerous," Petra countered. "They could have more Void spheres."

Kyle nodded grudgingly, then scanned the nearby streets again. There were lots of buildings all around them, and Ariana could've been taken into any one of them. It would take forever to search them all…and by the time they did, Ariana might be taken far away.

"Damn it," Kyle swore. He stifled a yawn, feeling suddenly exhausted. It had to be from using so much magic; he focused, sweeping his gaze over the town square again, then frowned. There was something…*off* about it, but he couldn't figure out what it was.

Then he saw it.

"Petra," he called out, pointing in the center of the square. There was a faint blue light there, so subtle as to be almost invisible.

"What do you see?" Petra asked.

"Something's down there," he stated. "Something magic."

They lowered themselves to the ground, and Kyle faced the blue light.

"Ariana?" he asked, stepping toward it. She might've used the invisibility field to...

And then something appeared.

"What the...!" Kyle blurted out.

It was a person, he realized. A man kneeling on the ground, clad from head to toe in full platemail armor... a night-black breastplate, helmet, gauntlets, and boots, with plates of deep purple armor everywhere else. He held a huge black shield in his left hand, with a white skull carved out of what appeared to be a single block of crystal in the center. In his right hand, he held a huge, black, spiked mace. Small runes were carved into his armor, his face hidden behind a full helmet in the shape of a skull. He wore a long cape over his shoulders, black on the outside and dark purple on the inside.

And there, lying motionlessly at his feet, was Ariana.

The man glanced up from Ariana, staring outward from the eye-sockets of that macabre helmet, his dark eyes focusing right on Kyle. Kyle glanced at Petra and Ariana, backing away from the man.

"Who are you?" Petra demanded, crossing her arms over her chest. The armored man's head turned slightly to face her.

"I am Gundar," he answered, his voice deep and gravelly. He looked down at Ariana. "She sleeps when she has no magic," he observed, seeming surprised. "Is she a Chosen?"

"Why are you here?" Petra pressed, ignoring his question. Kyle noticed blue light streaming from Gundar's body – very faintly – converging on Ariana. She began to stir. "I asked you a question," Petra growled.

The white crystal skull on Gundar's shield flash bright white, and rays of blue shot outward from Kyle, Petra, and Ariana. Ariana ceased moving, and Gundar lifted his gaze to Petra.

"I am here to take you."

Petra's eyes narrowed.

"Take us where?" she demanded.

"To your execution."

Petra took a step back, gravity shields appearing in layers around her. She clenched her fists.

"You'll find that harder to accomplish than you might think," she warned.

"Perhaps," Gundar replied. "Perhaps not."

"I'll give you one chance to stand down," Petra stated.

"A noble offer," he replied in that gravelly voice, inclining his head slightly. "I decline."

"So be it."

She flew forward with incredible speed, charging at Gundar. He intercepted her with his huge shield; the air in front of the shield rippled, a shockwave bursting out from it. Petra's shields vanished, and she shot backward, flying through the air above Kyle's head and slamming into the wall of the mansion twenty feet behind him. Luckily she'd managed to create more shields around herself before the impact; she ricocheted off the wall, then righted herself, coming to a stop in mid-air.

"Not bad," she admitted. "But I won't be so easy on you next time."

"Your time is limited," Gundar countered calmly.

"We'll see about that."

"I meant it literally," Gundar replied evenly. "A sedative was placed in your drinks."

Petra blinked, and Kyle glanced at her. They'd both drank the smoothies Candric's butler had offered them.

"You're bluffing," Petra accused. Gundar shrugged.

"Wait and see."

Kyle swallowed in a dry throat, backing up a step. He remembered how tired he'd felt just a minute ago. Indeed, he felt that same exhaustion even now...stronger than before. He stifled another yawn, feeling his eyelids growing heavy.

"Petra..." he warned. She glanced at him, her eyes widening.

"Kyle!" she cried out, flying toward him.

His legs wobbled, and he lowered himself onto his butt, so tired now that he could barely keep his eyes open.

213

"Kyle, stay with me," Petra urged. He felt her hands grip his shoulders, shaking him. He nodded, closing his eyes for a moment. But when he tried to open them, it was impossible to do so. His whole body felt like lead, his limbs so heavy he couldn't lift them.

He heard the *wump, wump* of heavy footsteps approaching him, and then he passed into oblivion.

Chapter 19

The hot sun beat down on Darren's scalp as he ran after the crowd of protesters fleeing the mayhem in the town square. He peeled off the black top of his Weaver uniform, throwing it aside as he sprinted toward the group ahead. He heard shouting from behind, and resisted the urge to look back, catching up to the nearest protesters and slowing down to be among them. He settled into a quick walk, continuing down the long street leading away from the governor's mansion.

More shouting from behind, fainter now. He closed his eyes, a vision of his sister coming to him. Of her standing in the town square, proudly holding the flag of Meros.

Of that guard's spear bursting through her chest.

His eyes snapped open, a wave of nausea coming over him. He resisted the urge to vomit, gritting his teeth and forcing himself to keep walking.

She's dead.

Darren's vision blurred, and he wiped moisture from his eyes, taking a deep, shuddering breath in. He felt a hand on his shoulder, and turned to see a young woman walking beside him, her eyes equally moist.

"I know," she said. "We all feel it."

He swallowed past a lump in his throat, nodding silently. There was no way he could tell her the truth. That none of them was feeling what he felt.

She's dead, and it's all my fault.

One of the most talented young Battle-Weavers of his generation, and he'd just stood there as the City Guard had murdered her. Just watched as they executed her in the streets. If only he'd acted sooner, if only he'd flown off of the balcony a few seconds earlier...

I let her die.

He felt another wave of nausea threaten to overtake him, and fought it, swallowing a surge of bitter fluid.

"Darren?"

He flinched, turning to his left. Another woman was walking beside him, staring at him.

"Darren!" she exclaimed. "Oh my god, I'm so sorry. I..." Tears welled up in her eyes, and she shook her head mutely. It took him a moment to realize that he'd seen her before...earlier that morning, at the Resistance headquarters where he'd visited Tessa. It was Gia, Tessa's second-in-command.

"Thanks," was all he could manage. His voice cracked, and he turned away from her, staring at the backs of the people walking in front of him.

"I still can't believe they did it," Gia admitted. "I mean, I expected them to arrest her. Even she expected it. But to *kill* her?" She shook her head. "It had to be a rogue guard, someone who..."

"No," Darren interrupted. She stopped, staring at him. "It was Apep, he explained. "It came straight from the top."

"You can't be serious," she countered. "Even *they're* not that corrupt."

"Apep was right there on the balcony with me," he retorted. "He even used a Neutralizer to drain me of magic while it was happening."

"My god," Gia said, her eyes widening. She put a hand over her mouth, a look of horror on her face.

"They're all corrupt," Darren muttered. "They were willing to kill Tessa to stop you. They were even ready to kill me," he added. He'd have fallen to his death from that balcony if it hadn't been for Kyle.

Gia lowered her gaze, staring at her feet as she walked. Then she looked up at him again. This time, her eyes were steely.

"We can't let them get away with this."

There was a shout from ahead, and Darren turned toward the sound. A full head taller than everyone around him, he was able to see two guards ahead; they ran toward the group of protesters, brandishing their spears.

"Shit," Gia swore, grabbing Darren's arm. "We have to run!"

"No you don't," he countered, feeling the *hum* of magic in his skull. He didn't have much, but he had enough. "You don't have to run anymore."

He pushed his way through the crowd, reaching the front of it and striding toward the guards, now only twenty feet away. They ran toward him, their spears glittering in the sunlight.

"You're under arrest," one of them yelled. "Get down on the ground, all of you!"

"On what charge?" Darren replied, forcing his voice to remain calm. He stopped, holding a hand out to signal the protesters to stop behind him.

"I said get down on the damn ground!" the guard shouted, walking right up to him and pointing his spear at Darren's chest.

"On what charge?" Darren repeated. He pulled a strand of magic into his mind's eye, weaving rapidly.

"Disturbing the peace," the guard stated. "Inciting a riot."

"As I recall," Darren countered, "...it was *you* who disturbed the peace. You know, when you murdered my sister."

The guard blinked, then glanced at the other guard nervously.

"That's right," Darren stated. "You're pointing your spear at a Battle-Weaver."

The guards stepped back, their eyes widening.

"It's never about the law, is it?" Darren inquired, taking a step toward them. "It's always about power. Who has it, who doesn't."

He smiled grimly at the two men. "And you thought *you* had the power now, didn't you? You thought you could just walk up to these people and charge them with bullshit crimes. Throw them all in jail, right?"

"Now hold on a second," one of the guards stammered. Darren put a finger to his lips.

"Shhh," he admonished. "Don't talk. It's not your turn anymore."

"We…"

"I said shut up," Darren growled. The guard's mouth snapped shut. "You had your chance," he admonished. "Now it's our turn."

"Just calm down," the guard urged, leaning down and setting his spear on the ground.

"Already tried that, remember?" Darren retorted. "My Dad was calm when the Empire stole me from my sister. My sister was calm when you murdered her."

"I didn't…"

"No, you didn't," Darren interjected. "Your government did. And you're complicit. I was too." He shook his head, feeling the knot of power pulsing in his mind's eye. "Not anymore."

"We can work this out," the guard pleaded, continuing to back away from him as he advanced. Darren felt a hand on his shoulder, and spun around to see Gia there. She shook her head.

"This isn't what Tessa would want," she told him. "She didn't believe in violence."

"Well they *do*," he retorted, pointing at the guards. "And now Tessa's dead."

"We need to do this the right way," Gia insisted.

"You mean *their* way," Darren shot back. "They don't get to murder us anymore, Gia. They don't get to do whatever they want and get away with it."

"Darren…" she began.

"Who's with me?" Darren shouted, gazing at the crowd of protesters. "You can fight for your freedom, or you can beg for it. Choose."

A full third of the crowd raised their hands, splitting from the others.

Darren turned back to face the guards, his lips set in a grim line.

"Darren, don't!" Gia pleaded.

"Come on," the guard he'd spoken to earlier pleaded. "It doesn't have to be like this."

"Too late," Darren growled. "This isn't a negotiation anymore," he added. "My sister was...*we* were celebrating our independence from Verhan today. And by tonight, we're going to celebrate our independence from the Empire."

"You can't..."

"Oh yes I can," Darren retorted. "Like I said, this isn't a negotiation." He felt the magic within him growing, the bones of his skull refilling with power. "This," he added, shoving the knot of power outward at the guards, "...is war."

* * *

Kyle groaned.

He opened his eyes, realizing he was lying on his side on a hard wooden floor. He was sprawled out by the rear wall of a small room, no more than ten feet wide and twice as long, with long wooden planks making up the floor and walls. A single closed door stood before him.

He heard a creaking sound, and felt as if the floor was tilting. He felt suddenly nauseous, and groaned again, picking himself up off the floor. It was then that he realized his wrists and ankles were bound by metal cuffs, with chains attached to them bolted to the wall behind him.

What the heck...

Kyle closed his eyes, trying to remember what'd happened. How he'd gotten here. A vision of him sitting next to Ariana on the balcony of the governor's mansion came to him...and of Tessa being murdered. A crushing guilt threatened to overwhelm him.

I should've saved her.

219

He rejected the thought immediately, knowing that he'd spent the last of his magic to save Darren from falling to his death. There'd been no good decision…no way to save them both. But he *had* given Darren magic afterward…and the Weaver had used it to murder all of those guards. Innocent men that had nothing to do with Tessa's death.

You couldn't known, he chided himself. But that hardly made him feel better. He still had the blood of innocent men on his hands, even if by proxy.

He felt the room tilt again, ever-so-slightly, and felt another wave of nausea.

There was a sound to his left, and he turned his head, spotting someone laying on their side on the floor a few feet away from him, their back to him. A woman in a jet-black uniform, with skin nearly as dark.

Petra!

Kyle pushed past his nausea, trying to walk to her. But he reached the ends of his chains quickly, pulling them taught.

"Petra!" he called out. But she didn't answer. She was snoring, he realized. He remembered the armored man who'd attacked them – the man who called himself Gundar.

They poisoned our drinks!

"Petra," he called out again. Still no response. He resisted the urge to do it again, knowing full well that someone could be listening. Better if they thought he was still unconscious. He needed time to think…and to regain his full magic power. Focusing inward, he *pulled* at the magic within his skull.

There was nothing there.

He frowned, trying again. Still nothing. Then he glanced at Petra again, noticing the tiniest ray of blue light shooting upward from her head. He followed the light upward, spotting a large white crystal embedded into the wooden ceiling a few feet above his head.

A Void crystal.

He cursed, lowering his gaze to Petra. With her Reaper vines, she was the only one who could possibly generate magic despite the Void crystal. Unless he could somehow slow the magic draining from his body, that was; he'd done so by covering himself with dirt in the past, insulating himself against magic loss. But there was only a thin layer of dust on the floorboards, hardly enough to be useful.

There was another creaking sound, followed by the nausea-inducing sensation of the room tilting yet again. At first he thought it might be a side-effect of the sedative he'd been slipped. But he'd felt this sensation before...and recently. It took him a moment to realize why it was so familiar.

I felt it on the Defiance, he realized. *We're on a ship!*

And then the door burst open.

Kyle flinched, lowering himself to his hands and knees. Four soldiers walked through the doorway, each dressed in purple chain-mail armor, with swords sheathed at their hips. Then a fifth person walked through the doorway...but it was no soldier.

It was a woman.

She was tall, even taller than the soldiers around her, and quite slender, wearing a simple white shirt sleeveless shirt and loose pants. Her skin was as dark as Petra's, and she had long, curly black hair that sprung wildly from her head. Her eyebrows were thin and arched, and one of them rose as she stepped toward Kyle.

"Well well," she murmured in a smooth, breezy tone, stopping a few feet from him. "The son of Kalibar awakens."

"Where am I?" Kyle demanded, glaring up at her. "And where's Ariana?"

The woman smirked, putting her hands on her knees and bending over until her eyes were level with his. A faint, sweet smell of flowers came to him.

"Now now," she chided, her eyes twinkling. "No need to be rude, darling." She stood up, gazing down at him. "You don't look anything like your father...not that I'm surprised," she added. "Kalibar's made it quite clear that he's impotent."

"I asked you a question," Kyle shot back.

"You asked me two," she corrected.

"So answer them."

"So demanding," she murmured with a little smile, putting her hands on her hips. "Very well. My name is Lady Damia. You're on my ship, a few miles off the coast of Meros."

"And Ariana?"

"Hmm?"

"My friend," Kyle clarified.

"You mean your sister," she corrected. "I'm afraid she's dead."

Kyle hesitated, realizing that this woman might not know Ariana's true nature. But Gundar had suspected she was a Chosen, so it was very likely that Lady Damia was aware of the possibility.

"Where is she?" Kyle pressed.

"Oh, I don't know," Damia answered with a shrug. "I had my men deal with her body. I imagine they did what they always do with dead bodies."

"And what's that?"

"Throw them into the ocean, of course," Lady Damia replied. She put a finger to her lips then, frowning slightly. "Though of course, if my Gundar is correct, and your 'sister' is a Chosen..." She arched an eyebrow at Kyle.

He stared back at her silently, refusing to take the bait.

"...then I suppose she's as good as dead anyway," she continued dismissively. "Can't scour the entire ocean for her, can you? And with no magic in the sea...well," she added, shrugging again. Kyle glared at her, straining against his chains.

"You didn't," he retorted. Still, a bolt of fear shot through him; if she *had* thrown Ariana overboard, then she was almost certainly right. There'd be no getting her back.

"True," Lady Damia agreed. "But my men might have. I suppose you'll have to ask them...not that you'll get a chance to."

"Let me go," Kyle ordered.

"But I'm not done with you yet," she replied, smiling down at him. "You've been *remarkably* useful, I have to say. Thank you for attacking those guards earlier. Such an unexpected and wonderful twist! I never imagined things would go so well."

Kyle frowned.

"What are you talking about?"

"Why, that whole fiasco back at the town square," she clarified. "Do you know how long it took me to arrange all of that? It was a lot of work, let me tell you. A symphony of murder, with so *many* people coming together to play their parts. And they all did wonderfully...especially you, my little one."

"Wait," Kyle said. "*You* did that?"

"Goodness no," she stated. "I had others do it for me. I'm a...conductor, if you will. I choose the music, the musicians...and they all play on my command."

"*You* had Tessa murdered?"

"Of course."

"But why?" Kyle demanded. "She was just trying to help her people!"

"So small-minded!" Damia declared, *tsking* at him. "Think of the big picture, darling." She paused, eyeing Kyle for a moment. "I'm going to have to spell it out for you, aren't I?" She sighed. "Ah well, I suppose you're just like your father then...woefully unprepared to play the game."

"What are you talking about?"

"I *supported* Tessa," she explained. "Gave her money...and lots of it. Set her up in a beautiful old church I own through a few...intermediaries." She leaned down, smiling at him. "If it weren't for me, her little Resistance would've been nothing."

"But why would you support her just to kill her?" Kyle pressed.

"Please understand, I supported the City Guard as well," Damia revealed. "A few bribes to the right people can go a long way. I pitted the guards against the Resistance for years, building them both up, watching as tensions escalated. As they went from peacefully co-existing to blaming each other for threatening to ruin the country they loved. A little push now and again, a little more kindling added to a smoldering fire, and *poof*," she stated, extending her arms out wide. "You ignite an inferno."

"You bribed Apep?"

"Oh no," Damia answered. "You never bribe a true believer, darling. Apep was more than willing to hate those upstart protesters...and to place a mole in the crowd, one of his guards in plainclothes, like I suggested. Through intermediaries, of course."

"And the guard who stabbed Tessa?" he pressed.

"One of my men, naturally."

Kyle lowered himself to sit on the floor, his chains rattling as he did so. He lowered his gaze to the floor, shaking his head slowly.

"Are you surprised?" she inquired. He looked up at her, seeing her smirking at him. "People are so *easy* to control, you see. Not individuals, of course...that's harder. But *groups* of people, ahhh...that's different. All you have to do is plant a few loud voices on either side, make them blame each other for all their problems. Then you fan the flames and watch them all burn." She smiled, kneeling down and putting a hand on Kyle's cheek. He jerked away from her cool touch, and she smirked. "Like my dear husband used to say," she added, "...divide and conquer."

"But I still don't get it," Kyle stated. "Why do all of this? What's the point?"

"The point is," Damia replied, standing back up, "...the Resistance has a martyr, the Empire will see the Resistance as the enemy, and now – thanks to you, by the way – the Grand Weaver's children are wanted criminals."

"*What?*" Kyle blurted out. "We're not criminals!"

"You helped Tessa's brother murder all those *helpless* guards," Damia countered. "And now half the City Guard will swear that you killed them yourself."

"That's a lie!"

"It hardly matters," Damia retorted. "People think you did. And that story will be repeated and repeated until it *becomes* the truth. And now, if Kalibar tries to rescue you, he'll be accused of using his station to subvert the law."

Kyle's eyes widened, a chill running through him. She was right, of course. He shook his head at her.

"You can't do this!"

"Oh but I already have," she corrected. "Your daddy has already all but handed me the crown. And now that the Empire has illegally assassinated the leader of the Resistance in Meros, all of the other chapters will rise up against the Empire in protest against their oppressor." She chuckled. "Kalibar's going to have his hands full with a full-on civil war…all the while having to choose between his office and his children. And all," she added, gesturing at herself, "…because of me. Beautiful, isn't it?"

"You're sick!" Kyle spat. Damia raised her eyebrows.

"Now you sound like my husband," she replied evenly. She sighed then, feigning sadness. "Rest his poor, tortured soul."

"Let us go," Kyle warned. "Or else."

Lady Damia's eyebrows rose, and she took a step back from him, putting her hands on her hips again.

"Or else what?" she inquired. "You'll get your daddy to come rescue you?" She laughed, a melodic sound that matched her beauty, but not her personality.

"He *will* come for us," Kyle warned. "He's done it before."

"Oh I hope he does," Damia replied. "That would be *marvelous.*"

"Not for you," he retorted.

"I beg to differ," she countered. "In a couple of days I'm going to be Queen of Verhan. If Kalibar tries to attack me, it'll be an act of war."

"Kidnapping us will be too," Kyle pointed out.

"Oh, I doubt it," she replied. "Kalibar would never risk the lives of hundreds of thousands of soldiers for one little boy." She sighed then. "That's why I'm going to have to kill you."

Kyle's eyes widened.

"What?" he blurted out.

"Nothing personal," she stated. "You're just a little, itty-bitty pawn in a very big game. And sometimes pawns need to be sacrificed."

"What are you talking about?"

"My people," she answered, "…the great citizens of Verhan, are all riled up. They hate the Empire now, thanks to you."

"Why?"

225

"Seems they still haven't forgiven you for viciously attacking one of our military vessels to save that pirate ship," she explained. "Murdering all those innocent sailors...*tsk tsk*."

"We didn't..."

"Oh but you *did*," she countered. "And as their future Queen, I can't very well deny them justice, can I?" She smiled then. "So, on the day of my coronation, I'm going to give them a little gift."

Kyle's eyes narrowed

"What gift?"

"Why you, of course," Damia revealed. "I'm going to stand you up in the Royal Mall in front of thousands of my people," she added. "And watch them cheer as I have your head separated from your shoulders."

Kyle felt another chill run down his spine, and he bolted upward and forward, stopped less than a foot away from her by his chains. He struggled against them, gritting his teeth.

"You can't do this!" he yelled.

"Oh but I can," she countered. "I can do whatever I want," she added. "I'm going to be Queen, after all." She gave him one last smile, then turned about, nodding at her soldiers. They began to move toward the door, but she stopped them, walking up to one of them and putting a hand on his shoulder. "Hold on now," she stated. "You've had a long day boys, haven't you? All cooped up in this ship with nothing to do."

The soldier glanced back at his colleagues nervously, then nodded. She smiled at him.

"Aww," she murmured. "You must be *terribly* bored."

Again, he nodded. Damia slid her hand down his arm, then dropped it to her side, turning to glance down at Petra, still lying unconscious on the floor.

"She's beautiful, isn't she?" Damia murmured, her gaze lingering on Petra. "Remarkable, really." She turned back to the soldiers, giving them a wicked smile. "Why don't you boys take her upstairs and...relax for a while?"

The men grinned, exchanging glances.

"Don't you dare hurt her!" Kyle shouted, straining against his chains, his heart pounding in his chest. Lady Damia turned to face him, arching one eyebrow. She seemed to consider this, then nodded, turning back to the guards.

"Listen to the boy, will you boys?" she stated. "Be gentle...but not *too* gentle. Wouldn't want her to have to wonder what'd happened to her while she was sleeping, would we?"

The guards' smiles broadened, and Lady Damia smiled back at them.

"Go on now," she urged.

Two of the guards strode to Petra's side, their boots *thumping* on the wooden floor. They unchained her, then lifted her up by the arms, dragging her across the floor and through the doorway. It was only then that Kyle saw a circlet around Petra's head, with a white crystal embedded in it at the center of her forehead. The rest of the guards followed, and Damia watched them go, waving at them.

"Have fun," she called out after them.

"Stop!" Kyle cried, pulling at his chains as hard as he could. He cursed, reaching into his mind's eye for a sliver of magic. He *pulled* as hard as he could, a sharp pain lancing through his skull as he did so, but it was futile. He had no magic whatsoever.

"Oh Kyle," Damia murmured, walking up to him and kneeling down, putting a hand on the back of his head. He tried to jerk away, but she gripped his hair tightly, holding him in place. She reached out with her other hand, sliding the backs of her fingers against his cheek and smiling at him with that infuriating way she had. "There's no stopping me now. You can fight all you want, but in the end, I'm going to win. I've waited such a long, long time for this," she added. "And now that I'm finally free, I'm going to enjoy it."

Chapter 20

The twelve members of the Council sat around the large circular table in the center of the War Room, Kalibar and Erasmus sitting side-by-side with them. Elder Runic Goran had called an emergency late-night meeting of the Council to discuss plans to deal with the situation in Verhan. Everyone seemed to have a different idea as to how to deal with Lady Damia, and, as usual, no one could agree on the specifics. And no one had asked Kalibar – or Erasmus, for that matter – their opinion. No doubt because they blamed Kalibar for being in this situation in the first place.

It was maddening.

"All right," Erasmus declared, standing up from his chair. He slammed both palms down on the table, glaring at the Councilmen. "Enough!"

All eyes turned to the portly Grand Runic.

"Your plans suck," he stated. "So there's no point in wasting all of our damn time arguing over them."

Elder Runic Goran glared at Erasmus, crossing his arms over his barrel chest.

"I'm sorry," he replied. "Did you have a better idea?"

"I do," Erasmus confirmed. Goran's eyebrows rose.

"Well then by all means," he stated. "Do tell."

Erasmus glanced at Kalibar, who nodded at his old friend. They'd both agreed that Erasmus should be the one to tell the Council of their plan. After what had happened, the less it seemed like it came from Kalibar, the better.

"We all know that Damia is going to become queen of Verhan," Erasmus began. Councilman Mudd's eyebrows rose.

"Only if we let her," he retorted. Erasmus glared at him.

"Because intervening the first time worked so well?" he shot back. "Let's say we *do* try to stop her. Then what? She knows we will, and she'll just use any attempt we make to show her people that the Empire is still trying to meddle in their election. That Verhan's enemy is so damn terrified of her becoming queen that we'll do anything to stop her."

"So we just let her become queen?" Councilman Hewes inquired incredulously. "That's your plan?"

"If you want my plan," Erasmus retorted, "…you'll quit interrupting me every two seconds."

"Our apologies," Councilman Goran interjected. He gestured at Erasmus. "Please go on."

"The goal now should be to build a strategy to manage Damia as queen of Verhan," Erasmus stated. "We have to castrate her, if you will."

"Poor choice of words," Councilwoman Hess replied with a smirk. "Or are you forgetting you're dealing with a woman as a ruler for once?"

Erasmus glanced at her, his cheeks turning pink. But he cleared his throat, trying his best to ignore her.

"We all know Damia's type," he continued. "And there are really only two ways this is going to play out. She's either just using anti-Empire sentiment to win the crown, after which she'll come around to being more pro-Empire, or she won't." He sighed. "And I have a feeling she won't."

"I have to agree," Goran said. "As long as she has an enemy, she can use the narrative of oppression to oppress her people for her own gain."

"The dictator scenario," Kalibar stated grimly. He'd seen it far too many times before. Dictators conjuring up false enemies to divert their own people from realizing that *their* country was their enemy.

"So antagonizing Damia directly will only increase her power," Erasmus continued. "We'll only be confirming that we're the enemy, just like she said. And then the fools will believe *anything* she says."

"To what end?" Councilwoman Hess inquired. "She's not stupid enough to risk a war with us."

"Of course not," Erasmus agreed. "We're more powerful than Verhan. Declaring war with us would threaten her rule…something she'd never stoop to."

"So again," Councilwoman Hess pressed, "…what's her endgame?"

"Diamonds," Kalibar answered. All eyes turned to him. He glanced at Erasmus, who nodded slightly. "Verhan has the largest diamond mines in the known world," Kalibar explained. "And peridot, and so on. For many countries in Orja, Verhan is their major source of precious gemstones. Without those gemstones, those countries won't be able to compete with the Runic technology of their neighbors."

"And since gemstones are by far the major export from Verhan," Erasmus concluded, "…Verhan's economy is absolutely dependent on them."

"I assume you're going to explain why this is relevant to her making us the enemy?" Councilman Mudd asked.

"I was getting there," Erasmus grumbled. "By creating enemies, she'll destabilize the region. Countries that worry about impending conflict spend more on their militaries. And their militaries…"

"Are dependent on large-volume runic weapons and armor," Goran deduced. He nodded, running a hand through his black beard. "Increasing demand for diamonds, and thereby raising the prices."

"And increasing her power," Erasmus agreed.

"So what's our strategy?" Councilman Mudd inquired.

"We isolate Verhan," Erasmus answered. "Make trade agreements with her neighbors, and sell them runics to bolster their militaries. Make them stronger, and they'll be threats to Verhan...and they won't need her diamonds as much if we're providing weapons to them."

"What about sanctions?" Goran inquired.

"Likely to backfire," Kalibar piped in. "They'll feed the narrative of oppression. We need to seem as neutral as possible toward Verhan, while establishing stronger alliances with her neighbors. If we isolate Verhan politically and cut her exports by increasing trade with her neighbors, her rhetoric won't matter."

"And after a while, people outside of Verhan will see her for the extremist she is," Erasmus concluded.

"Making her rhetoric a liability rather than an asset," Councilwoman Hess concluded. She nodded, issuing a rare smile. "Very clever."

"A good plan in theory," Goran agreed. "But it's the details that matter. Do you have a specific..."

There was a knock on the door, and everyone turned toward the sound. A moment later, a man strode into the War Room. He was tall, with long blond hair and green eyes, clad in black and silver armor and a long black cloak. It was High Weaver Urson, Kalibar's second-in-command when it came to his Battle-Weavers. Urson saluted sharply, his eyes locking on Kalibar's.

"Yes High Weaver?" Kalibar inquired, suppressing his annoyance at the interruption. Urson was as far from a fool as a man could be, and would not have interrupted the meeting without excellent cause.

"I need to speak with you, Grand Weaver," Urson stated crisply.

"Now?" Kalibar pressed.

"It's extremely urgent," Urson replied.

Kalibar sighed, pushing himself back from the table and standing up.

"Continue without me," he stated, nodding at Erasmus. Then he followed Urson out of the War Room, striding down the hallway. At length, Urson stopped, turning to face him.

"What's going on?" Kalibar asked.

"We have a situation on Meros," Urson answered.

A chill ran down Kalibar's spine, and he stared at Urson silently, feeling an all-too-familiar twisting sensation in his guts. He'd heard this tone from Urson before...when the man had revealed that Kyle and Ariana had escaped the Tower to travel to Verhan on the *Defiance* weeks ago.

"A local anti-Imperial terrorist group calling themselves 'the Resistance' protested during a parade near the governor's mansion," Urson explained. "The protesters attacked the guards, and their leader was killed during the scuffle. A fight broke out, and..."

Kalibar frowned at Urson; it was unlike the man to hesitate.

"What is it?" Kalibar asked.

"Sources say your children murdered over a dozen guards," Urson revealed, his tone grim. "Including the Captain of the Guard."

"*What?*" Kalibar blurted out. "That's preposterous!"

"My sources are reliable," Urson insisted.

"Where are they now?"

"Unknown," Urson answered. "The protesters fled, and your children and Petra are missing."

"Damn it!" Kalibar swore. He slammed his palm against the wall, making a loud *bang*. Urson just stood there, staring at him. Kalibar took a deep breath in, letting it out slowly. "Find them," he ordered. "Send Battle-Weavers to Meros and bring my children home."

"Yes Grand Weaver."

"And Urson," Kalibar continued.

"Yes?"

"My children did *not* murder anyone," he insisted. "I want you to find the truth. Gather evidence. I will not have my children endangered by these lies."

"Of course, Grand Weaver," Urson replied. He hesitated for a split second. "One more thing," he added. "I've just received word that Lady Damia's ship has been located."

Kalibar frowned; it took him a moment to switch gears, to remember that Damia's ship had been seen leaving Verhan the day before.

"Where is it?" he asked.

"Docked," Urson replied. "On Meros."

* * *

High Priest Kilson watched Jag as the man strode out of the Chamber of Communion, slamming the door behind him. Then he sighed, lowering himself to sit cross-legged on the plush prayer-pillow beneath him, setting his staff to one side. A necessity given his rapid weight loss; the hard stone floor of the chamber was too painful to sit on now that his flesh hung from his bones. A hidden cancer was eating away at his body, consuming him from the inside out. He sighed, closing his eyes for a moment, feeling a familiar emptiness in the pit of his stomach.

I've failed.

It was the same lamentation he always had after meeting with his wayward son. The same pattern that had plagued them ever since Jag had rejected the ways of the Priesthood. He'd always been a stubborn child, questioning everything. There was a bitterness inside the boy, an unwillingness to accept the possibility of a higher power. Of something greater than himself and his petty desires. That bitterness, that unwillingness to open himself to faith, had led him down a terrible path. A path of loneliness, of self-centeredness. The boy's – the *man's* – constant sarcasm betrayed his inner pain, the rift he'd created between himself and his roots.

And Kilson knew that, in the end, *he* was to blame for it.

I'm sorry my son, he thought, opening his eyes. He hesitated, then grabbed his staff, standing up and walking to the door. He opened it; beyond, he saw his daughter Sasha standing guard. Always the guardian, she. His protector. Jag's younger sister, she was everything that Jag was not. Kind, thoughtful, and in touch with her faith. *She* understood. She'd taken the pamaté within her body, had experienced the will of the Goddess.

233

"Father," she greeted, putting a hand on his shoulder. He grimaced; as much as he treasured her love for him, he hated any reminder of how frail he'd become. Loathed the bones protruding from his shoulders, covered with paper-thin muscles. He tolerated her touch, knowing that she was not disgusted by him, even if he was disgusted by himself.

"I'm alright," he reassured, forcing a smile. He turned his gaze to Jag, who was far down the hallway ahead, and retreating quickly. "I could use your help," he added.

Sasha glanced at Jag, then slipped her arm around Kilson's waist, walking forward with him. They followed far behind Jag…far enough that his son wouldn't know he was being followed.

"He's still the same?" she asked. Kilson sighed.

"I'm afraid so."

"You tried your best," she soothed. "He'll never see the truth. He doesn't want to."

"I know."

"It would destroy his anger," she continued. "He can't risk that…it's all he has now."

Kilson nodded, knowing that she was correct. Jag had built his entire life around the certainty that his father was wrong. That Kilson was foolish and naïve, clinging to a dying religion, praying to a false god. And even though Jag didn't realize it, everything he did – every terrible thing he'd done – was a result of that bitterness. An overwhelming need to prove his father wrong. To hurt Kilson in any way he could. It was not out of hatred, but out of fear.

Fear that Kilson could be right. That there *was* a true god.

And that, Kilson knew, was the real reason Jag refused to take the pamaté. For if he did so, and felt the presence of the Goddess, there would be no denying Her presence. His wall of pain would come crashing down.

They walked together, arm-in-arm, making their way after Jag, who would be rejoining the Imperial researchers soon, making their way to the Depths below.

"How long are you going to let them get away with this?" Sasha asked.

"I don't know," he admitted. He felt her tense up, and glanced at her. Her eyes were hard, her jaw rippling.

"Hasn't it been long enough?" she pressed. It was not a question, he knew. If it'd been up to her, Kilson would've confronted Jag long ago.

"The day your brother betrayed me," he replied wearily, "...was long enough."

"And yet we do nothing," she retorted angrily.

"They're taking trinkets," he countered dismissively. "Worthless junk."

"It may be junk to us, father," she retorted. "But it's advanced Runic technology to them."

"True," he admitted. He patted her on the small of the back. "Don't worry," he added. "The Empire will get what's coming to them soon enough."

"What about Jag?" she inquired. "Will he ever pay for his betrayal?"

Kilson sighed, turning to look out of one of the windows as they passed by. The high wall of the Citadel was visible in the distance, an impenetrable barrier created by the gods, an everlasting monument to their genius. Countless civilizations had risen and fallen since its creation, everything outside of the Citadel changing while the home of the gods remained forever the same. It was the one constant in this world, a reminder of a time when Man was ruled by beings whose wisdom far exceeded theirs. A time when Man would gaze up at the Citadel from afar, knowing that there was something greater than they, a power beyond their understanding. That humility was gone now, replaced by a selfishness that poisoned everything they did. Children left to themselves inevitably became rotten, just as Mankind had become.

Just as his son had become.

"He will," Jag promised.

Sasha stared at him as they continued down the hall, her beautiful eyes searching his. She had faith, he knew. Faith in his wisdom, that after years of communion with the last of the great ones, the Creator herself, he would possess the wisdom to do what was right.

It was an honor to be held in such esteem. He only wished that Jag could see as she saw. Could believe as *she* believed.

"When?" she inquired.

Kilson raised his gaze to the ceiling, to the sculpted godstone far above. Ten thousand years ago – a *hundred* thousand years ago – this ceiling had looked the same. The godstone was eternal, created by the gods themselves. It would be here long after he was dead, remaining even after everything that Man had created fell to dust. The gods themselves had stared up at this ceiling; that fact gave him a strange sense of peace. That something would endure the passage of time. That it could never be destroyed.

"In due time, my love," he replied wearily. "In due time."

Chapter 21

Kyle strained against his chains, watching as Lady Damia and her guards exited his makeshift cell, closing the door behind them. He heard a *click* as the door was locked, and then footsteps walking away.

"Let me *go!*" he shouted. He pulled against his chains as hard as he could, the metal bands encircling his wrists cutting into his skin. But it was no use...they were bolted to the wall behind him. He cursed, clenching and unclenching his fists, despair threatening to overtake him. Those guards were bringing Petra upstairs right now, and it wouldn't be long before...

Calm down, he told himself. *You need to think.*

He closed his eyes, forcing himself to breathe more slowly. Then he opened his eyes.

Okay.

Panicking wouldn't get him anywhere...and neither would brute strength. The only chance he had at helping Petra and Ariana was to *think* his way out of his predicament.

He turned around, staring at the chains bolted to the wall. If he had magic, he could rip the chains out. But with the Void crystal in the ceiling...

Kyle looked up, spotting the white crystal embedded in the ceiling. It was well out of reach...he couldn't get to it. He lowered his gaze, staring at his feet. No one made as much magic as he did, but he had none. That meant that the crystal was draining him faster than he could make magic. He had to reduce the rate at which magic was being drained from him. Insulating himself wasn't an option, not without access to dirt to cover himself in. So what else could he do?

He reached into his pockets, finding his crystal cubes still there; the magnetobombs and gravity grenades he'd brought with him. But like him, they were drained of magic...and therefore useless.

Closing his eyes again, he tried to remember what the late Master Banar had taught him. The slender Runic had been his first Runic teacher, the one who'd introduced him to the concept of magic vacuity. Transfer of magic between two objects was a function of the difference in magic between them, the magical vacuity of each object, and the distance between them.

His eyes snapped open, his heart skipping a beat.

Distance!

He looked up again; the Void crystal was directly above him. There was just enough slack in his chains to move a few feet to one side; he did so, then lowered himself to the floor, lying down on his belly and resting his forehead on the floor. He closed his eyes, focusing on his mind's eye, and waited. He forced himself to be patient, knowing full well that with every second that passed, the danger to Petra grew ever more dire.

Come on...

Focusing inwardly, he *pulled* at the bones of his skull...and saw a slender thread of magic pull into the center of his mind's eye.

Yes!

Still he waited, feeling his bones slowly filling with magic. He'd need more if he wanted to have a chance at breaking his chains. It wasn't long before he felt the power within him growing; he rolled onto his back then, studying where the chains were bolted to the wall. Four chains connected to a metal plate, which was bolted to a thick wooden beam of the wall.

Now what?

Heating the chains with the fire pattern wouldn't help, and it might set the room on fire. The light pattern wasn't helpful, and neither was the invisibility pattern. He might be able to pull the bolts out with a strong gravity field, but it might take the wall down with it. But the magnetic pattern could work, as long as the bolts had magnetic metals in them. He tested it, weaving a small amount of magic and sending it outward at the chains. They all pulled inward toward the magnetic field.

All right, he thought. Pulling more magic into his mind's eye, he wove the magnetic pattern again, this time throwing it out just before the metal plate. He streamed magic to it, pouring as much as he could for one large burst.

There was a loud *crack,* and the plate and bolts flew free of the wooden post, slamming into the opposite wall so hard they left dents in it.

Yes!

Kyle got to his feet, resisting the urge to go immediately to the door. He needed more magic…especially if he was going to take on those guards. He walked to one end of the room, as far away from the Void crystal as he could get. As predicted, magic began to fill his mind's eye at a more rapid pace. He stood there, picking at his fingernails, shifting his weight from foot to foot.

Come on…

An image of Petra came to him…of what those guards might be doing to her.

Kyle strode to the door, his chains trailing behind him, and opened it, seeing a long hallway ahead with closed doors on either side. He activated his gravity boots and created an invisibility field around himself. The gravity fields generated by his boots sucked his chains to his body, holding them against him. Which was all for the better, as they'd make a heck of a lot of noise otherwise. Then he levitated forward, cracking open each door as he passed and peering through.

The first room was empty; the second had two soldiers sleeping on a bunk bed. Kyle closed their door quietly, moving down the hallway. There were two more doors were on either side; he checked these, and found more soldiers sleeping inside.

It must be night-time, he reasoned.

Further down the hallway were two more doors, the last pair before a door at the end of the hallway. He checked the one to his left, but it was empty. He went to reach for the door to his right…

…and saw blue rays pulling outward from his arm, shooting forward into the door.

Another Void crystal, he reasoned. *Or…*

He hesitated, then pushed the door open, peering inside. There was a medium-sized room beyond, with two empty bunk beds. He spotted something on the floor by the far wall. Not something…some*one*. A figure lying on the floorboards. The rays of blue light were converging on this person; Kyle deactivated his gravity boots, stepping into the room and closing the door behind him. He strode up to the figure, then gasped.

It was Ariana!

He rolled her onto her back, then frowned. Someone had put a circlet around her head…one with a single white gemstone in the center of it, directly over her forehead. Another Void crystal, he knew…his magic was draining right into it. And so was Ariana's. With the circlet on, Ariana was effectively neutralized.

Kyle pulled the circlet from her head, and almost tossed it aside. But then he paused. Better to destroy it, or at least throw it into the sea. That way, no one could use it against her again. But if he carried it, he couldn't be able to wake Ariana…

You don't have time for this!

He climbed up to the top bunk of one of the bunk beds, shoving the circlet under the mattress. Then he dropped down, grabbing Ariana and sliding her as far away from the circlet as possible. Faint rays of magic issued forth from him toward the circlet…and slightly brighter rays converged on Ariana's forehead. She was draining him too.

Her eyelids fluttered, then opened.

"Shhh," Kyle warned, putting a finger to his lips. Her pupils converged on his face, and she blinked, then nodded. "We've been taken," he whispered. "We're on a ship. Petra's in trouble…we need to hurry!"

Ariana nodded again.

"Can you find her?" he asked. "She's with three guards." Ariana nodded a third time, her eyes unfocusing. She was listening, he knew; with her incredible senses, she could hear someone's heartbeat from across the room…and voices several stories above and below.

"I don't hear her," she whispered.

"She *has* to be here," Kyle insisted. "They said they were taking her upstairs."

"I know her heart," she explained. "It beats slower than most peoples'…like Kalibar's." She paused to listen. "She might be too far away for me to hear."

That made sense, Kyle knew. Both of them were the most physically fit people he'd met. But if Ariana couldn't hear Petra's heart, that either meant she was too far away…or something far worse.

"Come on," he urged. Ariana got to her feet, and he led her to the door, being sure to stay close to her. As long as she was close to him and far away from the circlet, she'd absorb his magic and stay awake. They stepped into the hallway, and Kyle led her toward the door at the end of it.

"There's guards in the rooms behind us," she warned. "They're sleeping."

"I know," Kyle replied in a whisper. "Ahead?"

"Two guards beyond the door," she answered. "And more above."

"I need more magic," he cautioned. She gave a grim smile.

"I don't."

She shoved the door open, bursting through the doorway!

There was a short, wider hallway beyond, with stairs leading upward at the other end…and two guards standing in front of it. Their eyes widened as Ariana dashed toward them, their hands going to the hilts of their swords.

They never had a chance to draw them.

Ariana rushed at the first guard, punching him square in the chest so hard that it left a dent in his metal breastplate. He flew backward, and hadn't even struck the ground before Ariana hit the other guard. Both of them fell to their backs on the floor, clutching at their chests, their eyes wide. Unable to breathe.

"Let's go," Ariana urged, making her way to the stairs ahead. Kyle following, glancing at the two soldiers she'd beaten. If he just left them there, they'd eventually recover…and alert Damia. But the only alternative was to kill them.

He hesitated, then ran after Ariana, taking the steps two at a time. There was a shout from behind, and he glanced back to see more soldiers pouring through the doorway they'd entered the room through. He grabbed a cube from his pocket, charging it with magic and tossing it behind him. The guards were sucked toward it violently, slamming into each other as the cube – a magnetobomb – pulled them into itself.

"That'll hold them for a while," Kyle stated, continuing up the stairs. The magnetobomb would not only hold them in place…it would also suck in anyone else that tried to come after them.

They reached the top of the stairs…and skid to a halt.

A long, narrow hallway greeted them, another stairwell going upward at the far end. And more soldiers standing in the middle of it. They turned to stare at Kyle and Ariana, then reached for their swords. Ariana stepped forward, but Kyle held her back with one outstretched arm.

"I got this one," he said.

And then he wove magic, creating a magnetic field in front of him. He shoved it through the soldiers, watching as it passed between them, sucking them backward and inward into itself. They screamed, landing on the ground in a heap, their limbs jerking uncontrollably. Nails shot out of the walls, floor, and ceiling, slamming into the soldiers. A portion of the ceiling collapsed, planks falling down to the floor with a clatter.

Ariana sprinted forward, leaping over the heap of soldiers and continuing toward the stairs ahead. Kyle ran after her, glancing at the soldiers as he passed. They'd stopped convulsing, and were just lying there, eyes wide open, foam at the corners of their mouths.

That's strange, he thought.

He sprinted to the stairs after Ariana; they led to a door at the top. She stopped before it, leaning against the door and closing her eyes.

"What do you hear?" he whispered.

"Just wind," she answered. "Come on."

Then she opened the door, stepping through the doorway…and froze. Kyle bumped into her from behind, and heard her sharp intake of breath.

"What?" he asked.

She grabbed his hand, pulling him through the doorway. The sky opened up before him, low, heavy clouds lit an angry red-orange from the setting sun. A chilly wind howled in his ears, whipping through his hair and clothes. He found himself standing on a long, broad wooden deck, nearly as large as the *Defiance's* had been. But something was wrong; the sails were down, secured to their masts…yet the island of Meros was nowhere to be seen.

He turned in a slow circle, feeling the deck tilt to the left slightly, throwing him off-balance. Luckily Ariana was holding his arm, and kept him on his feet. There was only the deck…and a two-story building behind them, probably the Captain's bridge. He gazed to his right, looking beyond the side of the deck, to the ocean.

Except it wasn't there.

"Uh…where's the ocean?" he asked.

Ariana shook her head, squeezing his hand tightly.

"I don't think this is a ship," she warned.

"What do you mean?" he asked. "It sure *looks* like a ship."

She didn't answer, but walked toward the rightmost edge of the deck, pulling him along with her. They reached the edge, and they both looked down over it. Kyle's eyes widened, and he gasped.

For there, where the ocean should have been, there was only a sheer drop…to the ocean thousands of feet below.

"Holy…" he blurted out. And then he heard a *thump* behind him. He turned around, spotting a dark figure standing in the center of the deck a few dozen feet away, silhouetted against the red-orange sky. A man wearing thick black and purple armor, carrying a huge mace in one hand and a massive shield in the other. A shield with a white skull carved of a single block of crystal in the center of it.

"We meet again," a deep, gravelly voice boomed over the howling of the wind. An all-too-familiar voice, one that set the hairs on the nape of Kyle's neck standing on-end. He swallowed in a suddenly dry throat, his heart hammering in his chest.

"Gundar," he replied.

And then the deck between them exploded.

* * *

At first there was darkness.

Then came the images, flashing in Petra's mind's eye, one melting into the other almost too quickly to process. Visions of trees, of her parents, of Mount Grimore. Of a man with a white, diamond-shaped crystal in the center of his forehead. Then of her brother laughing.

They came and went, fragments of memories, jumbled together in a vivid, ever-changing collage. Time meant nothing. She had no thoughts, only visions.

And then came the voices.

They seemed familiar, but far away. It was impossible to tell if she was hearing them or if they were memories of voices she'd heard. They spilled one on top of the other, senseless, without meaning.

She became aware of her body then, floating in the air. Felt hands gripping her arms and legs. She was moving, she knew. The *thunk, thunk* of footsteps came to her ears, boots drumming on a wooden floor.

The images in her mind's eye faded, her thoughts slowly coming into focus. A profound exhaustion gripped her, the desire to fall back into oblivion threatening to overtake her. She resisted it instinctively, fighting against that powerful urge. For it seemed unnatural, this compulsion. It was foreign to her, a force that sought to control her.

She fought it because she was a wild thing, born of the forest. She would *not* be tamed.

Her thoughts crystallized, the urge to sink into unconsciousness fading. She heard more voices, masculine voices. Coarse laughter, hands gripping her limbs more tightly. She heard grunting, then felt herself falling onto something soft.

The hands gripping her vanished, the voices becoming clearer.

"...clothes?" she heard a voice ask.

"Just cut them off," a gruff voice replied.

There was silence then. Darkness swam before her, and she realized that her eyes were closed. Her eyelids were heavy, so much so that even the idea of opening them seemed overwhelming.

She felt hands on her waist then, and a tugging on her Reaper uniform at her neck. There was a *thump*, the sound of something heavy landing on the floor to one side of her. She heard laughter, and felt a sudden jolt of fear. A realization that something was very wrong. She was in danger.

Petra focused, years of training kicking in. Day after day of honing her concentration, of perfecting discipline. She knew immediately that she'd been drugged, because she'd been drugged before. Had done it to herself many times, knowing that her tribe's enemies might try to do it to her. Forcing herself to be able to fight past it.

She felt a sharp pinch at her neck, heard the sound of a blade sawing against the fabric of her uniform.

Petra felt adrenaline course through her, her mind clearing instantly.

Her eyes snapped open, and she saw a man straddling her on a small bed, sawing at her uniform with a small knife. Two other men stood on either side, staring down at her, each in the process of pulling off their armor.

She reacted instantly, grabbing at the first man's wrist, pushing the knife to one side. He swore, fighting against her, obviously thinking he was stronger than she was. That he could overpower her.

He was wrong.

She brought one knee up as hard as she could, striking the man in the butt and forcing him to lurch forward over her. His head slammed into the wall behind the bed, and he grunted, his body going lax. She twisted to the left, shoving him off of the bed, and he landed on the floor with a *thud*.

The two other soldiers swore, frantically reaching for their swords lying on the floor.

Petra felt a pressure on her forehead, and reached up, feeling a thin metal band encircling it. She pulled the thing off, tossing it aside, then reached into her mind's eye for magic.

But there was none.

One of the men grabbed his sword, pointing it at her.

"Stop!" he shouted.

She rolled off the bed, landing on the soldier she'd pushed off earlier. Then she scrambled to her feet, facing the two soldiers. They both had their swords now, and were closing in on her.

"Get back on the bed *now*, bitch," one of them ordered.

Petra focused inward, on the *others* within her. The Reaper vines whose roots had embedded themselves into her skull, promising her a nearly infinite supply of magic…at a terrible cost. She made her request of them, and was answered with a sharp, excruciating pain that shot through her temples.

Power flooded her mind, magic overflowing the bones of her skull. She reached into the river of magic there, shaping it with her will, then throwing it outward.

The room *exploded*.

The men flew backward so violently they smashed *through* the far wall. The wooden planks of the floor and ceiling tore off, flinging outward from Petra even as she began to levitate above them, gravity shields appearing around her. The bed flew aside as well, smashing into the wall.

And as quickly as that, it was over.

Petra stared at the hole in the far wall, at the motionless bodies of the men who'd attacked her. Then she turned to the closed door leading out of the room she was in. There were voices beyond, men rushing to see what was going on.

The door flung open, soldiers rushing into the room.

Petra wove again, and a bolt of electricity shot out from her, slamming into the nearest soldier, then arcing to the next one, then the next. They flew backward, landing on the floor, their limbs convulsing. She levitated over them, flying through the doorway, finding herself in a hallway beyond.

More soldiers rushed toward her, their swords drawn.

She ignored them, looking upward at the ceiling, dipping her mind into the stream of magic within her, shaping it.

The ceiling above her exploded, and she flew upward through the hole she'd made, finding another hallway above her. She smashed through the ceiling there, accelerating upward...and emerged into the night air, low-hanging thunderclouds painted with orange and red by the dying sun greeting her.

She slowed her ascent, looking down to see a large wooden deck ten feet below her...and the ocean far, far below that. It took her a moment to realize where she was.

I'm on a ship, she realized. *An airship!*

Petra focused, spotting movement down below on-deck. Two figures standing near the edge right below her, facing a third figure standing in the middle of the airship. It was Kyle and Ariana, she realized...staring at a very familiar man. The man who'd attacked them back in Meros, before the sedative had claimed her.

"Petra!" she heard Kyle cry.

And then the skull on Gundar's shield flashed bright white.

Chapter 22

"Governor!" a voice cried.

Candric groaned, feeling hands gripping his shoulders, shaking him. He felt a flash of irritation at being so rudely awoken, and pushed the hands away, rolling onto his side. But the hands returned, shaking him again.

"Come on Candric," the voice urged. A gruff woman's voice. "Wake the hell up!"

And then his face jerked to the side as he was slapped full across the face.

He grunted, rolling onto his back again. The mattress was hard underneath him…far too hard. It wasn't a mattress at all, he realized.

It was the floor.

Candric opened his eyes, seeing a middle-aged woman keeling over him, her hands on his shoulders. It was Bae, his secretary. She looked uncharacteristically frazzled.

"There you are," she stated, sitting back on her heels and looking immensely relieved. "Get up sweetheart. We have to go…now."

"What?" Candric muttered, rubbing his eyes. He *was* lying on the floor…in his office, he realized. A few members of his staff were around him, all looking down at him.

All of them terrified.

"What's going on?" he demanded, sitting up. He felt a little woozy, and closed his eyes, waiting for the sensation to pass. Then he opened his eyes again, taking Bae's hand. She helped him to his feet. He glanced out of one of the windows, seeing the sun setting far in the distance, ominous clouds hanging in the darkening sky.

And then he heard a loud *bang*.

He jerked his head toward the sound, realizing it was coming from the door…and that his desk had been shoved against it.

"Open up!" a voice ordered from behind the door. "By order of the City Guard!"

Candric stared at the door, then at Bae, whose expression was grim.

"The city guards infiltrated the mansion," she warned. "They're coming for you."

"Why?" Candric demanded. He tried to remember what'd happened before he'd woken up, but his memory was foggy. He felt…scattered. Unfocused.

Then the door burst open, shoving his desk back a few feet, and guards spilled into the room, spears in their hands.

"Protect the governor!" Bae cried, throwing herself between Candric and the guards. Benton, his ever-faithful butler, came between them as well. One of the guards pointed his spear right at Bae.

"Step aside," he ordered. "We're taking the governor into custody. Anyone who gets in our way will be arrested."

"On what charge?" Candric demanded, pulling Benton and Bae aside and facing the guard. He was significantly taller than the guard – than all of the guards – and much stronger. His arms were bigger than their legs, shaped by years of rigorous exercise. The guard stared up at him, his confidence clearly faltering.

"Governor Candric," the guard replied, "…you are hereby charged with attempted murder, and conspiracy against the Empire."

"*What?*" Candric retorted. "I've done no such thing!"

"I saw you throw our captain off your balcony myself," the guard shot back. "And I saw your son destroy him."

Candric stared at the man, his fists clenched at his sides.

"Captain Apep was a traitor," he countered, forcing his voice to remain calm. "He engaged in conspiracy to start a riot. He had my daughter murdered!"

"Bullshit," the guard retorted. "Apep was right…you've been in league with the Resistance all along!"

"Is that what he told you?" Candric growled, taking a step forward. He stopped inches from the man's spear, glaring down at him. The guard stood his ground, but Candric saw beads of sweat on the man's forehead.

"Right before you tried to murder him, yes."

"I was acting in self-defense," Candric retorted. "Apep was in possession of a Neutralizer – illegally, mind you – and used it against my son and Grand Weaver Kalibar's children. My son almost fell to his death!"

The guard glanced at his fellows, shifting his weight from one foot to the other. Then he shook his head.

"Bullshit," he shot back.

"Is it?" Candric pressed. "What do you think Grand Weaver Kalibar is going to do when he finds out what you've done? What your precious *captain* did?"

"He'll thank us for protecting Meros from the Resistance," the guard shot back. "And arresting the traitor who conspired with them."

"You sure about that?" Bae interjected, crossing her arms over her chest. But the guard ignored her.

"You're coming with us," the guard growled. "We can do this the easy way, or we can do it the hard way. Your choice."

Candric stared at the man silently, his jawline rippling. If he allowed himself to be arrested, he'd be thrown in jail, and await trial…potentially for weeks, or longer. It was almost certain that many guards would testify against him…and with that many "credible" witnesses, he'd be hard-pressed to defend himself in court. He would almost certainly lose…and spend the rest of his life behind bars.

A vision of Tessa came to him, of the last thing he'd said to her. The final promise he'd made.

What if your way doesn't work, she'd asked.

I'll do it your way, he'd answered.

And he'd failed…not only to save his people, but to save his only daughter.

It was over, he knew. He could be governor no more. The guards were corrupted, many without even realizing it. Apep had won, turning them against him. Even after his death, the captain had gotten his revenge.

So be it, Candric thought.

He burst into action, grabbing the guard's spear and yanking the man forward. Then he swung his elbow at the guard's temple as hard as he could.

The man dropped like a stone.

Candric turned the spear around, stabbing at the nearest guard's face. The guard blocked the blow just in time, stumbling backward. Benton lunged for the man, knocking his spear aside and tackling him to the ground.

"For the governor!" the butler cried.

The other staff members burst into action, grabbing nearby objects and throwing them at the guards. The guards cursed, one of them rushing at Candric with their spear, thrusting at his belly. Candric dodged to the side, feeling a sharp pain in his belly as the tip of the spear grazed him. He ignored the pain, shoving the point of his spear into the man's face. It buried itself into the guard's left eye socket, making a sickening *crunch* as it thrust through his skull into his brain.

The guard fell to the ground, dead.

Another guard rushed at Benton, who was still wrestling the first guard who'd attacked Candric. Candric intercepted him, thrusting his spear at the man's chest. It bounced off the guard's metal breastplate, and the guard counterattacked, thrusting their own spear at Candric's chest. Candric managed to block the spear to the side, throwing the man off-balance.

And saw the guard Benton had tackled throw Benton off, grabbing his spear and scrambling to his feet.

"Benton, get back!" Candric cried, rushing at the guard, swinging his spear like a bat at the man's head. The guard ducked the blow, then thrust his own spear.

Right into Candric's right shoulder.

Candric cried out, stumbling backward. Another guard rammed into his side, throwing him onto the ground…then jabbed his spear at Candric's chest.

Then flew to the side as Bae smashed into him, tackling him to the floor.

Candric grunted, rolling onto his belly, then getting to his feet, ignoring the pain in his shoulder as he did so. He ran up to the guard Bae had tackled. The guard had managed to wrap his fingers around her throat, and was choking her.

Candric kicked the man in the temple. Hard.

The guard's head snapped to the side, but he clung on to consciousness, squeezing Bae's throat as hard as he could. Her face turned beet red, her eyes wide, vessels bulging in her forehead.

"Let go!" Candric shouted, kicking the man in the head again. But the guard held on tight. Candric knelt down, grabbing the man's temples and jabbing his thumbs into the guard's eyes. He pushed as hard as he could, feeling his thumbs slipping inward, hot blood welling up from the man's sockets.

The guard *screamed*.

Candric managed to pull Bae free from the man, and helped her to her feet. He heard a shout, and turned to see a guard rushing at him with a short sword. He swore, shoving Bae out of the way just as the man swung at him. The cruel edge of the sword glinted in the light of the magic lanterns, chopping downward at an angle toward Candric's neck.

"Governor!" he heard a voice cry.

And then Benton leapt in-between Candric and the guard, the blade slicing into the loyal butler's flesh in a spray of blood.

"*Benton!*" Candric screamed, stumbling backward. He stared in horror as his old friend fell to the floor, a massive, gaping wound extending from his shoulder all the way across his chest and belly to his opposite hip. "*No!*"

All reason left him then.

He leapt at the guard, reaching out with his bare hands and grabbing the man by the throat. His biceps bulged as he lifted the man clear off the floor, squeezing the man's neck as hard as he could.

Which was very, very hard.

Candric's powerful forearms rippled as he squeezed, the guard's face turning red, then purple. The man's sword fell from his hands, his eyes rolling upward.

There was a loud *crunch*.

The guard's arms spasmed, and then he went limp, never to move again.

Candric threw the man to the side like a rag-doll, his eyes wide, his breathing coming in short gasps. He spotted another guard cutting down one of his staff, and roared, charging at him like a madman.

The guard saw Candric coming, and his eyes went wide with terror. It didn't matter that he had a sword and Candric did not; there was madness in Candric's eyes. The guard was staring into the face of Death itself.

He dropped his sword and ran for the door.

Candric caught up to the guard, shoving him through the doorway into the hallway beyond. The man tumbled to the ground, and Candric leapt upon him, ripping off his helmet and holding it high in the air over his own head. He brought it down like a hammer on the back of the guard's skull, blood gushing as the man's scalp split open. Candric didn't stop, swinging the helmet again and again, smashing it into the man's skull until a large dent formed there, the guard's face buried in a pool of his own blood.

Candric chucked the helmet to the side, turning to look for his next victim. It didn't take him long to find one; the last guard, standing over the body of one of Candric's staff, spear dripping with blood.

He charged at the man.

The guard turned toward the sound, but by then it was too late.

Candric rammed into the man with his left shoulder, sending the guard flying into the far wall of the office. The guard ricocheted off, and Candric wrapped his arms around the man's waist, lifting him off the floor and turning toward one of the windows facing the town square. He rushed forward, tossing the man right at the window.

It shattered, glass exploding as the guard smashed through it. A blood-curdling scream echoed through the night air, followed by a loud *thump*...and then silence.

Candric stared at the broken window, his shoulders heaving with each breath, his pulse pounding in his ears. He looked around for something else to kill, his fists clenched so hard his knuckles were white.

But there was no one else. Only bodies littering the blood-soaked floor...and Bae, huddled in the corner, bruises already forming around her neck, her clothes spattered with blood.

Candric felt the blood-lust leave him then, the rage draining from his pores. He felt suddenly dizzy, and walked up to her, kneeling before her and reaching out to her, his hands trembling uncontrollably.

She leaned in, wrapping her arms around him, and he returned the embrace, holding her gently. Cradling her in his arms.

"It's over," he whispered, rocking her back and forth slowly. He felt her relax into him, closing her eyes and burying her face into his chest. He rubbed her back gently. "Everything's going to be okay," he murmured.

"I love you Candric," Bae replied hoarsely, patting him on the back. "But you're full of shit."

* * *

A strong, cool breeze whipped through Jag's long black hair, a sharp contrast to the warm, still air of the Temple of the Old Tree he'd experienced only seconds before. The great Wall of the Citadel stood before him, rising thousands of feet above God's Peak. Eternal. Immutable.

The only thing in this cursed world that would remain after everything else turned to dust.

He sighed, watching as men blinked into existence around him, the Empire's Runic researchers teleporting out of the Citadel now that the day was done. He ignored them, turning away from the Wall and gazing down at the island of Meros far below. The sun was already setting, casting the clouds above in a bright orange-red. It was as if the sky was on fire.

And below those clouds, he saw Osa.

It too was on fire.

He stared in disbelief at the flames engulfing the entire south end of the town. Black smoke rose from the burning buildings, rising into the air toward the angry clouds above. A chill ran down his spine. Those were the resorts, the massive buildings owned by the wealthiest men in the Empire. For one of them to be burning was bad luck. But for *all* of them to be on fire...

Shit.

He heard a gasp from behind.

"Oh my god," one of the Runics exclaimed.

"What's going on?" another asked.

Jag didn't bother to answer, reaching into his pocket and removing a spyglass. A childhood relic, one he'd once used to study the endless levels of the Citadel from his bedroom in the upper levels of the Temple. He brought it to his eye, peering through it.

It was just as he'd feared; the resorts were on fire. But not all of them. A few had been spared...and it was all-too-clear which ones.

Candric's.

Jag spotted something beyond the city, and shifted his gaze slightly. He saw the ocean within the reef, and the docks at the shore. A large ship was docked there. A Verhanian ship, obviously. But something was wrong.

It was *rising*.

He watched as it lifted out of the water, accelerating slowly upward.

What in hell?

He watched the ship for a moment longer, then lowered his spyglass, putting it back in his pocket. What a Verhanian ship was doing at port in Meros was beyond him, especially on the day of the Festival, the celebration of Meros's independence from Verhan. What a Verhanian ship was doing *flying* was even more troubling. Verhan didn't use magic…it was forbidden.

And a ship that size had to be part of the Royal Navy.

"What's going on Jag?" he heard Bopkin, the lead researcher, ask.

"Not sure," Jag answered. "But I got a few ideas."

"Like what?"

"Like you're in deep shit," Jag replied.

"What? Why?"

"See those buildings down there? The ones on fire?" Jag asked. Bopkin nodded. "Well, they're all owned by Imperial businessmen. See the ones not on fire?" Another nod. "Those are Candric's. He's a local."

"You're saying this is arson?"

"Damn right," Jag agreed. "And a whole lot of anti-Imperialists were planning to march at the Festival today."

"What does that mean?" Bopkin pressed. Jag grimaced, annoyed at the man's obtuseness.

"It means that something went wrong at the Festival," Jag replied. "*Very* wrong." He turned to face the Runic. "And it means that you and your friends better stay out of town for a while."

Bopkin swallowed visibly, then nodded.

"I see."

"After you help me get Ariana and Kyle out of there," Jag added. Bopkin frowned.

"Excuse me?"

"The Grand Weaver's kids are down there," Jag explained. "And if you and I don't make sure they're safe and sound, we'll have a lot more to worry about than a few burning buildings."

Chapter 23

A gust of wind tore through Kyle's clothes, the massive, black underbellies of the thunderclouds above flashing as lightning arced between them. A muffled *boom* slammed into the deck of the airship, drops of rain starting to fall from the sky, pelting his skin. He shivered, staring at the hole in the deck ahead...and the woman levitating above it.

"Petra!" he cried.

Petra turned to look at him, then at Gundar. The black-and-purple-armored knight stood there silently, seeming unsurprised by Petra's sudden arrival. The man's eyes – the only part of his body that was visible – flicked from Petra to Kyle, then to Ariana.

"We meet again," he stated, his deep voice somehow carrying over the howling wind.

"We were just leaving," Ariana replied. Gundar's eyes turned to her, the rest of his body as still as a statue.

"You are mistaken," he retorted.

"It is *you* who are mistaken," Petra countered, crossing her arms and glaring at Gundar. "We are not poisoned this time," she added. "I doubt you will find us such easy prey."

"Brave words," Gundar grumbled. "But I am not Lady Damia. Words mean nothing to me."

"Why do you work for her?" Kyle asked.

Gundar just stood there, rain pelting the man's armor. Another flash of lightning lit up the sky, a thunderclap blasting Kyle's eardrums. Kyle wove magic, creating a gravity shield around himself; the wind and rain vanished instantly.

"You do realize she's a psycho, right?" Kyle protested. "She's planning on murdering a couple of kids!"

"She does what she pleases," Gundar replied.

"But we didn't do anything!" Kyle pressed. Gundar shrugged.

"Life is a battle. Those that win earn the right to flourish. Those that lose are subjugated or die."

Kyle was about to respond when Gundar gripped his mace tightly, lifting it up, then slamming the butt of it onto the deck with a loud *bam*.

"I look forward to our battle," the man declared. "Fight well."

The crystal skull on his shield flashed bright white.

"*Back!*" Kyle cried, streaming magic to his gravity boots and bursting backward. Rays of blue light shot outward from his body, converging on Gundar's shield. Petra and Ariana flew back as well, connected to that shield by similar cords of faint blue. The farther they got from the shield, the weaker the light became.

A huge fireball burst outward from Petra, zooming right at Gundar.

Gundar raised his shield, and the fireball slammed into it, dissipating harmlessly. The skull on his shield stopped glowing, the rays of magic sucking out of Kyle, Ariana, and Petra vanishing. A triple-layer of gravity shields appeared around the man.

"You alright?" Kyle asked Ariana.

"Fine," she called back.

Then she burst forward, descending to the deck and sprinting at Gundar as fast as she could, a veritable blur in the darkness. Gundar pulled his shield close to himself, the runes inscribed upon it flashing blue.

A shockwave exploded outward from that shield just as Ariana reached him, melting her gravity shields and throwing her backward with deadly speed.

"Ariana!" Kyle cried. He wove rapidly, trying to create a gravity field to stop her, but she flew backward too quickly, slamming into one of the masts with bone-crunching force. She ricocheted off, landing belly-down on the deck with a *thump.*

Kyle stared at her, his guts twisting. The back of her skull had caved in, her neck twisted at an impossible angle. But as he watched, her skull re-formed, and she got to her feet, dusting herself off and glaring at Gundar.

"Not bad," she admitted. "But you'll have to do better than that."

Gundar's eyes narrowed.

"Interesting," he murmured.

A volley of red-hot fireballs shot outward from Petra, and at the same time, Gundar's gravity shields vanished, no doubt nullified by Petra's magic. Gundar stood there as the fireballs approached, unmoving as they slammed into him...or tried to. A blast of air exploded outward at the last minute, sending raindrops flying in all directions...and snuffing the flames instantly.

Ariana didn't even wait, rushing at Gundar again. A gravity field appeared to Gundar's left, pulling him toward the leftmost edge of the ship – but then his boots flashed, and he stopped sliding. Ariana leapt at him, punching him in the face...but he raised his shield, intercepting the blow. Ariana's fist slammed into the shield, bouncing off harmlessly. An explosion of lights shot outward from her automatically, her shard's defenses activating. But Gundar's armor seemed to respond in kind, nullifying her shard's attacks.

Ariana backpedaled, staring at her hand. Her wrist had crumpled with the force of the impact, bent at an impossible angle. It healed before Kyle's eyes, whole again in seconds.

"You're strong," Gundar observed, nodding at Ariana approvingly. "Sabin made you well."

"Sabin didn't make me," Ariana retorted. "And you have no idea what I'm capable of."

"Without magic," he replied evenly, "...you are capable of nothing."

The skull on his shield glowed bright white again.

259

"Back!" Kyle ordered, flying straight back. Ariana was already well out of range, Petra and Kyle following. But Gundar strode toward them, his metallic boots *thumping* on the wooden deck. A vision of the Void Chosen – the terrible being Kyle had fought on the Spine of Grimore – came to him. He'd nearly destroyed the creature, dousing it in flaming *punk* and creating an ultra-powerful gravity sphere around it. The only way the Chosen had survived was to teleport out of it...something Kyle was pretty sure Gundar couldn't do.

Alright then.

He *pulled* magic into his mind's eye, creating a gravity sphere before him, then creating a huge ball of *punk* within it. He set it on fire, then shot it outward at Gundar...and at the same time, he grabbed another thread of magic and wove the gravity sphere pattern. He threw this at Gundar, then *yanked* at the magic in the bones of his skull, pulling as hard as he could. A thick cord of magic appeared in his mind's eye, pulsing with power.

A sharp pain lanced through his temples, and he cried out, forcing himself to focus.

He threw the cord outward at the gravity sphere, streaming a torrent of magic to it, increasing its power. Power only *he* could generate...power beyond anything Gundar could have ever seen.

A sudden wind pulled at Kyle, the gravity sphere sucking inward, eager to consume everything around it. Flames shot inward, engulfing Gundar in a pressurized inferno. Planks tore free from the deck of the ship, sucked into the gravity sphere...and feeding the fire within.

A bright white light appeared within that inferno, blue light pulling free from Kyle and sucking into it.

Kyle ignored the magic vacuum, pulling more magic from his skull and sending it outward at Gundar. But a part of his magic stream diverted from the gravity sphere, pulling into the man's shield. Kyle felt the magic draining from him rapidly.

"Petra!" he cried. "I need more magic!"

But Petra didn't respond, unable to hear Kyle over the howling of the wind generated by the gravity sphere. He felt his power nearly drained, and stopped his stream, flying away from Gundar quickly…and out of range of the dark knight's shield.

The gravity sphere around Gundar vanished instantly, the flames surrounding him snuffing out. All around him, the deck lay in ruins, a hole twenty feet in diameter punched into the ship. Gundar levitated above that chasm, his eyes locked on Kyle's.

Utterly unfazed.

The skull on his shield went dark, and he nodded at Kyle.

"You are strong as well," he stated. "I've only met one other that was stronger."

"I'm just getting warmed up," Kyle lied, feeling his magic already starting to regenerate. He knew he needed time to fill his reserves…and that meant he needed to stall.

"We will see," Gundar replied…and flew upward and forward without warning, hurtling toward Kyle!

Kyle cursed, flying backward quickly, but Gundar flew right at him, swinging that massive mace at Kyle's head. Kyle cried out…and saw something slam into Gundar at the last minute, throwing him to the side.

Ariana!

Explosions burst from Ariana's shard, assaulting Gundar's armor as they both fell to the deck. Gundar slammed into it back-first, Ariana on top of him. His shield flashed, and a burst of white light shot out from it, flinging her high into the air…and setting her instantly ablaze. She arced through the night air, a fireball burning like a falling star, and fell to the deck with a dull *thud*. Kyle's heart leapt in his throat.

But then the flames vanished, and Ariana got to her feet. Half of her face was charred, her hair burnt away. But even as Kyle watched, her flesh mended, her hair regrowing.

"You know, fire used to scare me," Ariana admitted, stepping calmly toward Gundar, who was rising to his feet. She shook her head. "Not anymore."

"Yield now," Petra piped in. "You cannot win, Gundar."

Gundar glanced at her, then at Ariana.

"You impress me," he confessed. "That is not an easy thing to do."

"We warned you," Petra retorted. Gundar nodded.

"You did," he agreed. "I will remember this battle for many years to come," he added. "Long after you and everyone you know has turned to dust."

"Another idle threat," Petra replied dismissively.

"Not at all," Gundar countered. "I am eternal. Your lives will end, but I shall remain. As I have through the Ages of Man."

The skull on his shield began to glow again.

"Ariana, the sail!" Kyle cried, flying away from Gundar. He wove magic, creating a gravity sphere near the closest sail. It tore free from its mast, and Kyle flung it at Gundar, sending it billowing down over the man. At the same time, he sent a magic stream at Ariana, who dashed right at Gundar, grabbing one edge of the sail and sprinting in a circle around the knight, wrapping it around him. She stopped then, planting her feet on the deck and spinning in a circle...and spinning the sail as well. She spun faster and faster, then let go, sending the sail – and Gundar – flying off the edge of the ship.

The sail burst into flames as it fell through the night sky, arcing toward the ocean thousands of feet below.

And then the flames snuffed out, a shadow bursting from it, flying toward them with frightening speed!

Gundar shot at Ariana in an arc, rising high above the ship, then zooming downward right at her, moving so quickly he was a blur. He swung his mace overhead, bringing it down right on top of her head. The huge weapon smashed through her gravity shields, coming right down onto her skull. The sheer force of the impact sending Ariana right into the deck...and through it. The wooden planks below her shattered, a crater forming all around her.

Gundar flew upward, levitating above that crater, staring down at Ariana.

What remained of her.

Kyle's heart leapt into his throat, and he flew toward the crater, seeing Ariana's mangled head – and neck, and upper chest. He caught a glimpse of something green sticking out of what remained of her skull. A bolt of fear shot through him.

Her shard!

If it was damaged…

But before his eyes, Ariana reformed, flesh covering the shard once again. Within moments, she stood up, rising into the air above the crater, turning to face Gundar.

Who stared at her with what could only be described as awe.

"I can do this all day," Ariana stated calmly, crossing her arms over her chest. Gundar lowered his mace.

"You aren't a normal Chosen," he observed.

"Nope."

"I've never seen such magic," he admitted. "To heal so quickly. Sabin *didn't* make you."

"Nope," Ariana repeated.

"When I am done with your friends," Gundar said, "…I will drain you and study you."

"You're not done with us yet," Petra retorted.

Kyle saw blue light flash at her forehead as she wove magic, then heard a loud *crack*. The tall mast closest to her tore free from the deck, then swung downward – right for Gundar. Gundar raised his shield to intercept the huge wooden column.

A shockwave burst outward from the shield as the mast struck it, sending the mast hurtling backward through the air. At the same time, Kyle wove magic, creating another gravity sphere and sending it out at the knight. This one, however, was a *reverse* gravity field, pushing everything inside of it out…including the air around Gundar. He *pulled* a thick cord of magic into his mind's eye, throwing it at the gravity sphere.

A shimmering blue sphere surrounded the man, sucking the air out from around him instantly. As Kyle predicted, Gundar stayed put.

Kyle waited.

Gundar just stood there, staring at Kyle, not such much as blinking. Seconds passed, and then well over a minute, yet still Gundar did not fall.

There's no air, Kyle reasoned, feeling his frustration mount. *Why isn't he passing out?*

Then it came to him, a chill running down his spine.

The gravity sphere vanished.

"You cannot kill a dead man," Gundar declared.

"You're a Chosen," Kyle realized. Gundar nodded.

"The first of my kind," he confirmed. "Rendered immortal by Sabin twenty centuries ago."

Kyle glanced at Ariana, who glanced back at him. She looked terrified.

"But all of the Chosen are dead," he retorted.

"Sabin's slaves are," Gundar agreed. "We Prime Chosen are all that remains of his legacy."

"There's more of you?"

"Yes," Gundar confirmed. He lifted his mace, resting it on his shoulder. "Civilizations come and go, generations of Man rising and falling like the waves of the sea. Only we four remain."

"You're from the Barren tribes then," Petra deduced.

"I am."

"As am I," Petra revealed. Kyle turned to her, realizing that if Gundar *was* one of Petra's ancestors, then that meant they hadn't all been killed by Ampir like she'd thought. Their wisdom remained…something that Petra's tribe had sought after for thousands of years.

"Petra…" Kyle began, but Petra ignored him.

"We don't need to fight," she pleaded. "Teach us! Come back to the Barren forest and show your people…"

"You are not my people," Gundar interrupted.

"But…"

"No more talking," Gundar declared, swinging his mace downward and striking the deck before him. "Savor the next moments of your life," he added grimly. "They will be your last."

"Okay guys," Kyle stated, creating multi-layered gravity shields around himself. "Time to run."

Ariana nodded, glancing at Petra, who did the same.

"Fight or die," Gundar retorted, stomping toward them. "You cannot run."

Kyle continued to fly backward, staring at the Chosen as he lumbered toward them, his metallic armor shimmering as lightning shot down from the heavens. Then he had an idea.

Metal!

He closed his eyes, reaching into his mind's eye and *pulling* a thick cord of magic into the center of it. Weaving the magnetosphere pattern, he threw it outward at Gundar, then grit his teeth, steeling himself for the pain that was about to come.

He *tore* magic from the bones of his skull, pouring everything he had at the magnetosphere. A thick beam of blue light shot outward at it, making the magnetic field flash the brightest blue Kyle had ever seen.

"Petra!" he cried, pain shooting through his skull. His vision blackened, a wave of nausea threatening to overtake him. "Magic!"

He felt a burst of power flood his mind's eye, and redirected it to his magic stream. His vision began to clear, and he stared at Gundar.

The man's eyes were wide open, his arms pinned to his sides. The skull on his shield began to glow bright white, rays of magic pulling into it.

"More!" Kyle cried, sending a torrent of magic into the magnetic field. But though Gundar couldn't move, he did not seem hurt...and there was only so long that Kyle could keep him pinned.

Then he had an idea.

The last time he'd used the magnetic field, on the soldiers below deck, he'd shot it *through* them, and they'd fallen to the ground, convulsing. It hadn't made sense at the time, but now he knew exactly what'd happened.

It was simple physics, really.

When electrons moved – like electricity flowing through a wire – it generated a magnetic field. And when a magnetic field moved near a conductor of electricity, it made an electrical current. The soldiers had been *electrocuted*...by their own armor.

And magnetism was a far greater force than gravity…and therefore, gravity *shields*.

Kyle poured as much magic as he could through his magic stream, then flung the magnetic field to the side, well over the edge of the airship's deck. Gundar flew with it, sucked into the magnetic field's influence…and his body began to convulse, his armor glowing red-hot within seconds. Nails flew upward from the deck – and the masts, along with everything else metal – yanked from the wooden planks by the sheer power of the field. The planks burst upward as dozens of soldiers below deck were sucked in as well, hurtling into the air to the side of the airship toward Gundar.

And then Kyle could stream no more.

He cried out, collapsing in mid-air. He felt arms around him, and heard Ariana's voice calling out to him. His vision went black again, her voice muffled, unintelligible.

He felt himself rising.

Kyle's vision cleared slowly, the pain in his skull gradually abating. He stared down at the airship…or what remained of it. It was falling apart before his eyes, the metal that had been holding it together yanked out or destroyed by his magic. The giant ship disintegrated into a cluster of wooden planks, tumbling through the night air toward the ocean far, far below…and Gundar with them.

Kyle lifted his gaze, seeing Petra levitating in the air beside him. She was staring at him in disbelief.

"How did you do that?" she blurted out. Kyle grimaced, rubbing his forehead. He felt suddenly exhausted…and absolutely famished. Generating that much magic took a lot of energy.

"I'll tell you later," he muttered, activating his gravity boots and disengaging from Ariana. He glanced down at the falling ship. "We need to get back to Meros," he added. "And we need to warn Kalibar before it's too late."

266

Chapter 24

Rain fell in dense sheets from hulking thunderclouds high above the city of Osa, flooding its streets and whipping around buildings with each powerful gust of wind. That wind cast a chill over the city, draining the warmth Osa had absorbed during the day.

And braving that storm were hundreds of people, men and women who had chosen to defy the weather – and risk death by the hands of the people who had sworn to protect them. They marched down Main street, flames rising into the air behind them as the palatial resorts lining the shore burned. Resorts owned by the wealthiest businessmen in the Empire, men who had glutted themselves with the fruits of the natives' labor. Men who had taken the island from its own people, buying land and forcing the natives to work to death just to live there.

Darren marched down the street in front of the crowd, leading them down Main street toward the center of town. The people of the Resistance. The downtrodden, the oppressed.

There was shouting from ahead, a line of armed guards rushing toward them.

Darren wove magic, a gravity sphere appearing above the guards. They flew up into it, over a dozen men sucked into that powerful sphere. Darren lifted it higher into the air, until it was well above the rooftops of the buildings around them.

Then the sphere vanished, the guards plummeting to their deaths.

Darren heard gasps from the crowd behind him, and ignored them, levitating over the heap of bodies in the center of the street.

"They had a choice," he shouted without turning around. "The Empire or their own people." The crowd followed him, parting around the heap of bodies. "They chose wrong."

He spotted the governor's mansion in the distance, many blocks away...and more guards rushing down the street far ahead toward the building. His pace quickened, his lips drawn in a grim line.

He'd seen war. Fought against dictators that had sucked their countries dry, engorging themselves with riches while letting their people suffer and die. He'd seen the worst of Man. The Empire had taught him that it was different. That it was a shining beacon of hope and freedom, a bulwark against oppression and corruption. And like a fool, he'd believed it.

But not anymore.

He glanced back at the burning resorts behind him, clenching his fists at his sides. The Empire was as corrupt as any other government. But its corruption was more subtle, more sophisticated. It bled power from the people, draining their wealth and taking away anyone who could make magic. It was a nation of laws, of course. But those laws made for a rigged game.

Meros had been stolen from its people. The land was the Empire's. Its wealth was the Empire's. Its Weavers and Runics were the Empire's. And its people were veritable slaves.

But not anymore. Not if *he* could help it.

The governor's mansion loomed larger as he approached, scores of guards blocking the street ahead. They had to know who was coming for them. That Darren had magic and they did not. But they did not run...which either meant they were brave, fools, or...

One of the guards raised a hand, a white sphere clutched in it. "Stand down!" the man warned. "By order of the City Guard!" Darren shook his head, not so much as slowing down. *Fools.*

A Neutralizer could drain his magic at close range, and could prevent him from sending patterns near the guards. But dealing with Neutralizers had become part of his Battle-Weaver training, ever since the attack on Stridon by the Void spheres...and the Void Behemoth. He could still weave from afar.

Darren did just that, creating a massive ball of flaming *punk* thirty feet ahead of him...and used a gravity field to shoot it right at the guards. It sailed toward them, far too quickly for them to flee.

Too quickly for them to do anything but die.

The guards burst into flames, nearly a hundred of them splattered with sticky *punk*. Their screams pierced through the downpour as they were consumed by fire, not even the rain able to quench it. The awful stench of burning flesh reached his nostrils, and he ignored it, breathing through his mouth instead. He stopped, turning to face his people.

"They had a choice," Darren declared, sweeping his gaze over them. "We tried peace, and they killed us. We tried words, and they used spears. They took our power from us," he continued, rising into the air, levitating ten feet above the street for all to see. "Now we take it back!"

The crowd cheered, pumping their fists in the air.

"Ninety-nine percent!" they chanted. "We will represent!"

Darren turned back toward the mansion, flying forward, the crowd continuing to follow him down the street toward the burning guards littering the street. He wove magic, sweeping the bodies to one side, clearing the path for his people. They reached an intersection, and saw more guards on the side-streets. But these men made the correct choice.

They ran.

At length, Darren reached the high fence surrounding the governor's mansion, levitating over it...and weaving magic, tearing the fence down for his people. They walked on toward the entrance to the building, the double-doors already open. A guard burst out of the doorway, his eyes widening as he saw the hundreds of people marching toward him.

"Get back!" the guard shouted, brandishing his spear. "Now!"

"Make them," Darren growled from above.

The guard's gaze lifted up, and his eyes widened…right before a bolt of electricity slammed into his chest. He fell to the ground, convulsing. Darren turned to gaze down at the crowd.

"My father fought for Osa," he declared. "He fought for Meros. He obeyed the Empire's rules, played the Empire's game. And for that, they murdered his daughter."

The crowd booed, one woman wailing "Tessa!"

"They murdered my sister for exercising her rights. For fighting for *you*," Darren continued. "Now it's time we exercised our rights as people, to fight for our freedom…to fight our oppressors. And to take back what is ours!"

The crowd cheered, and Darren turned to the mansion, descending to the double-doors and stepping over the body of the guard he'd electrocuted. He strode into the foyer, his black boots *thumping* on the floor. The room was deserted, the other guards having no doubt fled the premises.

He took to the stairs leading to the third floor, the Resistance pouring through the doors after him. Up he went, reaching the third story, and found guards clustered in the hallway. The hallway leading to his father's office. Holding spears, pressing forward.

"Break down that door!" one of them barked to the others. "I want Candric alive!"

Darren cleared his throat, and the guards turned around, spotting him. He smirked.

"So do I," he stated coolly.

With a thought, they died.

Darren flew over the bodies strewn across the floor, making his way down the hallway to his father's office. He wove magic, and the door tore off its hinges. Beyond, he saw his father standing at the far end of the room, leaning against the wall with a shortsword in his hand, a middle-aged woman at his side. Candric's shirt was torn in several places, blood staining the fabric.

"Darren!" Candric cried. He limped toward Darren, dropping the sword and wrapping his arms around his son. Darren embraced his father, relief coursing through him.

"Are you okay?" Darren asked.

"Injured," Candric admitted. "But alive." He disengaged, holding Darren at arms' length. "We need to get out of here."

"I know," Darren replied. "I can take you back to headquarters."

"Headquarters?"

"Where we met Tessa this morning," he clarified. It was almost impossible to believe that it'd been only this morning that he'd seen his sister for the first time in over a decade. If he'd only know what was going to happen to her…

"I'm sorry," Candric murmured, his eyes moist. Darren swallowed past a lump in his throat.

"It's my fault," he confessed. "I could've stopped them."

"No," Candric retorted, gripping Darren's shoulders tightly. "Apep made sure of that. I thought I'd lost you too."

"Kyle saved me," Darren admitted.

"Where is Kyle? And Ariana?"

"I don't know," Darren confessed. "They disappeared after fighting the guards." He pulled away from his father's grasp. "But we can't worry about them anymore," he added. "We have to worry about *our* people now."

Candric hesitated, then nodded.

"I promised Tessa that if my way didn't work, I'd do things her way," he stated. "I'm with you."

Darren smiled, reaching in and hugging his father again. Candric accepted this, then pushed him back gently.

"The Empire *will* send Battle-Weavers – and the navy – to stop us," he warned.

"I know," Darren agreed. "I'm good…one of the best…but even I can't fight an army."

"We can," Candric countered. "And we will."

"How?" Darren asked. Dad smiled.

"The Resistance is bigger than Meros," he replied. He leaned on Darren then, limping toward the door. "Come on," he added.

Darren complied, helping his father out of the room, then down the stairs, walking out of the mansion. The stench of smoke and burnt bodies assaulted them as they emerged through the front

271

double-doors into the night air, the crowd of fellow Resistance fighters parting before them. In the distance, the line of resorts were engulfed in flames, thick black smoke rising to meet the angry clouds above.

He felt his father stiffen, and glanced at the man. Candric's eyes were locked on the burning buildings.

"What happened?" he asked, his mouth falling open. "How…?"

"I burned them father," Darren answered. "The Empire will no longer bleed our country dry, profiting off of our people. We're taking back our island."

Candric pulled away from Darren, staring at him.

"How could you do this?" he exclaimed. "Darren, there are *people* in those resorts!"

"People from the Empire," Darren retorted.

"And Verhan," Candric countered. "And other countries. They're innocent people!"

"Are they?" Darren retorted. He gestured at the burning resorts angrily. "They're helping the wealthy destroy our country!"

"They're just trying to get a break from their lives," Candric insisted. "They're on vacation, son. You can't just decide they all have to die."

"Isn't that what they did to Tessa?" Darren shot back. "They decided *she* had to die. They *decided* to rip me from my family. And when I didn't bow to their rules, when I fought back after they killed Tessa, they tried to kill *me*."

"Son…"

"No," Candric interrupted. "If we play by their rules, we give up our power. They *made* those rules, father. They made them so they'd always be able to win. I won't do it. Not anymore."

"Tessa believed in those rules," Candric retorted.

"Bullshit."

"She did," Candric insisted. "You think because you talked to her once that you know her? I talked with her plenty of times, son. Argued with her. I know what she believed, and she believed in her peoples' rights. The rights the Empire was *supposed* to give us. She

272

believed in the rule of law. She just hated that the laws had been abused by the wealthy to…"

"Make them slaves?" Darren interjected. "Allow outsiders to buy up all our land, our businesses? Meros isn't even *ours* anymore, father. The wealthy own us!"

"I'm wealthy," Candric reminded him. "I'm as wealthy as any of them."

"Then you're as complicit as the rest of them."

"Darren," Candric began, reaching out for him. He jerked back, shaking his head.

"No," he replied. "I've seen this all before. Governments rig the game, the people always lose. I won't allow it."

"This is a game you can't win with violence," Candric warned. "You're only one Weaver."

"I'll get more to join me."

"Not enough to stand against the Empire," Candric shot back. "Join me," he added, stepping forward and trying to put a hand on Darren's shoulder. Darren wove magic, creating a gravity shield around him. Candric's hand bounced off of it.

"No."

"Do it the right way," Candric insisted. "We can lead the Resistance like Tessa did. With organization, we can…"

"And let them kill us too?" Darren retorted.

"Maybe," Candric admitted. "But they can't kill all of us. And killing us will only draw more people to the Resistance."

"You go right ahead," Darren muttered. "But I won't be the Resistance's cannon fodder."

"If you go to war with the Empire," his father replied, "…then that's exactly what you'll become."

* * *

The wind howled in Ariana's ears as she flew through the rain with Kyle and Petra, raindrops scattering over their gravity shields, protecting them from the cold and wet. Neither of which bothered Ariana, who let the rain and wind assault her, hardly noticing any discomfort. Thousands of feet below, the ocean lay, endlessly churning.

And miles in the distance lay a large island, obscured by the darkness and the rain. But to Ariana's eyes, it might as well have been daytime. It took her a moment to remember that her vision was far better than Petra or Kyle's; they probably couldn't even see the island yet.

"I see Meros," she said, pointing ahead.

"How far away?" Kyle asked.

"A few miles," Ariana answered. Then she frowned. "There's something wrong," she added. Even from miles away, she could see the buildings lining the shore with remarkable clarity…and the tongues of orange coming from their windows and engulfing their roofs. Black smoke rose from these flames, rising at a sharp angle as they were carried sideways by the gusting wind.

"What is it?" Petra asked.

"The buildings at the shoreline," Ariana explained. "They're on fire."

"One may have been hit by lightning," Petra reasoned. "With this wind, the fire could spread quickly."

Ariana swept her gaze across the other resorts lining the shore. *Most* of them were on fire.

"It already has," she notified. She saw Kyle accelerate, felt the *hum* of magic as he shot forward ahead of them.

"Come on," he urged, flying forward and downward toward the shore. "There might be people trapped in those buildings. We have to help them!"

They zoomed toward the island, the howling wind rising to a shriek as they continued to pick up speed. The island grew larger as they grew closer, and even from a half-mile away, the stink of ash reached her nostrils. She wrinkled her nose, then stopped breathing. She hardly needed to breathe, after all, and only did so out of habit…and to speak.

"Only the resorts are on fire," Kyle called out. He was right; none of the other buildings nearby were.

"It looks like a lot of people escaped," Ariana noted, scanning the streets. There were crowds of people standing in a long line on the streets a block away from the resorts…and more standing on the shore in front of the burning buildings.

"Maybe not all," Kyle countered.

He swooped down toward the nearest resort – a large six-story building – cutting through the rain. As he flew over the building, a deluge of water fell from right below him, a magically-generated waterfall dropping to the rooftop below. The water struck the flames with a loud *hiss*, steam billowing up from the impact. He flew over the building slowly, pouring more water over the flames, until the roof was no longer on fire. But tongues of flame still leapt from the windows of the upper stories.

"Guys!" Kyle cried out.

Ariana and Petra were already on it, flying toward the windows and weaving magic, shooting streams of water through them. More steam burst from the windows as they worked, flying past each window and dousing the flames.

"Any survivors?" Kyle asked as they regrouped.

"I didn't see any from here," Ariana answered. "I'll go inside and check."

"Okay," Kyle agreed. "Petra and I will douse the other resorts."

Ariana nodded, then flew through one of the windows, landing on the charred floor beyond. She was in a small hotel room, a burnt-out mattress at one end. No one was on it, to her relief. She sprinted to the door, shoving it open so hard it blew off its hinges, clattering into the hallway beyond. She stepped into the hallway, pausing for a moment.

No cries for help…only the muted sound of the storm from outside.

She sprinted down the hallway, then stopped again to listen. Still nothing. That meant it was unlikely there was anyone on this floor…alive, anyway.

Ariana flew upward, smashing through the ceiling, her shard automatically protecting her from the impact. Not that it would've mattered; any injury would have healed immediately. She found herself levitating on the next floor up, in a hallway identical to the one below. She dropped to the intact floor, listening.

Still nothing.

She repeated the process, going up one story at a time, then listening, then traveling to the next story, until she realized she'd smashed through the roof to emerge outside. She went back down then, flying through the holes she'd made, until she reached the one she'd started on. She went down then, bursting through the floor. It was then that she heard something.

A faint crying sound.

To anyone else's ears, it would've been imperceptible. But not only could Ariana hear it, she knew instantly where it was coming from: the next story down, at the other end of the hallway. She smashed through the floor, then sprinted down the hallway below until she reached a door near the end of it. It was locked; she snapped the doorknob off, then slammed her palm into where the deadbolt went into the wall, smashing the doorframe and opening the door.

Another hotel room, but this one had been mostly spared from the fire. Still, a dark haze hung below the ceiling, the stench of smoke overpowering her. Ariana ignored it, stepping into the room. There was an elderly woman on the floor, lying on her left side and coughing violently.

"I've got you," Ariana called out, walking up to her and kneeling down. She tried to pick the woman up, but the lady screamed, shoving her away.

"My...hip!" she cried.

Ariana paused, studying the woman. Her hip was rotated outward, her leg slightly shorter than the other one. It had to be broken.

"I'm sorry," Ariana apologized, putting a hand on the woman's shoulder. "But I've got to get you out of here."

She picked the old woman up from the floor, trying her best to support the woman's hip. But the woman screamed as she was lifted from the floor, clutching onto Ariana, her breath coming in short gasps. Ariana ignored the woman's cries, walking up to a door leading to a balcony beyond. She flew over it, then dropped to the street below, walking to a nearby crowd of people. She lowered the woman to the street then.

"Can you take care of her?" she asked the crowd. A few people nodded.

She flew away then, back toward the resort, spotting Kyle and Petra flying over a resort one block away, dousing it with streams of water. There were many, many more resorts to go…and the longer it took for her to search each of them, the more likely that someone would die waiting. She had to be quicker. More efficient.

Ariana took a deep breath in, focusing at the task at hand.

* * *

Kyle stood beside Petra and Ariana on the street just outside of the resorts they'd saved, hundreds of people standing around them. He felt utterly drained, his head pounding from using so much magic…and hunger pains gripping his intestines. They'd managed to save sixteen people between the three of them, mostly young children and the elderly. In the process, he'd seen far too many bodies, some charred beyond recognition, others without a mark on them. Victims of smoke inhalation, they'd died trying to escape the fire…or lying in bed asleep, never to wake up again.

Despite all the lives they'd saved, it was the lives they hadn't that stuck in his mind.

You did the best you could, he told himself. And he had…they all had. But it was small consolation indeed.

"We need to get these survivors medical attention," Kyle stated, turning to the crowd. He pointed at one of the men. "How far away is the nearest hospital?"

"There's only one," the man answered. "It's half a mile away."

"I need volunteers to bring each of the survivors to the hospital then," Kyle decided. "Carry them if you need to."

"Yes sir," the man replied, turning to the men and women around him. Within moments, numerous groups of volunteers had assembled, each ready to help.

"We should help them," Ariana stated. "With our magic, we could carry quite a few at a time."

"We need to get to Candric," Petra countered. Kyle hesitated, then nodded reluctantly. The governor could be in trouble...and Darren was still on the loose. Someone in the crowd had told them that Darren had been seen marching toward the governor's mansion a half-hour ago. And that he'd been the one that set the resorts on fire. Of course it'd been to send a message to the Empire, but in the process, he'd murdered innocent people. People whose only crime was wanting to go on vacation someplace beautiful. Someplace safe.

And if Kyle didn't stop Darren, the Weaver might do it again.

"You okay?" Ariana asked, grabbing Kyle's hand. He glanced at her, realizing she was staring at him, looking concerned. He forced a smile.

"I'm okay," he reassured. She shook her head.

"No you're not," she retorted, giving his hand a squeeze.

"Come on," he prompted, activating his gravity boots, then flying upward and forward down the street. The governor's mansion stood in the distance, several miles away. Ariana flew upward with him, as did Petra. They left the crowd behind, accelerating forward. The rain had mostly subsided, a gentle drizzle all that remained of the storm that had raged for much of the night. "We need a strategy for dealing with Darren," Kyle stated.

"I can drain him," Ariana offered. "And then we'll detain him."

"He needs to answer for what he's done," Petra piped in. "We should bring him back to Stridon."

"Agreed," Kyle replied.

They zoomed down the street, passing each city block in a manner of seconds. Kyle glanced down at the street, spotting a cluster of dark objects ahead. They were bodies, he realized. Burned to a crisp. His stomach churned, and he grit his teeth, knowing exactly who'd killed them.

He flew past them, his eyes on the mansion ahead, flying until he reached the front double-doors. He deactivated his gravity boots then, dropping to the ground and walking into the foyer. Petra and Ariana followed close behind.

It was, he found, deserted.

"Can you find Candric?" Kyle asked Ariana. She frowned.

"He has a heart murmur," she replied. "It's pretty distinctive. I should be able to hear it if I get close enough."

"Alright," Kyle replied. "We'll stay here."

Ariana left, zooming up the stairs, leaving Kyle and Petra alone. He found her staring at him.

"What?" he asked, feeling rather self-conscious.

"How did you escape the ship?" she asked.

"They had me chained to the wall," Kyle answered. "With a Neutralizer in the ceiling. I got as far away from it as I could, then built up some magic." He shrugged. "Then I used a magnetic field to pull the chains from the wall, and found Ariana."

"Well done," she replied, nodding at him. He hesitated.

"How about you?" he asked. "Are you...okay?"

"I am fine," she reassured him. "I woke up with soldiers around me, and killed them all. Then I met up with you two."

"Good," Kyle replied, feeling relieved. The thought of those guards hurting Petra...

"I don't understand," Petra admitted. "Why did Gundar attack us? Why bring us aboard that ship?"

"It was Lady Damia's ship," Kyle answered. Petra just stared at him blankly. "Apparently she's going to become queen of Verhan soon," he explained. "She was planning on taking me and Ariana to Verhan to have us publicly executed."

"But why?"

"To get at Kalibar, I think," he answered. "I'm not sure what game she's playing, but we have to tell Kalibar about it."

Just then, Ariana came back down the stairs. She walked up to them.

"Look who I found," she announced, gesturing at the stairs. A man stepped down them...a very familiar man.

"Jag!" Kyle cried.

"Hey kids," Jag greeted. More men came down the stairs behind him. It was Bopkin and the other researchers...one of whom was helping Governor Candric limp down the stairs. The governor's shirt was bloodied and torn, and he looked utterly exhausted.

"Hello Kyle, Ariana," he greeted. "And Petra," he added, nodding at the three.

"Hell of a Festival," Jag mused, reaching the bottom of the stairs and strolling up to them. "Thanks for not being dead."

"Our pleasure," Petra replied coolly.

"Bet it is," Jag agreed with a smirk. "You guys better get the hell outta here," he added. "Meros's going to shit."

"We noticed," Ariana replied. "People outside said it was Darren that burned those resorts," she added, turning to Candric. "Is that true?"

Candric limped to the bottom of the stairs, then made his way toward them, his expression grim.

"I'm afraid it is," he confirmed. "He's gone rogue...thinks he can take Meros back from the Empire himself."

"By sacrificing innocent people?" Petra stated incredulously. "This is not the way to fight an enemy. It is unthinkable."

"I agree," Candric replied. "Which is why most of the Resistance broke from him and went to the headquarters."

"Saw a whole boatload of 'em marching back to God's Peak," Jag confirmed. "Seems there's a lot more of them after the parade. Great recruiting strategy, having their leader turned into a martyr," he continued. Then he glanced apologetically at Candric. "No offense, governor."

"None taken," Candric replied. "Unfortunately you're right." He sighed. "We need to get to them as soon as we can," he added. "And make it clear that they're not allied with Darren before the Empire arrives."

"The Empire is coming?" Kyle asked.

"Inevitably," Candric answered. "And I can guarantee that they won't take lightly to one of their provinces staging an uprising. Darren's killing of all those guards at the parade – and burning those resorts – will be all the reason they'll need to impose martial law and imprison anyone related to the Resistance."

"But wait," Kyle protested. "The Resistance had nothing to do with this!"

"I know that," Candric agreed. "But Darren is Tessa's brother, and he's claiming that *he's* the leader of the Resistance. The Empire will paint them with a broad brush, I'm afraid."

"We'll talk to them," Kyle stated. "I'll talk to Kalibar and tell him what really happened."

"You might not get the chance," Candric warned. "Word is the City Guard thinks *you* killed those guards at the parade with Darren. And I'm sure the Empire's spies will bring that news back to Grand Weaver Kalibar."

Kyle felt the blood drain from his cheeks, and he glanced at Ariana.

"That's what Lady Damia told me would happen," he admitted. All eyes went to him.

"What?" Jag blurted out.

"Lady Damia," Kyle repeated. "She's the one who planned all of this."

"Hold on," Candric stated. "Explain yourself. Start from the beginning."

Kyle did so, recounting how he'd woken in Damia's airship, and the conversation she'd had with him. And what Gundar had told him...that there were still a few Chosen left in the world, and that Gundar was one of them. No one said a word until he was finished. Then Jag gave a low whistle, shaking his head slowly.

"Damn," he muttered. "Just...damn."

"This is bad," Candric stated. "This is very bad." He ran a hand over his bald head, his eyes staring off at nothing. "That means Apep wasn't the one who ordered Tessa's death."

"It was Damia," Kyle informed them. "She paid off the guard that killed Tessa."

"Good god," Candric breathed, clutching at his chest. He lowered himself to the floor, sitting there. "Good god."

"If the Empire comes here and destroys the Resistance, then that means Damia gets her way," Ariana realized. "We have to stop that from happening!"

"Or maybe you wanna get the hell out of here," Jag countered. "You're wanted criminals, remember? This ain't gonna end well for you either."

"Kalibar won't..." Kyle began, but Jag cut him off.

"Damia was right," he interjected. "Kalibar can't do shit. If he does, he'll be interfering in a criminal investigation into his own children." He shook his head. "You're screwed."

"But..."

"You're saying that we'll be arrested too, along with the Resistance?" Petra asked. Jag glanced at Candric, who hesitated, then nodded.

"It's likely, yes."

"Then I am going back to the Barren Forest," Petra decided. She turned to Kyle and Ariana. "You can come with me," she added. "My tribe will protect you."

"We appreciate it," Ariana replied. "But we can't just leave the Resistance to take the fall for what happened."

"And we have to alert Kalibar about what Damia's up to," Kyle added. "And we have to stop Darren before he does something terrible."

"Agreed," Petra said.

"That's great and all," Jag butted in, "...but I'm betting the Empire gets here real soon, and with an army of Battle-Weavers. You stay here, they'll get you."

"No they won't," Ariana retorted. Jag turned to her, raising one eyebrow.

"Oh yeah girl?" he asked. "And what are *you* gonna do against an army of Battle-Weavers?"

Ariana gave him a grim smile, folding her arms across her chest.

"The question is," she replied, "...what are *they* going to do against *me*?"

Chapter 25

The sun was just starting to peek above the horizon as Kalibar finished his second lap around the campus of the Secula Magna. His black shirt was soaked with sweat, his legs burning after the ten-mile run. He'd taken it faster than usual, pushing himself. It was a run he'd been taking almost every other day since his twenties, but each year it'd gotten a little harder. Each year it felt like he had to fight just to keep what he had.

But not now.

Ever since Ampir had given him his eyes back – and healed him – he'd felt younger. Stronger. As if a decade of wear and tear had been taken from him. Now he felt like he could go for another lap, and almost did. But he knew the reason for the urge: to take his mind off of his children.

He sighed, turning inward from the high fence surrounding the perimeter of the campus, seeing the Great Tower in the distance. Two faint blue spheres followed behind him, his invisible elite guards trailing him. He kept up the pace until he reached the Tower, stepping through the double-doors, then making his way through the lobby to the riser. He took it up to the 42nd floor, to his suite, stepping inside and easing himself onto one of the couches there.

And immediately started thinking of his children.

He fidgeted, standing up and starting to pace. He hadn't had an update since yesterday, when Urson had told him about Kyle and Ariana being responsible for murdering guards in Meros. There was no way they could've done it...it had to be a mistake. Or they'd been framed.

Unless...

He turned, striding up to the huge window looking outward over Stridon. What if Ariana's shard had gone off, thinking she was under attack? Sure, she'd been learning to control her shard's reactions, but still...

There was a knock on the door.

"Yes?" Kalibar called out. "Come in," he added, streaming magic to deactivate the lock on the door. It opened, and none other than High Weaver Urson stepped through.

"Grand Weaver," he greeted, saluting sharply.

"Urson," Kalibar replied. "Any updates?" It was a rhetorical question, of course. Urson would not have bothered him otherwise.

"Several," Urson answered. "The terrorist group calling themselves the Resistance have a new leader. A Battle-Weaver named Darren."

"I've met him," Kalibar stated. Darren had been one of the Battle-Weavers that'd risked their lives fighting the Void Behemoth, using killerpillar guns on the massive war machine. "He was a loyal Battle-Weaver. Why'd he turn?"

"His sister was the previous terrorist leader."

"Ah."

"The terrorists burned down most of the major resorts, then laid siege to the governor's mansion. Darren has personally killed over a hundred of the City Guard. There's riots and looting."

"And my children?" Kalibar pressed.

"Your Battle-Weavers should have arrived late last night to retrieve them," Urson answered.

"Good."

"One more thing," Urson added. "Lady Damia's ship was seen leaving port last evening. By air."

Kalibar did a double-take.

"What?"

"It flew," Urson clarified. "...a few thousand feet above the ocean...then disintegrated."

Kalibar stared at Urson, hardly believing his ears. Damia's ship couldn't fly...magic was forbidden in Verhan. Which meant that if she *did* have an airship, it had to have been made illegally.

And if there were reliable witnesses that her ship *had* flown, he could use that against her. If she'd violated Verhan's most sacred law, exposing her would prevent her from ever rising to the throne. Assuming she was still alive, that was. If she'd been on the ship when it'd been destroyed, then the Empire's biggest problem had just solved itself.

"Ready a full contingent of Battle-Weavers," Kalibar ordered. "I want Darren neutralized and the terrorists arrested or killed, with a preference for the former. I'll send the navy to impose martial law and Runics to rebuild what the terrorists destroyed."

"Yes Grand Weaver," Urson replied. "With your permission, I'll go myself."

"Permission granted," Kalibar agreed. "I'll confirm the deployment of the navy with the Council. I can't imagine they'd offer any resistance, but even if they don't agree, we'll do it ourselves."

Urson nodded, waiting silently.

"Dismissed," Kalibar stated. Urson saluted again, then turned to leave. "And Urson," Kalibar added.

"Yes Grand Weaver?"

"Thank you."

Urson nodded, then left, the door closing behind him. Kalibar sighed then, turning to one of the communication orbs laying on an end-table nearby. He activated it, summoning Erasmus. He needed to convene an emergency meeting of the Council...and not just to coordinate a counterattack on the terrorists in Meros. There was also the matter of dealing with the owners of the resorts that had been torched. They were, after all, among the wealthiest men in the Empire...and vital donors to the Elitists in the Council. And they'd be mighty displeased that the Empire had failed to maintain order on Meros, allowing a rogue Battle-Weaver and a fringe terrorist group to destroy their property. Assurances would have to be made that any future investments would be insured against such destruction...and that the Empire would help finance the restoration of their resorts. As much as it annoyed Kalibar to use taxpayer dollars to appease wealthy businessmen – he was a Populist, after all – it was a necessary evil of doing politics.

Kalibar turned from the door, resuming his pacing. He found himself thinking of Kyle and Ariana again, and of Petra. They were staying at the governor's mansion, he knew. Which meant that they'd probably been there when Darren attacked. With Petra and Ariana there, he couldn't imagine that Kyle had been hurt, but still...

He stopped himself from that thought, knowing that it would only lead to crippling anxiety. Contemplating all of the terrible things that could happen in the future was the path to madness. He didn't have the luxury to engage in such foolishness.

Still, he found himself struck with the sudden urge to fly to Meros himself. To be with Petra and his children, to make sure they were safe. He could justify it by saying he wanted to make a speech in Osa after the terrorists were rounded up. To reassure its citizens that the Empire had not forgotten about them.

Yes, he thought. *I'll do just that.*

Which meant that he needed to go now, before the Battle-Weavers brought his children back.

He nodded to himself, then heard a knock on the door. It was Erasmus, as expected. Kalibar strode toward the door to greet his old friend, walking with renewed vigor. He would see his family soon...and Erasmus would stay behind to deal with the Council.

* * *

Sunlight streamed through the tall, narrow windows of the old church, sending golden beams through the dust swirling in the air. Kyle sat at a large round wooden table, Ariana on one side and Petra at the other, facing the remaining leadership of the Resistance.

Gia, Tessa's former second-in-command, and now the de-facto leader, sat opposite them, Candric seated to her left.

Kyle shifted in his seat, his back still sore after a night spent lying on one of the cots in the church. He hadn't gotten much sleep, having been woken up by Gia for an emergency meeting that morning.

"Darren took a quarter of our people," Gia was saying. "I still can't believe they'd abandon everything we fought for just to get back at the Empire."

"Some of them have had enough," Candric replied. "They think Tessa failed, and that it's time to fight."

"That's inane," Gia retorted. "It's suicide. We don't have the power to go to war with the Empire!"

"Darren is tapping in to their anger," Candric explained. "And right now they're angry about Tessa's murder."

"But this isn't what Tessa would've wanted," Gia protested. "We always obeyed the law – even when the government didn't. *Especially* when the government didn't. Tessa knew that by doing so, any violence against us would only expose the hypocrisy of the government…that the people could only have rights if they didn't use them."

"We all saw what Darren is capable of yesterday," Kyle piped up. All eyes turned to him, and he shook his head, lowering his gaze to the tabletop. Images of the dead bodies they'd found in those resorts after putting out the fires came to him. "We have to stop him."

"*Can* you stop him?" Gia asked. Kyle glanced at Ariana, then Petra, then nodded.

"We can," he answered.

"We need to make sure the Empire knows we're not with Darren," a woman to Tessa's left warned. "If they lump us all together, we're in deep trouble."

"Leave that to us," Ariana replied. Gia nodded.

"Thank you," she stated. "We're all in your debt."

"Anything we can do to help, we will," Kyle promised.

"We have a lot to do," Gia admitted. "After Darren's actions last night, rioters broke into stores in Osa, looting everything they could. A few shops were burned down...and most of those shops were small, and owned by natives. We need to organize fundraisers for them, and help them rebuild."

"I can spearhead that," Candric offered. "I'll help fund the effort personally." Gia nodded.

"We're in your debt," she replied. "We should also do a fundraiser for the families of the guards Darren killed," she continued. "He broke a lot of families yesterday, and they'll need all the help and support they can get."

Kyle found himself nodding, and glanced at Ariana, who smiled at him. She put a cool hand on his knee, leaning in until her lips brushed against his ear.

"This is good," she whispered.

He nodded, smiling back at her. This *was* good. These people were good...better than he was. He hadn't even thought about the families of the guards that'd been killed...yet Gia had. They truly *were* about the people, as Tessa had been. The Resistance was everything the Empire had proven *not* to be in Meros...a group of people who cared *about* the people. Not about power or profit.

I can make a difference here, he realized. *We all can.*

He had to keep his promise to Tessa, to let Kalibar know about the Resistance. And about how the Empire had forgotten about those who couldn't make magic. Kalibar would make things right.

He always did.

Just then, Jag strode into the room, followed by Bopkin and the other researchers. They'd slept at the headquarters as well. Jag leaned against the wall, nodding at Petra.

"Morning," he greeted. "Hope I didn't interrupt anything."

"We were just wrapping up," Gia replied. "Everyone know their parts?"

All heads nodded yes.

"Then let's do it," Gia stated. "Power to the people."

"Power to the people," everyone replied.

"Good luck with that," Jag muttered, almost too quietly to hear. Kyle stood from his chair, as did Ariana and Petra, walking up to the man.

"Hey Jag," Kyle greeted.

"Hey kids," Jag replied. "Petra."

"Come to help out?" Kyle asked.

"I came to bring you to the Citadel," Jag corrected. "We got work to do…and things're gonna get real dicey here soon. Better if you're not around when that happens."

"We have to stop Darren," Kyle countered.

"The Empire will stop him," Jag retorted. "Can't have you risking your necks fighting a damn Battle-Weaver. Your daddy would kill me if something happened to you…and I'm not about to piss off the Grand Weaver."

"We're not going," Kyle stated resolutely. "We're staying to help…and you should too."

"Yeah, I'll pass," Jag grumbled. Gia walked up to them then.

"We could really use your help," told Jag. "Our people need us."

"You're not 'my people,'" Jag reminded her. "I'm from the Citadel."

"But…" Gia began.

"This isn't my fight," Jag interrupted. "I'm not sticking my neck out for some hopeless cause."

"It's not hopeless," Ariana retorted. Jag rolled his eyes.

"Oh *really*," he replied. "Let me educate you then. See, this is all very simple. The Empire is a predator. Meros is the prey. Your daddy has all the power, and people with power don't just give it up. They're gonna come here, lock all you people up. Make examples of you."

"That's not true," Gia retorted. "We're not with Darren…we haven't done anything wrong."

"Think they give a crap?" Jag countered. "They won't give a damn *who* you are, or what you've done. They'll lump all you 'Resistance' people together, wait and see. You're guilty," he added, jabbing a finger at her, "…because the City Guard will say you are."

"Not if I can help it," Candric retorted, joining them. Everyone turned to face the governor. "I'll notify the Empire personally, and tell them the truth."

"You're Tessa's father," Jag reminded him. "Think they're gonna believe you? Word is you tossed the Captain of the Guard off a three-story balcony." He shook his head. "You're gonna be locked up too."

"It was in self-defense," Kyle protested. "Apep was trying to kill Darren."

"You mean the guy who just murdered a few hundred guards?"

Candric grimaced, saying nothing. It was a fair point.

"The Empire is better than you think," Kyle insisted. "They'll listen to reason."

"With all due respect," Jag replied, "...you're just a kid, kid. You have no idea what you're talking about."

"Then help these people," Ariana piped in. "Bring them into the Citadel so they'll be safe from the Empire, at least until we can talk to Kalibar and prove that they're innocent."

"Good luck with that," Jag grumbled. "Think my father is gonna help you?" He shook his head. "He doesn't care about anything but his precious gods."

"You're just like him then," Petra replied, crossing her arms under her chest and glaring at Jag. "You don't care about anyone but yourself."

Jag stared at her for a long moment, the color draining from his face. His jawline rippled.

"Think I need to take this from some backwoods *primate* and a couple self-important little shits?" he snapped. He jabbed a finger at Petra, his hand trembling. "You're *fools*, you understand me? You watch and see what happens." He glanced at Gia, then Candric. "All of you are *screwed*."

He turned then, stomping out of the room, and slamming the door behind him.

Kyle stared at the door, his mouth hanging open. He closed it with a *click*, then turned to Petra, whose expression was stony.

"Sorry," he mumbled.

"I can't believe he said that," Ariana added.

Bopkin and the other researchers stood there sheepishly, Bopkin glancing up at Candric.

"We'll stay," he offered. "We'll help in any way we can."

"Thank you," Candric replied. "We could use your magic to help defend this church, and your testimony to help prove our innocence."

"You'll have it," Bopkin promised.

"All right then," Gia stated, turning to the other members of the Resistance. "Any questions?"

There were none.

"All right," Gia stated. "Let's do this."

Everyone left the room, with Kyle, Ariana, and Petra leaving last. They made their way outside of the headquarters, emerging into the warm sunlight. Kyle took a deep breath in then, nodding at Ariana and Petra.

"Okay," he said. "Let's start organizing the church's defenses."

"I believe we can be of help with that," Bopkin replied with a smile.

Chapter 26

Kalibar gripped the armrest of his seat as his airship began to descend rapidly, his eyes on the window to his right. Blue sky lay beyond, and the occasional puffy white cloud. It was the calm after the storm, he knew…a storm that had only begun to pummel Stridon by the time he'd left the city for Meros. A fleet of airships flew in a circle around him, each carrying his Battle-Weavers.

And far below, he saw the island of Meros.

He turned away from the window, glancing at High Weaver Urson, who was seated beside him. The man hadn't said much during the trip, which was just as well. Kalibar had too much on his mind to deal with pointless banter. The Council hadn't been pleased with his decision to go to Meros, and neither had Urson himself, given that the island wasn't secure. But Kalibar hardly feared for his life. He was the most skilled Battle-Weaver alive, not to mention the fact that he had the ability to heal from almost any wound.

Not that the Council knew of that…or ever would.

He'd found himself thinking mostly of Damia, and how she'd managed to outwit him. Even his best spies had virtually no information on her. She came from an old family, one that had a tendency to keep to themselves, shunning the spotlight. Indeed, few had seen much of Damia until a few weeks ago.

Now it was impossible to go anywhere *without* hearing about her.

The ship continued to descend, and Kalibar looked down through the transparent crystal floor, spotting the governor's mansion directly below...and the town square just in front of the building.

The cobblestones below were stained with blood.

The ship slowed its descent, touching down gently inches above the square. Moments later, the airship's door opened, swinging down to form a ramp. Kalibar and Urson stood, and Urson went first, stepping down the ramp. Kalibar followed after, emerging into the hot air, the sunlight almost blindingly bright. Whereas Stridon was subtropical, located below the equator, Meros was a bit farther north. It was always hot...and almost always sunny. The perfect tourist destination.

Airships descended all around him, landing in the street behind the town square. Battle-Weavers streamed out of them toward him, thirty of his finest men. They surrounded Kalibar and Urson, waiting for orders.

"Team One, secure the mansion and search for the governor." Kalibar commanded. "Team Two, go to the resorts and search for survivors. Use your airship for medical transport."

Ten men saluted, leaving the circle.

"Teams Three through Five," Kalibar continued, "...coordinate with local law enforcement to find these terrorists. I want the location of their leader and all terrorist cells on the island."

More men saluted, leaving to their tasks.

"Team Six," Kalibar stated, "...deal with any remaining rioters. Protect businesses from looters."

The remaining Battle-Weavers left, and only Urson remained. The man turned to Kalibar, awaiting instructions silently.

"Urson, I want you to find the Weavers I sent to get my children and get a status update," Kalibar said. "I'll remain here in the mansion for the time being."

"Yes Grand Weaver," Urson replied. But the man hesitated.

"What is it?" Kalibar asked.

"Your safety," Urson replied. "This place is not yet secure."

Kalibar smiled, putting a hand on Urson's shoulder.

293

"I appreciate your concern," he replied. "I'll be fine."

Urson nodded, then flew up into the air to complete his task. Kalibar watched the man go, then sighed, turning to face the governor's mansion. Some windows were broken, mostly on the first floor, and the tall fence surrounding it was bent in some places. But the place was mostly intact.

How did this happen?

Meros had been peaceful since the Empire had colonized it two decades ago. Sure, there had always been people that had chafed under the Empire's rule, wanting Meros to remain an independent nation. But since becoming a part of the Empire, its economy had soared, businessmen from Stridon heavily investing in infrastructure. Osa, the capital of Imperial Meros, had been built up, some of the finest resorts in the world built upon its shores.

And the minute I bring my children here, he thought, *there's a damn revolt.*

He shook his head, turning to gaze out toward the sea in the distance. Where Lady Damia's boat had been docked the night before.

Why did she come here?

That was the question that'd been bothering him all last night. Why would Damia arrive at port the very night it descended into chaos? What role had she played here...and why Meros? It was such a small part of the Empire. There was no political gain in disrupting things here...at least not that Kalibar could see.

Unless...

A chill ran through him.

Unless she'd known somehow that Kyle and Ariana had been sent here.

He took a deep breath in, turning away from the sea and facing the mansion again. Striding up to the front double-doors, he stepped through into the foyer beyond. He had a job to do here, and worrying about Damia was not part of it.

But if she'd done anything to harm his children, he would make her pay dearly for it.

Personally.

* * *

It was less than a half-hour before Team One had finished scouring the governor's mansion. They'd found an abundance of corpses, most of them guards and a few members of the governor's staff. But no sign of the governor himself...or of Kyle, Ariana, and Petra. One of the governor's employees, a woman named Bae, reported that the City Guard had cornered the governor in his office, attempting to kill him. The governor – a man named Candric – had fought his way out.

When asked why the guards had wanted to kill their own governor, Bae had replied that they'd believed Candric to be secretly allied with the Resistance, the terrorist group responsible for the rioting and arson of the resorts...and now under control of Candric's own son.

Bae had adamantly denied Candric's involvement with the terrorists, saying that Candric had met many times with his daughter to convince her to leave the Resistance. As to where Candric was now, he'd been seen leaving with a man fitting Jagwell's description.

Kalibar sighed, leaning back in the governor's chair, staring across Candric's desk at the open door opposite it. He ignored the bloodstains on the floor and walls of the office, running a hand through his short hair.

Things were even more complicated than he'd imagined.

The easiest thing for him to do would be to take events at facevalue. With an order, he could crush the Resistance, institute marshal law, have Darren executed, and arrest Candric. He had the power to do so...overwhelming power.

And that was precisely why he had to proceed with caution...and with care.

Acting before having all of the facts might result in more tragedy, he knew. He could not afford to be swayed by the urge to attack those that had hurt the Empire. Justice had to be slow, deliberate, and above all, compassionate. And in this case, he was judge, jury, and if he chose, executioner.

Kalibar closed his eyes, running a hand over his goatee.

In these cases, he found it a useful exercise to consider events as each party might have.

Might as well start with Darren.

He'd met the man, by all accounts a loyal Battle-Weaver of considerable skill. Darren had won accolades for risking his life attacking the Void Behemoth over a month ago. The man's patriotism was not in question.

So what would drive such a man to murder?

The leader of the Resistance was his sister.

Surely seeing his own sister murdered would drive a man mad. And to have been murdered by the hand of the City Guard...no wonder Darren had gone berserk. But why attack the resorts? The answer eluded him.

Kalibar sighed, switching perspectives.

Candric had witnessed his own daughter's death at the hands of the City Guard...and by some accounts had thrown the Captain of the Guard off of a balcony. The captain had survived the plunge only to be killed by Darren...the first person Darren had murdered. By all accounts he should have targeted the guard that killed his sister first.

Two law-abiding men attacked the captain. Which could only mean they believed – or knew – that the captain was responsible for killing Tessa.

Kalibar opened his eyes, taking a deep breath in, then letting it out. Then he closed his eyes again.

Kyle, Ariana, and Petra had been with the governor during the celebration. They'd seen what'd happened...and had attacked the guards according to all reports. He could hardly believe that his children would've done so if the guards had acted lawfully.

And then Darren had taken over leadership, and burned the resorts, killed any guards in his way, then had gone to the governor's mansion. If Candric had still been there, Darren would've met with Candric. Had Candric then gone with Darren?

296

Kalibar heard footsteps approaching, and opened his eyes. A Battle-Weaver walked through the door, saluting sharply. It was a member of Team Two.

"Yes?" Kalibar asked.

"We went to the resorts," the Weaver stated. "Guests had already organized rescue efforts and found survivors. Local residents have helped house most of the displaced resort guests."

"Very good," Kalibar replied.

"Word is that the initial rescue efforts were coordinated by your son," the Weaver continued. "And that your children and Petra put out the fires."

Kalibar's eyebrows rose.

"Any word on their location?" he asked.

"No Grand Weaver."

"Very well," Kalibar replied. "Thank you," he added. The man bowed, then left.

The initial rescue efforts were coordinated by your son.

Kalibar smiled, shaking his head and gazing at the top of the desk before him. That was the Kyle he knew. Of course his children would be at the front of the line during a disaster, helping to save innocent lives. As much as his children looked up to him, he strove to be the kind of man that deserved their respect.

He thought back to when he'd first met Kyle, a confused, shy boy who'd been so helpless and scared. To think that, only a few months later, he'd grown to become the fine young man he was today!

"Grand Weaver?" he heard a voice prompt.

He glanced up, seeing Urson standing there.

"Yes Urson? Have you found my children?"

"No," Urson replied. "Our Battle-Weavers haven't located them. Eyewitnesses say they left the resorts last night, then came here."

"Well they're not here now," Kalibar stated, feeling rather irritated. Then an idea came to him. "They could be in the Citadel," he realized. "I want Jagwell found."

"Yes Grand Weaver," Urson replied. "I have news from Team Three."

297

"Go on."

"Darren was seen with a group of terrorists heading toward God's Peak, the mountain in the center of the island. The terrorist base is a refurbished church near there."

"Excellent," Kalibar replied. "Neutralize the terrorists. Do so with care, Urson. I want no casualties."

"Sir?"

"We have magic," Kalibar explained. "They do not. There is no reason to kill anyone, except Darren if absolutely necessary. We can't have the citizens of Meros see us as abusing our power…and we don't have a complete picture of what's really going on. We need to assume that all are innocent until we have proof of guilt."

"Yes Grand Weaver."

"That will be all," Kalibar stated. Urson bowed, then left, and Kalibar watched the man go, tapping his chin absently. He felt antsy, and knew it was because of his children and Petra. He'd expected to reunite with them quickly, after all. But it was not to be.

Of course, he could always go to search for them himself…

He resisted the urge, biding his time. It wouldn't be long before Candric was found, Darren was arrested, and the Resistance was neutralized. There would be days of interrogations, and the truth of the last twenty-four hours would be revealed. Justice would be served, and peace would be restored to Meros.

All he had to do now was wait.

Chapter 27

The wind whipped through Kyle's clothes as he flew toward God's Peak, the afternoon sun's hot rays baking his skin. He studied the mountainside, searching for a good-sized boulder. One big enough to store magic for the runic defenses Bopkin was creating for the headquarters, but small enough to fit inside the ancient building. It wasn't long before he found what he was looking for…a collection of boulders that had settled at the base of the mountain.

He streamed magic to his gravity boots, changing course to fly toward his target. In less than a minute, he reached the boulders, slowing his descent without even thinking about it and touching down on the packed dirt below. He strode toward the boulders, finding one that was just the right size. It looked to be a hunk of granite…hardly as good as a diamond for storing magic, but it would have to do. And since no one made as much magic as he did, he could fill the boulder up with magic to spare.

Kyle wove magic, creating a gravity sphere around the boulder. It had to weigh a ton, but with magic it was as light as a feather. He lifted the gravity sphere, and the boulder came with it.

Activating his gravity boots, Kyle flew back toward the church, the boulder in tow. The church was only a few miles away, at the southern end of the island. Ariana and Petra had been sent to retrieve more boulders for Bopkin; what exactly the Runic was going to do with them, Kyle wasn't sure. But he planned on finding out…and learning as much as he could from the Runic in the process.

Gia and Candric had convened another meeting earlier, assigning tasks to themselves and their fellow workers. Then Candric had left headquarters to travel to Osa. Despite Gia's – and everyone else's – protestations, he'd vowed to turn himself in to the authorities. He was innocent of Apep's murder, and believed that the Empire would recognize this in time…and that by staying with the Resistance as a wanted man, he was endangering them. He knew he would only be able to complete his daughter's work effectively if he was exonerated first.

It wasn't long before Kyle spotted the church in the distance, nestled at the foot of God's Peak. He aimed for it…then frowned, slowing his descent.

Something was wrong.

It took him a moment to realize what it was: faint blue spheres of magic a few hundred feet from the church, hovering above the ground…and closing in fast.

Probably the researchers, Kyle guessed. But if so, that meant they were using invisibility fields…and Bopkin and the other researchers had been on Meros for over a month now. The invisibility pattern had only been discovered a couple of weeks ago.

Which meant they couldn't possibly have learned it.

Kyle's heart leapt in his throat, and he shot forward and downward, speeding toward the church. The boulder he'd been towing fell toward the earth behind him, but he hardly noticed. The blue spheres reached the church, flying into it through the windows.

A moment later, smoke burst from the windows, followed a split-second later by a loud sound like a thunderclap.

No!

Kyle cursed, weaving a gravity shield around himself, then an invisibility field. He landed on the courtyard by the front door of the church, sprinting through the doorway into the large room beyond.

A cloud of dust hung in the air, broken furniture strewn across the floor. Beyond, he saw an open doorway leading to a long, wide hallway. Even with the dust partially obscuring his vision, he spotted glowing blue spheres hovering just above the floor, moving away from him into that hallway.

An ear-splitting shriek echoed through the church, followed by frantic shouting.

Kyle sprinted across the room and into the hallway after the spheres, *pulling* a thick strand of magic into his mind's eye and weaving it into a tight knot, throwing it outward. A blinding light filled the hallway, and Kyle squeezed his eyes shut, hearing shouting ahead. He flew up to the ceiling twelve feet above, creating a gravity field far below him, near the floor.

A very *powerful* gravity field.

He opened his eyes, a sudden gust of wind threatening to suck him down from the ceiling. Streaming magic to his gravity boots, he resisted the pull, watching as the three glowing spheres below got sucked into his gravity sphere. Then he created a gravity shield around them...not to protect them, but to trap them inside. One so powerful that only Kalibar himself could have escaped from it.

He dropped the stream to the gravity sphere, the shield still encompassing the three glowing spheres...which vanished, revealing three men. Men in black uniforms.

Battle-Weaver uniforms.

They got to their feet, pressing up against the wall of the shield, staring up at Kyle, who dropped from the ceiling to stand before them. Their eyes widened, and their lips moved, but of course no sound came out. The gravity shield was soundproof.

Kyle crossed his arms over his chest, glaring at the men. He hesitated, then dropped his magic stream to the shield trapping them.

"...us go!" one of the Battle-Weavers shouted. He blinked, then stepped forward, realizing the shield was gone. "Come on," he urged, "...we have to get you out of here!"

"Excuse me?" Kyle replied. "What are you talking about?"

301

There was a blood-curdling scream, and a Battle-Weaver burst through the door ahead, nearly taking it off its hinges. He fell onto his back on the floor ahead of them…and a pale figure appeared in the doorway, striding toward him.

"Ariana!" Kyle cried.

"What are you *doing?*" Battle-Weaver on the floor shouted. He scrambled to his feet, backing away from Ariana.

"Why are you attacking us?" Ariana shot back angrily.

"They're terrorists," the man protested. "We were…"

"They're *not* terrorists," Ariana interjected, striding toward him. He continued to back up, until he backed right up into Kyle. He spun around, then realized who he was looking at.

"Kyle!"

"She's right," Kyle stated. "They're not terrorists…they're innocent people."

"But…"

"Tell your men to stand down," Ariana warned, "…or we'll make them stand down."

The Battle-Weavers glanced at each other, then nodded, flying down the hallway into the next room. Kyle went after them, as did Ariana, passing through the open doorway into the large room beyond. He saw the men and women of the Resistance against one wall, a wall of blue light trapping them there. They all turned to face Kyle, Ariana, and the three Battle-Weavers, their eyes wide with terror. Gia was among them.

"Kyle!" she shouted, her voice muted by the magical wall. "Ariana!"

More glowing spheres hovered in the room, and five more Battle-Weavers winked into existence, staring at Kyle and Ariana.

"Let them go," Kyle ordered, gesturing at Gia and the others.

"Do as he says," the Battle-Weaver next to him insisted.

The magic wall vanished.

"You can come out now," Kyle reassured. Of course Gia and the others couldn't see the magic wall…or that it'd vanished. They hesitated, then stepped forward.

"What's this about?" Gia demanded. "Why are you attacking us?"

"They thought you were terrorists," Ariana said.

"We heard that Darren was your leader," one Battle-Weaver explained. "We were under orders to apprehend you." He turned to Kyle. "And to do so without harming anyone," he added.

Men in white robes came out of one of the doors opposite Kyle, gravity shields surrounding them. It was Bopkin and the other Runics. They stopped in their tracks, staring at the assembled Battle-Weavers.

"What's going on?" Bopkin demanded.

"We were acting on orders," one of the Battle-Weavers answered. "We were told that there was a terrorist cell here."

"What terrorists?" Gia pressed.

"The ones who burned down the resorts," he explained. "And led the riots, the looting…"

"That was Darren," Gia corrected. "Not us. We're trying to stop Darren…and help our people."

"That's not the intel we were given," the Battle-Weaver replied apologetically. "We didn't know," he added. "We were acting on orders."

"Orders?" Ariana replied incredulously. "From who?"

"From Grand Weaver Kalibar," the man answered. "Your father."

Kyle stared at the man.

"He's here," the Battle-Weaver continued. "Your father. He's at the governor's mansion." He smiled. "He's been looking for you."

"Wait," Kyle blurted out, his eyes widening. "He's *here?*"

"That's right," the man confirmed.

Kyle glanced at Ariana, who broke into a smile.

"Well what are we waiting for?" she asked. "Let's go!"

She turned to walk back into the hallway behind them, but Kyle grabbed her arm.

"Hold on," he said. "What about Petra?"

As if on cue, a woman strode through the hallway into the room, a boulder floating behind her. The Battle-Weavers' eyes all tracked

303

her as she stopped before them, the boulder lowering itself to the floor.

"What is going on?" Petra asked.

"It's Kalibar," Ariana answered, smiling from ear-to-ear. "He's here!"

Chapter 28

Gundar strode down the wide, ornate hallway, his metallic boots *clanging* on the white granite tiles underfoot. The sound echoed off the white marble walls and tall decorative columns rising to the ceiling twenty feet above. Statues made of pure gold stood against both walls, all of them of a tall, slender woman in various poses of triumph. Each statue rested on a dais wrought of pure diamond, sparkling in the light of magic lanterns bolted to the walls.

To anyone else, the sheer luxury of this hallway – matched by every hallway and every room in Lady Damia's palace – would have been mesmerizing. But Gundar had seen it too many times before...and displays of wealth meant nothing to him. They never had.

His sister had shared that quality once.

Gundar reached the door at the end of the hallway, stopping before it. The door was made of a single block of white crystal, a deposit created by one of the oldest Reaper Queens in the Barrens. What Sabin had called the Void crystal.

He reached out with one armored hand, placing his palm upon that smooth surface. Wove six threads of magic at once, twisting them into a single pattern and throwing it outward.

Nothing happened.

Gundar waited, knowing that the door could only be opened from the other side…and that his magic had merely notified those beyond of his presence.

Seconds passed, then minutes.

Gundar grimaced, knowing that he was being tested…and knowing full well that his irritation was exactly the reason he'd been made to wait.

A reason for everything.

He of course had not been born with that gift. The ability to see life for the game it was. To play it masterfully. He was a piece on the board, not the hand moving it.

Another minute passed, and at last the door swung open.

Gundar considered pausing, making *her* wait. But he rejected the idea immediately. It would only please her, to know that he'd been irritated enough to try to get back at her.

He strode through the doorway into the room beyond.

It was large, this room, roughly forty feet squared, with white marble walls rising to a golden domed ceiling high above. Light shone down from a single diamond in the center of the domed ceiling, a magical, miniature sun. It cast its rays down upon a large, circular bath in the center of the room, stream rising from its sparkling waters. Two larger pools flanked the hot bath in the middle.

And in the center of the middle pool sat a woman.

Her dark lips drew into a slight smile, her long hair falling in loosened curls over the front of her bare shoulders. The water was up to her collar bones, the rest of her body hidden beneath the water.

He ignored her, gazing at the huge paintings hanging on the walls all around them. Paintings of the Lady Damia throughout history. Riding a stallion into war with the Helsinks to the south. Sitting beside the throne of Verhan two centuries after the fall of the Ancient Empire, her king at her side. The first queen of Verhan, a kingdom rebuilt by the Outsider himself.

And there were so many other paintings, all of Damia. Beautiful. Elegant. Triumphant.

It was not a bath, Gundar knew. It was a shrine.

Damia said nothing, staring at him with her dark eyes. It was clear she wasn't surprised to see him.

He resisted the urge to squirm under that gaze, an all-too-familiar uneasy feeling coming over him. It was fear. A small fear, but fear nonetheless. A fear he'd become accustomed to ever since Sabin's army of Chosen had been destroyed. Since she'd been freed from this place.

A palace beyond compare, the most comfortable prison one could imagine.

A sanatorium for those who were beyond healing.

"They escaped," Gundar stated bluntly. She'd left the airship beforehand, flying to Verhan herself for an urgent meeting.

Damia arched an eyebrow.

"Oh really?" she replied. She stood up then, water dripping from her body. The bathwater only came up to her waist. He lowered his gaze, staring at the floor in front of him. She was, of course, unclothed. It was a calculated move, he knew. She enjoyed his discomfort, enjoyed the fact that she'd been the one to cause it. All planned, of course.

She planned *everything*.

"They defeated you," she surmised. Gundar said nothing, which was answer enough. She *tsked*, stepping out of the bath and strolling up to him. She pouted, putting a wet hand on his armored shoulder. "Beaten by a few children...how *humiliating*."

He lifted his gaze, staring back into her eyes. Not taking the bait.

"Your airship was destroyed," he notified her. "The boy is more powerful than we anticipated."

Her eyebrows rose, her hand slipping away from his shoulder. She crossed her arms.

"It was the boy?"

"He pulled apart the ship in seconds," he confirmed. "With a single pattern."

"My my," Damia murmured, considering this. "He seemed so weak. Pathetic, really." She smiled. "Fooled by a child...how marvelous!"

307

Gundar grimaced, finding nothing marvelous about it. They'd failed in their plan to bring the children back to Verhan for execution...and alerted Kalibar to their plot. He said as much.

"Oh, sweet brother," Damia scolded. "Always so *depressing*."

"I can retrieve them," Gundar offered.

Damia arched an eyebrow, one corner of her lips twitching.

"Can you?"

He held his tongue, refusing for her to hear his annoyance at being beaten...and knowing damn well that it didn't matter. She knew he was annoyed. She was trying to stoke it.

"Leave them be," Damia decided, waving the issue away with one hand.

"But Kalibar..."

"Will realize I've threatened his family," she interjected calmly. "That I've made it oh-so-very personal." She shrugged. "Let him know the stakes. Let him stew on it."

"As you wish."

"Naturally," Damia agreed. She turned away from him, stepping leisurely toward the bath. Immersing herself in the water, then turning to face him, sitting down once again. "Care for a bath?" she inquired, patting the water next to her.

"No."

"So dull," Damia accused. "Always so *serious*. What's the point of immortality if you refuse to enjoy it?"

"I'll leave that to you," Gundar grumbled.

She shrugged, splashing the water with one hand.

"Very well," she replied, giving him a little smile. "I suppose I'll just have to have enough fun for the both of us, hmm?"

Gundar frowned at her, knowing she couldn't see the expression behind his helmet. She stretched her arms over her head, then leaned back against the side of the bath.

"You know what?" she stated. "I've changed my mind. Be a dear and go fetch the little brats. And don't forget their babysitter...she'll make a wonderful toy for my guards."

"What are you plotting?" he inquired.

"You'll see," she promised with that mysterious smile of hers. "It won't be long before the whole world finds out what I'm capable of," she added. "And unfortunately for them, by the time they do, it'll be *far* too late."

* * *

The early afternoon sun cast its rays down on the ninth district of the Citadel, casting squat shadows of the tall godstone statues standing in the center of a small courtyard. Jag glanced at them as he walked down the black stone street. One of the statues was of a short, wiry with wild hair sprouting from his head and a long beard. Gazing down at a timepiece held in one hand.

Altair, the god of Time.

Jag sighed, setting his gaze on the street ahead.

How appropriate, he thought. For it was time that was weighing heavy on his mind at the moment. The seemingly great expanse of his life, forty years today.

Forty years, and what did he have to show for it?

He passed by the statues, glancing back at them as he walked. There was Altair, and standing nearby, a statue of a tall, willowy woman with long, wavy hair all the way down to her knees. She had one hand on Time's shoulder, the other holding a clump of dirt, a small seedling emerging from it.

The Goddess.

Jag grimaced, facing forward again. He stuffed his hands in his pockets, concentrating on putting one foot in front of the other. The Goddess. The Old Tree. To the Priesthood, they were one and the same. Legend claimed the goddess had transformed into the Old Tree during the Cataclysm. During the great massacre of the gods.

So went the story, anyway.

This place was full of legends. The priests memorized them, indoctrinating each generation. Corrupting young minds with silly stories. Ridiculous tales only a cult would believe in.

He'd believed, once.

Jag looked up, seeing the huge black platform of the eighth district high above. And above that, the seventh, and sixth. And so on, leading to the first, the home of the Temple of the Old Tree. His father had taught him all of the stories, of course. And he'd believed them as a child. He'd gazed at the statues of the gods, imagining himself living in their time, before the Cataclysm. Imagined their extraordinary power, beings beyond comprehension. Beings that could create the Citadel, something indestructible. Eternal.

Imagined that the Old Tree really was the last surviving god, and that by drinking the essence of the pamaté, the priests could speak with her.

Jag shook his head, a bitter smile on his lips. A man walked by on the other side of the street, waving at him. He nodded absently, hardly in the mood to converse. He supposed that's why he'd turned his father down today, refusing to have lunch with the old man.

It was tiring, being told every day that he was deficient. A thing to be pitied.

Have faith, his father always said.

And Jag supposed he *was* deficient, in that he couldn't believe in something he couldn't see. Something bigger than himself.

All you care about is yourself.

Jag grit his teeth, Petra's words repeating themselves in his mind. She'd been right, of course. His reaction had proven that. She'd hit him where it hurt.

It's not my fault.

He'd never had a chance, not with his father. The man had held his love hostage, demanding a ransom of Jag's faith. A ransom Jag had refused to pay.

There was an intersection ahead, and Jag turned left, hardly paying attention to where he was going. He couldn't stop, couldn't rest. Not with this feeling inside of him.

It was his birthday today, and no one was celebrating. Not even him.

Jag wandered, feeling hollow. Forty years old, half his life gone. No wife, no family. No real home. No real friends. Just acquaintances.

Just money.

The deal with the Empire had made him a rich man. They'd paid dearly for access to the Citadel's runic artifacts. For the possibility of smuggling advanced runic technology from the Depths.

Access that only Jag could give them.

He could retire now if he chose. There was no reason to keep coming back here. Yet for some reason he *did* come back, day after day.

Jag passed another small courtyard, more statues standing in the center of it. He stopped, staring at them. Trying to remember what it'd felt way back when he'd been a kid. When he'd believed in something…something other than getting his share. Than making enough money so that he wouldn't have to worry about making money anymore.

All you care about is yourself.

He sighed, shaking his head. He wanted to tell Petra that he'd learned not to waste his energy loving those who wouldn't love him back. Who couldn't. But it didn't matter what he told her, not really. The problem wasn't with what she'd said, it was with who he was.

Jag stopped in his tracks, taking a deep breath in. He pulled his hands out of his pockets, clenching his fists at his sides.

Then he turned around, walking back the way he'd come. Back to the Temple…and the teleportation circles that would take him outside of the Citadel.

Petra had told him that all he cared about was himself, but the truth was that he didn't care for himself. For who he was. On the day of his fortieth birthday, he hated who he'd become.

And if there was one thing he'd learned, it was that there was one thing he would never be able to run from. One thing that would follow him to the ends of Doma.

Regret.

And there was only one thing he could do about it.

Chapter 29

Kalibar paced up and down the hallway adjacent to Candric's office, his gravity boots *thumping* on the floorboards. It'd been over an hour since he'd gotten an update on his Battle-Weavers' progress, and he found himself feeling irritable. It was as much a product of not having eaten since that morning as anything else, he knew. But enjoying a good meal was the last thing on his mind at this point.

Governor Candric had arrived in Osa two hours ago, turning himself in to the authorities. Kalibar had interviewed him in Candric's own office. He'd found the man immediately likeable...and honorable to a fault. Candric had confirmed Kalibar's suspicions about this Captain Apep, and had revealed that Kyle, Ariana, and Petra had gone to the Resistance headquarters the night before.

And that the people of the Resistance were not terrorists at all...except those that'd decided to follow Darren.

Kalibar had considered reinstating Candric as governor, but he'd held off, knowing that many in the City Guard would rebel against Candric's command, some still believing the governor was guilty of murdering their captain. Kalibar would have to deal with that later, of course...and he still wanted to get collateral information from his children on what'd really happened the day of the Festival. If Kyle and Ariana could confirm Candric's innocence, then Kalibar would reinstate the man…even if it meant having to purge the City Guard and replace every one of them.

Kalibar sighed, feeling antsy.

Where are they?

If Kyle, Ariana, and Petra had really gone to the Resistance headquarters, then the Battle-Weavers he'd sent there should've found them by now.

Just then, he heard clambering coming from the stairwell beyond the hallway, and frowned, stopping in his tracks. A moment later, three very familiar people stepped into the hallway, striding toward him. He broke out into a wide grin.

"Kyle!" he cried, walking up to the boy and giving him a hug. "Ariana," he added, turning to give her a hug as well. They both beamed at him, their grins matching his. He turned to Petra then, standing behind them. She smiled at him, nodding slightly.

"Kalibar," she greeted.

"Petra," he replied. "It's good to see you." He stared at her for a moment, struck as usual by her beauty…and that warm feeling he got when he saw her. He realized he was grinning stupidly, and cleared his throat, turning to his children. "Where have you been? What happened?"

"That's a long story," Ariana said. "What are you doing here?"

"That's a long story too," Kalibar admitted, rubbing the back of his head. "I'd like to hear your story first. What happened here?"

"What have you heard?" Kyle asked.

"Start from the beginning," Kalibar requested, ushering them into Candric's office. He pulled up some chairs for them, then sat down behind his desk. They sat facing him. "Assume I know nothing."

They did so, Kyle starting, and Ariana and Petra filling in details as the story unfolded. Kalibar sat there, listening quietly, resisting the urge to interrupt them to ask questions. That is, until they revealed Lady Damia's involvement. His eyebrows went up.

"She *kidnapped* you?" he blurted out. "You spoke to her?"

313

"That's right," Kyle confirmed. "She drugged our drinks during the Festival somehow, and I woke up on her airship. She told me she was behind everything that'd happened in Osa."

"What did she say exactly?"

"That she'd financed the Resistance and the City Guard, pitting them against each other," Kyle answered. "She even paid off the guard that murdered Tessa."

Kalibar leaned back in his chair, running a hand through his hair. The fact that Lady Damia herself was behind all of this...it was unbelievable. What use was it to start a revolt in such a small island? And how could she be so bold as to kidnap his own children? Such a thing was tantamount to an act of war...and war with the Empire was something that Damia could hardly afford. Her rhetoric had always been inflammatory, and sure, kidnapping Kalibar's children would please her base. It was politically expedient...but practically suicidal.

"She was planning on bringing us back to Verhan," Kyle explained. "She told me she was going to publicly execute us."

"That doesn't make any sense," Kalibar muttered. "Executing the children of the Grand Weaver? We would've bring the full might of the Empire down upon her if she'd done that. She's not stupid enough to risk that."

Which meant that there was something he was missing.

"We fought a man named Gundar," Petra revealed. "He was a Chosen...he claimed he was the first of his kind." She hesitated, her jawline rippling. "He was one of my ancestors."

"From the Barren tribes?" Kalibar inquired. Petra nodded. "But I thought Ampir had destroyed all of the Chosen."

"He called himself a Prime Chosen," Ariana recalled. "Says he wasn't controlled by Sabin like the rest. He probably wasn't connected to Sabin's network. That's why Ampir's weapon didn't find him and kill him."

"I see," Kalibar replied, tapping his chin with one finger. If that was true...if this Gundar was a Chosen, and working for Damia, then things had just gotten a lot more complicated. Still, the fact that his children and Petra had defeated Gundar was reassuring.

They wouldn't have stood a chance against Sabin, after all. That meant that, as old as Gundar was, he wasn't nearly as gifted a Weaver. The man might already be dead, after all…and even if he was still alive, the fact that Kyle had beaten him meant that he'd be no match for Kalibar.

"Anything else?" he inquired. Kyle glanced at Ariana, who shook her head. Petra did so as well. "Very well then," he stated. "Thank you for everything…and good work in saving those people at the resorts," he added with a smile. "I'm proud of you."

"We did what we could," Kyle replied. "But it was too late for a lot of people."

"You did your best," Kalibar insisted. "And now I have to do mine." He stood up then, and everyone took his cue, standing as well. He stepped around the desk, hugging Kyle and Ariana, then hesitating when he faced Petra. She arched an eyebrow at him.

"I'm not covered in spikes," she stated.

He smiled, giving her a hug, then pulling away.

"It's good to see you," he admitted. "I…"

"I know," Petra interjected, putting a hand on his shoulder. "We'll talk tonight."

Kalibar nodded, turning to Kyle and Ariana.

"Why don't you go to the pools behind the mansion?" he offered. "You all deserve a rest."

"I'd rather help," Kyle countered, glancing at Ariana, who nodded in agreement. "What can we do?"

"Well, if this Gundar is truly as old as Sabin, he may have survived your attack," Kalibar reasoned. "Which means he may come for you again. There's no telling just how powerful he might be. Which means we need every advantage we can get to defeat him."

"The Citadel," Petra stated. Kalibar nodded.

"Exactly," he agreed. "The runic technology our researchers have excavated there is far advanced of ours. Right now, the best thing you can do is continue the original plan: go to the Citadel and help our researchers decode the runes there. Try to find something we can use."

"All right," Kyle agreed. Petra nodded as well.

"We should go now then," Ariana opined. "We don't want to waste any time."

"I think you should stay here with me," Kalibar countered. Ariana blinked. "Kyle and Petra will be perfectly safe in the Citadel," he reasoned, "...but I could use your help here in Osa. Governor Candric could use a bodyguard that doesn't sleep."

Ariana hesitated, clearly unhappy with being separated from Kyle. But Kyle touched her shoulder, giving her a reassuring smile.

"It's okay," he insisted. "Petra won't let anything bad happen to me."

"She was going to murder you if I didn't get that Void crystal from the cave a few weeks ago," Ariana reminded him. Kyle gave a rueful smile at that, glancing up at Petra, who shrugged.

"You retrieved the crystal," she replied.

"Well that's comforting," Ariana grumbled. She sighed, turning back to Kalibar and nodding. "All right, I'll do it."

"Good," Kalibar declared. "Kyle, Petra, meet up with the researchers and go to the Citadel."

"But what about Jag?" Kyle inquired. "They might not let us in without him."

"Try," Kalibar insisted. Kyle nodded, and he and Petra left, leaving Kalibar alone with Ariana. "Candric is at the pools on the mansion grounds," he informed her. "He's keeping a low profile until I deal with the City Guard."

"Gotcha," Ariana replied. She leaned in, giving him a kiss on the cheek, then waved goodbye, exiting the office. Kalibar watched her go, then sighed, sitting back down in his chair and leaning back into it.

For the first time since they'd left for Meros, he felt at peace.

It was short-lived, however. He found his mind quickly going back to Lady Damia...and her claim that she'd orchestrated all of this. Not just the double-cross over Lord Devlin, but the kidnapping of his children and fomenting chaos in Meros.

But why Meros of all places?

The island was small, after all, and hardly of any real political influence. Or economic influence for that matter, at least compared to the mainland. Why prop up the Resistance? Why pit them against the City Guard? Why assassinate this Tessa?

It made no sense.

Maybe it was to get to my children, he thought.

He rejected the idea immediately. There was no way Damia could have predicted he'd send his children here, and she'd clearly invested in Meros long before he'd made the decision.

So she'd funded both the Resistance and the anti-Resistance, ensuring escalating conflict. It was classic social warfare: weaken a nation by dividing its people. By making the people see each other as the enemy…all the while ignoring the *real* enemy lurking beyond their borders.

Remarkably effective, he knew…with potentially devastating consequences.

Which led him to believe that Meros had just been a test case for Damia. A proof of concept. Kalibar knew that there were anti-Empire groups on the mainland, even in Stridon itself. It was entirely possibly that Damia was going to target them next, supporting them and their enemies alike in hopes of weakening the Empire.

Divide and conquer.

Perhaps she'd already begun.

Kalibar sighed, rubbing his eyes, then staring down at the top of his desk wearily. The only antidote to division was unification…and in times of crisis, the people of the Empire would look to their leaders for guidance. The Council could not be trusted to provide a message of unification, he knew. But he and Erasmus could.

He would have to send a message of unity for his people, to lead them away from Lady Damia's clutches. And Meros would be *his* test case. If he could unify the people of this island after everything that Damia had done, then he could do it on the mainland.

If not, then the Empire was in deep, deep trouble.

Chapter 30

The air was musty and cool in the underground tunnel, the ceiling only a few feet above Darren's head as he strode down it. A few lanterns had been set on the floor in regular intervals, lighting the way toward the cavern ahead. He strode confidently forward, having long-ago memorized this path.

He'd taken it countless times as a kid, on weekends when Dad had been at work and he'd been home alone with Mom and Tessa. When Mom would inevitably start drinking. He'd taken Tessa here the minute she'd learned to walk, to a cave at the base of God's Peak. To escape the screaming and the beatings.

To reach their sanctuary.

How many days he'd spent here, claiming to be at a friend's house, or wandering the beach, he didn't know. Mom hadn't cared where they were, as long as they came home before their father did. And Dad had never come home until late, at least not in those days. Before Mom hadn't been able to hide it anymore.

Before he'd realized just how broken his family had become.

Darren had never told anyone about this cave except for Tessa. Their sanctuary had been theirs alone. Their own private playground, where they could get far enough away from reality that dreams of a better future would actually seem possible.

Dreams that had never come true...and never would.

Darren sighed, turning left as the tunnel did, spotting a brighter light a few dozen feet ahead. The cave...their sanctuary no more. For now it was the home of the Resistance.

He heard voices ahead, and continued forward, reaching the end of the tunnel. It opened up into a large chamber, as big as any of the city blocks on Osa, the ceiling well over forty feet high. A few beams of sunlight streamed through narrow gaps in the stone ceiling overhead, lighting the chamber in a soft golden hue. Men and women sat on boulders all around him, talking with each other.

But when they saw him, all eyes turned to face him, and the talking stopped.

"Afternoon," he greeted, his voice carrying easily across the cave. "I've confirmed our spies' reports...the Empire has sent Battle-Weavers to secure the island."

There was hushed whispering, followed by one woman raising her hand.

"Yes?" Darren inquired.

"What are we going to do?" she asked. "We can't fight Weavers. What if they find us?"

"They won't," he promised. "No one knows about this cave, trust me." Which was technically true. They didn't need to know that, at least theoretically, a Battle-Weaver could sense the magic Darren leaked. Magic absorbed into the stone leading to the cave, the tunnel, and even in the floor of this very cave. There was little natural magic in Meros, all magical plants and animals having been destroyed long ago when Verhan had owned the island. But it was unlikely that these Battle-Weavers would find the entrance to the cave in the first place; Meros was far too large for a small force to search it thoroughly, and chances were the Battle-Weavers would assume that any magic in the rocks was from themselves...if they were clever enough to follow magical trails at all.

And, knowing most of the Battle-Weavers from his days in the military, he wasn't too concerned. His only real worry was that one of his people would be dumb enough to lead the Empire here...which is why he'd forbidden that anyone leave or enter without him. The invisibility pattern had served him well, allowing him to ferry his spies to and from the cave, far enough away from the entrance that they wouldn't arouse suspicion, even if caught.

But if one of them *was* caught, and they talked...

"What about the rumors?" a man asked. Darren turned to him, keeping his expression carefully neutral.

"What rumors?"

"That Grand Weaver Kalibar himself is here," the man clarified.

"Confirmed," Darren replied.

There was more murmuring from the crowd, and Darren held up one hand for silence.

"Don't panic," he reassured.

"We can't do anything against Kalibar," someone complained. "Not even you could beat him!"

"True," Darren agreed.

"Then how..."

"I don't need to beat him," Darren interrupted calmly. "And it's unlikely he'll come for me personally. He's here to send a message...that revolution is unacceptable. That the Empire will not tolerate dissent from the people."

That Meros would never be free.

"But what if he does?" another person pressed.

"He can't fight what he can't find," Darren reminded them.

"So what, we hide here forever?"

"No," Darren replied. "I'll bring groups of you back to Osa, a few at a time. We'll go in the middle of the night. You'll stay there, live your lives as usual. Stay quiet, say nothing about the Resistance."

"You mean give up," one woman stated.

"Hardly," he retorted. "Some of you work for the City Guard, or in the governor's mansion. Some of you work for the wealthy pigs who own those resorts. Get access to those with power. Get access to the Battle-Weavers' food supply. Their water supply. Poison them."

Eyes widened, a hush coming over the cavern.

"You have power," Darren declared. "You just have to think bigger. Work smarter, not harder. You don't need magic to kill a

Weaver. They're human, just like you. They have to eat, and they have to drink."

"What about Kalibar?" a man pressed. "You want us to poison the leader of the Empire? They'll blast Meros to smithereens if we do."

"No," Darren answered, his tone sharp. "No one touches the Grand Weaver."

"But…"

"The Empire is corrupt, but Grand Weaver Kalibar is not," Darren insisted. "He's an honorable man. No one touches him. Or his children. Or my father. Understood?"

There were nods all around.

"We'll start evacuating tonight," Darren declared. "We'll do it over a few days."

"What about you?" a man pressed. "What are you going to do?"

"I'm going to leave Meros," Darren answered.

Eyes widened, voices calling out in protest. Darren raised a hand for silence.

"The Resistance lives in almost every city in the mainland," he explained. "Right now we're the only branch the Empire is targeting. We're too visible. I'm going to go to the mainland and drum up support for the other branches. We're going to recruit more people to our cause, and organize every branch to act together as one. We'll target every city in the Empire…stage protests, influence elections, remove those against us just as you'll do here. The Empire will have no choice but to direct its attention to the mainland…and away from Meros. And when they do, I'll return home…and we will rise up and take what is ours."

He swept his gaze over the assembled members of the Resistance, spreading his arms out wide.

"We will have our freedom," he promised. "Not today, not tomorrow. But one day, when the people rise up against the Empire in every town, in every city, when the majority rises to reclaim their rights, we will strike. And on that day, and every year thereafter, we will celebrate our independence!"

321

* * *

The sun had swung past noon by the time Jag reached the courtyard of the Resistance headquarters, nestled at the foot of God's
Peak. The rain from the previous night's storm had long since dried
in the hot sun, thank goodness. It'd made the trek down from the
Citadel far less onerous. In the city, a sprained ankle or a broken
leg was a nuisance, but on God's Peak – with the nearest soul over
a mile away – it could be a death sentence.

A few men and women were standing outside, near the entrance
to the church, and they turned to watch him as he approached. No
doubt surprised to see a stranger out in the middle of nowhere.

"Afternoon," he greeted, slowing as he reached the entrance.
"Who do I talk to about helping out around here?"

There were a few glances exchanged, and then one man stepped
forward.

"I'm Wilt," he greeted, extending a hand. Jag shook it.

"Jag."

"You know who we are," Wilt guessed. Jag smirked.

"It's my job to know things," he replied.

Wilt glanced at the other members, then turned back to Jag. He
had no reason to trust Jag, of course. After all, Jag could be a mole
from Darren's group. Or hired by one of the businessmen whose
resorts got razed. Jag was hardly surprised. If these people had wel-
comed him with open arms, they'd've been fools.

Just then, a woman stepped out of the church. A short woman
with curly black hair and piercing brown eyes. She stopped short,
staring at Jag.

"Jag," she greeted coolly, clearly surprised to see him. It was Gia,
the leader of the Resistance. Jag grimaced; they'd hardly parted on
the best of terms the day before.

"Gia," he mumbled. "Sorry about…"

"What can I do for you?" she interrupted. Her words were polite, but her tone was anything but.

"I'm more interested in what I can do for you," Jag replied. The
words felt strange coming from him. For most of his adult life, his

interactions with others had been purely transactional…to his benefit.

"Oh," Gia replied, clearly taken aback. "That's…I appreciate it. What did you have in mind?"

"What do you need?"

"Well, we have a lot of work to do. Right now our biggest problem is providing medical care to victims of the riots and the fires. There's only one hospital on Meros, and they're swamped. We've got treatment tents going up in Osa, and quite a few volunteers. But we need medical supplies, and people who know and can teach first aid."

"I got money," Jag offered. "And I know a thing or two."

"Any amount to help buy supplies would help."

"How much you need?"

"More than we'll ever get," Gia admitted ruefully.

Jag hesitated for a moment, the thought of dipping into his retirement fund suddenly terrifying. He'd worked hard for that money, risking his skin on more than one occasion. Too hard to just burn it all away on people he didn't even know. Didn't have any reason to care about.

Stop it, he told himself.

"Try me," he countered.

Gia raised an eyebrow, eyeing him for a moment.

"How much can you spare?" she asked. He hesitated again, then gave her a number. A number that hurt.

Her other eyebrow went up, joining the first.

"You're serious?" she blurted out. He nodded. "You'd give that much?"

"Not if you give me enough time to think about it."

"We'll take it," she stated instantly. "That could fund the whole medical relief operation," she added excitedly. "And pay for…"

"Just take it," Jag interrupted. "Where are these tents?"

"I'll show you," she answered. "I've got a carriage coming in an hour, they can take us there. We can stop by downtown and get supplies, then go there."

"All right."

323

Gia clutched her hands in front of her chest, a huge smile on her face. Then she stepped in, giving him a big hug. Jag resisted the urge to pull away, accepting it. She pulled back, holding him by the shoulders.

"Thank you," she said, grinning from ear-to-ear. "Thank you so much!"

"We all gotta do something," he replied awkwardly.

"If you do this for us," she countered, "...you'll have done more than enough."

Jag nodded silently, smiling with his lips but not his eyes. She didn't know him, not really, and he planned on keeping it that way. Because if she did, she'd know that, after the life he'd led, whatever he did here wouldn't even *begin* to save his soul. His fortune was made of lies and blood, every last cent earned at another's expense. Maybe, just maybe, using it to help the people of Meros would offer him some sort of redemption. Make him the kind of person others would like to have around...or even love.

But he'd have to do a lot more than hand over some coin if he ever wanted to feel like he deserved it.

Chapter 31

High Priest Kilson stepped out into the sunlight, passing well beyond the arched entrance of the Temple of the Old Tree. He took the wide godstone steps down, gazing at the immaculate landscaping on either side. Flowers in full bloom, pink and orange, blue and white. It was perpetual summer here, everything in the prime of life, robust and filled with color and beauty.

And here he was, in the last gasps of autumn, the winter of his life fast approaching.

He grimaced, feeling his clothes ripple in a slight breeze. Hating how they hung from his body, so loose. It'd only been a month since his tailor had made him new clothes, and yet now they were far too large for him. A reminder of the relentless disease consuming him from the inside out.

It wouldn't be long now.

Kilson reached the bottom of the stairs, and stopped there to catch his breath. The long path to the skybridge directly ahead was daunting, a distance that would sorely test him if he were to cross it. He spotted a few children running along the grass to his left, and watched them with no small amount of envy. To be able to move about with utter freedom, to be able to *enjoy* the use of one's body instead of dreading it, was a gift nearly all took for granted.

Until time took it away from them. Until their body started to betray them, one organ at a time.

Kilson sighed, waiting a moment longer, then continuing down the path toward the skybridge, the butt of his staff striking the ground with every other step. He would pay for his exertions tomorrow, but it hardly mattered. One day, very soon, tomorrow wouldn't come.

And then, at least, he would find peace. A final reprieve from the guilt he'd been carrying for so long now.

It still stung, Jag's refusal to meet him yesterday. He'd planned a birthday celebration, nothing spectacular. Just a meal between father and son, a time to talk. And more importantly, a time for Kilson to listen. To get to know his son…and to tell Jag how truly sorry he was. Kilson doubted he'd get another chance. This was the last birthday of Jag's he'd ever get to celebrate. Jag had to have known that too.

And the boy – the *man* – had refused him anyway.

It didn't take much introspection to know how badly Kilson had screwed up. How terrible of a father he'd been. He'd always been too busy to give Jag the time and attention the boy had craved. He'd put it off for another day, day after day, year after year, always thinking that what he'd been doing at the time was more important.

And now, at the twilight of his life, he could barely recall what he'd done that was so important to him back then, when he was busy neglecting his son. Jag had asked for love and not gotten it so many times that he'd stopped asking. And not just his father. Everyone.

Jag was a man who would never trust anyone, and it was all Kilson's fault.

You're a failure.

He stopped, realizing he'd made it to the start of the skybridge…and that he was terribly out of breath. He stepped onto the bridge, leaning against the railing and forcing himself to slow his breathing. A voice called out from ahead, and he blinked, spotting a woman on the bridge ahead, walking toward him. It was Marja, the Gatekeeper.

"Your Holiness," she greeted, stopping before him. She frowned, putting a hand on his bony shoulder. "Are you all right?"

"Just winded," he reassured, waving away her concern. "What...is it, child?"

"The Empire's researchers are requesting entrance," she answered. "And the Grand Weaver's son, and the tribal Weaver."

"So?" he replied. They'd requested entry almost daily...it was hardly something he should be notified of.

"Without Jag," she added. His eyebrows went up.

"Really?" he murmured. "Odd."

"They say he never showed up to take them."

Kilson considered this, dread twisting his guts. Had Jag denounced him entirely? He'd at least expected to *see* his son again before he died, but if Jag refused to return to the Citadel...

"Find him," he ordered.

"Yes your Holiness," she replied. She hesitated then. "Do you want us to bring him back?"

"No," Kilson answered. "Just make sure he's safe."

"I will," she promised. "And the researchers?"

Kilson sighed, gazing over the railing of the skybridge, at the high wall far in the distance...and the island of Meros beyond. Without Jag, he should bar the Empire's researchers from entering. They'd just continue plundering the Depths of the various trinkets there, trash they believed to be priceless treasure. On orders from a government that did what governments always did: take advantage of anyone they perceived as being less powerful than themselves. Entering into agreements in good faith, then stealing whatever they could in the cover of darkness. Behind a veil of lies.

They were like tapeworms, the powerful. Sucking the blood from their hosts for as long as they could. Their own peoples' blood, other peoples' blood. Taking what they pleased until the host was dead or managed to fight back.

But the Citadel was no helpless victim. The Empire believed itself to be stronger, believed it could steal from the Citadel with impunity.

Perhaps it was time he showed them just how very wrong they were.

"Let them in," he stated at last. "It's about time we showed the Empire the same…consideration and courtesy that they've showed us for the last few years."

* * *

Ariana and governor Candric sat side-by-side in white lounge chairs a few feet from one of the large in-ground pools behind the governor's mansion, the sun's rays baking their skin. Ariana hardly noticed the heat, just as she hardly noticed cold, or rain, or most other sensations that would've bothered her when she'd been alive. Her immortal body was above such things, it seemed, and she often had to remind herself that others still suffered from them. They'd been laying out here for the better part of an hour, neither of them saying very much. Silence didn't bother Ariana anymore either; a third of her life was spent in silence, when everyone else went to sleep.

Eventually Candric stirred.

"Tell me about yourself," he requested.

"What would you like to know?" she inquired.

"Where are you from?"

"Mortown," she answered. "A small town east of Stridon."

"How was it that you got adopted by the most powerful Weaver in the Empire?" he inquired. "If you don't mind me asking, that is."

"I don't mind," she replied. She told the story of how she'd been taken from her home by the Dead Man. How her parents had been murdered, and how she'd stayed in the Dead Man's underground prison for over a year."

"I'm sorry," Candric murmured. "I shouldn't have pried."

"It's okay," Ariana reassured. "I used to think keeping things inside would stop them from hurting me. Now I know it's better to let them out."

"That is very true," Candric agreed. He regarded Ariana with newfound respect. "You're very mature for your age, Ariana."

"I didn't have a choice."

"So Kalibar adopted you afterward," he prompted.

"Yeah," she replied. "After everything that'd happened, it was like I was finally getting a second chance. A second chance at having a life, and a family."

Candric sighed, and she heard his heart beating faster. She glanced at him, noticing his eyes were downcast.

"What's wrong?" she asked.

"I thought that would happen for me," he admitted. "When Darren returned after all those years, I thought I'd finally gotten a chance at having my family back. Whole again, you know? As whole as it could be after their mother's death."

Ariana put a hand on his arm, and he flinched.

"Sorry," she mumbled, withdrawing her hand.

"No, it's just that your hand is ice-cold," he explained with a smile. She smiled back ruefully.

"I have poor circulation."

"I often wonder what it would've been like if Darren hadn't been taken by the Empire so many years ago," Candric mused. "Tessa never forgave me for letting that happen, not that I had a choice in the matter. I thought I could change things by running for governor. I believed in the Empire, in the system. In the law. Tessa, well…"

He sighed, running a hand over his bald head.

"The Empire tore my family apart," he continued. "And the day it seemed like we were going to have our second chance, they killed Tessa. And Darren fought back, and now they're going to arrest him…and probably kill him too."

Ariana said nothing, staring at her feet. There was nothing to say.

"And here I am," Candric continued bitterly, "…the governor of Meros, doing nothing."

"It's not your fault," Ariana murmured, rubbing his arm. He glanced at her, a bitter smile on his lips.

"I know exactly whose fault it is."

Ariana held his gaze for a moment, then turned back to stare at the pool. She thought about how *she* had been taken, by the Dead Man. Forced from her home, her family. All because she could make magic. The same thing had happened to Darren.

Was the Empire really any better?

She shifted in her lounge chair, biting her lower lip. She knew the answer, of course. How could the Empire kidnap children – how could they tear families like Candric's apart – and be the good guys? How could Kalibar allow it, knowing full well what it'd done to her?

And how could she, with all of her power, just sit here and do nothing about it?

I can't, she knew. *I won't.*

And then she felt something in her mind's eye. Threads of magic weaving rapidly, automatically.

Her shard reacting.

Time slowed to a crawl, and she leapt toward Candric, wrapping her arms around him and rolling him off of his lounge chair. At the same time, she activated her gravity boots, feeling a jolt as she shot upward and to the side.

Just as Candric's chair exploded.

She heard Candric cry out, felt him clutch at her as they flew upward, accelerating rapidly. Looking back, she saw a black figure kneeling where their chairs had been. A man in night-black and purple armor, carrying a massive shield.

A shield with a white crystal skull in the center.

Gundar!

She streamed more magic to her boots frantically, soaring upward until she was above the roof of the mansion. Then she flew forward over it, spotting the third story balcony below, overlooking the town square. She descended toward it.

She had to protect Candric, but if Gundar drained her, she'd be done for. Which meant she had to stay far enough away from the Prime Chosen…and stay near the ground in case she *was* drained. Otherwise Candric would drop from the sky. She landed on the balcony...then felt the *hum* of magic in her mind. Her shard reacted, gravity shields appearing around her...and shoving Candric to the side.

Gundar's shield burst through the wall between them, debris exploding outward across the balcony. It shot past them, then arced quickly, coming right for Ariana!

She burst upward...but it was too late.

The shield slammed into her gravity shields...and then stopped there.

Ariana blinked, staring at the shield. At the white crystal skull staring back at her, only a foot away. Then she realized that something was wrong; her gravity shields were gone...and Gundar's shield had created a rippling sphere around her, so powerful that it bent the light, warping the image of everything around her.

A gravity sphere!

She reached out, touching the surface of the sphere. It was like touching stone.

Then the shield and the sphere shot backward, right into the wall of the mansion...taking Ariana with it.

Stone shattered all around her, the sphere smashing through wall after wall, destroying everything in its path. A man slammed into the sphere as she burst through room after room, careening off in a spray of blood.

And then she burst through the other side of the mansion into the open air, falling back toward the poolside, Gundar's shield flying right back into the man's left hand.

He stood there, only his eyes visible behind his black helmet, staring at her impassively.

"The boy," he demanded. "Tell me where he is."

"Go to hell," Ariana shot back.

She wove magic then, creating an invisibility field around her...and streaming as much magic as she could to it. If she drained her magic stores, the Void crystal inside her shard would activate, sucking magic from Gundar. Then the sphere around her would vanish.

"I could kill everyone in this building," Gundar offered.

"Not everyone," she heard a voice reply.

Ariana turned around, seeing a man standing nearby. A man dressed in a plain black shirt and pants, with short white hair and a goatee, his arms crossed over his chest.

"Kalibar!" she cried.

* * *

Kalibar stared impassively at the man holding Ariana captive, studying the glowing blue symbols emanating from the man's black and purple armor. Patterns woven by runes etched into the man's armor, many of them unfamiliar to Kalibar. No magic radiated from any part of Gundar other than those symbols, which meant that his armor prevented loss of magic, like Petra's Reaper uniform.

"You must be Gundar," he guessed.

"You must be Kalibar," the man replied.

"I hear my son defeated you," Kalibar stated.

"Temporarily."

"Release my daughter," Kalibar commanded, "...or I'll make it permanent."

Gundar said nothing...but the crystal skull on his shield began to glow, blue rays of magic *pulling* from Kalibar's body and converging onto it.

As expected.

Kalibar flew straight upward, so quickly that his vision blackened for a moment. He held on to consciousness, weaving magic in his mind's eye. Threads of magic would unravel if he sent a pattern outward too close to that shield...which meant he needed to weave from a distance.

He threw the pattern outward, far above Gundar's head...and a veritable waterfall appeared there, pouring down on the Chosen. The rays of magic streaming from Kalibar to Gundar's shield grew dimmer, the water insulating against magic loss.

Again, as expected.

Kalibar wove rapidly, throwing another pattern outward at the falling water. It froze instantly, trapping Gundar and Ariana in a

332

prison of ice. And ice, Kalibar knew, was a crystal…one that, utterly bereft of magic, would serve to neutralize Gundar's Void crystal. In theory.

The rays of magic leaking from Kalibar vanished.

He reversed direction then, flying downward at Gundar, weaving yet another pattern. The first one Kyle's K-Array had discovered: the killerpillar pattern. It shot downward in a flash of blue, striking the ice covering Gundar's helmet…just as Gundar broke free.

The ice *exploded.*

Kalibar ignored the hunks of ice pelting his gravity shields dropping to the ground before Gundar. He crossed his arms over his chest again, a smirk curling his lips. For the left side of Gundar's helmet had disintegrated, exposing the man's bald head and face. Gundar's skin was as black as night, tattoos adorning his temple.

"Now then," Kalibar stated. "I believe your shield won't be of any use to you."

Gundar glared at Kalibar, the white light shining from the skull on his shield fading…and the blue rays coming from Kalibar and Gundar's own exposed head vanishing as well. Gundar nodded at Kalibar.

"Impressive," he conceded.

"I believe I asked you to release my daughter," Kalibar stated coldly. "I won't ask again."

Gundar stood there for a long moment, then glanced at Ariana, still caught within that impenetrable sphere. It vanished, and Ariana fell to the ground. She got to her feet quickly, rushing to Kalibar's side.

"Leave us," Kalibar ordered, his eyes on Ariana.

"But…" she began.

"Ariana," he interjected, putting a hand on her temple. "Why don't you go inside and put on what Petra gave you. Then go disappear."

She hesitated, then nodded, giving Gundar one last glance before walking back toward the mansion. Kalibar kept his eyes on Gundar.

333

"A wise move," he stated.

"A strategic move," Gundar corrected. "Rest assured I will retrieve her after I am finished with you."

"You'll find that difficult when you're dead."

"You are mistaken," Gundar retorted. "I am already dead."

"In that case," Kalibar replied. "...it's time I buried you."

He wove magic rapidly, throwing the killerpillar pattern outward at Gundar. But the man dodged to the side almost too quickly to follow, a shockwave bursting outward from his shield...just as Kalibar's gravity shields vanished.

Decades of training kicked in, strands of magic weaving in Kalibar's mind without so much as a thought. The ground before him shot upward, a thick slab of stone and earth that intercepted the blast, absorbing its force. The slab shattered...but left Kalibar unharmed.

Kalibar burst upward then, creating a magnetosphere in the hole left by the slab he'd lifted...and streaming an enormous amount of magic to it.

Gundar slid on the ground toward the hole, falling right into it.

Kalibar wove a gravity field within the hole then, holding Gundar within the hole...and sucking the debris from the shattered slab back into it. The hole filled up quickly, burying the man.

He wove more magic then, throwing it downward.

The debris filling the hole burst into flames, the slabs of broken stone starting to glow red-hot. Kalibar streamed more magic, sweat beading on his forehead as he did so. He backed away from the hot air rising from the inferno, watching as the stone and dirt above Gundar began to melt, turning into a veritable pool of magma.

A geyser of liquid stone erupted into the air.

Kalibar flew backward, watching as a dark figure burst upward with the red-hot stone, landing near the edge of the pool two dozen feet away. It was Gundar, he saw...and the man was utterly unharmed.

"You are strong," Gundar noted. "For a mortal."

"I'm just getting started," Kalibar shot back. Gundar inclined his head.

"Show me."

Kalibar smiled, watching as blue light began to *pull* from Gundar's exposed scalp, converging onto a blue sphere hovering above the surface of the pool behind the man.

"Gladly," Kalibar replied.

Gundar's eyes widened, and he turned toward the glowing sphere behind him...just as Kalibar attacked, throwing out a magnetosphere between them. Gundar slid toward the magnetic field...then knelt, aiming his shield straight down

A burst of energy shot from the face of his shield, catapulting Gundar high into the air.

Kalibar saw Ariana blink into existence, clad in the Reaper uniform Petra had given her. Normally only her eyes would be visible through the black mask she wore, but she'd pulled it back to expose her forehead...and her shard. He smiled at her.

"Go get him."

She flew upward after Gundar, blue light streaming from Gundar toward her shard. Gundar turned in midair, looking down at her...and aiming the face of his shield directly at her. The crystal skull there glowed bright white, magic pulling from her toward it.

Ariana pulled her mask to cover her forehead, and the stream of magic leaking from her nearly vanished. She flew right at Gundar, slamming into him...and grabbing ahold of his shield. She yanked back on it, tearing it from his hands and tossing it aside. It fell...right toward Kalibar.

"Catch!" she cried.

Kalibar flew upward to grab the shield...and as his hands closed around it, a bright blue sphere surrounded him. His stomach lurched as he burst upward toward Gundar, who tossed Ariana aside, catching the shield. The Battle-Runic smirked at Kalibar.

"Predictable," he mused, his deep voice somehow penetrating the magical sphere imprisoning Kalibar.

And then Ariana slammed into Gundar from behind, wrapping her arms around the man's armored torso...and with her mask pulled all the way back, her hair rippling in the wind. She squeezed…and at the same time, magic leaked from Gundar to her shard, draining the man and his armor.

And the sphere surrounding Kalibar.

A few seconds later, the sphere vanished, and Kalibar flew back from Gundar, weaving the killerpillar pattern and throwing it out at the Battle-Runic's shield.

Gundar spun in mid-air, putting Ariana right in the path of it.

"Ariana!" Kalibar cried in horror.

She jerked Gundar around, spinning him in turn…and the killerpillar pattern struck them both in the flanks.

No!

Gundar's armor disintegrated there, exposing his torso…and Ariana's flank vanished to dust. Her hips separated from her waist, the lower half of her body falling toward the pool far below.

Ariana *screamed*.

A shockwave exploded outward from Gundar, flinging Ariana from him. She careened through the air, falling to the pool below and striking the surface so hard a geyser of water shot upward from the impact. Kalibar's shields absorbed Gundar's shockwave, knocking him backward but leaving him unharmed.

He flung another killerpillar pattern at Gundar, then flew down toward the pool below after Ariana. There was a *hum* in his skull, and he dodged to the side, creating a curved gravity field around himself. A beam of pure energy shot past his left shoulder…then arced around him, shooting right back in the direction it'd come. Kalibar spun around in mid-air, watching as the beam slammed right into Gundar's shield, scattering across its surface.

And conveniently distracting Gundar from the killerpillar pattern Kalibar threw right after it.

Gundar's shield *exploded*.

A burst of blue light seared Kalibar's eyes, and he felt a huge pulse of magic slam into him, filling his mind to overflowing with power. He harnessed the energy instantly, *pulling* threads of power into his mind's eye and tying them into a complex knot. He threw it outward at the thick cloud of dust where Gundar's shield had been, jagged bolts of lightning shooting through it at the shadowy figure beyond in rapid-fire sequence.

The dust cleared, revealing Gundar levitating above him. Holding what little remained of his giant shield, his mouth set in a thin line.

He tossed the mangled shield aside, grabbing his huge mace in both hands, his exposed jawline rippling.

"Enough," he growled.

Kalibar lowered himself to the poolside, watching as Gundar did the same, touching down a dozen feet away. They stared at each other, neither of them moving a muscle.

"I underestimated you, mortal," Gundar admitted. "I will not make that mistake again."

"You hurt my daughter," Kalibar retorted. "That was the last mistake you'll ever make."

Gundar grunted, swinging his mace over his head and bringing it down on the ground between them.

Boom!

The ground all around them shattered, hunks of stone bursting into the air. Kalibar felt himself flying upward and backward from the impact, debris ricocheting off his gravity shields. A few hunks of rock managed to penetrate his shields, slamming into his chest and back with bone-shattering force.

His vision blackened.

Kalibar felt himself falling, then felt a sudden jolt as his gravity shields struck the ground. His vision cleared slowly, and he blinked spots from his vision, realizing he was lying on his back, floating above the ground. He levitated upward, righting himself, his wounds from the attack already healing.

The poolside was destroyed.

A large crater stood in its place, twenty feet in diameter and five feet deep. And standing in the center of it was Gundar, his mace buried in the shattered stone before him.

Gundar yanked his mace free, lifting it up and resting it on his shoulder.

"Now you die," he promised.

"It's a shame you have no talent," Kalibar mused, facing Gundar defiantly. "I've seen many like you. People with raw power, but no mind for using it." He shook his head. "You could have been extraordinary."

"Spare me," Gundar grumbled.

"I'm afraid that's out of the question," Kalibar replied calmly.

Gundar ran toward him, lifting his huge mace high above his head, then swinging it downward at Kalibar. Kalibar wove the light pattern, creating a blinding flash between them...and created a magnetic field to Gundar's right, pouring magic into it. Gundar's mace was yanked toward the field, and he stumbled to the side, falling onto the ground...and sliding right into the magnetic field.

Kalibar wove another pattern, and the ground rose up around Gundar, fingers of earth reaching up and grabbing the Prime Chosen, wrapping around his body. Gundar grunted, his armor flashing blue...and the earthen tendrils shattered.

Just as Kalibar wove the killerpillar pattern.

It shot outward in a flash of blue, slamming into Gundar's neck and upper chest. The armor there disintegrated...just in time for the second killerpillar pattern to strike.

Gundar's upper body turned to dust.

The Chosen's head rolled free from his mutilated body, stopping face-up on the shattered ground. Kalibar stepped up to the man's head, staring down at it.

Gundar's eyes turned to look at him.

Kalibar grimaced, realizing the man was still alive...or still undead, anyway. With no need to breathe and no need for blood, Gundar's head could live on without his body.

"I warned you," Kalibar stated, kneeling before the head. Gundar's lips moved, but no sound came out...yet Kalibar heard words in his mind.

"My death means nothing," Gundar declared. "Damia will destroy you."

Kalibar frowned; Gundar's shard had to contain a universal translator, like Ariana's...and like the earring Kyle wore to understand what people were saying here. As long as Gundar thought the words he wanted to say, it would translate, allowing others to hear. Deaf and mute people in the Empire used the technology similarly to "hear" and "speak."

"Your death means nothing only if your life meant nothing," Kalibar retorted. Gundar gave a grim smile.

"I am a pawn, like you," he stated. "A puppet. Our names will be lost to history, our stories forgotten."

"And Damia?"

"She is the puppetmaster," Gundar answered. "She holds the strings that move the universe."

"We'll see about that," Kalibar retorted, crossing his arms over his chest.

"You cannot defeat her," Gundar warned.

"I defeated you."

"She is different," Gundar countered. "Even Sabin could not defeat her."

A chill down Kalibar's spine, and he lowered his arms to his sides.

"She's more powerful than Sabin?"

"In her own way."

Kalibar heard a splash, and turned to see Ariana stepping out of what remained of the pool. To his immense relief, her body was whole once again, her midriff exposed where the killerpillar pattern had blasted her. She stepped up to his side, staring down at Gundar.

"Hey honey," Kalibar greeted, putting an arm around her shoulders. Gundar's eyes flicked over to her, his eyebrows rising.

"Impossible," he breathed. Kalibar gave him a grim smile, kneeling down before his disembodied head.

"You have no..." he began...and then his shields melted away, a burst of green mist slamming into his face and chest. His skin began to burn, his shirt blackening and peeling away, his flesh turning red, then bubbling upward. It blackened then, smoke rising from his arms and chest, and from his face.

The pain was unimaginable.

"Kalibar!" he heard Ariana cry.

339

And then his vision blurred, fading to black as his eyeballs melted.

He heard Ariana's voice, seeming far away now. The burning stopped, fading to numbness. He felt nothing, saw nothing.

Then the pain returned, as did his vision.

Kalibar looked down, seeing his flesh repairing itself in front of his very eyes, growing and knitting together until it was whole once again, his bare, muscular chest and arms visible through the huge holes in his uniform.

Gundar's eyes widened.

"How...?" the headless Chosen blurted out. Kalibar gave a grim smile.

"We have something Lady Damia doesn't," he answered. "A very powerful friend." He turned to Ariana then. "Would you like to do the honors?"

"Thought you'd never ask," Ariana replied, kneeling down beside him. She reached out to Gundar's forehead, her pale fingers sinking into the Chosen's flesh.

Chapter 32

"All right," Bopkin declared at last, lifting his arms over his head and stretching his back. "I think that's a wrap for today everyone." Kyle gave the man a relieved smile, jotting down the last rune in the artifact he'd been studying, then standing up. He'd been kneeling over artifacts for hours now, with only a short lunch break to stretch and walk around a bit. He and Petra had gotten quite a lot of work done…and had found a few artifacts that could potentially be weaponized. Kyle swore Bopkin had spent as much time praising Kyle as he had working…much to Kyle's discomfort. Still, Bopkin meant well, and it was nice to be appreciated.

"Thanks for all your help," Bopkin stated, beaming at Kyle and Petra.

"Our pleasure," Petra replied.

The other researchers got to work putting the artifacts away, setting them in a pile near the high wall. No one tried to stuff artifacts into their bags, he noted, unlike the last time. When they were done packing up, Bopkin led them away from the dig site and back up the tunnels to the surface of the Depths. They flew upward then, passing the seemingly endless godstone platforms of the Citadel until they reached the Temple of the Old Tree thousands of feet above. They touched down near the steps leading to the massive building, making their way toward the entrance…

341

…and found High Priest Kilson waiting for them there, a dozen men and women in white robes on either side of him. Two guards covered from head to toe in jet-black armor stood behind Kilson, holding long black spears and black shields. The entrance to the Temple was closed.

"Good evening," Bopkin greeted, stopping before Kilson.

"Evening," Kilson replied, leaning on his staff and inclining his head slightly.

"Thank you again for allowing us in," Bopkin stated. "I'm still not sure where Jag went."

"He will be found," Kilson promised.

"We've finished for the night," Bopkin notified him.

Kilson just stood there.

"Is…is something wrong?" Bopkin inquired. Kilson raised an eyebrow.

"What an interesting question," he mused.

Bopkin blinked, then glanced back at his fellow researchers before returning his gaze to Kilson.

"I'm afraid I don't understand," he admitted.

"So you're a liar," Kilson observed coolly, "…as well as a thief."

Bopkin's mouth fell open, and he took a step back.

"I don't…"

Kilson slammed the butt of his staff against the ground, the sharp sound of the impact making Bopkin flinch.

"Please," he interjected. "Don't waste your breath, and don't waste what little time I have left." He snapped his fingers. The two black-armored guards strode forward, marching up to Bopkin and the researchers and tearing their packs from them.

"Hey!" one of the researchers yelled. "You can't…!"

"Oh *really?*" Kilson shot back, glaring at them. "You violate the covenant we had with your government, stealing artifacts from our home and smuggling them out of Meros, and *you're* indignant?"

Bopkin's face paled.

"Tell me, do you think me a fool?" Kilson inquired.

Bopkin swallowed visibly.

"I asked you a question," Kilson insisted.

"No sir."

"Then how stupid of you to assume I wouldn't notice your crimes," Kilson replied.

"We thought, you see," Bopkin stammered. "Jag, he said it was okay..."

"Oh did he now?"

"Yes," Bopkin insisted. "And we thought, well, since he's your son, that it *was* okay."

Kilson just stared at Bopkin for a long moment. Bopkin squirmed under that gaze, lowering his own eyes to his feet.

"I seem to remember your government having signed a written contract detailing the parameters of our agreement," Kilson reminded him. "Did Jag have you sign another one?"

Bopkin shook his head.

"Then you violated the contract," Kilson concluded. "You have committed crimes against the Citadel, and have broken the covenant between our governments."

"But Jag..." Bopkin began.

"Will be dealt with later, I assure you," Kilson snapped. "By the laws of the Citadel, I hereby find you guilty of theft and breach of contract. Your sentence," he declared, "...is death."

Bopkin's eyes widened, and he took another step back.

"*What?*"

"You are all hereby sentenced to death by execution," Kilson declared. He turned his gaze on Kyle and Petra then. "All of you."

Kyle felt his blood go cold, a chill running through him. He exchanged glances with Petra, who crossed her arms under her chest.

"We have stolen nothing," she stated coolly. "I doubt Grand Weaver Kalibar will appreciate you attempting to murder his son," she added. Kilson gave her a withering glare.

"Spare me the veiled threats," he retorted. "Kalibar has no power here. The Empire is nothing to us. Your armies cannot breach our walls. The Citadel is eternal, a fortress made by the gods."

"And yet *we* are inside," Petra countered icily. "And if you attempt to harm us, you will regret it. Deeply."

"Oh *really*," Kilson sneered.

He held his staff up high then, the loose sleeve of his robes slipping down to expose his frail arm. A bright blue-white light flared to life atop the staff, so bright that it hurt to look at. Kyle took a step back, shielding his eyes with one hand...and grabbing Petra's arm with the other.

"Run!" he cried, streaming magic to his gravity boots.

He burst upward and to the side, bringing Petra with him...just as the light atop Kilson's staff grew, enveloping the High Priest. Kilson levitated off the ground, his whole body glowing now, his robes rippling around his emaciated body. Bopkin backpedaled, layered gravity shields appearing around him and the other Runics.

And then it happened.

A tsunami of pure white light shot outward from Kilson, slamming into Bopkin and the other researchers...and missing Kyle and Petra by less than a foot. An ear-splitting *boom* echoed through the Citadel, so loud that pain shot through Kyle's ears.

Bopkin and the other Runics *disintegrated*.

Kyle felt himself angle downward sharply, Petra yanking him below the edge of the godstone platform the Temple sat upon. They burst downward, flying toward the next platform some ninety feet below. He saw her lips moving, but her voice was muffled, his ears ringing loudly.

Kyle glanced back over his shoulder, spotting two black figures leaping off the side of the platform above. The armored guards, their black spears glowing like Kilson's staff...and pointed right at him.

"Dodge!" he cried, streaming magic to his gravity boots and lurching to the right, pulling Petra with him. Twin beams of light shot past them, slamming into the godstone platform below.

"...fly out of here!" he heard Petra say. He felt her reverse course, flying upward toward the part of the Citadel wall nearest them.

"We'll be sitting ducks if we do that," he warned.

"What?"

"They'll shoot us out of the sky," he clarified. "And Jag said there was no way out except through the Temple."

Petra hesitated, then reversed course, flying almost straight down, but dodging left and right as more beams of light from the guards' spears shot down at them.

"They'll find us anyway," she pointed out. "We cannot run forever!"

Kyle grimaced, dodging another volley of attacks from above. She was right, of course. Unless...

He wove the invisibility pattern, creating a sphere around them.

"That should hold them off," he stated, looking back and upward. He spotted the guards flying through the air after them, and swooped to the right around a godstone pillar. But they followed him without hesitation.

Damn!

"It is not working," Petra warned.

"Got that," he grumbled. "You fend them off," he ordered. "I'll fly."

He felt Petra pull him in close, climbing onto his back and wrapping her arms around his torso. Then he felt the *hum* of magic, and turned to see Petra shoot a massive fireball at the rapidly-approaching guards, who dodged out of the way of the inferno, flying ever quicker...and gaining on them.

Fast.

Kyle turned forward, accelerating rapidly, dodging around another pillar, then flying straight downward. Beyond platform after platform below, he spotted the surface of the Depths...and the tunnel leading below ground, back to the dig site.

Suddenly, Kyle had an idea.

"The dig site!" he exclaimed.

"What about it?" Petra asked, lobbing another volley of fireballs at the guards. Kyle dodged to the left, a beam of white light shooting past him.

"The wall," he explained. "The one with the secret entrance."

"They won't be able to get in," she realized, following his train of thought. "Bring us there," she ordered. Another volley of white

345

beams shot toward them, and Kyle barely managed to dodge out of the way in time. "Quickly!"

"Hold on," he warned.

He streamed more magic to his gravity boots, shooting downward so quickly that his vision blackened. He grit his teeth, focusing on the Depths, still at least five hundred feet below. He curved to the right, then jerked leftward, trying to make himself a difficult target. It worked; the guards' attacks went far wide of their mark.

The image of Bopkin disintegrating in the wake of Kilson's monstrous attack came to him, that white light bursting through the poor Runic's shields as if they hadn't even been there.

If it's the same weapon, he thought darkly, *these guards will only have to hit me once.*

He passed a godstone platform, then swerved under it, putting it between him and the guards above. If he could keep putting the platforms between him and the guards, they wouldn't be able to hit him. It worked; no more beams of light passed by him. He passed one platform, then another, moving with dizzying speed…until there were no platforms left. The rubble of the Depths approached rapidly.

"Hold on!" he cried, shifting his magic stream to another crystal on his boots. Their descent slowed rapidly, Kyle's guts lurching as he decelerated. He leveled out at the last minute, his boots slamming into the ground a few feet from the tunnel leading further into the Depths. Petra jumped off his back, sprinting to the tunnel, and Kyle followed after her. He glanced up, spotting the two guards descending toward them, only a few hundred feet above.

"Quickly!" Petra urged, levitating a foot off the ground and flying down the tunnel. Kyle did the same, following the tunnel as it wound its way deep into the earth.

"Think we can fight them?" Kyle called after her.

"Too risky," she replied. "Their magic is far advanced of ours. I hit them a few times," she added, "…but their armor seemed to absorb the blows."

"Great," Kyle grumbled.

"When we get to the wall at the dig site," Petra warned, "...you'll need to open the door quickly."

"Got it."

"We won't have much time."

"I said I got it," Kyle repeated.

"Do you remember where it is?" she pressed.

Kyle didn't respond, concentrating on flying through the winding tunnels without smashing into any walls. After nearly a minute, the tunnel opened up into the giant cavern of the dig site.

"This way!" Kyle ordered, bursting past Petra and flying right toward the wall ahead. He spotted the runic artifacts Bopkin and the other researchers had piled up near the wall...and coincidentally, almost directly under the secret door in the wall some one hundred feet above.

At least he *thought* that's where it was.

He swooped forward and upward, reaching the wall in seconds, then flying straight up...and streaming magic at the wall as he went.

There was shouting from behind, and Kyle glanced back, spotting the two guards flying into the chamber after them.

"You focus on the wall," Petra snapped. "I'll hold them off!"

He obeyed, slowing his ascent while continuing to stream magic to the wall. But he saw no telltale blue glow of runes...and he was farther up than he remembered them being.

Which meant the door had to be to the right or left...and if he chose wrong...

Boom!

He glanced back, seeing a rapidly expanding shockwave of rippling air shoot outward from Petra, slamming into the guards. They were thrown backward, their spears flying from their hands.

"The wall!" Petra shouted.

"Working on it," Kyle grumbled. He moved to the right a few yards, then descended, continuing to stream magic to the wall...and saw runes light up in front of him. "Got it!"

"Unlock it, quickly!"

The guards recovered from Petra's blast...and their spears shot right back into their hands. They pointed them at Petra, who flew to the side just as beams of deadly white light pierced the air where she'd been a split-second earlier. She counterattacked, the rubble between them exploding, a veritable wall of dust and debris flying upward…and blocking their view of her.

Kyle resisted the urge to watch, focusing on the runes. Sweat dripped into his eyes, stinging them, and he wiped the moisture away hurriedly, pulling magic into his mind's eye. He wove quickly, tracing each of the runes, then throwing the patterns outward.

The door swung inward.

"Petra!" he cried. "It's open!"

"Go in!" she shouted, turning away from the guards and flying toward him. He flew into the tunnel beyond, glancing back to see the guards bursting through the cloud of dust after them. Their spears flashed, beams of light striking the wall…and missing Petra by mere inches.

"Hurry!" he cried, backpedaling deeper into the tunnel.

She reached the entrance…just as the door began to swing shut. Another beam of light shot right at her.

"Petra!"

She narrowly dodged the deadly attack…and slammed into the edge of the closing door in a spray of blood, careening into the tunnel and smashing into him. He flew backward, landing on his back with her on top of him, air exploding from his lungs. He gasped, stars floating in his vision…and felt something hot and wet on his chest. He grunted, rolling Petra off of him.

She screamed.

Kyle froze, his vision clearing. He saw Petra lying on her back next to him, her Reaper uniform – and his shirt – soaked with blood. The black fabric at her left arm had torn off completely, exposing a deep gash in her upper arm…and a jagged white bone end jutting out of it.

The door to the tunnel slammed shut.

"Petra!" Kyle cried, kneeling before her. He stared at her broken arm in horror, watching as blood flowed from the gaping wound, forming a rapidly expanding puddle beneath her. She grit her teeth against the pain, her breath coming in short gasps. Sweat poured from her brow.

"Pressure," she ordered. "Put pressure on it!"

He nodded, remembering what he'd learned from his parents, both of them emergency physicians. He had to stop the bleeding first, which meant either applying direct pressure to the wound, or compressing the artery upstream from the break. He could do that with his hands, but it would be much easier to use a tourniquet.

He pulled off his shirt, then wrapped it around Petra's arm above the break, tying it tight, until the bleeding stopped.

"Okay," he stated. "Bleeding's stopped." Now he had to find some way to splint the arm. He looked around, knowing full-well that there was nothing in the tunnel to use as a splint. Then he looked down at himself, at his bloodstained undershirt.

A sling!

Kyle peeled off his undershirt, looping it behind Petra's neck, then under her mid-forearm, tying it loosely there until her elbow was at a ninety-degree angle.

"Better?" he asked. Petra grimaced, then nodded. But she didn't *look* better.

"Help me up," she ordered, reaching up with her good arm. He grabbed her by the elbow, helping her to her feet. She bit off another scream with the movement, rising to her feet, then leaning against the wall. More sweat beaded on her dark skin, dripping down her tattooed temples.

"Petra…" he began. But she cut him off with a gesture.

"We go," she interjected. "Forward." She pushed herself from the wall. "You lead."

Kyle nodded, walking down the tunnel to the room beyond. An eight-by-eight-foot room, the ceiling fifty feet above. He glanced at Petra, noting the blue light around her exposed bone.

"Can you fly?" he asked. She nodded, of course. It'd been a dumb question.

He flew upward, Petra following close behind, and reached the top quickly, streaming magic to the door he knew was on the wall before him. Three runes flashed bright blue, and he traced them quickly, opening the door. He went through first, followed by Petra, finding himself in the familiar tunnel beyond. This led to another eight-by-eight-foot room, but with a much lower ceiling. The same room they'd come to the other day...the one with the trap.

Kyle streamed magic to the far wall ahead, seeing three more sensory runes light up. Then he tried the floor.

More runes lit up across the floor, each connected to the sensory runes.

"Right," he mumbled, recalling what he'd discovered before.

"What?" Petra asked. She grimaced, clutching onto her bad arm. "What's wrong?"

"It's starting to ache," she admitted. "I think it's the tourniquet."

"It'll be okay for now," he reassured. It could take up to six hours without a blood supply for a limb to start dying...if he remembered correctly. "We can try loosening it in a bit. I don't want it to start bleeding again."

"Okay," she agreed. "This room was trapped," she remembered.

"Yeah," Kyle agreed. "The runes on the door are connected to more runes all over the floor. Which means if we open the door, something bad might happen."

"A third test," she reasoned. "Can you describe the runes on the floor?" Kyle shook his head.

"They're complicated," he answered. "Real complicated."

"Then we must protect ourselves while opening the door," she reasoned.

"Protect ourselves from what?" Kyle countered. "There's no telling what this place will throw at us. And if we get it wrong..."

"We either go forward, or go back."

And they both knew what was waiting for them if they did the latter.

Kyle sighed, running a hand through his hair.

"Okay," he said. "We can open the door and use gravity shields to protect us from whatever traps are here, but that'd be too easy...these traps probably won't be stopped so easily."

"Agreed."

"And I can't open the door without triggering the trap," he continued, tapping his chin. "Unless…"

"Yes?"

He reached into his pockets, rummaging around…and finding a few small cubes inside. He pulled one out; it was one of the crystals Master Lee had given him, for practicing making runics. A blank one, unlike the few magnetobombs and gravity grenades he had left.

"Unless we don't need to be in the room to unlock it," he reasoned, breaking out into a smile. "That's it!"

"What's it?" Petra asked.

"I can't send the pattern out to the runes from too far away by myself," he reasoned. There were three runes to trigger, and the further away a sensory rune was, the harder it would be to trigger all three accurately. "But I can inscribe the patterns to unlock the door in this cube, and stream magic to it from far away…from back in the tunnel," he added, pointing back the way they'd come. "We'll be far enough away from the room to avoid the trap, and the cube will be close enough to the door to trigger it."

"Maybe," Petra replied. She nodded grudgingly. "It is a good plan."

"We should still shield ourselves," Kyle stated. "Just in case."

"All right," she agreed, backing up into the hallway. "Do it."

Kyle got to work, pulling a small brown cube from his pocket and streaming magic to the three sensory runes locking the door. They lit up again, and he inscribed them quickly into the cube.

"All right," he declared. "It's done." He set the cube near the secret door, then backed up into the hallway with Petra, who stood behind him. He wove magic, noting that he still had quite a bit left despite the magic constantly draining from his body. There had to be Void crystals or something like them around here somewhere, but they were no match for his unparalleled ability to produce magic.

Multilayered gravity shields appeared around them.

"Okay," he stated, taking a deep breath in, then letting it out. "Ready?"

"Ready."

He hesitated, glancing back at her.

"If we don't make it," he said, giving her a weak smile, "…I just want to say I appreciate everything you've done for us." He swallowed past a sudden lump in his throat. "You could've left us at any time, you know. When things got rough. You could've gone back to the Barren Forest to be with your family."

"True," she admitted. He hesitated.

"Why didn't you?"

"Because I care about you," Petra answered. "And I promised Kalibar I would look after you."

Kyle nodded, blinking back sudden moisture in his eyes.

"If I die," Petra stated, "…promise me you will tell Kalibar…"

"Tell him what?"

She grimaced.

"Tell him that I know how he feels about me," she requested. "And that I feel the same."

Kyle nodded again.

"I will," he promised.

She took a deep breath in.

"Do it."

Kyle turned to the tiny cube near the far wall of the room, pulling a cord of magic into his mind's eye. He held it for a moment, closing his eyes and gritting his teeth.

Then he threw it outward at the cube.

Chapter 33

Long rows of tents had been erected a block away from the burnt-out remains of the palatial resorts lining the emerald waters of the lagoon in Osa, shielding the victims lying on makeshift cots beneath the tents from the last rays of sun peeking from above the endless ocean. The air was starting to cool, for which Jag was grateful; it felt marvelous on his hot, sweaty skin. He stood by the tent, watching as the man he'd treated walked away.

"We got one more," Hana called out as she walked up to him, towing a young man carrying a child. A short, elderly woman with long silver hair, Hana was a retired nurse. She was no-nonsense, but with a warmth that surprised him.

"What we got?" Jag asked.

"This is Ennis and Favia," Hana introduced. "From one of the resorts. Favia's got a burn."

"Have a seat," Jag told Ennis, gesturing at one of the cots under his tent. The man sat on the edge of the cot, putting the girl on his knee. "Show me," Jag requested.

Ennis gestured at Favia's left arm, which had been wrapped in a piece of cloth. He began unwrapping it, and Favia immediately began to cry, trying to bat her father's hands away. When Ennis unwrapped the last layer of cloth, she screamed…and Jag soon saw why.

Some of her skin peeled off with it, exposing raw, burned flesh beneath.

"Okay," Jag stated, taking a deep breath in. He inspected the wound as Hana had taught him. The skin was beefy red, with some ruptured blisters oozing clear fluid. Other blisters remained intact. "Hold her tight," he instructed Ennis. "This is going to hurt."

Jag touched the edges of the burn, ignoring Favia's screams as he did so. Applying pressure made the skin blanch, and when he let go, it pinked up again. That meant it would heal pretty well. He saw a patch of grayish skin, and pressed on that. Favia didn't yell, and the skin didn't blanch.

That was bad.

"Don't pop the blisters unless they pus up," Jag instructed. "Most of this is gonna heal well, but we need to get rid of that gray skin."

"Get rid of it?" Ennis asked, clearly alarmed. "How?"

"Gonna have to scrape it off," Jag answered. "She might not even feel it," he added, trying to sound as comforting as possible. Something he'd had very little practice doing in his life.

"I don't know…"

"More likely to get infected if we don't," Jag warned. Hana had taught him that as well. Burns that blanched and hurt were good, but gray skin was burnt deep enough to be a problem. It would scar – badly – and the dead skin would invite infection.

And infection, Ennis had to know, could lead to amputation. Or even death.

"All right," Ennis decided. He hesitated. "What do I do?"

"Lie her flat," Jag instructed. "Turn her head so she can't see me and lie on top of her, except the arm."

Ennis complied, and Favia began to scream again, struggling as her father did as he'd been instructed.

"I'll hold her arm," Hana offered, coming to the side of the cot and grabbing Favia's arm, pulling it taut. Jag grabbed a clean knife from the table beside the tent, then knelt before Favia's small arm. He took a deep breath to steady himself, then placed the edge of the knife against the grayish skin.

"Ready?" Jag asked Ennis.

"Ready."

Jag glanced at Hana, who nodded at him encouragingly. Then he grit his teeth, pressing the edge of the knife into Favia's flesh. It sank into the dead skin a good quarter of an inch...with no bleeding.

Another bad sign.

He sawed near the edges of the gray area, then peeled the dead skin off. Underneath, there was some bleeding; he dabbed at it with a clean cloth, seeing yellow fat below...and a hint of rust-colored muscle with some gray spots on it.

Like cooked meat, he thought, feeling a little nauseous.

He cut the gray parts out, making Favia shriek. The sound tore at his very soul, but he kept going, knowing that he had to hurt her to make her better. They'd run out of narcotics an hour ago...and would've run out sooner if Jag hadn't bought more. At ten times the usual price, of course. Shopkeepers making a mint off of tragedy.

Non-native shopkeepers, of course.

Jag finished, then grabbed a jar of honey, scooping a generous amount into the hole in Favia's arm, then grabbing a fresh roll of bandages and wrapping her arm.

"Ok," he stated. "That should do it. Change the bandage twice a day. Clear or pink fluid is normal, white fluid is bad. If it swells or red streaks go up the arm, or she gets a fever, get help."

"Yes sir," Ennis replied, clearly relieved it was over. He got up, holding Favia in his arms. She shot Jag a venomous glare, clinging to her dad. "Thank you," Ennis stated, shaking Jag's hand. "Thank you so much. The gods smile on you."

"You're welcome," Jag replied, smiling at him. "Sorry Favia," he added, waving at her. She turned away from him, of course. The two left, leaving Jag alone with Hana.

"Not bad," Hana admitted, giving him an approving look. "You learn quick...and you got balls. Lots of men wouldn't've been able to do that to that poor girl."

"It felt awful," Jag confessed. "I wanted to stop."

"But you didn't," Hana pointed out, patting him on the shoulder. "You helped a lot of people today, kid. We would've run out of supplies hours ago if you hadn't bought more."

"I just wish we'd had more pain medicine," he muttered.

"You did everything you could," Hana reassured. "Must've cost you a fortune."

Jag gave a rueful smile. It *had* cost him a fortune, at least a small one. Months' worth of earnings for a single day.

"It'll take another fortune to keep it up tomorrow," Hana mused, turning to gaze out at the other tents.

"Luckily I got a few," Jag replied. She glanced at him.

"You've done enough," she scolded.

"I can make more," he countered. She eyed him sidelong for a moment.

"Just make sure you take care of yourself too," she counseled. "The sickest ones we've already seen, at least until the infections start coming in. That'll be in another couple of days."

"I spent my whole life taking care of myself," Jag retorted. "I want to do this." He hesitated. "I *need* to do this."

"All right kid," Hana replied. She smiled at him, leaning in to give him a hug. She let go then, patting his cheek with one rough palm. "Thank you."

"Thank *you*," he said. "For teaching me."

"Oh, I'm not done with you yet," she replied with a wicked grin. "You'll never be a nurse, but we'll get you close enough."

"Looking forward to it."

"I'll pack up," she stated. "You go on home."

"I can…"

"Go," she interrupted, waving him away.

"All right," Jag mumbled. "Bye Hana."

"Bye Jag."

He turned away, walking between the rows of tents until he'd left them behind, continuing down the street. It struck him that he didn't know what to do now. He had a home just outside of Osa, a small cottage by the shore. It was only a few miles away; if he ran, he could make it by sundown. He hardly felt like running though, not after the day he'd had. He was exhausted…but in a good way. In fact, he felt better than he had in a long, long time.

For the first time in his adult life, he'd done something for someone else. Without expecting anything in return. And they'd truly appreciated it. He'd gotten more hugs in this afternoon than he'd gotten in a lifetime.

It'd felt *amazing*.

His father had always told him that being part of something greater than oneself was the path to the divine. And he'd been right, in a way. But Jag didn't need to drug himself into a stupor to become part of something bigger. He didn't need to conjure up false gods to experience the divine. Being with the gods meant nothing.

Being with *people* meant something. Meant everything.

And that's exactly what he'd yearned for for so many years growing up in the Citadel. A connection with his father, one that wasn't transactional. One that wasn't conditional. He'd given up on that, and even led himself to believe that he was just like his father. Broken, unable to truly love.

Maybe I'm not.

He strode more quickly down the sidewalk, a smile on his lips. Despite the long day, he felt a new energy coursing within him, a giddy feeling both foreign and wonderful.

I can be the man my father never was, he realized.

And that was the real crux of it. For all the times he'd defied his father, hating the man, he'd almost turned out exactly like Kilson. Pretending to be a good man, but doing everything for himself, never letting anyone in unless it was to get something from them.

No more.

He didn't need his father. He didn't need the Citadel or its gods, or the heaps of money he'd lied, cheated, and stole to amass. The life he'd imagined for himself – one of impossible luxury – would never fill his heart. Not like it'd been filled today.

He smiled to himself, gazing at the setting sun in the distance, sending its long reflection across the water.

Then heard footsteps behind him.

357

The sound jerked Jag out of his thoughts, and he resisted the urge to turn around, continuing to walk, forcing himself to move casually. He felt the amulet he wore around his neck bouncing on his upper chest, and focused on it. A gift from his father, a minor runic device from the Citadel. Illegal to bring it out into the outside world, but his father had allowed it.

The footsteps followed, faster now.

Jag focused inward, willing the vibrations within him to focus into a single point in the center of his awareness. He held it there, waiting.

"Jag?" a voice called out.

Jag spun around...and saw a dark figure approaching him, hidden in the shadows.

"If I were you," he warned, "...I wouldn't get any closer."

"Jag!" the figure exclaimed.

Jag frowned; it was a woman's voice. The figure approached, and it was then that he saw starlight shining on a pale face. A very familiar face.

"Ariana?" he blurted out.

"It's me," Ariana confirmed. "I've been looking all over for you."

"And now you've found me," Jag replied warily. "What's going on?"

"Grand Weaver Kalibar wants to talk to you," she explained.

"I'm a little busy to fly back to Stridon," he grumbled.

"No, he's here," Ariana insisted. "In Meros, at the governor's mansion."

"He's *here?*"

"He came earlier today," she confirmed. "He needs to talk to you."

"What about?"

"It's about Kyle," Ariana answered. "And Petra. They went to the Citadel this afternoon, but they haven't come back yet."

"What?" Jag exclaimed. "They got in without me?"

"Yes."

He stared at her for a long moment, then grimaced.

"In that case," he replied at last, "...they're in deep shit."

Jag stood in governor Candric's office, before the large desk behind which Grand Weaver Kalibar himself sat. He was, as usual, struck by Kalibar's intensity, and his vitality. Nearly as old as his own father but appearing decades younger, the Grand Weaver was distinguished, handsome, and possessed of remarkable self-confidence. One that was earned, of course. A rarity, to have a man with confidence equaled by his competence.

"Tell me your concerns," Kalibar urged, folding his hands atop the desk. He then fell silent, waiting for Jag to respond.

"The original contract stipulated that I accompany your Runics to the Citadel each time. They aren't supposed to be able to go in without me." He paused, waiting for Kalibar to say something, but the man didn't. Jag cleared his throat. "They're also contractually obligated to leave before sunset," he continued.

Still, Kalibar said nothing, listening intently.

"You understand the, ah, agreement I reached with your researchers?" Jag inquired, shifting his weight from one foot to the other.

"I do," Kalibar confirmed.

"There's a possibility my father caught them…helping themselves to some runic artifacts," Jag explained. "If that's the case, the law says the punishment for that is…"

He trailed off, glancing at Ariana, who was leaning against the wall near the door. Then he turned back to Kalibar, who still said nothing.

"…death," Jag concluded with a grimace.

"You're saying there is a possibility my son and Petra have been detained by the Citadel," Kalibar stated.

"Yes," Jag replied. "Or, well, we don't exactly detain the guilty," he corrected. "The High Priest acts as judge, jury, and…executioner. If he has proof of any crime, he'll act on it sooner rather than later."

"So my son may already be dead," Kalibar deduced. He'd stated it mildly, but the intensity of his expression was anything but. There was a sharp intake of breath from Ariana.

Jag shrugged helplessly.

"Can you retrieve them for me?" Kalibar asked.

"Sir?"

"I would ask you to go back to the Citadel. Talk to your father. If my family is still alive, find some way to negotiate the terms of their release."

"I...uh..."

Kalibar stood then, stepping around the table to stand before Jag, who felt immediately intimidated by the man's presence. Kalibar reached out, grabbing Jag's shoulders gently but firmly.

"I love my son," he stated, his eyes glittering with moisture. "I love him more than my office, more than my riches. More than I could possibly communicate with words." He gripped Jag's shoulders more firmly. "I would die for him, Jag. If your father requested that I take his place, I would do it without hesitation."

And the way Kalibar said it, Jag knew beyond a doubt that it was true.

He swallowed past a sudden lump in his throat, knowing full well that his own father would never say such a thing. Had never loved him the way Kalibar loved his son.

And he wished, at that moment, that Kalibar had been his father. That he could've had a father like this.

"If I go back," Jag warned, "...I might be sentenced too. I'm as guilty as they are."

Kalibar stared at Jag for a long moment, then lowered his gaze, his shoulders slumping.

"I understand."

Jag stared at the man. Two futures spread out before him, one where he walked away, and one where he didn't. And he knew with sudden, utter certainty that if he left this man, that if he didn't help Kalibar, that he'd have to live with that for the rest of his life. It would follow him everywhere he went. It would be there when he went to sleep, and would be waiting for him when he awoke.

Regret. Shame.

He hesitated, then put a hand on Kalibar's shoulder. Kalibar lifted his gaze, staring into Jag's eyes. Tears were streaming down the Grand Weaver's cheeks.

"Then again," Jag stated, "...maybe not."

"You'll do it?" Kalibar asked. Jag nodded.

"I have to."

"You will have every reward," Kalibar vowed. "Ask your price and you'll have it."

"I don't want your money," Jag countered. "I just want to live a life I can be proud of."

Kalibar stared at him for a long, silent moment. Then he nodded, a smile on his lips.

"That," he stated at last, "...is the greatest wealth of all."

Chapter 34

Kyle stared through the blue shimmering surface of his gravity shields at the small cube at the far end of the eight-by-eight-foot room ahead, holding a pulsing knot of power in his mind's eye.

Then he took a deep breath in, and threw the magic outward.

A stream of magic shot forward, striking the cube.

The runes on the secret door beyond flashed bright blue, and then the floor ahead shot upward like a giant piston, slamming into the ceiling above with an ear-splitting *bam!*

A rush of air screeched around Kyle and Petra's shields, the view ahead obscured by a wall of stone from the piston-like floor. A few seconds passed, and then the floor began to sink downward, eventually reaching its original position. Beyond, Kyle saw the secret door, now open…and the crushed remains of his cube scattered across the floor.

"Go!" Petra urged.

They flew forward, bursting out of the tunnel into the room, then flying straight through the open doorway on the other side. They were just in time; the door swung closed behind them a moment later.

Kyle found himself in a long, dark hallway, the stone floor and walls rising to a ceiling ten feet above. Petra smiled at him.

"Good thinking," she congratulated. He smiled back, then focused on the hallway ahead, casting one of his magical lights forward.

He froze.

For there, not twenty feet from where they stood, was a large metallic man-ant. One of the emissaries...staring right at them.

"Back!" Kyle cried, creating more layers of gravity shields around them. But the emissary didn't attack. Instead, it turned away, skittering down the hallway and vanishing into the darkness beyond. Kyle watched it go, then glanced at Petra.

"Perhaps it wants us to follow," she proposed.

"Think that's a good idea?"

"What choice do we have?" Petra countered.

"Fair point."

Petra nodded at him, and he strode forward, casting his magical light ahead of them. The hallway stretched onward as far as he could see; they continued down it, eventually reaching a dead-end.

Kyle frowned, slowing as they reached the wall ahead.

"Maybe there's another secret door," Petra guessed, grimacing and grabbing her arm. Kyle glanced down at it, noting that her hand was much paler than the good one.

"We should loosen the tourniquet," he stated. "Maybe the bleeding stopped."

"Try it."

He did so, untying the knot, then unwrapping the makeshift tourniquet and watching the gash in her arm. Blood began to ooze from it, though much more slowly than before. Petra grimaced.

"It's tingling," she informed him, her jaw rippling as she grit her teeth. "Ooo," she added. "Hold on."

They waited, and Kyle saw that her hand had pinked up considerably. She clenched and unclenched it.

"Better," she stated. "Wrap it around the wound, but not too tightly," she instructed. Kyle did so, applying pressure to the wound, but not enough to cut off her circulation completely.

"I'll try the wall," he offered, turning to the dead-end wall before them. He walked up to it, streaming magic to the stone. But nothing happened...no runes lit up. "Damn, he muttered.

And then the floor dropped out from under them.

"Whoa!" Kyle cried, instantly activating his gravity boots. But it was unnecessary; the floor was descending, but in a controlled fashion, like an elevator. Downward it went, until Kyle wondered if it would ever stop. Eventually it did, slowing, then stopping...and revealing another long, dark hallway beyond.

They stepped off the elevator, Kyle casting his light forward. This hallway looked identical to the first. He walked down it, Petra close behind. He spotted a bright golden light ahead, and the emissary waiting for them just before it. It watched them with its lone eye as they approached; Kyle slowed, then stopped a healthy distance from it, eyeing it warily. Petra stopped beside him.

"What are you?" she demanded.

No response.

"Can you talk?" she pressed. Still, the creature did not respond. But it turned away from them, continuing down the tunnel toward the golden light streaming through an archway beyond. Kyle and Petra glanced at each other, then followed behind it. They passed through the archway...and Kyle gasped.

The room beyond was *enormous*.

They were standing on a wide ledge with a short stone railing directly ahead, overlooking a huge space. A room that must have been a few hundred yards squared, with a stone floor forty feet below the ledge they were standing on. Bright golden lights illuminated the space, suspended in mid-air all around the room at varying heights. More emissaries skittered around below, dozens of them, weaving around various metal tables and heaps of what appeared to be scrap metal around the periphery of the room.

And in the center of the room was the largest tree Kyle had ever seen.

Its trunk was truly massive, maybe two hundred feet in diameter, with large roots plunging into the stone floor around it. Huge branches extended upward hundreds of feet, piercing through the stone ceiling that looked to have been built around them. The tree's bark was thick and rough, and the golden lights all around it cast it in otherworldly glow.

"Whoa," Kyle breathed, staring at the tree. A chill ran through him, goosebumps rising on his arms. He turned to Petra, seeing her staring at the tree, her eyes wide, her mouth hanging open. She realized he was staring at her, and she blinked, her mouth snapping shut.

"This must be the Old Tree," she reasoned.

Kyle nodded mutely.

Smaller branches came off the main trunk and larger branches, large leaves identical to the ones he'd seen at the surface sprouting from them. And the pamaté fruit hung from many of them, just as they had above, when Kyle had first seen them near the top of the Citadel's massive walls.

Which meant that this tree was thousands of feet tall.

"Welcome," a smooth, deep voice greeted. It seemed to come from everywhere and nowhere, echoing through the massive chamber. "Please, come down."

A stairway lit up to their left, and Kyle glanced at Petra, who shrugged. They walked to the stairway, then took them down, eventually reaching the floor of the chamber. Tables were laid out in neat rows ahead, metal and crystal gadgets of all kinds sitting atop them. Emissaries skittered around the huge chamber, paying Kyle and Petra no mind.

"Hello?" Kyle called out.

He felt the *hum* of magic in his mind, and looked up. A dark figure was descending from the upper branches of the Old Tree toward them.

"Greetings," the figure replied. The voice was similar – smooth and deep – but this time it clearly came from…whoever it was. A man, Kyle saw as the stranger dropped gently to the floor before them. A bald man with skin as black as night, his well-muscled chest bared. For he wore no shirt, only loose black pants. His feet were bare, his body covered in black tattoos from head to toe, like Petra. And like Petra, he bore long, raised scars on his temples. The mark of the Joined, those who became one with the Reaper vines. He had another diamond-shaped scar in the center of his forehead.

Kyle felt a chill run down his spine.

"Who are you?" Petra demanded, stepping in front of Kyle and glaring at the man. He smiled, reaching out with one hand. He looked to be about thirty, but it was difficult to say.

"My name is Calef," he answered. "What is yours, my child?"

Petra hesitated, then shook the man's hand.

"I am Petra," she replied. "Of the Barren tribes."

"But of course you are," Calef stated, his black eyes twinkling. "To think that I would find my kin in this place," he added, gesturing around the chamber. "And a Joined! I am delighted to have you as my guest."

He turned to Kyle then.

"And you as well," he added. "You must be Kyle."

"Yes," Kyle confirmed. Then he frowned. "How'd you know that?"

"My friends tell me," Calef answered, gesturing at one of the emissaries. "Or rather, I hear through them, and see through them. They are my eyes and my ears."

"Your...friends?"

"I made them," Calef admitted. "They are poor conversationalists, I must confess. But they are my only company...except of course for her," he added, gesturing at the tree.

"Her?" Petra asked.

"Oh yes," Calef replied. "The Mother."

"How did you get here?" Petra asked. "And what are you doing here?"

"I could ask the same of you," Calef countered. "I have not had anyone manage to pass my trials for a very long time." Then he broke out into a grin. "Come," he added. "Let us bask in the light of the Mother. I will explain everything to you...after you tell your tale to me."

He strode toward the tree with remarkable vigor, and Kyle and Petra followed him, struggling to keep up with his fast pace. Calef's excitement was obvious; he led them to one of the huge roots coming from the tree trunk, flying up twenty feet to land atop it. He turned around, sitting down and hanging his legs off the edge of the root, patting the spot beside him.

"Come!" he urged.

Kyle flew up to join Calef, sitting down to his left, and Petra did as well, sitting on the man's right. The root's bark was surprisingly warm, and Kyle felt the *hum* of magic all around him, filling him instantly.

"Now," Calef stated, putting an arm around each of their shoulders. The man's skin was as cold as ice, like Ariana's...and Petra clearly was not pleased with the gesture. "Tell me your story!"

"Well," Kyle began, "...we came from the Empire to the Citadel to..."

"Oh no, no," Calef interrupted. "From the very beginning. I want to know who you *are*."

"Uh..." Kyle mumbled. "That might be a while." Calef smirked at him.

"Time I have," he replied.

"Why should we?" Petra interjected. Calef turned to her. "We don't know you," she explained. "You could be an enemy."

"I am *no* one's enemy," Calef countered. "My life is here, in this great place, the birthright of our people. My heart is with the Mother. I will not hurt you unless you would hurt me."

Still Petra stared at him, clearly unconvinced. Calef's expression became deadly serious.

"You are safe here," he insisted earnestly. "In my care, under the light of the Mother, no harm will come of you."

Kyle glanced at Petra, who hesitated, then nodded grudgingly.

"I guess I'll start at the beginning," Kyle said. "Or at least as close as I can."

He told his tale then, starting with his life on Earth, and how his parents had divorced. How he'd gone to school, played with friends. Kyle thought for sure he'd bore Calef with the details, but it was quite the opposite; Calef seemed utterly fascinated, asking questions at every turn. Not just about Earth, or Kyle's family. But how Kyle *felt* about them. His inner thoughts, his experience of his own life. Kyle had never had to tell anyone such things. Never had anyone even ask. At first he was protective of these innermost thoughts and feelings, but as Calef greeted each revelation with warmth and encouragement, Kyle found himself letting go of his concerns. He opened up, eventually reaching the point where he'd come to this world. How he'd met Kalibar and Ariana, fought the Dead Man, struggled to survive against Xanos, and eventually destroyed Sabin. He kept the details light when it came to Ampir, of course.

When he was done, Kyle felt exhausted...but good. Really good. Other than asking questions, Calef hadn't interrupted once, or seemed impatient in the least.

"What a tale," Calef murmured, shaking his head. He smiled at Kyle, patting his upper back. "You have given me more than I could have imagined, Kyle. Other worlds! And with such amazing technology!"

"Wait," Kyle said. "You believe me?"

"Of course," Calef replied. "The Mother has shown me the many worlds beyond our own. And," he added, winking at Kyle, "...perhaps she has shown me yours."

Kyle blinked.

"What?"

"That is for later," Calef stated. "You say Ampir destroyed Sabin?" Kyle nodded. "Good," he declared. "I trust death will be kinder to him than life ever was," he ventured. "Sabin was a good man, a brilliant man, but a tortured soul."

"Wait," Petra interjected. "You knew him?"

"I knew *both* of them," Calef corrected. "Ampir and Sabin." He leaned back with a smile, shaking his head wistfully. "To think that Ampir found immortality...but of course he did. He was beyond Sabin. Beyond anyone of his time. I wonder if..."

He fell silent then, and Kyle raised an eyebrow at him.

"Ampir was very curious about this place," Calef admitted. "He visited me here. Only once, very soon after I came to the Citadel. I showed him the Ambrosia, and he took some with him. I suspect this has something to do with his immortality."

He fell silent again, considering this. Then he realized they were both watching him with confused expressions on their faces. He smiled, turning to Petra. "But I prattle on. I would hear your story now, Petra."

Petra told her story, remaining cagey when it came to more personal details. Then she grimaced, clutching at her right arm.

"You're injured," Calef noted. "Is it bad?"

"I broke my arm," Petra answered. "It is bad."

"I will see it," Calef stated. He began untying the cloth Kyle had wrapped around the wound, and Petra winced, pulling away.

"I don't..." she began.

"Come now," he interrupted, finishing unwrapping it. His breath drew in with a hiss. "That is a bad break," he observed. "It will become infected and this will kill you."

"You are very comforting," Petra grumbled.

"Have no fear," Calef replied with a smile. "I will save your arm and your life. Or rather, the Mother will!"

With that, he leapt down from the root, floating to the stone floor below. Kyle and Petra stood up, but Calef waved them down.

"Stay, please," he instructed.

He grabbed a section of the root's bark then, peeling it off and throwing it aside. Then one of the emissaries came to his side, plunging a metallic fist into the flesh of the root underneath. The emissary stepped back, and Calef cupped his hands, putting them into the wound, then flying up to Kyle and Petra. A white, gooey substance was in his hands.

"This is Ambrosia," he explained. "The sap of the Mother. Drink it and it will heal you."

Petra hesitated, then lowered her lips to the Ambrosia, drinking of it. After a few swallows, she glanced up at him.

"That should be sufficient," he declared. "Your wounds will heal with time...and the Reaper vines in your skull will be repelled for a time."

"How does it work?" Kyle asked.

"The Mother is the Goddess of Life," Calef explained. "Now, let me tell *my* story."

He cleared his throat then, staring off at the tree in the distance.

"The world had gone through thirty cycles since my birth," he began. "I was the son of the leader of my tribe, a great woman. She was Joined, as you are," he added, nodding at Petra. "I was given the gift of magic and the talent to use it, and all agreed I would become Joined one day myself."

"How long ago was this?" Petra asked.

"Two thousand and twenty-one cycles," Calef revealed. Petra's eyes widened.

"You are one of the Immortals," she realized. "One of my ancestors!"

"Oh yes," Calef agreed, flashing her a smile. "And how wondrous to see that my people are still strong, and still carrying on the traditions we cherished!" He shook his head in wonder. "If I could pluck you from this time and bring you to my past, no one would know you were not from our time."

"But..." Petra said. She hesitated. "My people worshipped the Immortals for thousands of years, hoping one day to speak with them. I...I did so, met two of them, and they only tried to kill me." Her expression hardened. "They treated me like I was nothing. Like my people were nothing."

"I am sorry," Calef stated solemnly. He sighed. "It is a reflection of their blackened souls, not yours." He smiled at her. "You are not nothing, my child. I am grateful to meet you, and honored to have the opportunity to help you."

"Thank you," Petra murmured. Her eyes became moist, and she lowered her gaze. "Thank you."

"As I said, my fate was to become Joined," Calef continued.

"Wait," Petra interrupted. "You were thirty and not yet Joined?" she asked incredulously. "We do it much earlier."

"Things change," Calef explained. "This is nature's way. That which remains the same is often worth keeping, and that which changes is often not. So it is with the species of animals and plants, and so it is with our cultures."

370

"Go on," Petra urged.

"One day, a man in golden armor came to us," he continued. "His name was Ampir, and he was sent to destroy us. You see, his tribe had attacked our land, trying to kill us and steal from our mines. The Barrens drained them of their magic, and the Joined destroyed them. They were nothing before us, but Ampir...ah, he was different. He was their golden warrior, a man who defied the Barrens! Such was his power that he held his magic, and could have defeated us."

"But he didn't?" Kyle asked.

"He was a man sick of war," Calef explained. "He had seen enough of it to give him pause. We attacked him and he did not attack back. Our magic could not hurt him. He found us fascinating, and humbled himself before us."

"I find that hard to believe," Kyle grumbled. Ampir was anything but humble.

"Why?" Calef inquired, seeming genuinely surprised. "Ampir was a warrior, but also a philosopher. He had great power and great wisdom."

"He's...different around me," Kyle admitted.

"Then he is teaching you," Calef concluded. "Ampir was a student and a teacher. He learned our ways, and taught us his ways. He protected us in secret, battling his own tribe without their knowledge. And we gave him the gift of the Reaper vine bark, that he blackened his armor with."

Calef sighed then.

"Eventually Ampir left, and our tribe never saw him again. And then one day, many cycles later, several cycles before I became Joined, another man of his tribe came to us. A man named Sabin."

Kyle's expression darkened, and Calef noted this, but did not comment.

"Sabin was a good man, a brilliant man, but unwise. His mind was forever in the past. When he came to us, he was mad, his mind diseased with loneliness and despair. We healed him as best we could, and in return he opened his heart to us. He took a wife among our people, a beautiful woman with a heart big enough for both of them."

"He sure changed," Kyle muttered. Calef paused, then nodded.

"In a way," he agreed. "Sabin studied the Reapers and their Queens, and through this study he discovered a path to immortality. The tiny crystals within the brains of each Reaper are similar to the crystal within mine," he explained, tapping the scar on his forehead.

"Wait," Kyle stated. "You're a Chosen?"

"Of course," Calef replied.

"But…"

"Patience," Calef admonished gently. "Rest assured I am not one of Sabin's slaves, nor am I in league with the others that attacked you."

"Okay," Kyle replied. "Sorry."

"Sabin made Immortals of animals first, perfecting the process. Then he offered to make Immortals of us. I had since become Joined, and was the second to agree."

"Why?" Petra asked.

"As Joined, my time was limited," Calef explained. "Sabin insisted he could keep the Reaper vines from my brain with the same crystal that would make me immortal. To become an eternal protector of my tribe…it was an honor I could not refuse."

"Must've worked," Kyle said. Calef nodded.

"It did. And it does," he agreed. "Others offered after me, and one before me. Sabin made the first Immortal out of his wife's brother, a man you know as Gundar."

"*He* was Sabin's brother-in-law?" Kyle blurted out. Calef nodded.

"A proud man even then," he replied. "Immortality changed Gundar, made him believe he was greater than his people. Strength was all that mattered to him. He began to look down on his tribe, and on my mother who led it."

"Well, he works for Lady Damia now," Kyle stated.

"So you have taught me," Calef replied. "As it was then, so it is now."

"Huh?"

"You will see," Calef promised. "After Gundar and myself, a third man was chosen to receive the gift of immortality. A man named Yafatka, our medicine man. He was to preserve our knowledge of herbs and healing for eternity, so that we would never lose this wisdom."

He sighed then, shaking his head.

"And then came the fourth," he stated. "And the last of what Sabin was to call his 'Prime Chosen.'"

"Who?" Petra inquired.

"Sabin's wife," Calef answered. "She requested it, and requested that he join her afterward. So that their love could last forever. You see, Sabin was older, and plagued with illness, a disease our medicine man knew well. Incurable. In any case, he agreed, and made her the fourth Immortal. But...something went wrong."

"What's that?" Kyle asked.

"It worked – she was immortal – but her mind was damaged, and her heart. From that moment on, she saw others as...things. Her heart was closed. Love became foreign to her, including her love for Sabin."

He sighed again.

"After that, Sabin refused to make more Immortals. His heart was crushed, and his illness claimed him. One morning we found him unable to move, barely breathing. We took him to the cave where you found him, and executed his instructions to make him an Immortal. And so it was."

"What then?" Kyle pressed. "How did you get here?"

"Sabin took a long time to become what you saw," Calef answered. "And in his absence Gundar and Sabin's wife banded together, murdering my mother and father and declaring themselves leaders of the tribe. I attacked them, but Sabin had given his wife a more powerful crystal than mine. I had a choice: escape, or die. So I escaped."

"And came here?"

"Yes," Calef answered. "It was the one place I knew I would be safe from them, the true home of our people."

373

"What are you talking about?" Petra retorted. "The Barren forest is the home of our people."

"The second home," Calef corrected. "The first was what you now call the Citadel. This was the home of the gods first, and of the Mother. After the Cataclysm, it became our home."

"The what?"

"The Cataclysm," Calef repeated. "I have seen it in the memories of the Mother," he explained, gesturing at the tree. "Her fruit holds her memories, and those that eat of them can experience them. Imperfect, like a blind man seeing with his fingers, but still enlightening. I have spent the last two thousand cycles eating of the fruit my friends collect for me," he added, gesturing at an emissary. "I wish to know the mind of the Mother, and like you," he stated, gesturing at Petra, "...I wish to follow my roots to their creation."

"So there *were* gods here?" Kyle asked. Calef nodded.

"Oh yes," he confirmed. "Five great gods and many, many lesser ones. The Mother was the strongest of the five. They came here long, long ago, from another world. Ruled this world for many cycles, far more than I have been alive." He sighed. "I don't know the details," he admitted, "...but one day the lesser gods rose up against the five, killing all but the Mother, who cannot be killed. She had long before transformed into this tree, and posed no threat to the lesser gods. Still, they tried to kill her, and could not. So they buried her, small as she was at that time."

"What happened then?" Kyle inquired.

"The lesser gods were made immortal by the Mother," he explained. "They did not know this. When they attacked her, their immortality was revoked. They grew old and died...but had children, in the way of mortals. These children beget children, who beget children, and eventually the magic and knowledge of the gods was lost. These were my ancient ancestors. This is where we come from," he stated, nodding at Petra."

"We're..."

"The children of the gods," Calef confirmed. "The Citadel is our birthright...and the Mother is our mother. You see, the lesser gods were borne of the five great gods, and the Mother was the only woman."

Petra turned to stare up at the massive tree, her eyes wide. Calef patted the bark of the root.

"You are a child of the Goddess," he declared with a smile. "As am I. The tree you sit upon, the tree standing before you, is the beginning of our people. These roots are the roots of our very existence. Our ancestors were borne of her womb."

"I…" Petra said, staring at the tree, her jaw slack. She shook her head slowly. There were no words.

"You must bring this knowledge to our people," Calef urged. "Tell them of their heritage."

"I will," Petra promised. Tears streamed down her cheeks, and she took a deep, shuddering breath in, lowering her gaze to match Calef's. "Thank you," she murmured. "This…is everything to me."

"You are very welcome," Calef replied. He leaned in then, embracing her. They held each other for a long moment, and then Calef pulled away. "Would you…like to know your Mother?"

"What?"

"Eat of her fruit," Calef clarified. "It is your right to know your Mother."

"Yes," Petra replied instantly. "Please."

"A moment," he requested. And it was only that long before an emissary came up to them, climbing up the side of the root with their ant-legs, carrying a glowing white fruit in their hands. They gave it to Calef, who handed it to Petra. "Each fruit contains a fragment of a memory," he explained. "Eat only a little at a time, for to eat too much is poison. A single bite will do."

Petra nodded, then hesitated.

"Now?" she asked.

"Share it with your tribe," he instructed. "So that they may see the truth of their heritage."

"Thank you," Petra stated. "For everything."

"Of course," Calf replied. He stood up then, offering a hand to Petra, then Kyle. "Now we must go."

"Where?" Kyle asked.

"The people who have claimed our home wish you dead," he explained. "I am still a Joined, sworn to protect my people. So protect you I shall."

"What if they attack us?" Petra asked.

"My friends will accompany you," Calef answered, gesturing at some nearby emissaries, who stopped what they were doing, turning to look up at them. "The occupiers cherish them, and will not dare interfere with them. If they do, I will act through them to ensure your safety."

"Act through them?" Kyle asked.

"Pray it does not come to that," Calef replied. He jumped down from the root then, landing on the floor twenty feet below. Kyle and Petra followed, and within a few seconds, they were surrounded by a half-dozen emissaries. Calef hugged Petra one more time, then embraced Kyle, to Kyle's surprise.

The emissaries turned toward the stairs leading back up to the walkway above, skittering toward them.

"Follow them," Calef instructed.

"Thank you again," Petra stated. "Will…can I see you again?"

"Of course," he replied. "I insist that you do. And you as well, Kyle. The grandson of Ampir is welcome here anytime."

They smiled, then turned to go. But Kyle paused, glancing back. "Why don't you let anyone else in?" he asked.

"Only a Joined could make it through this temple," Calef answered. "Or Ampir. Or, in this case, you," he added. "Sabin himself could not enter without my consent, even if the occupiers were to let him within the Citadel walls. Nor the other Prime Chosen."

"Ah," Kyle replied, although it hadn't really answered his question. He turned away, following Petra to the stairs.

"One more thing," Calef stated. "Get as far away from Gundar and Damia as possible. And warn Ampir about them if you can."

"I get warning Ampir about Gundar," Kyle replied. "But why Damia?"

"Because," Calef answered. "She's far more dangerous."

"Really?"

"Oh yes," Calef replied. "You see, Damia was Sabin's wife."

Chapter 35

High Priest Kilson glared at his two Holy Sentries, men clad in godstone armor within which the ancient runic magic of the gods had been inscribed. The armor made them nigh invincible, his agents of justice and death. Their spears, imbued with the power to destroy almost anything, were clutched in their hands as they stood before him in the Chamber of Communion, staring at him silently.

"They *what?*" he blurted out.

"They escaped into the Ruins," one of them repeated. "The boy found a way in."

"How in the hell did they 'find the way in?'" Kilson demanded. The Ruins, the great structure built around what most believed was the very heart of the Old Tree, was impenetrable to everyone and everything other than the mysterious emissaries, those creations believed to be as old as the gods themselves. The keepers of the Old Tree, servants of the Goddess. Some believed they'd been created by Her...and only they had access to the Ruins.

"We don't know, your Holiness," came the reply.

"Of course you don't," Kilson muttered. He turned away from them, taking a deep breath in, then letting it out. "Keep watch at the Ruins," he ordered. "They can't stay in there forever."

Which was a guess, of course. No one knew for sure what lay beyond the Ruins. But every calculation insisted it was the Goddess herself. To think that these outsiders might have gained access to her when, in a thousand years, his people had not!

It was unthinkable.

"I will be notified when they emerge," Kilson stated, straining to keep his voice calm.

"Of course, your Holiness."

"Go," he growled.

They bowed, then left him, exiting the Chamber of Communion. Kilson watched them go, then stood there, staring at the door. He lowered his gaze then, shaking his head. Nothing was going as simply as he'd planned. But it was immaterial if the boy and that woman had made it into the Ruins. They couldn't stay in there forever, and they couldn't leave the Citadel. And if they'd made it inside the Ruins, they could be made to tell Kilson how they'd done it.

And then the Priesthood would finally gain access to the Ruins…and perhaps even the Goddess herself!

He smiled at the thought, feeling his shoulders relax. Either way, he would benefit. This was a happy accident; fortune smiled upon him. To see the Old Tree before he died…

There was a sudden knock on the door.

"Yes?" he called out, irritated at the interruption.

"Your son," came a feminine reply.

Kilson blinked, taking a moment to process what he'd heard.

"Bring him in," he ordered. A moment later, the door swung open, and none other than Jagwell stepped into the room. The boy – the *man* – walked up to Kilson, stopping before him. No bow, not even a handshake or a hello.

"Father," Jagwell muttered.

"Son," Kilson replied, unable to help himself from smiling. "I didn't think I'd ever see you again after last night."

"Neither did I."

"Happy birthday son," Kilson stated, ignoring Jag's comment. He paused. "I know you didn't come just to see me," he added.

"I came to ask you to let Kyle and Petra go," Jag revealed. Kilson's eyebrows went up.

"Really," he murmured. "Let me guess…Kalibar sent you?"

"I sent me," Jag retorted.

"I doubt that."

"Doubt all you want," Jag shot back. "Kalibar asked me to go, but I was the one who agreed to."

"And how much is the great Kalibar paying you to convince me to get his children back?" Kilson inquired.

"He isn't."

"Oh bullshit," Kilson retorted. "I know money is the only thing you care about now."

Jag shook his head, a smirk curling his lips.

"Oh how wrong you are, father."

"Really?" Kilson pressed. "What do *you* care about these outsiders?"

"They're innocent," Jag answered. "They had no idea what the Empire was doing. What I was doing."

"So you admit to your crimes," Kilson observed. Jag nodded.

"I do."

Kilson eyed Jag silently for a long moment.

"Why did you do it, son?" he asked at last. "Why did you forsake us?"

"I wanted to hurt you," Jag answered bluntly. "I wanted to get back at you, and make enough money to never have to work again."

"Did you?"

"I did," Jag confirmed.

"So you got everything you wanted," Kilson concluded. "Why come back? Why vouch for two strangers? Don't tell me you care about them."

"Their father does," Kilson retorted. "Which is more than I can say about you."

Kilson stiffened, glaring at his son.

"I could have you executed for your crimes," he shot back. "That's what the law demands."

"I know."

"And yet you came back," Kilson continued. "You must have known I wouldn't do it."

"Not true," Jag countered. Kilson raised an eyebrow.

"Then why return?" he demanded. "Why risk your life for these two? Because you felt bad for the Grand Weaver?"

"He loves his children more than he loves anything," Jag answered. "He would give up his fortune for them. His throne. Even his life."

"I would do the same," Kilson countered.

"No," Jag replied. "You wouldn't."

"And how do you know that?"

"Because you didn't," Jag answered.

Kilson just stared at him, unable to respond. It was true, and he knew it. Or at least, it *had* been true. How many times had Jag asked to spend time with him, and Kilson had told him to wait? That he would spend time with the boy another day? He'd always been too busy, always putting his work first. To be honest, he'd always believed he'd have more time, but Jag had grown up in a flash. And by that time, it'd been too late.

"I've learned my lesson," Kilson stated quietly. "I know I failed you."

"Let them go," Jag insisted. "They're innocent, father."

"Kalibar knew what he was doing when he made the decision to steal from us," Kilson retorted. "Now that he pays the price, he demands leniency? No. There must be a price to pay for his treachery."

"Choose a different price."

"Like what?" Kilson inquired.

"Kalibar is offering to give back all of the runics they took," Jag answered.

"How comforting."

"I'll give back the money I earned helping them," Jag pressed. Kilson's eyebrows rose.

"Oh really?" he murmured. "You're willing to sacrifice for these outsiders?"

"I am."

"I don't understand," Kilson admitted. "Why help them now? Why start caring now? The only thing I've ever know you to care about is yourself."

Jag's jawline rippled, and he glared at his father. But then his shoulders relaxed.

"You're right," he confessed. "I learned from the best."

It was Kilson's turn to stiffen, and he felt a flash of anger. But he let it pass, knowing that Jag was not incorrect. He *had* been selfish. Self-absorbed. All the while believing it was for a higher cause. For the gods. But the gods were dead, save for the One Tree. And she would be here long after he was gone.

"You did," he admitted at last. "That was not the lesson I intended to teach you."

"Too late now."

"Maybe so," Kilson agreed. "So you'll give up the money, return the runics, and Kalibar will get his children back. Is that the deal?"

"It is."

"Very well," Kilson decided. "On one more condition."

"Go on."

"You stay here, in the Citadel with me," Kilson stated. "You must promise to never leave."

Jag's eyes widened, and he took a step back.

"You can't..." he began.

"I can."

"But...that's not fair!" Jag insisted. "You'd keep me a prisoner here?"

"Those are my terms," Kilson declared, crossing his arms over his chest. Jag stared at him incredulously, his mouth working silently. A long, uncomfortable moment passed, and then Jag took a deep breath in.

"Fine," he muttered. Kilson frowned.

"What?"

"Fine," Jag repeated. "I agree to your terms."

"Really," Kilson stated. "You'll stay here for them?"

"I will," Jag replied. "But I'll always hate you for it."

Kilson lowered his arms to his sides.

"Why?" he asked. "Why are you doing this?"

"Because I realized I was just like you," Jag answered. "For the first time in my life, I decided to do something about it. Today, in fact. I helped people, father. I did something for someone other than myself. And you know what?" he added. "It made me feel more alive than I'd ever felt in my life."

Jag crossed his arms over his chest.

"If I let Kalibar's son die, I'd be able to go wherever I wanted," he continued. "But no matter where I went, I wouldn't be able to live with myself."

Kilson stared at Jag, swallowing past a sudden lump in his throat. Jag's eyes were moist, for the first time in years. Tears dripped down the man's cheeks, but Jag did not wipe them away. Did not try to hide what he was feeling. He was not ashamed that he *was* feeling.

Kilson paused, then stepped forward, putting a hand on Jag's shoulder.

"I accept your terms," he decided. "I'll let the boy and the woman go free."

Jag inclined his head slightly.

"Will that be all?" he inquired, his tone flat.

"Yes."

Jag turned, walking toward the door and opening it.

"And Jag?" Kilson called after him. Jag turned around.

"What."

"You can go free as well," Kilson stated. "All I ask is that you stay the night, and have one last supper with me before I die."

Jag stared at him, swallowing visibly. More tears welled up in his eyes. His lips trembled.

"Thank you father."

"I love you son," Kilson stated. "Now more than I ever have. I failed as a father, and I can never change that. That is my greatest regret." He hesitated then. "I'm proud of you, Jagwell."

Jag stood there, the door partly ajar, staring at him. Then he nodded slightly.

"I'll see you tonight father."

And then he stepped past the door, closing it behind him.

Chapter 36

Kyle stood in the tunnel leading outside of Calef's temple, some twenty feet before the stone door separating him from the dig site…and the black-armored guards that almost certainly stood beyond waiting for him. He glanced at Petra, who was standing beside him, then at the half-dozen emissaries crowding the hallway ahead.

"Ready?" Petra asked. He hesitated, then nodded, weaving magic to form layered gravity shields around himself.

"Ready."

"Stay close," Petra instructed. "If anything happens to me, go back to Calef."

"But…"

"No buts," she interjected. "If I fall, you must run."

Kyle hesitated, then nodded.

"If you're hurt, I'll bring you back to the Mother," he offered. She nodded.

"Deal."

They both turned forward then, and Kyle watched as the runes on the stone door beyond the emissaries glowed a bright blue.

It swung open.

"Stay behind the emissaries," Petra ordered. The emissaries started leaping out of the tunnel one at a time, and Petra and Kyle followed after them, stopping at the edge of the tunnel. The large cavern of the dig site spread out below them; Kyle peered through the relative darkness, but couldn't see any black-armored guards.

"Go," Petra urged. "Before it closes!"

She leapt down, sailing through the air toward the cavern floor a hundred feet below. Kyle joined her, and just in time; the door swung closed right behind him. His stomach lurched as he accelerated toward the ground, and he activated his gravity boots at the last minute, slowing his descent for a gentle landing beside Petra. The emissaries skittered ahead, moving quickly toward the tunnels leading to the surface.

"See any guards?" Kyle whispered. Petra peered through the darkness, then shook her head.

"No."

Kyle activated his gravity boots, levitating a few feet off the ground and accelerating to catch up with the emissaries, Petra flying at his side. They reached the tunnel quickly, taking it forward and upward. It wasn't long before they reached the surface of the Depths, the seemingly endless layered platforms of the Citadel far above their heads.

"Coast is clear," Kyle observed, gazing upward. "All we have to do now is get to the Tem…"

BAM!

There was a blinding light, and he felt himself flying backward. His back slammed into something hard, the breath exploding from his lungs. A sudden, intense pain shot through the right side of his chest to his back, his vision blackening.

He gasped for air, but it would not come.

Kyle's vision returned slowly, and he saw Petra flying up to him. Her eyes were wide with fear, her lips moving. But he couldn't hear her. Couldn't hear anything.

She grabbed him by the shoulders, shaking him frantically.

Kyle gasped, finally managing to suck in some air. Petra shook him again, her eyes brimming with tears.

"Kyle!" she shouted. "Kyle!"

He groaned, blinking away the last of the spots from his vision. Then he tried to sit up, but Petra pressed him down firmly.

"What happened?" he mumbled. Petra broke out into a relieved smile.

"You are okay?" she asked. He nodded, looking down at himself. A hole had been burned in his shirt on the right side of his chest, but the skin underneath was intact.

"I think so," he answered. He tried to sit up again, and this time Petra let him. Then she swore, grabbing him and flinging herself to the side.

Boom!

Another shockwave struck them, and the world spun around Kyle wildly. He felt Petra stop abruptly in mid-air; they were levitating some forty feet above the ground, a plume of dust flying upward to their left.

A black-armored man burst out of that cloud, flying right at them!

"Left!" Petra cried...and dodged to the right. The black-armored guard aimed their spear at them, a beam of white light shooting outward and missing them by a wide margin. Petra counterattacked, a bolt of lightning shooting out from her and slamming into the guard's chest.

It didn't even faze him.

Kyle wove magic, creating a gravity sphere around the guard. But the pattern unraveled when it reached the man, tendrils of blue light absorbing into his armor.

What the...

"His armor is absorbing my patterns!" Kyle shouted, dodging out of the way of another blast from the guard's spear.

"Mine too," Petra revealed.

The guard burst toward them...and then a large silver *thing* crashed into him in mid-air. It was an emissary; the creature wrapped its ant-legs around the guard, falling back toward the ground. They slammed into the debris of the Depths, the emissary pinning the guard to the ground. It grabbed the guard's helmet, yanking it off.

And then the tip of the guard's spear burst through the emissary's insectoid thorax.

The emissary leapt off the guard, the spear still impaling its metallic body. It grabbed onto one end then, pulling the spear out of itself and aiming it at the guard's head. A beam of white light shot from the tip, taking the guard's head clear off his shoulders.

He slumped to the ground, never to move again.

"Incoming," Petra warned, glancing upward. Kyle followed her gaze, spotting a half-dozen more guards falling through the air toward them.

"Get to the tunnels!" Kyle cried, grabbing Petra and flying down to the gaping maw of the tunnel below. He flew in a zig-zagging pattern, beams of white light missing them by mere yards, scorching the packed earth below. Kyle flew right into the tunnel, letting go of Petra and traveling a good hundred feet before dropping to the ground. Petra landed beside him.

"What are you doing?" she demanded.

"Let the emissaries take care of them," Kyle replied. "If the enemy follows us, those spears won't be as useful in these winding tunnels."

"A good point," Petra admitted.

There was a shout from behind, and Kyle turned to see several guards flying toward them, emissaries chasing right behind them.

"Back!" he cried, flying further down the tunnel. He glanced back, seeing the guards coming after them. There was no way to cast a pattern directly at them – their armor would unravel the magic threads – but if he were to keep his patterns far enough away...

Kyle wove a flat gravity field, flinging it out directly behind him and streaming a huge amount of magic to it.

A blast of air slammed into him, threatening to fling him backward into the gravity field. He accelerated, resisting the powerful vortex, and glanced back. The wind smashed into the guards, sending them flying backward into the emissaries rushing at them from behind.

The emissaries leapt at the guards, plucking them out of the air and smashing them into the ground, tearing off their armor.

"Well done!" Petra shouted over the howling wind. Kyle cut off the stream to the gravity field, then slowed, dropping gently to the tunnel floor. Petra followed his lead, glancing back. Two of the guards had their helmets torn off by the emissaries, their spears ripped from their hands. But one guard managed to escape, blasting the emissary atop him with his spear. The white light blasted a hole through the emissary's silver head.

It dropped like a stone.

The guard scrambled to his feet, blasting another emissary off of one of his colleagues.

"Kill the damn things!" the guard shouted, blasting a third emissary, then grabbing a nearby spear from the ground, tossing it at a freed guard. "I'll get the boy and the woman!" He turned to Kyle and Petra then, flying through the air toward them with frightening speed.

Kyle burst backward away from the guard, and Petra followed, weaving magic. The ceiling ahead of the oncoming guard collapsed, a deluge of rocks and dirt smashing into him from above…and burying him alive.

"Four more to go," Kyle called out.

A guard flew over the mound of rocks that had fallen, pointing their spear at Kyle and Petra.

"Watch out!" Kyle cried, flinging himself to one side as a white beam shot at him. He slammed into the side wall, feeling a sudden, burning pain in his opposite shoulder. A hole had been burned into his shirt there…and into his flesh. The beam had only grazed him, but a small hunk had been taken out of his skin, the edges of the wound black, the surrounding flesh seared.

"Kyle!" he heard Petra cry.

"I'm okay," he replied, leaping away from the wall as another beam shot at him, missing him by mere inches.

Then he had an idea.

He created a gravity field in front of him, then wove the water pattern, pouring as much magic into it as he could. He thrust it outward at the gravity field.

Water shot outward at the approaching guard like a veritable water cannon, nearly as large as the tunnel itself. It slammed into the flying guard, tossing him backward and upward.

"Freeze it!" Kyle shouted at Petra, activating his gravity boots and flying up from the deluge of water pouring back down the tunnel toward them.

"Get back!" Petra ordered, following her own advice.

Kyle complied, zooming back away from the deluge…and then felt the air turn ice-cold instantly. The column of water flash-froze, then fell to the tunnel floor, breaking into large hunks of ice. So large that they took up two-thirds of the height of the tunnel.

Kyle hesitated, then flew upward and forward over the ice, shivering in the sudden cold. He spotted a dark shape in the ice ahead, embedded several feet down in a frozen tomb. It was the guard, of course; Kyle stared at the man grimly, putting a hand on his burnt shoulder. It wasn't the first time he'd killed a man. Still, he expected to feel something, but all he felt was numb.

"Good work," Petra stated. Kyle flinched, realizing she was levitating beside him.

"There's more coming," he warned. Two more guards were flying over the ice toward them. He wove magic again, sending another blast of water shooting up the tunnel at them. But one of them shot at him with their magic spear, forcing Kyle to dodge out of the way…and breaking his concentration. The water stopped, the guards flying right at Kyle.

"Back!" he cried, flying down the tunnel away from the rapidly approaching guards. He weaved left and right, twin beams of deadly light shooting past him and smashing into the walls. He dipped down low, flying a foot above the tunnel floor, then swooped upward, another volley of attacks missing him by less than a yard. Petra flew ahead of him, following the tunnel as it slithered deeper into the earth.

And then one of the beams of light shot past Kyle, striking Petra in the back.

"Petra!" Kyle cried.

She spun out of control, careening into a wall and ricocheting off, then falling to the ground in a mad tumble. Kyle swooped down after her, reaching into his pocket and activating the last of his gravity bombs, then tossing it back at the approaching guards. Then he flew to her, picking her up and bursting forward through the air as fast as he could.

Behind him, the gravity bomb triggered, sucking the guards into itself, then sending a shockwave outward, tossing them into the walls on either side with bone-shattering force.

Kyle focused on following the tunnel, taking it back down toward the dig site he knew was ahead. He looked down, seeing Petra staring up at him, her eyes wide, sweat beading up on her forehead. He looked at her belly, and his guts twisted in terror.

There was a large hole there, in her lower belly...all the way through to her back. Blackened, cauterized flesh lined the ghastly wound.

He felt a hand grip his shoulder, and saw Petra's eyes bore into his.

"Leave me...behind," she ordered. "Go back....to Calef." She grimaced, clutching at her wound. "I'll slow them down."

"No," Kyle retorted, his eyes blurring with moisture. "I won't leave you."

"Kyle..."

"We're almost there," he interrupted. "I'll take you back to Calef."

Petra swallowed visibly, then nodded.

"Take me back," she agreed. "I want...to die by my Mother."

"You're not going to die," Kyle shot back. "Not today."

But he knew that, as confidently as he'd said it, that he was most assuredly wrong.

He glanced back, seeing the two guards flying after them, a third joining the chase.

"Go!" Petra urged. Kyle complied, accelerating rapidly, whipping through the winding tunnel as fast as he could without smashing into the walls. The tunnel opened up ahead, the dig site visible in the distance...with the wall of Calef's temple beyond. Kyle aimed for the entrance to the chamber, shoving magic into his gravity boots. He burst forward...

...then saw a flash of white light smash into the ceiling ahead.

The ceiling caved in, huge boulders falling down atop him. Kyle cried out, swooping downward and weaving magic, creating gravity shields around himself and Petra. The boulders slammed into his shields, shoving him to the ground. More rocks piled on top of him, barely held back by his multi-layered shields.

And then there was darkness.

Kyle tried to fly forward, but it was no use; the rocks were pinning them down. He created a light within his gravity shields, and saw boulders and dirt surrounding them. The tunnel had collapsed all around them...they were trapped!

He felt panic rising within him, his breath coming in short gasps. The sphere of rock seemed to crush inward, the air thinning rapidly with every breath he took. It wouldn't be long before he ran out of oxygen completely. Before he started to suffocate. His concentration would waver, and he'd end up dropping his gravity shields, and then...

Calm down, he told himself. *Focus.*

He forced himself to slow his breathing, considering his options. He still had magic, after all...and lots of it. He could create a reverse-polarity gravity sphere past his shields, lifting the rocks around him, then...

Suddenly the rocks began to lift off of him, silver metallic arms wrapping around each boulder and hauling them away. Kyle stared; it was a literal army of emissaries, filling the entrance to the large chamber ahead and swarming through the tunnel all around him. They cleared the rocks in seconds, then formed a ring around Kyle and Petra, facing the oncoming guards.

Who stopped in mid-air to stare at the army of half-humanoid, half-ant machines.

And then a dark figure approached, walking amongst the emissaries. A man with skin as black as night, his dark eyes glaring at the guards. He stopped before Kyle and Petra, crossing his arms over his bare chest.

"Leave," he ordered.

The three guards hesitated, levitating in the air above the army of emissaries, exchanging glances.

Then they pointed their spears at Calef.

"STOP!"

The word echoed through the tunnel, the voice deep and powerful. A bright light pierced through the darkness behind the guards, lighting the tunnel like a miniature sun. A man in white robes levitated in the air toward the guards, a black staff in his right hand.

The guards descended to the tunnel floor, kneeling before this man. Before their master, the High Priest Kilson.

Kilson stared down at the guards, stopping in mid-air before them. Then his eyes went to Kyle and Petra, then Calef and the emissaries.

"No harm is to come of the child," Kilson stated authoritatively, "...or the woman. Leave them be."

"Yes your Holiness," the guards replied in unison.

"Leave us," Kilson ordered. The guards hesitated, glancing back at the emissaries and Calef, then complied, flying down the tunnel back toward the surface. Kilson kept his gaze on Calef. "Who are you?" he demanded.

"I am Calef," Calef answered. Kilson's eyebrows rose.

"*The* Calef?" he inquired. "The Keeper of the Old Tree?"

"The same," Calef confirmed.

Kilson stared at Calef for a moment, then descended, touching down lightly on the ground in front of Kyle and Petra. He glanced down at Petra, noting the wound in her abdomen, and grimaced.

"I've come too late," he muttered. "My apologies."

"You murdered Bopkin!" Kyle accused. "You tried to have us killed!"

"Jag vouched for your innocence," Kilson explained. "He offered to give up his life and his freedom in return for yours."

"Tell that to her," Kyle retorted angrily, gesturing at Petra, who was lying on the ground in the fetal position. She grimaced, trying to sit up, but could not.

"I'm sorry," Kilson apologized. "I came as quickly as I..."

"Well you didn't come quickly enough," Kyle interrupted.

"Kyle," Calef interjected, striding forward and putting a hand on Kyle's shoulder from behind. "Be at peace."

"But Petra," Kyle protested. "She..."

"Drank of the Mother," Calef stated calmly. "Her wound is cauterized; she will not die of bleeding. Her wound, like her arm, will heal."

Kyle stared up at Calef, rising to his feet.

"You mean...?"

"She will live," Calef confirmed, smiling at him. Kyle broke out into a huge smile, relief coursing over him. Then he felt his knees wobbling, and would have collapsed if Calef hadn't grabbed him by the shoulders. The man was incredibly strong, his grip like iron.

"You are the Keeper the legends describe?" Kilson inquired, stepping up to Calef and Kyle. The man looked even frailer than when they'd first met him, his flesh hanging from his bones.

"I am," Calef confirmed.

"But you're..." Kilson stated, gesturing at Calef. Then he grimaced, glancing down at Petra.

"Like her?" Calef inquired coolly. Kilson nodded. "We are from the same people," Calef explained. "Our ancestors were borne of the Mother. This," he added, gesturing at everything around him, "...is *our* home."

"My people have lived here for a thousand years," Kilson retorted. Calef smirked.

"And I have lived here for two thousand."

Kilson considered this, glancing at the emissaries all around the chamber.

"We both worship the Goddess," he declared at last. He inclined his head respectfully. "I mean you no harm."

"I as well," Calef agreed. "You have eaten the fruit of the Mother," he added. "You know her heart. Would she condone revenge and murder?"

Kilson grimaced, lowering his gaze.

"You have much to learn," Calef scolded.

"And no time left to learn it," Kilson countered grimly. He sighed, his shoulders slumping. "The last days of my life, and I've learned that I failed as a father, and now as High Priest." He shook his head. "I'm sorry."

Calef smiled, stepping around Kyle and Petra and putting a hand on Kilson's frail shoulder. Kilson flinched at his touch, but accepted it.

"Great failure is the path to great wisdom," he reassured. "You realize your failure, and therefore you are not one."

"That's…kind of you to say," Kilson stated.

"My friends," Calef stated, gesturing at Kyle and Petra, "…may leave. And I expect that, when they come to visit me in the future, they will be greeted with open arms."

"You have my word," Kilson agreed.

"Then this is goodbye," Calef declared. He inclined his head at Kilson. "We will not meet again."

"Wait," Kilson blurted out. "The ruins…does the Goddess…?"

"She is there," Calef confirmed. "And I am with her."

Kilson hesitated.

"Can I see her?"

"No," Calef answered. But he said it gently. "You are welcome to the Citadel," he added. "I allowed your ancestors to take it as their home, as I allow you to live within it, as long as you revere the Mother. But that is all."

Kilson sighed, then nodded.

"Very well"

"Goodbye," Calef stated. Then he glanced down at Kyle and Petra. "Take her home, Kyle. I look forward to seeing you again."

And with that, he left, vanishing among his army of emissaries, who escorted him back to the ruins. To the Mother, his home.

Chapter 37

Starlight shone through the narrow gaps in the cavern ceiling far above Darren's head, pale silver beams slicing through the air to the rocky ground below. He gazed up at the narrow sliver of night sky he could see, then lowered his gaze to the dying campfire in the center of the cavern. With a thought, he snuffed out the flames, smoke rising from the glowing embers. He glanced at the men and women sitting around the cavern, most of them already fast asleep on blankets in the darkness. Their gentle snoring filled the cavern, a peaceful end to a long day.

There were fewer people in the cave than that morning, a result of Darren sending small groups out every few hours to return back to Osa. Each with instructions on what do to once they got home, each entrusted with an integral part of a larger plan. One that would – through targeted poisonings, guerilla tactics, and sabotage of the reconstruction of the resorts – bring the Imperials to their knees.

Tomorrow more would leave, and more the next day, until no one was left but him.

He sighed, rubbing his eyes, then stepping quietly away from the campfire toward the tunnel leading out of the cavern. Every night, he used magic to place large boulders to block the tunnel. An unnecessary precaution perhaps, but his Battle-Weaving teacher,

Master Owens, had trained him to be paranoid. Underestimating one's opponent was a sure-fire way to die.

Darren reached the tunnel, which was shrouded in darkness. He created a small, pale light, then followed the tunnel it as it wound to the right. It was then that he noticed something on the left wall...words carved into the rock. He paused before them, kneeling down and tracing the words with one finger.

D & T.

He and Tessa had used a small rock to carve their initials there long ago. To mark their home away from home, their sanctuary. A place where they knew they'd be safe. A reminder that they'd always have each other, even when it seemed like the whole world was against them. He sighed, standing up, his knees popping.

How wrong they'd been.

Darren turned away, continuing down the tunnel. It wasn't long before he found what he was looking for: a few large boulders set in a small alcove in the rightmost wall. He stopped before them, weaving magic again. The nearest boulder lifted upward, and he swung it over to the tunnel ahead, setting it down to block the way. He repeated the process with the second boulder, setting it gently atop the first.

And then the boulder *exploded.*

Darren wove magic instantly, years of training kicking in. Gravity shields appeared around him, but not before he was pelted with a few hunks of rock. One struck him in the chest, knocking the wind out of him, another smashing him in the nose.

He stumbled backward, pain shooting between his eyes, his vision going black. Threads of magic *pulled* into his mind's eye, and he wove rapidly, sending pattern after pattern outward. Muffled explosions battered his shields, and he activated his gravity boots, flying backward, bouncing madly off the tunnel walls.

His vision began to clear, and he shot a large fireball down the tunnel, the flames casting the walls in a deep orange-red.

The fireball stopped in mid-air, then flew right back at him.

Darren cursed, shooting a blast of water at the fireball even as his shields vanished, creating more shields to protect himself. He flew forward then, bursting through the water before it even had a chance to fall, spotting a man standing in front of the remaining boulder ahead. A man in black and silver armor and a black cape, with long blond hair and piercing green eyes.

His blood went cold.

Urson!

He flew right at the man, trying to ram him, but Urson dodged, creating a gravity field that threw Darren to the side, smashing him into the wall. He ricocheted off, his shields protecting him. What few remained; they were winking out again, one-by-one, Urson using his magic to snuff them out.

Darren flew back away from Urson, landing on the ground and glaring at the man.

"High Weaver," he greeted, inclining his head slightly.

"Darren," Urson replied.

"Come to take me in?" Darren inquired, his tone casual. But his heart was pounding in his chest, sweat trickling down his flanks. Urson was good. Very good. One of the few Battle-Weavers that could challenge Darren.

"If you behave," Urson replied.

"And if I don't?"

"Then I'll be taking your body in," Urson answered. Darren smirked.

"You're awfully sure of yourself."

"I have reason to be," Urson retorted calmly. And again, Darren knew it was true. Urson was maddeningly self-assured, but he'd earned the right to be.

"You always were a cocky son-of-a-bitch," Darren muttered. "The Empire's faithful dog, executing orders without question."

"Grand Weaver Kalibar's faithful dog," Urson corrected. "He ordered me to retrieve you. Personally."

"With all due respect to the Grand Weaver," Darren replied, "...I must decline."

"You can come with me," Urson stated, "...or I can ask Kalibar to fetch you himself."

Darren felt the blood drain from his face, and he swallowed in a suddenly dry throat, taking a step back. Urson he had a chance against, but if Grand Weaver Kalibar came for him…

"The Empire murdered my sister," Darren accused. "They tried to murder my father!"

"I don't care."

"You should," Darren retorted, taking another step back. "They kill and enslave anyone who dares to challenge them. Anyone who tries to stand up for their rights."

"I," Urson repeated, "…don't care."

"That's the problem with you people," Darren shot back. "You *don't* care. That's why we protest. That's why we fight back, even when you try to silence us. When you kidnap our children. When you murder us!"

Urson just stood there.

"I fought for the Empire," Darren declared, glaring at Urson. "I risked my life for the Empire!" He clenched his hands into fists. "And they repaid me by enslaving my people, by attacking my family!"

Still, Urson said nothing. Darren stared at him, shaking his head.

"You really don't care, do you?" he muttered.

"Save it for the judge."

Darren took a deep breath in, then let it out, his shoulders slumping.

"All right," he replied. "I'll…"

He *shoved* magic at the weak light hovering before him, covering his eyes with one arm as it flared into a miniature sun. He wove then, shoving a pattern out at the walls flanking Urson; an electrical field that separated the charges between the rock. Lightning arced between the walls, with Urson caught in the middle.

Or so he thought.

Darren flew backward, blinking away the afterimage of the blinding light, and saw the High Weaver hurtling through the air after him. He threw a gravity field to one side of Urson, sucking the man right into the wall…while nullifying his gravity shields.

Urson smashed into the rock, ricocheting off.

Darren continuing flying backward, watching Urson tumble to the floor. But he was unharmed, a new set of gravity shields already surrounding him.

"You're quick," Darren observed.

"You're predictable," Urson shot back.

Darren cast another pattern outward, past Urson, to the boulder further down the tunnel. It shot toward them...and right at Urson's back.

"Oh really?" Darren replied.

The boulder disintegrated right before it reached Urson, rocky debris shooting around him and slamming into Darren. Or rather, his shields.

"Really," Urson retorted.

And then Darren felt a sudden, unbearable pressure in his ears, and the hunks of stone shot into him from all sides, a powerful vacuum sucking the air and the debris inward...and right through his shields. Rocks pelted him, and he grunted, creating a gravity field to nullify the vacuum...and shoot the debris back at Urson.

Who simply dodged out of the way.

"Like I said," Urson stated. "Predictable."

"Are you trying to toy with me?" Darren inquired, smirking at him.

"You'll know when I start trying."

Darren wove rapidly, tossing the pattern out at the rock wall to his right. The rock there seemed to shrink, darkening to a dull red color as the very substance of the rock transformed into pure iron.

And then he created a magnetic field behind Urson...forcing the hunk of iron to shoot out of the wall, hurtling at the man.

Urson flew backward past the magnetic field, the hunk of iron stopping in mid-air in the center of it. Then it began to glow red-hot, and shot right back at Darren!

He deflected it to one side with a gravity field, ignoring the debris flying at his shields from the hunk of iron's impact with the wall.

"Now who's predictable?" Darren inquired.

And then the ground beneath him *melted*, molten rock shooting upward all around him. The sudden heat was unbearable; Darren cried out, increasing the power of his gravity shields to keep out the heat.

The air turned ice-cold without warning, and he was plunged into darkness.

Darren created a light before him, and found that the molten rock had flash-frozen, creating a smooth, stony tomb around his spherical shields. And, rather cleverly, severely limiting his oxygen supply.

Well played.

He cast a pattern outward, superheating the wall of stone ahead, then creating a gravity field to send it flying back at Urson. But as quickly as he heated it, the stone cooled again. Darren grimaced, pouring more magic into his pattern, but it was no use; Urson was doing the same, using brute force to match him.

Except Urson had an unlimited air supply, while Darren did not.

Darren tried to ignore the rapidly thinning air within his stony tomb, moving his pattern to the section of stone wall behind him instead. The stone glowed red-hot for a moment...then darkened.

Damn it!

He gasped for air, feeling suddenly lightheaded.

Don't panic, think!

It was Master Owens' constant precept. A Battle-Weaver's power lay in strategy, not brute power. Panic shut off the mind, making a Weaver useless. He forced himself to slow his breathing, thinking it through. Urson knew he would try to melt the stone, or use powerful gravity fields to try to break it. But if he *transformed* it instead...

He wove magic, throwing it toward the leftmost wall. The stone shrank, turning red. Transforming into iron...and by shrinking, causing the stone around it to crack.

Air – sweet air! – rushed in, and Darren lowered his shields for a split second to let it surround him. Then he created a magnetic field beyond the iron, attracting it...and pulling it free from the stone around it. He burst through the hole, spotting Urson ahead, and used magic to whip the hunk of iron at him.

Urson deflected it, inclining his head at Darren.

"Not bad," he conceded.

"Thank you," Darren replied, more calmly than he felt. "That means a lot coming from you."

"I doubt it."

"Don't," Darren retorted. "I meant every word." He gave a bitter smile. "I looked up to you, you know, growing up."

Urson didn't reply.

"I still believe in the Empire," Darren continued. "In what we fought against Xanos for. But people without magic need the same rights and representation that *we* have."

"Tell it to the Grand Weaver," Urson grumbled. Darren smirked.

"Hard to speak with a rope around my neck."

He focused inward, realizing he was running low on magic reserves. Urson almost certainly had more magic, much of it stored in crystals embedded in his armor. But Darren had prepared for this; he'd filled rocks in the tunnel closer to the cavern behind him with magic yesterday. If he could get to them, and keep Urson away…

"You knew the law," Urson stated. "You broke the law."

Darren wove magic, creating a powerful gravity field in front of Urson. A sudden, powerful gust of wind shot through the tunnel, tossing Urson backward. At the same time, Darren flew backward against the wind, toward the cavern entrance only a hundred feet away.

Urson caught himself, then burst forward after him!

Darren shoved even more magic into the gravity field – and his gravity boots – the wind howling through the tunnel and slowing Urson's advance. The magic-filled rocks were only fifty feet away now…forty. Thirty.

And Urson was burning through magic to chase him, expecting Darren to run out of magic first. But when he got to his magic stores…

He heard a loud *crunch* from behind, and turned to see the tunnel collapsing behind him.

No!

He shot backward, falling stone smashing into his gravity shields. One managed to break through before being flung away, clipping his left shoulder. Pain shot through his arm, and he lurched to the left, ricocheting off the wall.

His concentration faltered, and he lost control of the gravity field ahead.

The wind died down instantly, and Urson sped down the tunnel toward him, ramming him. Their shields collided, and Darren saw the world spinning around him crazily. He slammed into one wall, then the other, trying desperately to maintain the streams to his gravity shields.

Then the world stopped spinning abruptly, and he found himself lying on his back, his shields levitating him inches above the ground.

A green gel appeared on the floor all around him, rising upward to envelop him.

"No!" he shouted, streaming magic to his gravity boots. But his gravity shields vanished, the gel surrounding his back, his arms, his legs. Covering his boots, making it impossible to stream magic to them. It continued to rise, enveloping his belly and chest, leaving only his face uncovered.

Then the gel began to harden.

He felt it shrink as it did so, tightening around his limbs…and his chest. Shoving the air out of his lungs, and making it impossible to take a breath in.

"N…" he gasped, struggling wildly. He tried to suck air into his lungs, but it was no use. Dark spots appeared in his vision, expanding rapidly.

Don't panic. Think!

He *pulled* at what little magic he had left, weaving it rapidly. But he fumbled with the pattern, the threads untangling and sucking back into the bones of his skull. He tried to get them back, but the world was fading away.

I'm sorry Tessa.

He saw a figure appear, levitating in the air before him. Saw a face lowering itself down to stare at him. Green eyes. Then they disappeared, lost in swirling darkness.

I failed you.

And then he saw nothing at all.

Chapter 38

The sun had long-since vanished below the horizon, countless stars shining in infinite space above the city of Osa by the time Kyle and Petra made it back to the governor's mansion. Kyle had flown Petra from the base of the Citadel all the way to the city, carrying her in his arms. In the hours since their harrowing battle – and Petra's terrible injury – the gaping wound in her belly had already shrank considerably. High Priest Kilson had given Petra a few leaves to chew, and they'd relieved her pain. Which was just as well, given that she still had a hole through her body...one that Kyle could still see all the way through.

They descended to the town square, his gravity boots touching down on the cobblestones there. He lowered Petra, placing her on her feet gingerly.

"Can you stand?" he asked. She hesitated, then nodded.

"I can," she answered. "The pain is bearable."

They began walking toward the front door, and Kyle looked up, realizing there was a large hole in the mansion a few stories up. Debris littered the square, shattered glass and broken pieces of furniture scattered over the cobblestones.

"Jesus," Kyle muttered. "What happened here?"

"We will find out," Petra replied. They walked up to the front door, which was flanked by two armored guards. The guards bowed

403

immediately, then opened the door and stepped aside. Kyle and Petra continued into the grand foyer, making their way to the spiral staircase.

"Can you make it?" Kyle asked.

"I will fly."

She did just that, flying up through the center of the spiral staircase, and Kyle followed below her. They reached the third floor, making their way to the governor's office. Or rather, Kalibar's office. Two Battle-Weavers stood by the door, their faces lighting up when they saw Kyle.

"Kyle!" one of them exclaimed. He knocked on the door, then opened it. "Grand Weaver, your son is here!"

Within moments, none other than Kalibar himself burst through the doorway. He spotted Kyle and Petra limping toward them, and broke out into a huge grin.

"Kyle!" he exclaimed, rushing up to Kyle and giving him a bear hug...and lifting him up so his feet dangled above the floor. Kyle grinned, hugging Kalibar back. His adoptive father lowered him gently, cupping Kyle's face in both hands. "Are you okay?"

"I'm fine," Kyle replied. Kalibar's eyes went to Petra, who limped up to them. Kalibar's smile vanished, his eyes going to the hole in Petra's lower belly.

"My god," he exclaimed, rushing up to her. He examined the wound, then turned to one of the Battle-Weavers. "Fetch the surgeon at once!"

"No," Petra stated, pulling away from him. "That won't be necessary."

"But..."

"I will heal," Petra interjected.

"It's okay," Kyle reassured. Kalibar glanced at him quizzically. "She's right," he added. "But it's a long story."

"For you," Kalibar replied, "...I have all the time in the world."

Kyle heard footsteps behind him, and turned to see none other than Ariana running toward him. He braced for impact, preparing himself for a rib-shattering hug, but she skid to a stop before him, leaning in and embracing him gently. She kissed him full on the lips, then smiled at him.

"Hey," Kyle mumbled. "We…"

"I heard everything," Ariana interrupted. Which of course she had. He often forgot that she could hear people's conversations, even from a few floors away. "What happened? Did Kilson let you go?"

"Like I said…" Kyle began.

"It's a long story, right," Ariana finished for him.

"What happened to Jag and the researchers?" Kalibar inquired. Kyle grimaced, glancing at Petra.

"Kilson executed the researchers," he answered grimly. "I don't know what happened to Jag."

"I see," Kalibar replied.

An image of Bopkin and the other Runics being struck by that awful white light, their bodies disintegrating in a split-second came to Kyle, and he shoved the memory aside, swallowing past a lump in his throat.

"By the way," he asked, "…what's with the huge hole in the mansion?"

"It's a long story," Ariana answered.

"Gundar attacked," Kalibar informed them. "He tried to kidnap Ariana, and was looking for you as well," he added, nodding at Kyle.

"What happened?" Kyle asked.

"He lost," Kalibar replied.

"His head," Ariana added with a smirk.

"It seems we have a lot to discuss," Kalibar stated wearily. "Perhaps it would best to do so after a good night's sleep."

"Agreed," Kyle replied. It'd been a long day, after all. But after all the magic he'd used, he was starving. "I could use something to eat first." He glanced at Petra. "You hungry?"

"I will wait for the hole in my intestines to heal first," she answered. Kyle grimaced; it was a fair point.

"All right then," Kalibar decided. "Kyle, you go get something to eat. Everyone else try to get some sleep. I'll be reinstating Candric as governor tomorrow, and we'll head on back home in the morning."

"I'll go with you," Ariana decided, hooking Kyle's arm in her own, then leading him down the hallway toward the stairs. Kyle smiled at her. He had no doubt she was glad to see him, and wanted to spend time with him, even if it meant just watching him eat. But he also knew she was going to ask him all sorts of questions about what'd happened while he did so. Which was all right by him.

"So you're going to stare at me while I eat?" he inquired.

"Yep," she confirmed. "And stare at you while you sleep, too."

"Creepy."

"I'm a creepy girl," she replied, leaning her head against his. Her hair tickled his neck. "What'd you expect? I *am* kinda dead you know."

"I guess you can't help it then."

"Nope," she agreed, turning to kiss his cheek. "Would you have it any other way?"

"Not on your life," he replied with a grin.

* * *

Kalibar watched Kyle and Ariana go, watched Ariana lean in to kiss Kyle. He smiled, shaking his head slowly. A most unlikely couple; a boy from another world and an immortal, undead girl with a heart of gold. They would do anything for each other, he knew…and already had. A love like that was one-in-a-million.

He sighed then, glancing at Petra. She was staring at him, her expression unreadable, as usual.

"I suppose I'd better get to bed," he stated wearily. "Goodnight Petra…I'm glad to see you well."

Her eyebrows rose.

"Is that it?" she inquired. He blinked.

"I'm sorry," he apologized. "What do you…"

She strode up to him, shoving him backward through the doorway into his office, then pinning him against the wall. She kicked the door closed behind her, then leaned in, kissing him full on the lips.

It felt *amazing*.

She held the kiss for a long moment, holding his face in her hands, then pulled away, staring into his eyes.

"I love you," she stated bluntly.

Kalibar stared back at her, his mouth dropping open. She arched one eyebrow.

"Is the great Kalibar speechless?" she inquired, a smirk curling her lips.

"I thought you…" Kalibar stammered. "You said…"

"Shut up," Petra interrupted, putting a finger to his lips. "Tell me you love me too."

"You know I do," Kalibar replied, his eyes moist. "More than anything."

"I'm sorry I pushed you away," she murmured, dropping her gaze. She shook her head. "I thought it was pointless to…"

"I know," Kalibar interjected, putting a hand on her shoulder. "We both have to be there for our people."

"Yes."

"I've been thinking about that," he admitted. "A lot. After you left for Meros, I…well, I started thinking hard about what was really important to me. What I wanted out of the rest of my life."

She lifted her gaze to match his.

"And?"

"I became Grand Weaver to protect my family from Xanos," Kalibar explained. "But now that he's gone, all I really want is to spend time with my children…and…"

Petra waited silently.

"And you," he confessed. "I've done what I wanted to do as Grand Weaver. And you have to go back to your people to protect them. So I think I should…"

"Quit?"

"Step down," Kalibar corrected.

"You protect millions of people," Petra countered. "I protect less than one hundred." She sighed. "I should be the one to step down."

"Petra…"

"My tribe will choose another to become Joined," she insisted. "I will train them myself." She smiled. "I would not endanger one family for a chance at another."

"So that's what you want?" Kalibar asked. "A family?"

She nodded.

"When I watched over my people, I spent most of my days alone," she explained. "I was like you, sacrificing myself for my people. I was ready to spend the rest of my life that way."

"Me too," Kalibar admitted. "Until I met Kyle and Ariana. And you."

"I almost died today," Petra revealed. She gazed down at the wound in her belly. "When I thought it was over, I told Kyle to leave me behind. I was ready to spend the last minutes of my life protecting him."

Kalibar gazed at her, at a loss for words.

"I've been wondering why," Petra continued. "Why I did that."

"It was the right thing to do."

"No," Petra countered. "It was more than that." She hesitated, as if searching for the right words. "All my life I've been trained to be a protector, to save my people. My family." She smiled, putting a hand on his chest. "I saved Kyle because he *is* my family now. And I want you to be too."

She leaned in again, kissing him a second time. The faint, woody scent of her Reaper uniform mixed with the intoxicating smell of her skin, a pleasant medley that, combined with her warm, soft lips on his, was simply divine. He lost himself in it, feeling everything else melt away.

At length she pulled away, staring at him with those lovely black eyes.

"You'll have to put up with my daughter then," Kalibar warned, a smile on his lips. "She's a terrible sleeper." She smirked.

"Your children I can handle."

408

"Can you handle three?" Kalibar inquired, raising one eyebrow suggestively. She gave him a look.

"Are you suggesting we make one?"

"Worth a try," he ventured with a grin. She rolled her eyes, stepping back from him and putting her hands on her hips.

"And I thought you were tired," she grumbled.

"A man is never *that* tired," he countered.

"You haven't changed since our first dinner together," she mused. "Back when my parents invited you to their home. Still with the dirty mind."

"Can you blame me?"

She smirked at him, clearly catching him admiring her form.

"Mother warned me about people like you," she admitted.

"Like me?" he inquired.

"Men," she clarified.

"Ah."

"Get some sleep," she ordered, leaning in to give him one last kiss. "You have a long trip ahead of you tomorrow."

"But…"

"And I still have a hole in my abdomen," she continued. He glanced down at her wound.

"Right," he mumbled. "Forgot about that." He hesitated. "It's really going to heal?"

"It is," she reassured. "I'll tell you more in the morning."

"All right," he agreed. "Good night, Petra."

She smiled at him, putting a hand on his cheek.

"Good night Kalibar."

And then she stepped through the doorway, and was gone.

Chapter 39

The gray stone walls and floors of row after row of holding cells were dusty and bleak, the air damp and musty. Located deep within the earth below the ODC – the Osa Detention Center – these cells had been designed to hold the most dangerous criminals of all: Weavers and Runics, those with the power to escape any normal jail. With the power to kill any normal guard.

But these cells were far from normal.

Large crystalline rods had been shoved into the earth below the floor of the cells, each attached to a runic device that used any magic the crystals stored, generating water that flowed through pipes underground, helping to supply the city with fresh water. This drained the crystals, which – hungry for magic – drained everything around them in turn. Including the prisoners who were kept in these cells.

Like Darren.

Governor Candric took the last steps down to this room, grimacing at the mustiness of the air. He paused at the bottom of the stairs, then took a deep breath in, letting it out slowly. Preparing himself. Then he strode down the long hallway, gazing at cell after cell flanking him on either side. Most were empty, of course; Meros was not often visited by Weavers, much less Weavers charged with a crime. But there was one cell at the end of the hallway directly

410

ahead. A cell with a lone figure seated on a stone bench by the far wall.

Candric swallowed past a lump in his throat, wanting nothing more than to stop. To turn around and leave this place. But he kept walking. Put one foot in front of the other until he reached the tall vertical bars of the cell.

The figure lifted their head, dark eyes staring into his.

"Hello father."

Candric grimaced, nodding slightly.

"Son," he replied.

Darren stood, brushing the dust from his black pants, then stepping casually up to the bars, his eyes on Candric's.

"Come to see me one last time before I die?" he inquired. "Or can I expect you at my execution?"

Candric lowered his gaze, shaking his head.

"I've already watched one of my children die," he replied. "I won't do it again."

"You could do something about it," Darren stated, gripping the bars with both hands. Candric lifted his gaze.

"I can't."

"You can," Darren insisted. "You're still the governor."

"You're being court-marshalled," Candric retorted. "It's out of my hands."

"Then help me escape," Darren pressed.

"No."

"No?" Darren blurted out. "No?"

"You killed innocent people, Darren," Candric reminded him.

"The guards that murdered Tessa, then attacked us?" Darren retorted. "Please."

"*That* I could have helped you with," Candric stated. "We could have explained that away. But you burned those resorts, son."

"Resorts owned by corrupt businessmen bleeding our island dry," Darren argued. "Buying all of our land and pushing the natives out of their own damn country!"

"There were innocent people in those resorts," Candric countered, more loudly than he'd wanted. He took a deep, steadying

411

breath. "You killed children," he added quietly. "Burned them alive…and wounded many more."

"They weren't innocent," Candric retorted. "They were complicit."

"Children?"

"Casualties of war, father. How many innocent families do you think the Empire has killed over the years, hmm?" Candric sneered at him. "You have no idea what I've had to do for them. No *idea* how many innocent people we've 'inadvertently' killed."

"We're not at war," Candric shot back.

"Oh yes we are."

"Tessa wasn't at war," Candric insisted. "She…"

"Was murdered because the Empire couldn't have her riling up the people," Darren interjected. "Couldn't have the little people get it in their little heads that they had power, could they?" He let go of the prison bars, crossing his arms over his chest. "You know damn well that the Empire has us right where they want us. Exploited. Weak. Disorganized. Helpless. All so they can steal from the poor to give to the rich."

"Darren…"

"It's the same story everywhere," Darren continued. "Every tinpot dictatorship, every kingdom, every damn government I've ever seen. I used to think the Empire was different."

"It is, son."

"They kidnapped your son!" Darren almost shouted, lunging forward and gripping the cell bars. "They murdered your daughter! How can you still *believe* that?"

"Because they *want* to do what's right," Candric replied evenly. "I've spoken to Grand Weaver Kalibar. I know his heart's in the right place."

"You're a fool."

"Maybe so," Candric agreed. "But so was Tessa then. She believed in the Empire…in the rights we were supposed to have. *She* believed we could show them a better way."

"She showed them," Darren agreed. "And they killed her for it."

412

"You don't know everything," Candric retorted. "Verhan was behind Tessa's death. Lady Damia ordered it."

"Bullshit," Darren spat. "Did Kalibar tell you that?"

"He did," Candric replied. "And I believe him."

"So you'll keep being governor," Darren muttered. "The Empire's lap dog."

"No," Candric countered. "I'm going to run for mayor of Stridon. And then I'll run for the Council."

"They'll never let you into the Council," Darren shot back. "You don't make magic, remember?"

"That will change too."

"Who's gonna change it?" Darren demanded. "You?"

"The people will," Candric answered. "And I'll show them why they should change it…that they have the *power* to change it. Just like Tessa did."

"And they'll kill you too."

"Maybe," Candric conceded. "But I promised your sister I'd do it her way if my way didn't work. And that's what I'm going to do…even if I have to make the ultimate sacrifice, like she did."

Darren stared at his father for a long, silent moment, not so much as blinking. Then his shoulders slumped.

"So that's it," he muttered. "You're just going to let me die."

"You killed children, son," Candric stated. He felt a horrible pang in his heart, as if someone were squeezing it. He blinked sudden moisture from his eyes. "I saw their little bodies."

Darren turned away from him, staring at the cell floor.

"I love you," Candric insisted.

"No," Darren replied, his tone flat. He turned to gaze at Candric, his expression stony. "You don't."

"That's not true."

"When did you love us?" Darren retorted. "When you worked until sundown almost every day while we were growing up? When you let Mom beat us and scream at us?"

"I didn't know…"

"You weren't *there*," Darren shot back. "You were *never* there! You wonder why Tessa hated you? You wonder why *I* hated you?

413

Because you always loved your *damn* work more than you loved us." He sneered at Candric. "If you'd really loved us, you would've chosen us over your damn businesses."

"I made mistakes," Candric confessed. "But…"

"But what?" Darren demanded.

"Family is all that matters to me now, son."

Darren's eyebrows rose, and he stared at Candric. Then he stepped forward, leaning in and pressing his face between the narrow bars, his nose inches from Candric's.

"Too late Dad," he muttered. "You don't have a family anymore."

Chapter 40

The flight from Meros back to Stridon was a long one, but Kyle, Ariana, and Kalibar had no problem filling it. After all, a great deal had happened during their few days on the island, and everyone had a different perspective on the adventures they'd experienced. By the time their flying carriage passed through the Gate Shield surrounding the Secula Magna and came to a gentle stop a few feet above the verdant lawn near the Great Tower, everyone had been filled in.

It'd been good to sit and talk...to try to process everything that'd happened. And how everyone felt about it.

Kyle felt a cold hand on his, and turned to see Ariana smiling at him. He smiled back, then watched as the door of the carriage swung downward, forming a ramp leading to the campus lawn below. Kalibar stood, and – ever the gentleman – gestured for everyone to disembark before him. They all got off, then made their way across the grass to a cobblestone pathway leading to the front double-doors of the Great Tower. Kyle lifted his gaze to the crystalline pyramid at the top of the Tower, glittering like a diamond in the waning sunlight. He smiled, feeling the tension of the last few days draining out of him. It felt good to be back.

But even so, something felt...different.

He sighed, lowering his gaze, realizing that Kalibar was walking beside him, eyeing him silently. Kyle gave him a forced smile, then felt a cold hand grab his. It was Ariana, of course, walking beside him, his ever-faithful companion. She gave him the same look Kalibar had.

"Hey you," she prompted. "Something wrong?"

"Just...thinking," he answered. She stared at him, waiting patiently for him to elaborate. "It doesn't feel the same."

"What doesn't?"

"Being home," he clarified.

"Yeah," she agreed. They reached the double doors, passing into the lobby of the Tower.

"You feel it too?"

"I do," she replied.

"Why is that?" Kalibar inquired. Kyle turned to his adoptive father, hesitating a moment. Kalibar gave an encouraging smile. "You can tell me," he reassured.

"We were the good guys before," Kyle replied.

Kalibar grimaced, falling silent. Kyle glanced at Ariana, who was staring at her feet as she walked, and sighed, concentrating on putting one foot in front of the other.

"Kalibar!"

Kyle glanced forward, spotting a very familiar man in a white uniform rushing across the lobby toward them. A bald man with bushy white eyebrows and an impressive white beard...and an equally impressive belly bouncing as he ran.

"Evening, Erasmus," Kalibar greeted. Erasmus practically collided with Kalibar, giving his old friend a big bear hug. Then he pulled back, grinning from ear-to-ear.

"Thank god you're back!" he declared. "If I had to work another day with Goran," he added, practically spitting out the Elder Runic's name, "...I'd have hung myself from the rafters!"

"And probably pulled down the whole Tower on top of you," Kalibar replied with a grin of his own. Erasmus harrumphed, but his eyes twinkled.

416

"In that case, I'd hope Goran was in the building so I could take him with me!"

"It's only been two days," Kalibar reminded him. Erasmus snorted.

"Have you *met* Goran?"

"Trust me, I'd prefer Goran any day over what happened on Meros," Kalibar replied. Erasmus frowned.

"What the hell is that supposed to mean?" he demanded Kalibar glanced about the crowded lobby, and Erasmus nodded.

"Ah, yes," he muttered. "Come on then, let's go somewhere more private. Your retirement suite?"

"Sounds good to me," Kalibar agreed.

Erasmus walked side-by-side with Kalibar, the two men leading Kyle and Ariana across the lobby toward the riser at the end of the long hallway ahead.

"Any news on your end?" Kalibar inquired.

"Oh nothing really," Erasmus replied. "Other than the un-washed masses uprising against us and all."

"Excuse me?"

"Seems the leader of a bunch of protesters in Meros got killed," Erasmus explained. "News of it reached the mainland, and now protesters all over the damn Empire are getting their undies in a twist."

"I was afraid of that," Kalibar admitted wearily.

"These people live in the safest, wealthiest country in the world," Erasmus grumbled, "...with the most advanced runic technology, the most opportunity, and what do they do with it?" He shook his head, throwing up his arms. "Complain! Protest!"

"It's a bit more complicated than that," Kalibar countered.

"Is it?" Erasmus shot back, his eyebrows raising.

"I was there in Meros," Kalibar explained. "The people there just wanted equality."

"Equality?" Erasmus replied. "With who? Weavers and Runics?"

"That's right."

"Preposterous!" Erasmus spat.

417

"Why is that preposterous?" Kalibar inquired, stepping onto the riser ahead. Erasmus joined him, as did Kyle and Ariana. "Our Constitution states that all citizens are equal."

"Under the *law*," Erasmus countered. The riser shot upward, zooming past each floor of the Tower with dizzying speed. Then it slowed abruptly, and stopped at the 41st floor. Everyone got off, continuing down the hallway toward Kalibar's retirement suite.

"I'm not seeing your point," Kalibar admitted.

"Just because we're equal under the law doesn't mean we're *equal*," Erasmus explained. "Is a genius equal to a dullard? A lazy, blood-sucking bastard equal to a man who busts his rump all day, every day? Is a man capable of flying and leveling cities equal to a potter? Is a man who runs ten businesses equal to a homeless man?"

"Erasmus…" Kalibar began, but Erasmus cut him off.

"It's always the same with you Populists," Erasmus complained. "Filling everyone's heads with fanciful ideas about everyone being the same, about no one being better than anyone else. It's poppy-cock and you know it!"

Kalibar smirked, patting Erasmus on the back.

"Hit a nerve, did I?"

"It's these protesters," Erasmus complained. "No matter how much they have, they'll always want more."

"I could say the same for the wealthiest Elitists," Kalibar countered, his eyes twinkling. Erasmus paused, then nodded grudgingly.

"I'll give you that one," he grumbled.

Kalibar stopped before the door to his retirement suite, unlocking the door and opening it, ushering everyone in. Erasmus walked to the nearest table, sitting down on one of the chairs.

"Enough politics," Erasmus stated. "How'd your little vacation go?"

"That's a long, long story," Kalibar admitted, grabbing the chair beside Erasmus and sitting down. Kyle and Ariana joined them, sitting opposite the two men.

"Well go on," Erasmus urged. "Tell me."

Kalibar did so, piecing together most of what he'd learned from Kyle, Ariana, and Petra. And Candric…and even Darren, who'd he'd briefly interviewed. To Erasmus's credit, he listened without interruption, other than the occasional curse word. When Kalibar was done telling the tale, Erasmus leaned back in his chair, running a hand over his bald pate.

"Well now," he muttered. "That's a fine mess, isn't it."

"Tell me about it," Kalibar agreed.

"So Petra left to go back to her tribe?" Erasmus inquired. Kalibar nodded.

"She did," he confirmed. "But she said she'd be back."

"Good," Erasmus replied with a grin. "I missed her too...maybe even more than I missed you."

"She was right about you," Kalibar stated, shaking his head at his old friend. "She said..."

"Don't tell me," Erasmus interrupted. "Leave me my illusions," he added. "They're all I have!" He sighed then, running a hand through his long white beard. "I don't know about you," he grumbled, "...but I could use a little wine."

"More than a little," Kalibar agreed. "And a meal at that."

"I'll summon that butler of yours," Erasmus decided. He got up then, walking to the nearest communication orb and sending a stream of magic to it. Within moments, there was a knock at the door.

"Come in," Erasmus and Kalibar called out in unison.

The door opened, and none other than Jenkins appeared, walking up to the table and bowing crisply. Kyle smiled, catching Ariana doing so as well. It was good to see the butler again...and to be sitting at this table with Kalibar and Erasmus, like old times.

"Good evening," Jenkins greeted. "What may I..."

"Roast duck," Erasmus replied immediately. He glanced at Kyle and Ariana. "I assume you're all right with that?" There were nods all around...except for Ariana, of course. "And more than a little wine," he added with a sly wink.

"But of course," Jenkins replied.

The man left with his customary efficiency, the door closing behind him. It wasn't long before he returned, steaming trays filled with silver platters in his arms...and a shorter man following behind him, more than a few bottles of wine clutched in his arms.

"Marvelous!" Erasmus declared, rubbing his hands together eagerly. "Jenkins, it's criminal that Kalibar here won't give you a raise."

Jenkins lowered the trays to the table, and the wine bottles were given similar treatment. Kalibar rolled his eyes at Erasmus.

"Not twice in one month," he retorted.

Jenkins laid a silver platter in front of Kyle, whisking away the lid, and Kyle was immediately rewarded with the mouth-watering aroma of roasted duck. He dug in immediately, as did everyone else, the sound of lips smacking and silverware scraping every last morsel of food off of their plates the only sounds in the suite. It seemed only moments later that Kyle's plate was empty. Jenkins, with his customary genius, had already anticipated such a disaster, whisking away Kyle's plate and offering seconds. To the delight of all, everyone received similar consideration, and it was a considerably longer period of time before everyone finished this second course. When the gruesome remains of devoured fowl were finally taken away, everyone leaned back in their chairs, their bellies a bit bulgier for their efforts. Except for Ariana's, of course.

"I think we forgot to drink the wine," Erasmus realized, and quickly made up for this oversight, filling glasses for himself, Kalibar, and even a little for Kyle. Kyle sipped at his, more out of politeness than anything else. It tasted terribly bitter, and burned his tongue and throat on the way down. How adults could stand the stuff – much less enjoy it – was beyond him. But enjoy it they most certainly did...and as usual, a few glasses loosened their tongues.

"So your little vacation was a bust, eh?" Erasmus stated, eyeing Kyle and Ariana. He turned to Kalibar. "A few days away from home and they still managed to create another international incident."

"I wouldn't say we created it," Ariana countered.

"More like got caught up in it," Kyle agreed.

"Oho!" Erasmus declared. "Little cherubs are defending themselves now." He elbowed Kalibar. "Your children are growing up!"

"Indeed they are," Kalibar replied, smiling at Kyle and Ariana. "And I couldn't be prouder."

"Yes, well," Erasmus stated. "I doubt the Council will share your enthusiasm. Consorting with a bunch of protesters, attacking city guards...it doesn't look good."

"We'll manage the narrative," Kalibar reassured.

"Bull," Erasmus retorted. "That so-called 'Lady' Damia will spread the story far and wide, and you damn well know it." He pointed one chubby finger at Kalibar. "She has it out for you."

"Don't remind me," Kalibar grumbled.

"If it makes you feel better, our spies say she'll almost certainly be crowned Queen tomorrow."

"Oddly enough," Kalibar replied, "...it doesn't." He sighed then. "That's the least of our worries, I'm afraid."

"The hell it is!" Erasmus retorted. But he leaned forward, his bushy eyebrows furrowing. "What haven't you told me, Kalibar?"

Kalibar grimaced, taking a long draught of his wine, then setting his glass on the table with a *clink*.

"Damia," he replied, "...was Sabin's wife."

Erasmus's mouth fell open.

"*What?*"

"His *original* wife," Kalibar clarified. "She was one of Petra's tribal ancestors two thousand years ago...and one of Sabin's first Chosen."

"You're saying that witch is a damn *Chosen?*" Erasmus nearly spat.

"Afraid so."

"And how do you know this?" Erasmus inquired, crossing his arms over his belly.

"Kyle and Petra met another of these original Chosen – Prime Chosen, they call themselves – in the Citadel. An enemy of Damia's."

"So you're saying Lady Damia is an immortal like..."

Erasmus hesitated, glancing at Ariana.

"It's okay," Ariana reassured. "No offense taken."

"That's correct," Kalibar confirmed.

"And now she's about to be crowned Queen of damn Verhan," Erasmus muttered, shaking his head grimly. "Wonderful."

"Her brother was also a Chosen," Kalibar continued. "A man named Gundar. I was able to defeat him, thank goodness…I suspect their shards are far less advanced than the Dead Man's, for example. Sabin created them when he was still a mere mortal, after all."

"So you think you could beat Damia?"

"Perhaps," Kalibar answered. "Not that I'll get a chance. Assassinating the democratically-elected leader of one of the most influential countries in the world won't endear us to our allies…or our enemies."

"Might be worth it though," Erasmus ventured with a wink. Then his eyes widened, his face turning pale. "Well shit," he swore.

"What?"

"If she's immortal, that manipulative little tart is going to be Queen for…"

"Ever," Kalibar finished grimly. "My thought exactly."

Erasmus just sat there, looking thunderstruck. Then he shook his head slowly.

"What the hell are we going to do?" he asked. Kalibar drummed his fingers on the tabletop, taking another gulp of his wine. The cheery tone of the dinner was clearly over…and it wasn't coming back.

"First we tell the Council," Kalibar answered. Erasmus gave him a sour look.

"That'll just solve everything," he muttered.

"Then we continue our strategy of containment," Kalibar continued. "She's going to use us as a foil for as long as she can."

"Which is forever," Erasmus reminded him. "She'll have all the time she needs to build her power, until she's *really* a threat to us. Shouldn't we just invade Verhan now, kill the damn witch, and get out?"

"That's one option," Kalibar conceded. "Believe me, I've considered it."

"Well if we don't, she'll win," Erasmus warned.

422

"She's already won," Kalibar pointed out. "I have to give her credit," he added ruefully. "Her strategy was a stroke of genius. Trick me into neutralizing her political rivals, ruining the Empire's reputation, installing herself as Queen...so by the time we realized what she really was, it'd be too late." He sighed. "Any move against her now would be an act of war...and could lead to the deaths of thousands, if not millions."

"Cheery thought," Erasmus grumbled. Then he frowned. "Didn't you say she used a magic airship? Can't we accuse her of using magic? It's forbidden in Verhan, after all."

"We can try," Kalibar replied. "But if I were her, I'd simply deny it and claim it was a smear campaign by the Empire."

"And her people will believe it," Erasmus muttered. "You're right...she's untouchable now. Anything we do, she'll use against us."

"As proof we're truly the enemy of Verhan," Kalibar agreed.

"Which she'll do anyway," Erasmus pointed out. "If we don't give her a reason, she'll make one up."

Kalibar sighed, leaning back in his chair and rubbing his eyes.

"Yes, well, I don't plan on solving this tonight," he stated wearily. He stared at his empty wine glass then. "And I don't know about you, but I'm ready for bed."

"Spoilsport," Erasmus grumbled, pouring himself another glass of wine. "I was just getting started!"

Kalibar pushed himself from the table, then stood up, putting a hand on Erasmus's shoulder.

"Good night old friend," he stated.

"Night," Erasmus mumbled, taking a gulp of his wine.

"Are you two staying up?" Kalibar inquiring, looking Kyle and Ariana's way. Ariana smirked.

"I know I am," she replied. Kalibar chuckled.

"I meant you, Kyle."

"I think I'll go to bed," Kyle decided. It'd been a long day, after all, and he hadn't slept very well the night before. It'd taken him a long time to wind down after everything that'd happened in the Citadel.

"All right then," Kalibar stated. He gestured for Kyle to stand, and Kyle did so, walking up to Kalibar and giving him a hug. Kalibar held him for a moment longer than he'd expected, then pulled back, holding Kyle by the shoulders.

"I heard what you said back there, Kyle," he admitted. "To Ariana, when we were in the lobby."

Kyle's mind drew a blank, but of course Ariana remembered instantly.

"That things didn't feel the same coming home?" she asked. Kalibar nodded.

"And that when you left for Meros, we were the good guys," he added. Both Kyle and Ariana lowered their gaze, and Kyle felt a glumness come over him.

"What I meant…" Kyle began, but Kalibar cut him off.

"Sometimes we're the good guys," he stated. "And sometimes we're not." He sighed. "We don't always do the right thing…and sometimes we hurt people. *Really* hurt people, without meaning to."

Kyle nodded mutely.

"No one is perfect," Kalibar continued. "And no government is either."

"That's for damn sure," Erasmus concurred, swigging a gulp of his wine. Kalibar ignored the man.

"The Empire is guilty of a great deal of wrongdoing…as am I," Kalibar admitted ruefully. "But I try to do the right thing…and when I don't, I try to make amends."

"We know," Ariana piped in, getting up from her chair and hugging Kalibar's side. He smiled, wrapping an arm around her.

"I'd like to think that when we're not the good guys, it's out of ignorance," he continued. "And I like to think that the difference between us and the 'bad guys' is that we *want* to be better." He squeezed Kyle's shoulder. "And we *will* be better."

"Will we?" Kyle asked. Kalibar nodded.

"You have my word."

He gave them both one last hug, then bade them goodnight, leaving the suite. Erasmus left with him, bringing a fresh bottle of wine with him…and leaving Kyle and Ariana alone in the empty suite. They glanced at each other, and Ariana leaned in, gently but firmly grabbing his head in her hands and pulling him in for a kiss.

"G'night," she murmured.

"Night," he replied with a goofy smile. He still got all warm and tingly when she did that, no matter how often she did. She smiled back, ruffling his hair, then pushing him toward his bedroom door. They went to his room, closing the door behind them.

"Get in bed," she ordered. "I'll watch you until you sleep."

He did as she requested, stripping to his underclothes, then hopping into bed. She tucked him in, then laid beside him, gazing into his eyes.

"I still don't get why you like watching me go to sleep," he grumbled. It made him feel terribly self-conscious.

"I like spending time with you," Ariana replied. "And I like seeing you get comfy. There's something...peaceful about it."

"If you say so."

He felt her fingers running through his hair, and smiled as she massaged his scalp. It'd become their nightly ritual, and already he found himself yawning.

"Hey," she said.

"Hmm?"

"What do you think," she asked. "About what Kalibar said, about us not being the good guys?"

Kyle sighed, rolling onto his back and staring up at the ceiling.

"I don't know what to think," he admitted.

"Me neither," Ariana agreed. She fell silent for a long moment, until he began to wonder if the conversation was over. "The Empire isn't what I thought it was," she confided.

"Yeah."

"I think I thought everyone was like Kalibar," she continued. "That everyone in the Empire really believed what he believes." She sighed. "But in some ways, we're no better than the Dead Man was."

Kyle frowned, turning to face Ariana.

"What do you mean?" he asked.

425

"We kidnap kids for their magic just like he did," she explained. "Take them from their families. *Destroy* families, like Candric's. We take advantage of people less powerful than us and say it's fair."

"We're not like the Dead Man," Kyle countered. "And *we* didn't do any of this stuff," he added. "We tried to help people."

"Yeah, well, about that," Ariana muttered. To his disappointment, she stopped scratching his head. "Kalibar was right. We've been the bad guys too."

"What?" Kyle blurted out. "How?"

"When we killed those sailors on that warship," Ariana clarified. "The one that attacked the *Defiance*."

"They were trying to kill us," Kyle retorted.

"They were trying to incapacitate a ship full of smugglers and criminals," Ariana corrected. "They were innocent men, acting on orders, enforcing the law. And we killed them."

"They shot at us," Kyle reminded her. "They shot you in the head!"

"Only because we attacked," Ariana countered. "We could've just flown away and tried to make it to Verhan."

"How were we supposed to know the *Defiance* was full of criminals?" Kyle asked. Ariana gave him a bitter smile, massaging his scalp again.

"We weren't," she answered. "And that's just the thing. We killed innocent people because we didn't know any better."

Kyle considered this, feeling terribly troubled. He hadn't thought about it that way, not really. The thought that someone out there, the wives and children – and even friends – of the men he'd killed might think of him the same way he'd thought of the Dead Man...

He lay there, staring at the ceiling, feeling numb.

"We saved the Captain," Ariana continued. "And Slim, and Grotes. And a lot of other people. Good people."

"You just said they were criminals," Kyle muttered.

"Good people do bad things," Ariana countered. "Just like we did."

Kyle sighed, suddenly wanting nothing more than to turn away from her, curl up into a ball, and go to sleep. But she stopped him with one small, cool, and impossibly strong hand.

"We're still the good guys," she reassured him, giving him a smile. But he didn't smile back.

"Are we?" he shot back.

"We are."

"How do you know that?" he pressed.

"Because we want to be better," she answered, leaning in and kissing him on the cheek. "And we *will* be."

Chapter 41

Jag walked up to the stairs leading up to the front door of an old, two-story home, the washed-out red of the bricks contrasting sharply with the pristine black of the godstone platform supporting it. He stopped before the stairs, gazing up at that front door. Its bright brown paint had long since dulled to a brown-gray.

It was old, and until recently, had been abandoned. Uncared for, neglected, it was fading away.

He sighed, gathering himself, then ascending the steps, the boards creaking under his boots. Then he knocked on the door.

"Come in," came a muted voice from beyond.

Jag hesitated, then turned the knob, and the door swung inward, its hinges squeaking. He saw a familiar narrow hallway beyond, with a small living room to his right and stairs going up to his left. The hallway led to a tiny kitchen, and it was there that the voice had come from…and where an old man in a plain shirt and pants stood, stirring something in a pan.

"Ah!" the old man said, spotting Jag. "Come in, come in."

Jag stared at him, hardly believing his eyes. It was his father, the High Priest of the Temple of the Old Tree…dressed as a normal person.

"Food's almost ready," Kilson notified. The smell of vegetable soup and fish and fruit medley came to him, an aroma that instantly took him back to when he was a boy, coming home from the Temple after a long day to be greeted by his mother – and a tasty supper. Jag stared at his father, at the clothes hanging off the man. A skeleton with skin draped over him. Yet he hadn't seen Kilson this lively in a long time. Kilson tended to the stove with a smile on his face, stepping from oven to sink to the kitchen counter with a little bounce in his step. As much as the old man could muster, that was.

In that moment, he looked...human.

"Do you need, ah, help?" Jag asked, walking into the kitchen slowly. Kilson smiled at him, shaking his head.

"No no," he replied. "I'm almost done, and the table's already set. Sit down and relax...I'll pour you some tea."

Jag stood there for a moment, watching his father completely ignore him, going about his business with zeal. Then he walked into the dining room, where their old table sat, just as it had thirty years ago. Barely large enough to seat four people. He sat down, staring at the tabletop, then the walls, the old paintings still hanging there.

Even the one of his mother and father on their wedding day.

He stared at this, remembering his mother. Not as he'd last seen her, pale as death, eyes vacant, breath coming in gasps as she succumbed to the pneumonia that had struck her down only two days before. But as the vibrant, warm woman she'd been. Thirty years ago she'd died, leaving Jag with a father who'd thrown himself into his work, drugging himself to escape the pain...and the responsibility of picking up the pieces of his son's soul.

"Here we are," Kilson declared, limping into the dining room, carrying a cup of tea in his withered hands. He set it down before Jag, steam rising from it. Eleva tea, made from a fragrant leaf that had grown in the garden outside when Jag was a kid. His favorite.

"Thanks," Jag mumbled. He sipped it, watching as his father limped back into the kitchen. "You sure you don't need help?"

"Quite sure," Kilson replied.

Jag watched him, sipping at his tea. It was delicious, and spot-on. He hadn't even known his father knew how to make it...or had remembered that it was Jag's favorite. Kilson moved about slowly, almost painfully so, and it hurt to watch him. His father was as near to death as any man Jag had ever seen, hanging onto life years after his illness had reared its ugly head. The opposite of Mom, who'd gone from healthy to dead within a single weekend.

Jag felt a twinge of sympathy for the old man, and shoved it aside. He refused to feel sorry for Kilson…just as he'd learned to stop feeling sorry for himself.

"Thought you'd want to meet in the Temple," Jag ventured as Kilson brought a large tray into the dining room.

"I wanted it to be here," Kilson replied, reaching the table. "I've got it," he insisted as Jag tried to stand to help him. He set the tray down, giving Jag a plate, then himself. Then he walked the tray back to the kitchen, returning to ease himself into the chair opposite Jag's.

"You cooked," Jag noted, looking down at his food. It actually looked pretty good…like mom used to make. "I didn't know you knew how."

"I don't," Kilson replied with a smile. "I'm not the cook your mother was, but I did my best." He gestured with his fork. "Dig in," he insisted.

Jag did so, stabbing a piece of fish and fruit with his fork, then putting it in his mouth. Again, he was surprised; it tasted pretty good, other than a slight bitter aftertaste.

"You're right," he stated. Kilson raised an eyebrow. "You're not the cook Mom was."

Kilson chuckled, and despite himself, Jag did too.

"It's pretty good though," Jag admitted. "Not bad for a first try."

"First try?" Kilson scoffed. "I've been practicing for weeks!"

"Oh," Jag replied. "Well then forget I said anything."

"It was your fortieth birthday," Kilson reminded him with a smile, taking a bite of his own food. "I wanted to surprise you."

"You have."

They ate in silence for a while, and Jag found himself staring at the painting of Mom. Kilson noticed the object of his attention, and turned to look at it.

"I miss her," Kilson admitted. "Every day. Sometimes I still expect to see her in the morning when I wake up." He turned to Jag, his eyes moist, but twinkling. "A few times I've called out to her, and tried to find her in the morning. Must be getting senile."

Jag nodded, saying nothing.

"Thirty years alone," Kilson mused, shaking his head.

"I miss her too," Jag confessed.

"Do you have anyone?" Kilson inquired.

"No," Jag answered. "No one serious, anyway."

"Haven't met the right person yet?" he pressed. Jag smirked.

"Haven't been looking for the right person."

Kilson chuckled, smiling at him.

"Still sowing your oats, eh?" he mused. "That can be good fun."

"It gets old after a while," Jag admitted. Kilson nodded.

"I suppose it would," he agreed. Jag waited, but his father didn't say anything more. He raised an eyebrow.

"No judgement?" he asked. "No lecture about getting married?"

"Oh no," Kilson replied. "I just want to spend time with you, that's all. I don't need to be your father today."

"Were you ever?" Jag replied automatically, and immediately regretted it. A low blow. But Kilson didn't seem offended.

"I think I was, before your mother died," he replied. "After that, I was…lost. The Goddess gave me purpose again."

"Instead of me."

"Instead of you," Kilson agreed. "Yes." He took another bite of his food, chewed, then swallowed. "And then I spent the next thirty years trying to share my purpose in life with you instead of trying to get to know you. Instead of finding out what *you* wanted to do."

Jag nodded. It was true. All of it.

"If you ever have children," Kilson stated, pointing his fork at Jag "…don't be like me."

Jag sighed.

"Spent my whole life trying not to," he replied. "And it took me until yesterday to realize that's exactly who I'd become."

Kilson nodded, staring off at nothing for a long moment. Then he stirred.

"We teach our children with what we do, not what we say," he stated. "A pity I'm learning all of this at the end of my life."

"You spent most of your life…"

"Experiencing another's," Kilson finished. "Yes. I never gave myself time to *be* myself."

"But you still insist on trying to convert me," Jag noted. "To 'experience the Goddess.'"

"No, no," Kilson retorted, wiping his mouth with a napkin. "I don't want you wiling your years away like that, not anymore. I want you to live your own life…the life *you* want."

"Really."

"Really," Kilson insisted. "All I ever wanted to do was share my experiences with you."

"Too late now."

"Yes, well," Kilson replied. "I got to spend time with you today, and for that, I'm grateful."

Jag hesitated, then inclined his head slightly.

"And I'm grateful you spared Kyle and Petra," he replied.

"You're welcome."

They continued eating, until at last their plates were empty. Jag sipped more of his tea, then set his cup down, leaning back in his chair and crossing his arms.

"So what now?" he inquired.

"Hmm?"

"After tonight," Jag clarified. Kilson sighed.

"Oh, I don't know," he admitted. "Preparing the Priesthood for my passing, I suppose. Wonderfully morbid, let me tell you."

"Anything else?"

"Not likely," Kilson answered, not without a tone of regret. "I don't think I have many days left. I doubt I'll last the week, honestly."

Jag nodded silently, lowering his gaze. He'd been expecting his father's death for years now, but the reality of it – of Kilson not being there anymore – was still difficult to process.

He felt a dry hand on his, and looked up, resisting the urge to pull away.

"I know I have no right to ask this of you," Kilson stated. "And if you tell me no, that's alright. But…if you could be there with me, when I die…"

Jag swallowed past a lump in his throat. Despite himself – despite everything – he found himself nodding.

Kilson smiled, his sunken eyes brimming with moisture. Tears dribbled down his cheeks, and he patted Jag's hand, easing back in his chair and sighing. He didn't say 'thank you,' didn't say anything at all. But it was there, hanging in the air silently between them.

They sat there for a while, neither man saying anything. Then Jag yawned, feeling suddenly exhausted. It'd been a long day after all.

"I suppose I'd better get going," he stated. Kilson sighed, nodding at him.

"I suppose so."

Jag slid his chair back, then stood up…and stumbled forward, gripping the edge of the table.

"Whoa," he muttered, steadying himself. "Feel a little dizzy."

Kilson nodded.

"That's how it starts," he replied.

Jag frowned, staring at his father.

"How *what* starts?"

Kilson stood up from his own chair, stepping around the table to Jag's side. Jag felt his father's hands grip his upper arms.

"Let's lie you down," Kilson prompted.

Jag resisted, trying to pull away from his father. But the movement made his head swim sickeningly, and he froze, closing his eyes against a sudden wave of nausea.

"What's…" he began, then felt a chill run down his spine. He opened his eyes, staring at his father, horror gripping him. "You…poisoned me?"

"Took me weeks to find a way to mask the flavor," Kilson admitted. "The pamaté is a bit bitter, I'm afraid."

"You *poisoned* me!" Jag shouted, backing away. But he tripped over his own feet, falling onto his buttocks on the floor. Kilson knelt down beside him, pushing him backward gently.

"Lie down son," he urged.

"No," Jag retorted. His vision began to blur, the edges turning bright white, as if looking through a long white tunnel. "No!"

"Shhh," he heard his father soothe. The voice seemed to come from far away, and echoed in his head. His vision went completely, his body numb. He tried to get up, tried to resist his father laying him backward, but it was futile. Jag felt the cold, hard floor against his back, felt a warm hand cradling the back of his head.

He tried to speak, but his mouth didn't exist anymore. His body vanished, his consciousness expanding, flowing outward in all directions. Formless, unconstrained within the prison of his flesh.

No!

Shadows moved within the whiteness, blurry at first, then sharpening. Four men standing before a huge ring made of black stone, runes etched into its surface…serving as the border for a wall of utter blackness. The first Door, creation of Altair, the Traveler.

The men stepped into that blackness, vanishing from sight.

Jag followed, seeing his arm reach out to the black wall. Saw chocolate-brown fingers where his hand should be, clad in golden rings glittering with crystals, fingernails painted blue-green. Intricate tattoos on the back of the hand, extending to each finger up to the nails.

The hand plunged into the wall of black, vanishing from sight.

The vision faded into white.

Jag felt his consciousness shatter like a glass smashing into the floor, pieces of his mind flying outward, tumbling through space and time. Then they pulled together, re-forming. His vision sharpened, the whiteness fading.

He was standing on a mountaintop, great forests spreading outward far below him in all directions. The four men were standing around him. Altair, the Traveler. Rastaban and Rabakan, the Twins. Menkar, the Transformer.

He looked down at himself, seeing a baby clutched in brown, heavily-tattooed arms clutched to his breasts. *Her* breasts. He knew at once what he was. Not Jag. Not anymore.

The Goddess.

Menkar held out one hand, and the rugged rock of the mountaintop before them began to cave inward at the middle, a massive crater forming within.

We'll start over, the Goddess thought, gazing down at her baby. *This is our home now.*

The vision faded, a memory lost to time.

He saw worlds then. More Doors, archways surrounding that inky blackness, gateways to other worlds. Altair taking her by the hand and bringing her through one after the other. To the far reaches of the universe, one dead world after another.

He saw the barren landscape of one world, the atmosphere thick with red dust, obscuring the silver light of three moons in the heavens above. Saw that brown hand touch the earth, primordial green and brown spreading outward across the surface. Looked up to see Altair smiling.

Another dead world brought to life.

Jag's vision blurred, his consciousness spreading again, growing rapidly. The universe stretching outward before him, awesome in its sheer scope, beyond all comprehension. He felt a *humming* in his mind, a vibration so powerful that it overwhelmed him. World after world flashed before his eyes, scenes of such awesome beauty that he wanted to weep.

And for a moment, for a fraction of an instant, he felt the mind of the Goddess. Her knowledge, her wisdom. Vast, unknowable.

It was beyond description.

He heard a voice from far away, and knew at once that it was his own.

"Beautiful…" he gasped. "Beautiful…"

"I know son," came the reply. "I know."

Epilogue

The bleached white stone of the Royal Mall extended outward from the east wing of the Castle Verhan, a raised platform three feet high, shaped like a pentagon. And beyond this, a truly massive crowd stood, packed shoulder-to-shoulder for as far as the eye could see. Heavily armored guards stood in front of the raised platform, lining the entire Royal Mall. The sun shone down on the bleached stone from the cloudless sky above, a cooling breeze in the air. A perfect day.

And near the end of the pentagon, Lady Damia stood, Lord Zellus at her side. The High Judicator stood before them, facing the crowd, a large white envelope in his hands. He turned to face Damia and Zellus, who both nodded at him. Then he turned back to face the crowd, raising one hand for silence.

The crowd hushed.

"We are gathered here today," he announced, his powerful voice booming over the crowd, "...to witness the succession of our late King Lorius the Seventh." He bowed his head, and the crowd bowed theirs for a moment of silence.

Damia lowered her own gaze, knowing that eyes were upon her. She felt nothing for the old king – another in a long line of her late husband's pawns – but the great Game had to be played. Politics, as always, was all about appearances. A great magic show, with spectacle diverting the attention of the masses while the trick was executed just out of sight. And the trick was always on them.

Always.

The High Judicator lifted his gaze, sweeping it over the crowd.

"The people have voted," he declared. "And your votes have been tallied. Not once, not twice, but thrice. Each count to the same end, an overwhelming consensus that cannot be questioned."

Damia resisted the urge to smile, knowing that, even if the counts had been only one vote different, the Judicator would have said the same. There could be no doubt in the peoples' minds that the vote was decisive. Again, the Game. People were by and large trusting, believing that everyone was as mindful of the rules of human engagement as they were. Never suspecting that those they elected to represent them, the rich and powerful, paid these rules only superficial respect. True wealth – *true* power – only came to those unconstrained by the truth. By decency. Came to those to who did not – or could not – feel the influence of the most powerful force of all: the opinion of others.

And the people would never believe, not even if they were told, that this could be true. That such monsters existed, flourishing among them.

"The people have spoken," the High Judicator declared, holding up the envelope for the crowd to see. "You have chosen the successor to the throne, they who shall be crowned ruler of all Verhan!"

The crowd roared, a sea of fists rising in the air. Damia smiled, knowing that none dared shout the name of the Lord they expected would win. To be wrong would be to invite the wrath of their fellows upon them. The mob would not tolerate dissent.

Utterly fascinating that, if they wanted to, the people could swarm the Royal Mall, overwhelming the guards and killing everyone on the stage. Except for Damia of course. But they did not. They had no understanding of their own power. They played by the rules, bending themselves to the will of those who dared to lead. Sheep, all of them. Weak.

Pathetic.

437

The High Judicator lowered the envelope, opening it, then pulling out a neatly folded sheet of paper within. He unfolded it slowly, gazing down upon it. Then he placed it back in the envelope, just as the sheriff came to his side to collect it...and hand the king's crown to him. The High Judicator thanked the sheriff, then returned his gaze to the crowd.

"I shall now announce the one whose head shall wear the sacred crown until their dying breath," he declared, holding the golden, jewel-encrusted crown high above his head. "It's weight on their head will signify the great weight of their responsibilities. To you, the people, and to this great country."

He paused, lowering the crown to his breast.

"I now declare the next ruler of Verhan to be..."

He turned to Damia and Lord Zellus.

"...Queen Damia!"

The crowd burst into applause, cheers echoing off the great walls of the castle behind the Royal Mall. Damia smiled as the High Judicator knelt before her, holding the crown up for her to take. She paused, gazing at the crowd, then lifted the crown from his hands, placing it upon her head. It rested there rather uncomfortably, fit for its previous owner.

That, of course, would be rectified.

The High Judicator continued to kneel, and Lord Zellus knelt before her as well. The crowd bent to one knee, as did the guards, who turned to face her, prostrating themselves before her. She gazed at the massive crowd, a smile playing at her lips.

It felt just as marvelous as she'd imagined.

She waited, forcing them to kneel for just a little too long. Just long enough to be uncomfortable. No one would dare stand without her order. She could make them kneel for an hour if she liked, and they would do it.

But they were not to be punished, her loyal subjects. Not when there were so many others more deserving of such a fate.

"Rise," she ordered, her voice carrying easily over the crowd. They did so, as did the High Judicator and Lord Zellus. She smiled.

"I was elected by the will of the people," she declared. "And the will of the people will serve as my guide."

She stepped forward, to the very edge of the platform, mere feet away from the first row of people in the crowd.

"For too long," she continued, "...Verhan has suffered in the darkness of the shadow thrown by the Empire. Forced to concede to its demands. Forced to compromise." Her expression darkened. "The Empire destroyed our country, enslaved our ancestors. Yet we struck back. We overcame. And we rose from the ashes," she added, raising her hands slowly, palms-up. "We rebuilt this kingdom, brick-by-brick, heart-by-heart. And here we stand."

The crowd cheered, and she allowed this, waiting a long moment before gesturing for silence.

"We are strong," she declared, sweeping her gaze over the crowd. "We are free. But there are those that hate our freedom. That fear our strength."

She made a gesture, and the sound of wheels rolling on stone came from behind. A long, rectangular wooden platform five feet high being pushed forward by a row of guards, she knew. She turned to face it; several beams rose up from the platform, supporting a long horizontal beam from which four nooses hung. A burly man wearing the grotesque mask of an executioner stood on the platform, a large axe resting on one shoulder.

The platform rolled to a stop ten feet behind her.

"Ladies and gentlemen," Damia announced, "...I present to you the disgraced lords of Verhan."

Guards marched out from the castle onto the Royal Mall, each escorting a lord. Utterly nude, their arms tied behind their backs, their feet chained loosely together. Lords Farwell, Tristan, Lindon...and of course Lord Devlin. They were led up wooden stairs to the platform, then forced to stand before each noose, facing forward.

The crowd booed.

"When the Empire's spies learned of the will of the people," Damia declared, "...that I should become your Queen, the Empire conspired to silence you. It bribed these…*men*," she continued, gesturing at the lords, "…to deny you your voice. The Empire," she added, "…conspired to crown a puppet that would dance to its every whim."

She paused, her lips curling into a smile.

"They tried to take away your voice, yet you have spoken," she continued. "They tried to silence you, yet you have been heard. Let me hear your voices now, and I, as your Queen, will execute your will."

She gestured at the lords.

"Shall we show these traitors mercy, and forgive them for their sins against you?"

The crowd roared "NO!"

Damia arched an eyebrow.

"Shall we let them rot in jail?"

"NO!"

She smiled, nodding at the executioner.

"My people have spoken," she declared.

The guards standing behind each lord shoved them forward, pulling the nooses around their necks. Then the executioner gripped his axe with both hands, lifting it high in the air.

"Hold!" Damia shouted.

The executioner paused, lowering his axe, and Damia stepped up to the side of the platform, ascending the stairs. She walked right up to Lord Devlin, standing before him. He glared at her, barely recognizable without his fine uniform, resembling nothing more than a common beggar.

He spit right in her face.

She didn't even flinch, the spittle striking her in the cheek. She smirked, cupping his chin in one hand. With a simple squeeze, she could shatter his jaw.

"Bitch!" Devlin cursed.

"Now now," Damia scolded. "That's no way to speak to your queen."

"Just get it over with," he growled, jerking his chin out of her grasp. She smiled, leaning in to whisper in his ear.

"A pity about your wife and daughter," she murmured. "I hear the guards…played with them before they died."

Devlin's eyes widened, and he struggled against his chains. The guard behind him yanked Devlin backward, and Damia gave the former lord a wicked smile. It wasn't true, of course; Devlin's wife and daughter were fine. But to know that that image had been burned into his mind right before his death…

It was *perfect*.

She turned away from Devlin, walking back across the platform toward the stairs, glancing at the executioner as she went.

"Drop them gently," she ordered. "Give us a show."

She made her way down the steps, walking in front of the platform, then turning to face the four lords. The executioner untied each rope from the beam above, lengthening them slightly, then forcing the lords to their knees. That done, he returned to his original position.

She nodded at him.

The executioner lifted his axe up above his head, bringing it down on a section of rope stretched over a wooden block set before him. The rope snapped, trapdoors beneath each lord falling open. The lords fell through, jerking to a sudden stop as their nooses went taught. Far enough a drop to crush their windpipes, but not so drastic as to break their necks.

Damia watched as they flailed helplessly, the veins on their faces bulging, their eyes wide with terror. Their mouths open in silent screams.

The crowd roared.

Still the lords struggled, every one of them fighting for their short, pathetic lives. Then, one by one, they went still, until all four of them hung there motionlessly, swaying slightly in the cool breeze.

The crowd cheered, the sound carrying on for what seemed like an eternity. Damia allowed this, waiting patiently for their voices to die down. At length, they did.

The executioner cut down the lords one-by-one, their bodies falling unceremoniously to the stone below.

"My people," Damia stated. "I would hear your voices one more time." She gestured at the bodies of the lords. "Do these traitors deserve a respectful burial?"

The crowd booed.

Damia sighed theatrically, but nodded.

"Very well," she decided. "It's only right that you should decide their fates." She turned to the guards still standing on the wooden platform. "Give the lords to their people, will you?"

The guards obeyed, stepping down from the platform, then grabbing the lords' bodies one-by-one, bringing them to the edge of the Royal Mall and tossing them into the crowd. The crowd caught each body, lowering it to the ground, then swarming over it, kicking and punching the corpses. Tearing at the bodies with mad, unfettered glee.

So-called civilized men and women, acting like the animals they were.

Damia smiled, enjoying the show for a while, then turning away, walking across the great expanse of the Mall to the east wing of the Castle Verhan. She passed through the doorway, a group of guards walking behind her. She waved them away, continuing through the long hallways of the castle, her footsteps echoing off the stone walls.

She smiled to herself, gazing at the paintings hanging on the walls on either side, a seemingly endless line of monarchs that had ruled Verhan for the last thousand years.

And in all that time, she'd been waiting. Pinned under the thumb of her almighty husband, a prisoner within the palace he'd built for her. She'd been afforded every luxury, of course. Riches beyond imagination, almost anything she could ever want just a snap of the fingers away.

It'd been *dreadfully* boring.

But now, at long last, she was free. And now she could get to work undoing everything her late husband had worked so tirelessly to achieve. What he'd endured millennia of pain and suffering to accomplish.

Order. Control.

She ran her fingers across the wall to her left, letting them strike the frames of each painting as she passed, rotating them slightly.

Now it was time to *play*.

She'd nearly reached the end of the long hallway when a man came through the doorway ahead. A man wearing the purple uniform of a Royal courier, a large box in his arms. He stopped before her, bowing sharply.

"My Queen," he greeted. She stood before him, one hand on her hip.

"Yes?"

"A package for you, my Queen," he explained, holding the box out before her. She stared at it for a moment, then waved him away.

"Put it in my chambers," she commanded.

He bowed again, then left as quickly as he'd come, vanishing through the doorway ahead. She watched him go, then followed in his footsteps, passing into another hallway. She walked through a maze of hallways, passing guards as she went, until at last she reached the Royal Chambers. *Her* Royal Chambers. A large room with a massive four-post bed, its rich purple sheet and blankets contrasting with its golden frame. Huge paintings adorned the walls, commissioned by former kings and painted by the greatest artists in Verhan's long history.

She smiled, stepping up to the bed, running her fingers over the fine purple blanket. So much better than the boring white the previous monarch had preferred. Black and white, Sabin's favorite colors. Everything black and white.

It was high time she added some *color*.

A guard approached from behind, and she didn't bother to turn, caressing the sheets with her fingertips. She heard him clear his voice.

"Your Majesty?" he asked.

"Yes?"

"Lord Zellus requests an audience with you, as you requested."

"By all means," she replied, turning to face the guard. "Bring him in."

A moment later, Lord Zellus himself stepped into the bedroom. He bowed before her – deeply, to her satisfaction – then cleared his throat, just as the guard had. He was clearly nervous around her…everyone was. Because no one knew much about her.

Sabin had seen to that.

"You requested me?" Zellus inquired.

"Who else would I request?" she replied smoothly, a hint of a smile playing on her lips. Zellus squirmed, unable to tell whether she was being sarcastic or sincere.

Delicious.

"Of all the lords," she continued, stepping up to him and putting a hand on his chest, "…you were the only one who didn't betray your country. You're a loyal man, Zellus…and I just *love* loyal men."

Zellus swallowed visibly, bowing slightly.

"Of course, my Queen."

"The recent…events on Meros have gone remarkably well," she informed him. "We will use this momentum. Send our people on trade ships traveling to Stridon and Eastport. Have some integrate with the Resistance across the Empire…and others with the city guards."

"Yes my Queen."

"Frame the Empire for the murder of a few prominent Resistance leaders. Then frame the Resistance for the deaths of a few government officials." She traced a circle on his chest with one finger. "Stir things up a bit, will you?"

"At once, your Majesty."

"I'll leave you to it," she stated. He bowed, then left, and she nodded for her guard to close the door to her bedroom, leaving her alone. She sighed, turning back to her bed…and spotting the large box the courier had presented to her earlier lying atop it. She stared at it, resisting the urge to grab it and open it. Savoring the intrigue, the mystery of what might be inside.

The mystery was almost always better than reality, the anticipation of something far more poignant that the thing itself, good or bad.

She thought back to Lord Zellus, and smiled. He was no doubt confused by her orders, but he would not question them. Her aim was remarkably simple. Framing the Empire for murdering Resistance leaders would ignite the passions of the people, growing the Resistance and radicalizing it. Framing the Resistance for the deaths of a few politicians would force Kalibar to order the Resistance quashed, or be seen as a weak terrorist sympathizer, flouting the rule of law. He would be forced to act, forced to use overwhelming force to silence the poor, the downtrodden, the ones without magic...the very people the Resistance fought for.

And in doing so, he would play right into her hands.

She stared at the box, waiting for a moment longer, then giving in at last to her curiosity. Walked up to the bed and grabbed the box, pulling it closer. She felt no magic emanating from it; of course it would have been subjected to Void crystals prior to her handling it.

Not that she feared this Age's primitive magic.

She pulled the lid off, setting it aside, and found tissue paper within. Sheets of crumpled purple and black.

"Well, *somebody* knows me," she murmured.

Damia pulled the tissue paper out, then froze, her breath catching in her throat. She stood there, staring into the box.

A face stared back at her.

It was a decapitated head, with skin as black as hers. Tattoos running up its temples. Black eyes staring lifelessly upward. And in the center of its forehead, a large hole...within which molten gold had been poured.

Damia stared at it. At the head of her brother, the man who had been her constant companion for the last two thousand years. Faithful to the bitter end.

Then she smiled.

"Well *well*," she murmured. "What a wonderful surprise."

She lifted Gundar's head from the box, gazing at it for a long moment. Reliving the moment she'd seen it, that marvelous feeling of shock and surprise. A rare feeling indeed. One to be treasured. Savored.

At length, the feeling faded, as they always did. She sighed, staring at Gundar's head a moment longer, trying to rekindle the feeling. But it was gone.

Damia walked up to the mantle above the large fireplace opposite her bed, setting her brother's head atop it, making sure to have him face the bed. So that when she woke up every morning, she would see it.

Then she looked at the box, turning it upside down and shaking it. Just more tissue paper, nothing else. No letter, no message. But of course the head *was* the message.

"Bravo, Kalibar," she murmured. Then she turned toward the door. "Guard," she called out. The door opened at once, her guard bowing.

"Yes my Queen?"

"It seems Grand Weaver Kalibar has sent us a message," she declared. She smiled then, feeling positively giddy. "It'd be downright rude not to send one back."

Made in the USA
Middletown, DE
12 December 2021

55291781R10272